NEVER

LEAVES

ME

CJ MORROW

Copyright © 2017 CJ Morrow

Tamarillas Press

ISBN: 1983480630
ISBN-13: 978-1983480638   ˎ

Cover artwork: Tithi Luadthong/Shutterstock
Design: © A Mayes

For my family, who always believe.

Also by CJ Morrow

Romantic Comedy
Blame it on the Onesie
A Onesie is not just for Christmas
Mermaid Hair and I Don't Care
Little Mishaps and Big Surprises
We can Work it out

Stonehaven – Hidden magic, romance and mystery
The Finder – Stonehaven book 1
The Illusionist – Stonehaven book 2
The Sister – Stonehaven book 3

Short Stories
Party Time and Twelve

ACKNOWLEDGMENTS

As always, I'd like to thank my family for their patience and support during the writing of this book.

A special mention must go to Keely Fulford for her expert medical advice.

Also, Chloe Dodgson, my patient proof reader and sense checker.

And finally, to you, the reader, without whom there would be no point. Thank you!

ONE

Gasp. I wake. My heart pounds in my chest.

I was having that dream again. The one where the car rolls over and over, spinning out of control.

The alarm is sounding; that's what woke me. Its persistent beeping doesn't stop. What time is it? It's still dark outside, so it must be early. Do we have to get up extra early today? I can't remember. It's Robin's alarm because it's on my right. It's his phone. I wish he would turn it off. It's driving me insane. I bet he's already up. He does that, sets his alarm then wakes before it goes off. I bet he's in the bathroom. Yes, I can hear the water hissing. That's why he can't hear his damn alarm, he's standing under his power shower and deaf to the world.

The jets come from the sides and the back, sharp tingly darts that feel as though they will pierce your flesh. Even the waterfall showerhead at the top is hard on my skin. I never use it. *It wasn't meant for you.* I prefer a quick dip in a warm bath, you can wash your feet so much easier in a bath, no precarious balancing to soap your toes. Robin likes to stand in the shower letting the hot jets pummel his skin. He called me a wimp after I tried it and complained, but secretly he was pleased because he wanted to keep it all to himself.

Still, I wish he would come back and turn off his damn alarm. I suppose I could reach over and do it.

It's stopped. Thank God. Maybe it's run his phone battery flat. He won't be happy, but it'll teach him a lesson. Not that I will say so.

It's still dark outside, very dark. Not a chink of light getting in. So, it must be very early. Too early. I can't think why we need to get up so early today. Maybe it's just Robin who needs to be up early but he'll still want me to drive him to work. I'm just going to have another ten minutes. He'll wake me when he needs me. Maybe he can get his own breakfast today.

Gasp. I wake.

Oh, my God, that dream. It's making my heart pound. Bang, bang, thump in my chest. It's painful. The car was rolling – roof, wheels, roof, wheels. So fast, such speed.

I try to breathe easy. I try to calm down.

I feel sick.

For God's sake; it's just a dream.

Robin's alarm is going off. Why doesn't he turn it off? It's doing my head in. He's in the shower; I can hear the water hissing down on him. *My shower.*

The alarm's stopped. Thank God. I'm so bloody tired. It's too dark to get up now. Just five more minutes.

I wake.

The car is red.

My car is red.

I've counted the spins. Three. Wheels, roof, wheels, roof, wheels, roof. It landed on its roof. I hate this dream. It's horrific.

My whole body feels as though it has been thoroughly shaken. My heart throbs in my ears.

The damn alarm is going off. That's Robin's phone alarm. I wish he would turn it off. He's probably in the shower. Yes, I can hear the water running. He'll be ages. He loves to stand under that shower. *Power shower.* I hope he has the extractor fan on otherwise he won't be able to see his face when he cleans his teeth and he'll be irritated and grumpy when he comes out of the bathroom. He always cleans them after his shower. I clean mine before – not that I have a shower, I prefer a bath. He says I should do my teeth after; I agree with him and say I do, but I don't. I don't see what difference it makes.

The alarm has stopped, probably flattened his phone battery. He won't be happy about that. I'll need to remind him to charge it in the car on our way to work. I can still hear his shower hissing.

Why are we getting up so early? It's still dark? I don't remember there being a reason to start early today. What day is it? I can't remember; I'm still half asleep. I think it's Friday.

I like Fridays. Everyone at work is looking forward to the weekend. Everyone is happy in anticipation. Not like Mondays, when everyone is grumpy and lamenting the loss of their freedom. Robin says it's the same where he works, except that it is intensified by ten because they are always counting down to the next half-term break. He says it's worse after the summer holidays. The kids look sad but the teachers look sadder – some are off sick within a week. The only ones who don't look sad are the parents dropping their offspring at the gates, pushing them out of their cars and waving cheerfully. Who wants a stroppy teenager festering in bed all morning, hanging around the house all day and staying up all night?

Stroppy teenager. Robin never called me a stroppy teenager.

I can hardly remember being a teenager, even though it's less than ten years ago. I don't think I ever festered in bed. I'm sure I didn't, though I can't really remember.

I'll get up when Robin comes out of the bathroom. I'll just catch a few more minutes until then. Thank God, it's Friday.

I'm watching that car now. I know it's a dream. I'm watching it spinning, rolling. I wouldn't like to be inside that car. Imagine what that must feel like, seeing the world turning over when it isn't the world at all, it's you. Imagine when it finally stops, landing on its roof. You'd be hanging there, suspended by your seatbelt. Hanging there feeling sick and helpless. Supposing you're hurt. God, that would be awful.

When it lands on its roof it just rocks, like a cradle. Side to side. Gives motion sickness a new meaning. Horrific. Frightening.

I wonder what it means.

Gasp. I wake.

It's just a silly dream. I know that. My mind knows that. My body doesn't. Calm down heart. Shut up alarm. Get out of your shower, Robin. Stop that damn hissing.

It's just a dream. I wonder what it means? Isn't a car a metaphor for your life? I remember, when Mum and Dad were being particularly difficult about me and Robin – they liked him then, they just didn't like him for me – I had that dream, several times, where you're trying to drive your car from the back seat. Your feet don't quite reach the pedals, your arms aren't long enough to steer properly. *Your parents were trying to control you.* After Robin said that, the dream stopped. He was right. I had to live my own life. They meant well, but it wasn't up to them what I did, who I was with. I was an adult.

Legally.

The car is red. It's definitely my car.

Gasp.

The alarm. My heart.

This is too much.

Just too much.

I'm petrified.

Calm down. Calm down.

It's just a dream.

A stupid dream.

Breathe. Breathe. Calm. Calm.

That's better. The alarm has stopped. If his battery's flat, that's his own fault, but I couldn't stop it because he hates me touching his phone. No doubt he's set it and gone in the bathroom before it's gone off. He does that.

Why are we getting up so early today? What's going on? It's still dark outside. Which means it's before dawn. What time is dawn?

I can hear Robin's shower, its power forcing the water into his skin. He likes it. I hate it. *It's not for you, Juliette.*

What's that smell? Is it a new shower gel or deodorant? Not sure I like it. It smells antiseptic. That's not a good smell. And alcohol. What do they put in those products? It must be very strong to work its way along the landing and into our room, even if Robin has left the bedroom door open. I bet he has.

He likes the main bathroom; it's bigger. I use the smaller ensuite; I'm grateful it has a bath.

He'll be in here in a minute telling me to get up. *Lazy Juliette.*

I'll get up before he comes back, best way to avoid annoyance.

In a minute.

Wake up Juliette. You're dreaming.

The car is red and mine. It's on its roof. I'm running away as fast as my leaden legs will carry me. But I have to look back. I have to do that, don't I? I couldn't just carry on running. Why couldn't I just keep going? My car is burning now. Flames lick the doors, engulf the roof. The stench of burning petrol and metal singes my nostrils. Acrid smoke. I want to cough.

And I stand there and I watch. And nothing is happening except the car burning. I look around for people, for other cars. There are none. Just me. Alone.

I check myself. Am I on fire? No. I'm fine. I'm wearing my black coat, the one with the too-big buttons; it's tight across my chest now. I've had that coat a long time, Robin bought it for me for Christmas – our first Christmas. My parents weren't pleased when they finally found out. Mum said it was wrong of him to buy it and wrong of me to accept it. Too late, I'd chirped back at her. Dad didn't say anything, just glanced at me and glanced away. He looked sad. I've noticed how Dad always looks sad. I wonder if I've done something to upset him. Recently, I mean. I know I upset him before, but that's years ago now. Ten years. Probably more. And it's all worked out fine, so he had no reason to worry. Did he?

Perhaps it's not me. *Yes, the whole world doesn't revolve around you, Juliette.* Perhaps it's Mads. I suppose she's got to that age now; fifteen. I can't imagine Madeleine being stroppy, she always seems so sweet. Maybe that's just for me. She'll always be my baby sister, no matter how old we get. She's twelve years younger (well thirteen sometimes, depends on which month we're in) and I remember the day she was born like it was yesterday.

I remember the day Mum and Dad told me they were having a baby too. It was my birthday, my twelfth. They thought it would be a nice surprise for me, a nice present. I was repulsed. Disgusted. Looking back it seems hilarious now, but when you're twelve you really don't believe your parents have sex. I really thought they were far too old to be having another baby. My mum did too. I heard her telling Sally next door. She was forty, dad was forty-three. They weren't expecting *that* to happen.

I was embarrassed. I didn't tell my friends at school. But then I was spotted out shopping with Mum; we were in big Tesco. We were looking at the clothes. Mum was enormous by then but it was all out front, her skinny legs dangling from below her immense bump. There was no mistaking she was pregnant; it couldn't be passed off as just fat. I wanted the ground to open up and swallow me as Angie and Cara waved at me across the underwear aisle. They smiled. I smiled. Mum said her back was aching and we needed to get home. Then she marched us straight past them towards the tills.

I dreaded going into school the next day. How

could I hide the fact that my parents had sex? The evidence was there. Disgusting. But nobody said anything. Nobody cared. Angie waved to me across the room in Maths and never mentioned it. Nor did Cara. They had their own lives to live.

Two days later Madeleine arrived. Blue eyes in an angry, red face stared out at me when I went to visit mum in hospital.

'I like her hair,' I said, moving to touch the crusty halo that stuck out from her head.

'Don't.' Mum shuddered and batted my hand away. 'She hasn't had a bath yet.'

'She's perfect,' Dad said, putting his arm around Mum's shoulder. He glowed with pride. I'd never seen him like that before. 'All my girls are perfect.' He put his other arm around my shoulder and Mads stared at us as if she knew what Dad meant.

I suppose I fell in love with Mads that day. She was my baby sister. Mum let me hold her for five minutes before putting her back into the safety of the clear Perspex crib.

Mads was the perfect baby, apparently. Fed well, slept well, grew well. 'Just as well,' Mum told Sally when she visited from next door. 'Given my age, I couldn't cope with a difficult baby.'

I remember wondering if I had been a difficult baby. I tossed that remark around in my head for days. But, surely Mum would have said *another* difficult baby, if I had been. Wouldn't she? In the end, I asked Dad. He smiled and said I was perfect, just like my little sister.

Yes, it's probably Mads who's making him sad now. She's got to that age.

'Come on, Juliette. Wake up.'

I'd better get up before Robin gets annoyed. He's not known for his patience. Well, not with me anyway. He's patience personified with his pupils. He says he has to have the patience of a saint to teach Maths. Especially now because pupils are getting lazier.

That's how we met.

Not at school. He wasn't my teacher at school. Our meeting wasn't tacky or sordid like that.

I will get up any minute now. I will.

Oh God, I've dozed off again. I'm back in this bloody awful dream. My car just keeps on rolling and burning. I run and stop and look back. Why don't I just keep running?

As I stand there, staring at the flames, I see a body on the grass verge.

Dreams are amazing really, aren't they? One second you're running away, next you're watching from afar, then suddenly, you're right there, close up, staring at a body. And all without any effort from you. If only waking up was so easy.

She's wearing a coat like mine; the buttons are too big. And it's a bit tight on her. She's not fat. Not what I call fat anyway. Robin might, but he's far too critical. But the coat is tight, she probably should have bought a bigger size. I bet that's what mine looks like. I don't think I'll wear it again. I haven't worn that coat for years. It's been in the back of my wardrobe forgotten and unworn. I should have got rid of it, stifled back sentiment and stuffed it in the charity bag. I did consider selling it on eBay but it wasn't that good, I mean it wasn't expensive or good enough, or fashionable, or even classic enough that anyone would buy it. But donating to charity would be a good thing to do. I've only kept it because of the sentimental value; it was the first thing Robin ever bought me.

'Wake up, Juliette,'

I wish I had some energy. I am just so tired. I wonder what the hell the time is? It's still dark outside. I'm surprised Robin hasn't put the light on. He'll be shaking me in a minute to wake me up.

Was I drinking last night? I can't remember. I think I must have been because I do have a headache. Not a cranking, hanging one. Just a dull, persistent thud. It's dehydration, I know that. A pint of water and a strong coffee and I'll be fine. And my mouth is dry. Dry and sore. That's definitely too much wine. Actually, my throat is sore too. Maybe I'm ill. Maybe I've got a fever. That would explain why my muscles and bones ache, why I can't summon the energy to get up. I've got flu. Not man-flu like Robin had last Christmas. No, just normal flu, woman-flu. A couple of paracetamol and I'll be right as rain for work. I'll have to go. You can't be off sick on a Friday, it looks like you're skiving. When you go back in on Monday everyone gives you that smirky sideways look. They know you are lying. So everyone drags themselves in on a Friday and spreads their germs. That'll be me today.

If it's not flu, it's definitely a hangover. No one dares take time off work for a hangover. But everyone knows. If you've got a hangover that bad, apart from the tell-tale signs, the wan face, the slow movement, apart from that, you can smell it. The alcohol oozes out of your pores.

That's what it is. I can smell alcohol. We were drinking; correction, I was drinking because Robin rarely does.

I wish I could remember.

My God, that's bad.

My feet are cold.

And my hands. Like ice.

Maybe that's why I keep dreaming about a burning car, it's because I want to be warm. The world of dreams doesn't always make a lot of sense but that could explain it.

Mmm. I might pop over to Mum and Dad's over the weekend. Check Mads will be there for a catch up – I haven't seen her for ages. It must be weeks and weeks. Maybe I can persuade Robin to come with me. Maybe. Maybe not. Perhaps it's not a good idea for Robin to come. There's always an atmosphere when he comes to my parents. Everyone's very polite and nice but it's strained. My dad doesn't say much and Mads usually disappears up to her bedroom and my mum makes too many cups of tea and keeps trying to make us eat cake so we can be a normal family.

We are a normal family.

Mmm. I'll see how it goes. I can't remember the last time Robin came to Mum and Dad's.

Never mind the weekend, I've got to get on with today. I've got to get up and get dressed and drop Robin off at school on my way to work.

The face is mine. The face is mine. No wonder she's wearing my coat. She is me. I am her.

I'm the body by the burning car.

She's just lying there. I'm just lying there. My eyes

are closed. I look fine. No blood. No horrible twisted limbs.

This is a nightmare.

The alarm is going. I need to get up. Robin's in the shower. I should get up, make the bed, lay out my clothes, before he comes back. He gets annoyed if I stay in bed. *Lazy Juliette.*

I need to get up so I can shake that horrendous dream out of my head. I'm definitely getting rid of that black coat. It doesn't fit me anyway. It's too tight. The buttons are too big. It's old and outdated. Can this dream really have been about that coat?

Don't be stupid.

I'll drink plenty of water to get rid of the hangover. I'll wash my hair; will I have enough time to dry it? What time is it, anyway? It's still dark; I don't know why we're getting up so early.

I'll see what my parents are doing this weekend. Catch up with Mads. Maybe we could go shopping, Mads and me, buy some clothes. She'd like that. I'd like that. It'll make a change. Robin always comes clothes shopping with me, chooses what suits me. He has a good eye. He jokes he's created my style. I laugh and frown but I think he's probably right. He's got such good taste in clothes; always has. That first night, when my dad brought him home, he had on a dark coat over stonewashed jeans. He was wearing Timberland boots. With his trendy dark hair, his tall, lean build, those cheekbones and lashes, he didn't look like a teacher, he looked like a model.

And my dad brought him home to be my Maths tutor. He reached across to shake my hand when Dad introduced me. His hand was warm and large. Mine was small and sweaty. I'd bitten off the turquoise nail varnish I'd been wearing, but not completely. I felt like a piece of shit. He looked like a god.

'Hi Juliette.' That was all he said and I felt my heart flip, my spine tingle, the hairs on the back of my neck stand up. If love at first sight exists, that was it. I couldn't even manage a reply, other than a stupid grin.

Later, much later, when it all got a bit nasty, Mum said it was just a stupid schoolgirl crush. She said I'd get over it. I didn't.

I didn't have to, did I?

Look at us now.

Oh. Here's Robin.

He's left his shower running. That's not a good sign. And I haven't even made it out of bed yet, despite my good intentions. It means there isn't enough time for me to have a bath, I have to have a quick shower – he knows it will be quick because I hate his power shower. No time to wash my hair either. I hope we have enough time for breakfast. I'm starving. And thirsty. I must have a coffee before we go. I hope I'm all right to drive. Surely, I didn't drink that much? I wish I could remember.

I try to move. Really, I do. But the hangover is just too bad. It's paralysing me.

'Wake up, Juliette.' Robin does his trick with the duvet; he flips and shakes it. He lets it fall back down on me, which is better than normal; usually he just rips it off completely. I'm grateful for small mercies. As the duvet lands back on me it settles over my feet first, despite them still feeling cold the duvet burns me as it scrapes over the ends of my toes. My feet flinch and flex.

What a hangover.

'Wake up, Juliette.'

I'm trying. I really am. I try to speak but my mouth won't work. I try to open my eyes wide, but they won't comply. All I see is blackness.

'Juliette. You need to try. Come on.'

Robin rubs my arm, I wish he wouldn't do that. The smell of alcohol is strong now, it must be on his breath too. Was he drinking? Surely not.

'Come on. Wake up.'

He's pressuring me now and I don't like it. Does he think I'm playing at being asleep? Doesn't he know that I wouldn't do that?

Am I still dreaming? Is that what this is? All part of the same horrible, repeating car crash dream?

I groan. Then Robin's alarm goes off again. What the hell? The shower is still running and the alarm is going off and it's making my headache worse and I'm so very confused.

A sharp sting in my arm and it all stops. It's silent. I'm calm.

A hand strokes my forehead. It's not Robin's hand. Too small.

I sleep.

Gasp.

I wake.

'You need to wake up, Juliette. You're in hospital.'

I'm in hospital?

TWO

What a disgrace I am.

I am in hospital with a hangover. That's disgusting. What a criminal waste of NHS resources. What the hell is going on? How did this happen? How did I drink so much that I am in this state? I must have alcohol poisoning. As soon as I get over this I'll be scuttling out with my tail between my legs. I am so embarrassed. What the hell was I drinking? It must have been some potent stuff.

This is awful.

I've never done anything like this before. Three glasses of wine is my usual limit. Invariably I don't drink at all as I'm always the designated driver. Robin rarely drinks but he doesn't like driving unless he's forced to. Though he does have a nice car, just in case.

It wouldn't be so bad, well yes, it would, but it might help if I could even remember last night. If it's Friday today, whatever possessed us to drink on a Thursday evening? We both have work today. Actually, Robin seems okay.

This is insane.

And I feel so tired.

'You just need to wake up, Juliette.'

Yes, soon.

The dream again, the burning car, the black coat

with the too-big buttons, the body. What a nightmare.

I know where I am. In hospital. I can't open my eyes or move anything. I feel dreadful. And sorry for myself. What a sorry state I am in.

I feel ashamed.

I can hear machines beeping – it was never Robin's alarm. That's what the hissing was too, I suppose, not Robin's power shower.

'How is she?' That's my mum's voice. Oh no. What is she doing here? Why did Robin tell her? Why has he dragged her in here for a hangover? This is just getting worse.

'The infection is slowly responding to treatment.' That's a voice I don't recognise. A nurse? A doctor? Not Robin.

'Any sign of …' Mum's voice trails away.

'Still unconscious. But we did see a little movement in her feet earlier. We've started to wean her off sedation, so we'll see how it goes.'

'Ahh. That's good news.' Mum's voice sounds hopeful yet tentative.

'Early days.' A noncommittal reply.

Infection? Infection? I have an infection? Not a hangover. Thank God. I'm not a complete idiot. Hang on, wouldn't a hangover be better. An infection sounds serious. It IS serious; I'm in hospital. What kind of infection would put me in hospital? Meningitis? Sepsis? Isn't sepsis the one everyone is talking about and fearing now? Isn't it a silent killer? No wonder I'm delirious and having nightmares.

I think I'd rather have a shame-laden hangover.

'Now your mum's here I'm going to nip home and shower.' Robin's breath is soft on my cheek. If I could move, if I could speak, I'd turn and smile and say thanks. He must have been up here all night. Have I been here all night?

I hear the scrape of a chair, I feel pressure on the bed. I imagine Robin moving his chair so that Mum can have it. I imagine her putting her bag on the bed. I hear a soft flump as she sits down. There's no conversation between Mum and Robin. That's a shame. I imagine strained smiles across my prone body.

Mum's probably blaming Robin for this. She's spent a lot of time over the years blaming Robin for anything and everything. It didn't start out like that. She liked him in the beginning.

Everybody liked him.

It had been Mum's idea to get me a tutor after the mock GCSE results, when my Maths had been so poor and everyone was horrified.

'How can this be? Your father's a deputy head.' Mum was so angry, angrier than Dad. I didn't see what the problem was, I didn't go to Dad's school. But Mum said it was shameful and embarrassing for Dad. He said he would give me extra tuition. Just for Maths, everything else was okay.

We lasted two sessions, well, one-and-a-half really. Dad was tired. I was tired and irritable. I hated Maths. What did it matter if I didn't get a good grade? I was good at other stuff. I tried not to have a tantrum, but I didn't succeed. I *was* a stroppy teenager that day.

'Don't you want to go to university?' Mum's voice took on a tone of confrontation.

'Yeah,' I muttered. Did I? Yes, I probably did, all my friends would probably be going. But we had these exams to get through, then two years of

A'levels. It was too far away to think about.

Later, when I was in the kitchen and Mum and Dad were in the lounge I heard them discussing me.

'It's too much, on top of your job. You need to unwind when you get home, not start work again. And she's so ungrateful.'

Was I ungrateful? No. I just wasn't grateful enough. Not for Mum. I see it now, all these years later, but back then I just didn't want to know. I hated Maths. Everyone did, but they didn't seem to struggle like I did. Algebra – what was that about? I'd never use that in real life, would I?

Dad didn't respond to Mum; or, if he did, his voice was too quiet, too low for me to hear.

Two days later he brought Robin home. He came for tea, so Mum could check him out and make sure he was suitable. Mads was three then, she insisted he sat next to her, insisted he play *My Little Pony* at the table until Mum tactfully removed the ponies; citing hygiene as the reason. Robin looked relieved when the toys were gone but was happy to chat to Mads. He was really sweet with her.

With his on-trend clothes and looks, he didn't seem like a teacher. My dad looked like a teacher, his body wore that weary look of forced, extended periods of patience, his clothes were professional, if ironed out. Dad wore a shirt and tie, Robin didn't. I thought he was amazing, wanting to spend his evenings tutoring after a day teaching. Later, I heard Dad telling Mum that Robin had just bought a house and needed the extra cash. Dad was paying him cash-in-hand. I didn't know what that meant at the time.

We began our first session in Dad's study – quite an honour, I was rarely allowed in there – this was where he did his marking and planned his lessons.

Robin told me a little about himself, he'd only been at Dad's school for a term, having spent five years in a private girls' school. I did a lot of nodding and smiling that first evening, too shy, too intimidated by his appearance, and my own shabby clothes – my washed out uniform – to say much.

After an hour and a half of Maths tutoring my head was aching and I was relieved when he finally left.

After that, when Mum declared that he seemed trustworthy and reliable, she agreed the arrangement; he would come twice a week, have tea with us first.

Twice a week! Tuesdays and Thursdays.

I felt both lucky and horrified. I spent every Monday and Wednesday evening washing my hair, ensuring my nails were good and I stopped wearing the turquoise nail varnish after Robin commented that it looked a bit tacky. I stuck to clear after that. I spent so much time on my appearance on those evenings that my other homework began to suffer. When she found out – my school rang her – Mum banished hair washing to the weekend and she supervised my homework at the kitchen table every evening.

'You'll thank me later,' she said, when I whinged about it. 'You shouldn't be washing your hair that often anyway, it makes it more greasy.'

Mum decided that Robin would only have tea with us once a week. I think she would have preferred to stop it altogether, but the pattern had been set. She made up some excuse about Thursdays being difficult, Robin didn't seem to mind.

I lived for Tuesday and Thursday evenings. I spent

the whole week imagining Robin's large, expressive hands spread across my dad's desk as he explained Maths to me. Eventually it even started to make sense.

Over the course of those glorious three months from March to May I learnt a lot, and not just about Maths. I had started wearing make-up in year nine, the same as all my friends, nothing too garish for school of course. But even at weekends we didn't go over the top, the main aim was to look flawless, to hide our lumpy, red, spotty, teenage skin; to increase our eyelash curl and to enlarge our eyes with the aid of a few eyeliner flicks.

'You don't need all that on your face,' Robin had said one Thursday evening after we had crunched through a dozen equations and I had fully understood them.

I touched my face self-consciously. I felt myself blushing.

'What I mean is,' he said, smiling, he looked so devastatingly gorgeous when he smiled that I felt my stomach flip. 'Is that you're a good-looking girl, you don't need any artifice.'

I blushed even more then.

'I'm sorry. I've embarrassed you.' He laid his hand on my arm before standing up to leave; it sent a tingle so strong running up and down my arm I almost gasped. 'I'll see you next week.'

Next week couldn't come fast enough.

After he'd gone I hurried up to my bedroom and looked up artifice.

'Well,' my mum says, patting my hand, which I can feel. 'It's a struggle to know what to talk about.'

Right. Well. If I were able, I'd laugh. My mum never has any problem talking, or offering advice; especially when it's not asked for.

I hear her rummaging in her bag.

'What I thought,' she continued. 'Well, that is, we've been told to chat to you all the time, that you can probably hear us, but even if you can't hear us all the time, some of it might get through. So, I've pretty much exhausted all my topics of conversation during the last two weeks…. Her words fade away.

Two weeks. Two weeks. Does she mean I've been here for two weeks? That can't be right. Can it? I stop thinking and start listening to Mum again.

'And because it's just me coming during the day now, because as we explained yesterday your dad has had to go back to work, what with the Ofsted and him being the Head and everything, well, I thought I'd read to you. What do you think?'

I wish I could respond. I wish I could nod. I wish I could ask what the hell is going on. What is this infection that has wiped two weeks of my life out?

'So,' Mum's voice is slow and deliberate now. 'I went into your bedroom, your old bedroom at ours not yours obviously, and had a look through your books.'

My books? I didn't even know I had any books there. I thought I'd given them all to Mads, including the ones she had sneakily borrowed. In fact, doesn't Mads have my old bedroom now?

'And I found this.'

I feel a breeze on my face as she waves something across it. I wish I could see. Why can't I see? I don't think my eyes are open. But it's too dark. Even with my eyes closed I should be able to detect light and dark, I should be able to tell the difference. Oh, my God, am I blind? Is the infection in my eyes? I feel a wave of horror and panic creeping through my body.

An alarm goes off. I feel the presence of several bodies around me. Medical staff? I can't hear anything except the rush of air and the alarm. Then a sharp sting coursing through my veins and I'm gone.

The car is spinning, spinning, roof, wheels, roof, wheels, roof. I run, I stop, I go back. Why must I go back? The body is in the road. My body, in my black coat with the too-big buttons. The face is mine. There are no eyes. Just skin where the eyes should be.

I'm blind. I'm blind. How will I be able to live if I'm blind? How will I be able to carry on with my life, my job, if I'm blind? How will I be able to drive, take Robin to work, if I'm blind?

'Calm down, Juliette.'

Robin's soft voice is whispering in my ear.

'You're going to be fine.'

Okay.

'You just got a bit distressed.'

Okay. Where's Mum?

'Your mum was here, she was going to read to you before… Anyway, she got upset. She'll be back later.'

Okay.

'You need to concentrate on getting better. You need to wake up.'

Okay. I'm trying. I really am. I wish you could hear me.

'It's going to be fine. You'll get through this. Trust me, Juliette.'

I do. I do. I always have. And that trust saw me though some tough times.

My parents were delighted when I passed my Maths GCSE with an A*. I was elated. Robin was quietly proud. We all glossed over the less than stellar results of my other GCSEs, though they were all above grade C, but not quite as good as had been expected. I was supposed to be a straight A student. I was carrying my dad's reputation.

Dad was philosophical about it, Mum bit her tongue and I jokingly said to Robin that it was a shame he didn't tutor other subjects. He laughed. We both did. Together.

Soon I was into A'levels – Maths, of course, but without Robin's diligent tutoring I was struggling again.

'I'm not as good at this as I thought,' I wailed to him one evening on the phone. I had a pay-as-you-go mobile by then – a present for passing my exams, maybe it would have been a contract phone if I'd done even better. I sat in my bedroom facing the window, hopeful that my parents wouldn't hear me.

'You are. You just lack confidence. You are good. Trust me.'

'Would you tutor me some more?'

There was a silence, followed eventually by an 'umm.'

'I'm sure I can persuade my parents to pay.' My bravado had no substance.

'Okay,' he said, though his voice sounded reluctant.

'I'll talk to my parents.' I sounded so sure of myself.

It took two days before I was able to broach the subject, then Dad gave me the perfect opener.

'How are you settling into sixth form?' Dad said, as we sat around the dinner table waiting for Mads to finish. We all watched her stab individual peas with her fork and eat them one by one. When one fell on the floor, she dropped down from her chair and retrieved it before popping it into her mouth

'Urgh. Gross,' I hissed.

'We all have to learn.' My mother lifted Mads back onto her seat. 'Anyway, answer your dad.'

'I'm doing okay. Thought it's harder than I expected.'

'But you're doing your favourite subjects. You excelled at Maths.' This was Mum speaking while Dad looked on, studying us both.

'Yeah. I know.' I shrugged.

'Is it harder without your tutor?' My dad's eyes looked at me with a mix of pity and concern.

'Yeah.' I looked down.

'We find that at our school. I mean, that A'levels are a lot harder than expected. Some say even harder than university.' He wiped his napkin across his mouth. 'Come on, Madeleine, eat up,' he said, as though diverting the conversation. He sighed, he looked weary.

'You should have gone to college instead of staying on at school.' Mum smiled at me with that *I-told-you-so* look on her face. I don't know why she felt the need to say that, I don't know what relevance it had. I'd only stayed at my school because all of my friends had.

I shrugged. I looked down again, running my finger along the rim of my empty plate. Now was my opportunity, if I didn't say it now, I might never get the chance again.

'Robin says he's still willing to tutor me.'

Mum's eyebrows shot up, she exchanged a look with Dad.

'You're still in contact with him?' Dad frowned.

Oh shit.

'Not really. Not in contact with him. Not really. You know. I I,' I stuttered in my lie. 'I bumped into him. In town. Last week.' Some of it was true, though I'd never bumped into him anywhere. I had his number, he'd given it to me on our last tutorial before the last exam, but we weren't in regular contact. He'd been the first person I'd rung immediately after it had finished, the first person I'd rung with my A* result, but we weren't chatting daily or anything like that. *He* never rang me, it was always me who rang him.

Neither of my parents spoke, just looked at me, glanced at each other before my mum whipped my little sister's plate away, while she howled that she hadn't finished. She soon shut up when apple crumble and ice cream was put in front of her.

Every mouthful of that pudding stuck in my throat. I wanted to kick myself for saying anything. I wanted to rewind time, snatch back the words, but it was too late. Dinner was over, the table was cleared, the conversation not resumed.

A week later, Mum caught me on the landing, I'd just come out of the bathroom, she was sorting through an already tidy airing-cupboard; she'd been waiting for me.

'Your dad spoke to Robin,' she said, her eyes watching my face closely. I felt my heart beating in my throat. 'They've agreed he'll tutor you.'

'Cool.' I tried to downplay my elation.

'Yes. Once a fortnight. Thursdays. He won't be coming for tea.'

Once a fortnight. Oh. I didn't dare express my disappointment but Mum read it in my eyes.

'You don't need to see him more than that, do you? You've got two years to get through. Anyway, you focused too much on Maths last year, you need to focus on your other subjects too. History used to be your strongest.' Mum closed the airing-cupboard door.

'Of course.'

'Good.'

'I've already joined the History study group.' It was true, I had. But it met on Thursdays, so I would be missing every other week now, but I didn't tell Mum that.

She smiled. 'Good. Well done.'

'Thanks mum.' I half skipped into my bedroom, but before I closed the door, she was there, in my face, speaking.

'Don't be taken in by Robin's smooth looks and charms,' she said. 'He's far too old for you.'

'Urgh, Mum. Gross.' I groaned. I hoped I was conveying sufficient horror at the very idea that Robin could charm me. I don't know if she was fooled. Looking back, I don't even know if I was fooled. I knew how old he was. He'd told me. I was fifteen when he started tutoring me and he was twenty-eight. He was still twenty-eight but I was sixteen now. I'd told him I was catching up with him. He'd laughed and said if I believed that then he hadn't done a very good job teaching me Maths. I loved it when he laughed; his eyes crinkled at the edges. He had the sort of laugh that came from his throat, a bit like a growl. I thought it was so cool.

I still find it sexy, even now.

I hear Mum coming back onto the ward. I assume it is a ward, though without being able to see I don't know if there are other patients nearby. I can't hear them, just the radio, it's on all the time, low, but ever present. I hear Mum's voice as she speaks to someone, not me, not Robin. Then she approaches the bed, her steps slow.

'Hi Lyndsey,' Robin says to Mum. 'I'm just going. Give you two some time together.'

I hear the chair scrape. I hear Mum slump down into it. You'd think they'd have more than one chair for visitors.

'You all right now, love?' She pats my hand and pauses as though I might answer. Would that I could. 'Maybe it was the book choice.' She laughs.

I don't remember her telling me which book she'd brought and I couldn't see it, because I'm blind. I wonder if anyone knows I'm blind.

'Anyway. I'm not going to read that one now. Not Harry Potter.'

Harry Potter? How old does she think I am? I'm twenty-eight, not eight. Thank God for that, then. I didn't even know I had that book. Which one was it? There are so many. I don't think I've ever read one. I've seen all the films. I think that was Mads's book.

'They've got a bit of a book depository in the corridor. You can borrow, or donate. You know. So, I picked up this.' She waves another book in front of me. I wonder if my eyes are open. Wide and staring. She obviously thinks I can see the book. 'It's Jane Austen. We love a bit of Jane Austen, don't we?'

Do we? I hear the pages turn as she finds the first chapter. She doesn't tell me what the title is before she starts to read.

'*It is a truth universally acknowledged, that a single man in possession of a good fortune, must be in want of a wife.*' My mum is reading Pride and Prejudice.

I've never read that book either, but everyone knows that opening line. I suppose it's a distraction from this misery, this infection that I can't remember catching. I've seen the film with *Keira Knightly*. I think we watched it together, me and Mum when Dad had a school governors' meeting one evening, Mads was in bed, and there was just the two of us alone in the house.

Mads would have been five by then. She went to bed at seven-thirty every evening. Good as gold, Mum used to say, implying, or perhaps it was just me inferring, that *I* hadn't been good as gold. I still had that feeling of being troublesome, difficult, though I'd never tackled Mum about it. Maybe I was afraid of the response. Maybe I had been a demonic little girl. Anyway, Mum and I sat down to watch Elizabeth and Darcy exchange meaningful looks and splintered words and neither of us noticed that Mads had sneaked back downstairs and was crouching in the corner behind us watching it too. It was ten by the time it finished and Mum had screeched in shock, then annoyance when she'd found Mads wrapped in the panda fleece she kept on her bed and sound asleep. Mads had woken with a scream and Mum had chivvied her back to bed.

'I don't know how long she'd been there,' Mum said, when she came back. 'What do you think she saw?'

'There's nothing in it.' I laughed, but Mum's stern face showed she didn't think it was funny.

'Juliette, she's only five.'

'She probably slept through most of it.' I said that to make Mum feel better because of course, I had no idea what she'd seen or not seen.

'Yes. She probably did.'

I got the truth out of Mads the next day before tea, while Mum was in the kitchen, Dad in his study and we were watching TV in the living room.

'I saw it all. All of it. Kissy, kissy.' She laughed, her eyes twinkling with mischief as she giggled.

'You were asleep.'

'I was just pretending.'

And I knew that she was telling the truth. Good as gold? No, just better at hoodwinking our mum. She climbed onto my lap and looked into my eyes, holding my face with her little hands. 'Kissy, kissy,' she giggled before kissing me on the nose.

I'd giggled with her. I've always loved my little sister but I loved her more than ever that day. Little devil.

'"*Oh!*" said Lydia stoutly, *'I am not afraid; for though I am the youngest, I'm the tallest.'*" My Mum's voice brings me back to the present. I had drifted off and I've missed her reading. Lydia, if I remember rightly, was the younger, feistier, louder Bennet sister. Reminds me of Mads a bit. She's never afraid to say what she thinks. And she's that age now. Fifteen. I wonder if Mum still thinks Mads is as good as gold.

'I think that's enough for now.' Mum shuts the book, its pages slap closed. 'Your dad's hovering in the car park for me. He's not coming in tonight, it's been a long day for him, what with the Ofsted. He'll try and come tomorrow.'

Okay.

She leans in and kisses me on the forehead. I can't smell her perfume, perhaps she's not wearing any.

'Bye love.' I hear her walk away, in the distance a door closes and I am left in silence, silence except for the slow hissing that is some machine somewhere, pumping air.

I am alone.

'Hello Juliette. Good visit from your mum?' Robin's back. Has he been hovering in the corridor waiting for Mum to leave?

Footsteps come towards me.

'Hello Juliette. How are we this evening?' The voice is friendly, unfamiliar and booming. 'I'm Sue. We have met before but you might not remember. I say this every night, so I hope you'll forgive me if you've heard it before.' She chuckles to herself.

'Hi Sue,' Robin says, his voice cheery. 'This one is very loud.' Even though he's whispering in my ear, I do worry that Sue will hear his comment.

'I'm going to get you ready for the night, bit earlier than usual but we're busy tonight. I'll apologise now for the indignities, but we're all girls together.' She laughs then lifts the bedcovers from me and a chill descends.

Ready for the night. I don't like the sound of this.

THREE

I hear curtains as they are whipped around me. Am I in a ward with other people? I haven't heard anyone else, just the relentless sound of a radio, though never loud enough for me to hear it properly.

'Ooo, your eyes are looking very sticky today. Have they been done?' Sue leans over me and I can feel her breath on my face. 'Tut, tut.' I hear her pulling on rubber gloves. She starts to dab at my eyes with something wet. A wipe maybe. It seems to go on for ages and as it progresses I realise that my eyes have been shut tight, glued almost. After much diligent wiping by Sue, she pulls up my left eyelid. 'Now for the drops, I think.'

The liquid, as it hits my eye, feels cooling and soothing. She pulls the lid up and down a few times as though rubbing the drops in. She keeps my eyelid open and I can see light.

I'm not blind. I'm not blind. Well, not completely, anyway.

Sue lets my lid drop and I am unable to force it open. She repeats the process on my right eye. This time I see the skin on her face, its pores magnified, when she peers in after administering the drops.

I am not blind.

I may not be able to open my eyes but I am not blind.

Sue wipes my face, my neck, my hands. Then she

lifts whatever I'm wearing – I imagine some hideous crunchy hospital gown – lays a towel completely over my bottom half and proceeds to wipe down the top of my body. I can feel her actions but not the sensation of hot or cold. I think she's using a wet flannel, because I'm sure I hear her rinsing it and wringing it out.

'I hear your physio was a bit harrowing this morning,' Sue says.

I don't know what she's talking about.

'You've got a bit of a bruise on your chest. Still, it could be worse.' The last part is muttered to herself. 'Your chest is so much better.'

I really don't know what she's talking about. I don't remember any physio.

Robin hasn't said anything since his first comments about Sue's loudness, so maybe he's gone now. I hope he has, because I have a feeling this indignity is about to get worse.

I am right; it does. Sue covers up the top half of me and exposes the bottom. Oh God, the indignity. She's wiping me. Everywhere. Turning and twisting me so she can gain access. I try to think of other things, try to zone out. Remind myself that this is good, that I am being looked after. But, oh, the indignity. I imagine this is what it must be like to have a baby. I remember Clare at work, after coming back from maternity leave, had joked with another new mother that she had parked her dignity on the hospital doorstep and picked it up on the way out. They'd laughed together about it. Maybe I'll be able to laugh about this.

Thank God Robin isn't about. I hope.

Finally, the indignity is over. Sue covers me up

with the towel, or it could be a blanket; I can't really tell.

'Okay, Juliette, catheter doesn't need changing, so you're done once I get you a clean gown.'

Catheter? Catheter.

'How you doing, Juliette? Has she finished yet?'

Robin is back. He asks the question as if expecting me to answer. I wish I could.

'Here we are, Juliette. A nice clean gown.' Sue is back, lifting my right arm and threading it through the sleeve. She doesn't put my left arm in it, just tucks it around my shoulder. Then tucks it around my body and legs. 'I just need to reposition you. I'll apologise now for any discomfort.'

She heaves my legs to the side, then pulls my body to follow them. I think I might fall out of the bed which wobbles, and hisses its displeasure. I wait for Robin to say something, to tell her not to be so rough, to defend me. But he doesn't.

My chest feels as though it is being crushed. I am in pain.

'Sorry, Juliette.' Sue pats my arm. 'All done now. It's for your own good. These air-stress beds are good, but we still need to move you. We don't want you to get pressure sores.' She pulls the bed clothes over me and I try to relax into my new position as gradually the pain in my chest subsides. 'I'll be back in a few hours to turn you again. Try to get some sleep now.'

If I could groan, I would.

How does she know I'm not asleep? Maybe, she doesn't. Maybe, she just hopes I can hear her.

'It's for your own good, Juliette.' Deep down I know that Robin is right, but I don't want to hear it. I hurt all over. I didn't hurt so much before. The effort of all this has exhausted me.

After what seems like minutes, Sue is back.

'It's her again. Big mouth.' Robin's voice sounds loud to me, but maybe that's because he's right by my ear. I hope Sue hasn't heard, no need to offend her.

'Sorry, I've been so long. I'm running late but we've been really busy tonight.' Sue's voice *is* loud. We're just going to reposition you.'

We?

The bed clothes are removed and two pairs of hands grab at me.

'How are you, Juliette? All right?' It's a new voice, a male one.

I'm heaved into a different position and the bed covers are pulled back up.

'Those eyes have definitely improved since I was last on. The swelling has really gone down.' I hear the rustle of paper. 'And I see your pneumonia is much better, last day of antibiotics tomorrow. Soon have you back to normal. See you later.' The last few words are said as he moves away. So, while I'm not familiar with him, he is with me. I shudder. I have no dignity. No privacy.

'I've told them it's not appropriate for a male nurse to look after you, but I was met with blank stares.' Robin sounds annoyed.

Part of me agrees with him but a part of me doesn't care. I'm tired. I'm aching. Maybe it shows, because Robin pats my left arm to reassure me.

'The sooner you wake up the better for all of us, Juliette.'

He's right. I'm forgetting how many hours he must be spending in that chair. I bet it's a rigid plastic one.

And my poor mum, trawling up here every day. She must be off work. How long will they put up with that?

Robin might as well go home tonight, though, because I can hardly stay awake. I'm exhausted.

I'm awake. But my eyes don't open and I still cannot move. I'm on my back again. Have I been moved in my sleep?

I was having that dream again; the car turning and turning. The flames, my body in the tight black coat with the ridiculous big buttons. It's just a dream. It's over.

And I have pneumonia. I've just remembered. That's what the male nurse said. Is that how I got to be in this mess? How did I get pneumonia?

'Morning, Juliette.' It's him again. The male nurse. What's his name? 'Did you hear what the doctor said? He said they're so pleased with your progress they're going to try taking the tube out today.'

What's he talking about? Tube? Does he mean catheter? I never heard any doctor.

'That'll be so much better, won't it?' He starts to dab at my eyes. Lifting the lids like Sue did. I get a glimpse of him. His skin is dark, his eyes are caramel. He smiles. He looks friendly, kind. 'I'm Jeff, by the way, but you already know that.'

I don't.

'Hi Jeff,' Robin says, a smile in his voice. He's back, or maybe he never went away. 'Don't be taken in by his charms,' he whispers in my ear.

He always says things like that. If we meet someone new, on holiday, at a party, anywhere really, and I comment that they seem nice, he'll always argue. He says you can't judge people by their looks, you can't tell what people are like by their exterior. He always says I'm too ready to think people are nice. In his experience, most people aren't nice.

I always counter that with how I thought he was nice when I first saw him, and I was right.

I still get a thrill when I think about our first meeting. Our first proper meeting, I mean, not the ones at my parents' tea table or my dad's study. I mean our first meeting on our own. It was the following week after our first A'level tutoring session, the Thursday when he wasn't tutoring me. I told Mum I was going to History study group, but Robin was giving me extra tuition at his house, for free. He said I was worth it.

He picked me up from the end of our street; he drove a little sporty car then, I don't know what it was, but it was grey. We'd agreed not to tell my parents about the extra tuition; Robin said they might feel obliged to pay him and insist he come to our place. Or stop us. I didn't want them to stop us.

'Buckle up,' he said as I lowered myself into his car. I was wearing jeans, new dark ones and a soft, floaty top. Underneath I wore new underwear, bought with money I'd been saving for a new coat. I had my school bag on my lap. 'Aren't you cold?' I wasn't wearing a jacket and it was October, and windy.

'No,' I lied. I was hardly going to wear my coat, the hideous navy thing I wore to school every day.

He was wearing jogging bottoms, and a soft grey hoodie over a white t-shirt. I'd never seen him so casual; he'd always come to our house straight from school. His hair was wet, dark curls licked around the back of his neck and across his forehead. The air in the car smelled of shampoo and shower gel as though he'd just jumped out of the shower. Had he done that just for me? My heart skittered in my chest.

'Excuse the wet hair,' he said, noticing me studying him. 'Just been to the gym.'

I had to stop myself from gasping. I imagined his gym toned body beneath the while t-shirt.

'Cool,' I said as he pulled away, one large hand on the gear stick, both eyes on the road, but I saw the little smile that lifted the corners of his mouth.

He pushed a CD into the car stereo, something blared out that I wasn't familiar with.

'You like this?'

'Yeah.' I'd have said anything to please him.

His house was brand new. Two-up, two-down, was how he described it. But that didn't account for the bathroom upstairs. It was sparsely furnished, just a sofa and TV in the lounge, a table and two chairs in the kitchen-diner.

'Good job the kitchen was fitted, and the carpets included,' he joked as we sat down at the table. He sat opposite me before pulling off his hoodie and dropping it on the floor. His six-pack was visible through his t-shirt. He noticed me noticing and smiled. 'It's why I do the tutoring. So I can afford furniture.'

'How many others do you tutor?' The thought had suddenly occurred to me and I felt jealous.

'Two at the moment. Plus you.' He watched my face as he spoke.

'Oh.' I looked down. What right did I have to be jealous?

'Yep, a boy of fourteen on Mondays, and a girl your age, no she's younger,' he looked away, then back at me. 'In your old spot on Tuesdays.'

'Cool.' I flicked open my Maths textbook. 'I was struggling with this in class.' I pointed at the page.

His hand went over my finger, wrapping around it, his skin hot, mine cold. It felt as though electricity sparked between us. 'Really? We wouldn't want you struggling.'

I felt sick. Sick with excitement, sick with anticipation.

He whipped his hand away.

We spent the next hour working on my Maths problem. We behaved as though nothing had happened. I began to wonder if it had. Wondered if I had just imagined it or read meaning where there was none.

'I think you've grasped it.' He stood up. 'Fancy a coffee?'

'Cool. Thanks.' I couldn't look at him; I'd spent the previous hour concentrating on my textbook, my pen, anything rather than look at him. I didn't really like coffee.

'I think we should call it a night after this. I'll drop you off home.'

'Cool,' I muttered into my chest.

He made coffee, dribbled milk into then asked if I wanted sugar. Before I could answer, he said, 'No, sweet enough already.'

I blushed, I knew my neck was blotching as he looked at me.

He placed the coffee on the table in front of me and sat back down in his place. I didn't look up.

'So, how's school in general? Are you happy you made the right choice staying at school and not going to sixth-form college?' He sounded like my mum. I wondered if my dad had put him up to this.

'Yeah, it's cool. All my friends are there.' I concentrated on my coffee, blowing across the surface before taking a sip.

'Boyfriends?' Robin let the word linger on his lips, the questioning intonation hanging in the air.

'No. Can I use your loo?' I put the coffee cup down and stood up.

'Up the stairs, straight ahead.'

The bathroom was neat and tidy, folded black towels on the towel rail, a single bar of black soap – I'd never seen black soap before – in a black soap dish. After I flushed the toilet I looked through the cabinet above the sink. I saw the cologne he wore; I stopped myself from touching the bottle in case some leaked onto me. How would I explain that? There would be no escaping the smell; delicious and strong. Robin.

He was waiting for me at the bottom of the stairs, twirling his keys and wearing his hoodie again.

'Okay?'

'Sure.' I collected my books from the table and we headed out to the car. I hadn't drunk the coffee.

He opened the car door for me and made a show of ushering me inside before leaping round and jumping into the driving seat. As we pulled away I stared straight ahead and didn't say anything.

'Good session tonight. I thought. Didn't you? Did you get what you wanted from it?'

'Yes. Thanks.'

'Good, I don't want you thinking that because it's free it's not as good.'

I nodded. 'Course not.'

He dropped me at the end of the street and roared

off.

Twenty minutes after I got home he messaged me: J, jst checking u got hm ok. Gr8 sesh 2nite. C u nxt wk at urs. R xx

Wow. Two kisses. And he called me J, signed off as R. Wow. I agonised over my reply, it took fifteen minutes and several attempts before I finally pressed send: R, hm ok. Gr8 sesh! J x

I kept his text as long as I could, cherished it. That following week, I must have looked at it a hundred times. It was the first of many, even though it sounds odd now with its text-speak. Now Robin writes messages so long they're like essays, and the grammar is always perfect. That's technology progression for you, he says, when I tease him about it.

'Hi Juliette.' The voice, female and yet another new one, says to me. 'I'm Jo Pandy. I've been looking after you. We're going to have a go with this tube now, it's helping you breathe but you don't need it now. We've weaned you off all sedation. It's hard for you to let us know because you can't speak and you can't open your eyes, but we think you're having periods of wakefulness.'

I am. I am.

'We'll give it a go, shall we? We'll take the tube out and see how you get on. Don't worry, we can always put it back in.' She turns away from me and speaks to someone else. 'What time is Mum due in?'

'In the next half hour,' Jeff, my male nurse, says.

'We can't wait. Obs all good?'

'Yes. Good.'

'Okay. Juliette,' she's talking to me again. 'We're going to start.'

'Just clearing out some of the mucous,' Jeff says as something is poked into my mouth. It reminds me of the dentist. That's when I realise that they mean I have a tube in my mouth. I hadn't noticed. How can I not have noticed?

Is this tube breathing for me? Have I been unable to breathe myself? Is it the pneumonia? I'm confused. What if I can't breathe on my own? I'm confused. I'm afraid.

'It's okay, Juliette. You're doing really well.'

I can hear clicks and rustles on my chest. What are they doing?

'Okay. Everything's good. Just going to pull it out now. Cough when it comes out, if you can.'

It feels as though I'm being turned inside out, as though they're pulling my lungs up through my throat. It's horrible. Jeff is rubbing the back of my hand telling me I'm doing well.

Where's Robin? I wonder if they sent him out. Probably just as well, he's squeamish, he couldn't stand this. It's horrible.

Then it's over and I cough twice, small coughs. 'Well done. Well done. Just popping this oxygen mask on.'

I breathe. I breathe by myself. The air I breathe hurts on its way in, and it's cold. My chest aches. My throat feels as though it's on fire. But I am breathing. I am breathing. Tears roll down my face.

'You did really well.' Jeff wipes the tears from my face. 'Your throat will be sore for a day or two. You're doing really well. And here's Mum.'

I hear Mum gasp. I suppose it's shock or relief. The chair scrapes on the floor as Mum sits.

'Poor darling,' she says, wiping my hair to one side.

'You'll be able to talk now.'

Talk? Talk? I've only just learnt to breathe.

I'm exhausted. I can't hear any more. I don't want to hear any more. I sleep.

When I wake, Mum is still here and she's reading Pride and Prejudice again. I've lost track of where we are in the story but she's just mentioned Mr Collins – he's the relative that will inherit everything when Mr Bennet dies, because daughters weren't allowed to.

I suppose if I'd died Robin would have inherited everything I own. Not that I own much. My car, my clothes, my *stuff* – he always calls it my stuff, he means make-up and handbags and, well, my stuff. And, my half of the mortgage. Not that much to show for my life really. No children. That saddens me. I inhale deeply.

Mum jumps and calls a nurse. Jeff appears.

'She gasped and shuddered. Is she in pain.'

Jeff pokes around, presses buttons on machines that beep, and declares that I'm fine.

I'm not fine.

I'm never going to have a baby.

Even though I can't remember much that's happened recently, I remember the night I found out.

'I'm late.' I had a smile on my face that made my jaw ache.

Robin glanced at his watch and shook his head. 'No. We're not leaving for another ten minutes.' He was reading the newspaper at his desk, we'd just moved and he now had his own study. The house was brand new, Robin liked brand new, not soiled or spoiled by anyone else. The walls were painted magnolia, clean and fresh.

We were going to the cinema, I can't remember what we were seeing because it was Robin's choice; we never went in the end.

'No, silly. I mean I'm late.'

He frowned. I sighed.

'I think I might be pregnant.' I'd been fantasising about it all day, imagining his delight when I told him.

'No. You can't be.' He didn't even look up from the paper. This wasn't quite the reaction I'd expected.

'I think I might be. I'm nearly a week late. I'm never late.'

He didn't answer so I carried on prattling, but now he was watching me. Intently.

'I know we haven't planned it, and I know we've just moved and we've taken on a big mortgage and everything, but it'll be fine. I can go back to work later and ...' I stopped.

He was shaking his head. His eyes had narrowed and his face was red.

'If you are,' he said, between gritted teeth, 'it's not mine.' He stood up.

'Of course it is. Who else's could it be?'

'No. It's not mine.'

'But why are you saying that?' I remember a hiccup that turned into a sob. I was crying. He'd made me cry.

'If you are pregnant, it's not mine.' He pushed past me and strode to the kitchen. I followed to find him at the sink downing a glass of water.

'I don't understand.'

'If you've been unfaithful, I can't have you in my house.'

'Our house,' I corrected, forcing the words out between sobs. 'Our home.'

'Huh.' He pushed past me again and marched back to his study. I galloped along behind him.

'I don't understand. I thought you'd be pleased. You've always played with Mads and said what a delight she is.' Mads was eleven then, cheeky and funny and almost as in love with Robin as I was. I was twenty-four and we'd been married six years. Robin was thirty-six. We were the perfect ages to start a family.

'It's not mine.'

'Why do you keep saying that?'

'Because . . . because I can't have children.'

I slumped down onto the floor, my back against the wall, my legs splaying out in front of me.

'Why not?'

'Because I can't. Because of something that happened in the past.' He turned away from me, I saw his shoulders rise and fall. I imagined some illness, an accident maybe.

'But maybe you can now. Maybe it's, you know, healed, or something.'

He spun round, he looked at me in horror.

'It doesn't work like that. If you're pregnant, it's not mine.'

I pulled myself up from the floor. 'Yes. It. Is.'

He barged past me again; I heard him grab his keys from the hall table and storm out. Seconds later his car was roaring down the road which was frightening, because, since I'd passed my test, he rarely drove.

I went into the lounge, sat down and seethed and sobbed.

He came back two hours later. I was sitting in the dark. He flicked the light on.

'God, look at the state of you.'

My face was a mess of snot and tears. I didn't care what I looked like.

'Okay,' I spat. 'Tell me this. If you can't have children why have we been using condoms all these years?' I'd had plenty of time to think in his absence.

'Keeps it neat and tidy. And clean.'

'What?' I screeched.

'Like I said, it's not mine; we've been using condoms and I'm fucking infertile. There, happy now you've made me say it? How could it possibly be mine?'

I suppose I could see it from his point of view. But I hadn't been unfaithful. Why would I? He's the love of my life. Always has been, always will be. How could he even think that I would do that? I started sobbing again, great big, ugly, snotty howls.

He looked down at me, sneered, turned and stomped up the stairs, slamming the bedroom door behind him.

I slept fitfully on the sofa. We had spare bedrooms but there were no beds in them.

In the morning, I was stiff and aching.

I didn't go to work for the rest of the week. I wasn't pregnant. I was bleeding profusely.

Mum slaps the book shut.

'There. That's a good place to stop. Don't you think?'

I still can't move or open my eyes, but I manage a grunt through the mask.

'Well done, well done.' Mum pats me and hugs me. I feel overwhelmed and crushed. I grunt my disapproval and she understands. 'Sorry, Juliette. It's just so good to know you're back with us.'

I grunt again, because I know it will make her happy.

Mum starts bustling about, a cupboard door opens.

'I brought your hairbrush up,' she says to the sound of rummaging. 'Here.'

The brush caresses my hair, Mum is so gentle. I'm soothed and calmed by it. I'm a little girl again.

'That's better. You look more like you now.' She opens the cupboard again, then closes it. I imagine her putting the brush away. 'I'm going to get off now, sort out your dad's tea, and we'll both be back this evening. He'll be so pleased to hear you're really on the mend. He'll really notice the difference in you, just in the few days he's not seen you.' She kisses me. Her hand straying to my hair again, pushing it to one side across my forehead. 'Once your hair grows back on that shaved side, those scars won't even show.' She turns on her heels and leaves.

I grunt after her but she doesn't come back.

What does she mean? Scars? Shaved? Hair?

FOUR

Robin loves my hair. That's why I keep it long. I've had the same style since I first met him; side parting, elbow length, straightened, dark brown. A few years back I casually mentioned that I was thinking of getting it cut, that I was toying with something more sophisticated. He begged me not to.

'I love your hair.' He began to stroke it and lift it up, letting the strands drop to allow the light to play through them. 'It's one of your best features.

'Really?' I wasn't too sure if I was happy about that or not.

'I think I fell in love with your hair the very first time I saw you.' He smiled at the memory.

'What? At the tea table at Mum and Dad's.' I found that hard to believe; I remember it as being greasy the first time he tutored me – although it never was again.

'Yes.' He smiled again, a look of pleasure in his eyes. 'It was so silky, so innocent.'

'Innocent?'

'I mean you hadn't done things to it like so many women do. Colours, curls.'

'No, because I was fifteen and not allowed; you've met my mum.' I laughed.

'Well, it looked good then and it looks good now. Don't change it.'

So, I didn't; even though sometimes it felt a bit

dated. I did, however, start wearing it up for work, which Robin frowned at the first time but ignored thereafter, as long as it was down at home.

I've kept the same style, but when I go for my trim, I've started having a semi-permanent colour applied. My hair won't stay that dark, dark brown forever, it's already starting to fade. But Robin doesn't need to know that.

I wonder what the hell it's like now. Part of my head shaved – Robin won't like that. I'm surprised he hasn't said anything; he must be feeling very sorry for me not to have mentioned it.

When I'm better, when I'm out of here, it might be the time for a new hairstyle. I can hardly go around with long hair on one side and a shaved head on the other. He wouldn't like that either and neither would I.

Hair's a funny thing. I've always loved Robin's hair. It's even darker than mine and even though he keeps it short, it manages to curl and flick along his collar. He doesn't like it doing that, says it makes him look too exotic. Sexy exotic, I always correct. He's got quite a few silver hairs mixed in with it now, some around his temples, which he's accepted, albeit reluctantly, after someone at school told him it made him look distinguished. I daren't tell him he has more at the back of his head; I'm not sure how he'd react to that.

He has an abundance of chest hair too.

Every other Thursday, when he picked me up for our illicit tutoring session, it would always be on his way back from the gym. His hair was always damp and a bit tousled and the necks of his t-shirts never quite prevented his chest hair from peeping out.

I imagined a thick mat of hair, running my fingers through it, stroking it, twirling it. I imagined all these things as I sat next to him in his car or opposite him at his kitchen table.

It took until Christmas before that fantasy became a reality.

It was raining and cold when he picked me up from the end of the street. I jumped in and shivered as I dropped Mum's wet umbrella in the foot well.

'No coat?'

'No.'

'You must have a coat. What do you wear to school?'

'A hideous thing that I wouldn't be seen dead in anywhere else. And my denim jacket is too tight.' Despite my slim build – I was barely a size eight then – the jacket didn't fit because I'd had it since I was thirteen. Mum said it was fine, but I thought it gaped across my chest. I felt self-conscious in it. It had pink trim and embroidery on the sleeves; I was sixteen now and I thought it babyish. I had other childish jackets too, but I wouldn't wear them either.

And Mum wouldn't be buying me a new coat anytime soon, especially as the hideous one was new in September. Despite my dad having a good job, Mum hadn't worked since Mads arrived and we lived in a money-pit, according to Dad. We had a large, rambling house that always needed work doing; the plus side was that both Mads and I had our own bedrooms and a bathroom between us.

I was saving up for a new coat, or a jacket, I hadn't decided. It had taken longer than originally planned after I'd spent some of the money on new underwear but now I only needed to work two more shifts and I would have enough to get something in the January sales. It had been Mum's idea for me to get a Saturday job and our local Tesco had been very convenient. Not that I had told Robin about it. I didn't want him knowing I worked in a supermarket.

'So, no, I don't really have a coat,' I added.

An absent smile passed over Robin's face as he drove.

We dashed indoors and I took my shoes off in the hall; he had new carpets and didn't like them getting soiled. As I padded through to the kitchen I prepared myself for a few hours in Robin's company, even if it did mean equations and algebra, because I knew I wouldn't see him again for a few weeks. I would hardly be going to study group during the Christmas break – Mum wouldn't fall for that one. Anyway, I'd been asked to work extra hours at Tesco.

On the kitchen table was an elaborate present, large and wrapped in gold metallic Christmas paper. Red, curling ribbons spiralled out from the top. Robin would need to move that before we began.

'Been doing your wrapping?' I imagined some lovely girlfriend that he'd never mentioned – why would he – whooping with joy on Christmas morning. My heart sank, so did my shoulders and my spirit.

'Yes.' He had a faraway look in his eyes.

'Do you want to move it?' I dropped my school bag onto the table and let out an audible sigh, immediately wishing I hadn't.

'Not really.'

I looked at him. What was that supposed to mean? Did he expect us to crowd into the small space left? It was hardly a big table to start off with. I was beginning to wish I hadn't come. 'Oh.'

'It's for you.'

'What?'

'It's for you. Happy Christmas.'

I didn't know what to say, at first. Then I said that stupid thing that people always say when caught out. 'But I haven't got you anything.'

He laughed. Threw back his head and really laughed, exposing his throat; his chest hairs rising higher above the neck of his t-shirt.

'Don't be silly. I wasn't expecting anything.'

'Neither was I.' How ungrateful I sounded.

Its metallic paper twinkled at me. I didn't know what to do. It was enormous. I wondered how I could sneak that into the house. Then I saw the tag.

Juliette
Merry Christmas.
Robin
xxxx

Four kisses. Four. I smiled at him, all the while feeling my face redden.

'Aren't you going to open it?'

'It's not Christmas yet.' How stupid I sounded.

'That's okay. Open it.'

I let my fingers drift over the paper. 'It seems a shame to spoil it. It looks so beautiful.'

He laughed again. 'Come on, open it. I want to see if you like it.'

My fingers trembled as I turned it around and around, looking for the opening. I didn't want to ruin it; somewhere there should be Sellotape I could peel away carefully. But there wasn't. Robin was watching me intently. I looked into his eyes and forced a smile.

'What are you doing?' He patted my shoulder. I

flinched, but not because I didn't like it.

'I don't want to wreck it; it looks too lovely.'

'Pull the ribbons, that's what's holding it together.' He took my hands in his and guided them towards the red-ribbon curls. I felt my heart beating in my chest and my ears. Could he hear it?

Together we pulled the ribbons and the parcel opened, the paper floating down with elegance to reveal the treat within.

The coat. The black coat. The one with the too-big buttons.

I gasped. It was gorgeous. I'd seen it in a magazine only the week before. Had I mentioned it to Robin? Of course not.

'Oh my God.'

'Try it on. Here, let me help you.' He held the coat up for me to slip my arms into the sleeves, then turned me around to button it up. I felt the pull of the fabric across my breasts. 'Perfect,' he pronounced, standing back to admire me. He guided me into the living room, stood me in front of the mirror. His hands stayed on my shoulders as he hovered behind me.

The coat looked great. But not as great as him standing so close, smiling, his reflected eyes twinkling as they looked into mine.

'Gorgeous.' The word was whispered into my ear. I shuddered. 'Do you like it?'

'I, I, love… it.' I stuttered. I had almost said, I love you.

'I knew you would. I knew you'd look amazing in it.' He kissed me on the cheek. My knees buckled. And he caught me.

As he spun me around it was me who made the

first move, me who thrust my face towards his, me who kissed him. I expected him to push me away, I was petrified he would be repulsed. Why would he, a grown-up, drop dead gorgeous man who could have anyone, want a swotty sixteen-year old? I decided to enjoy the experience while it lasted and suffer the humiliation afterwards.

He did step back. He held my hands and pulled them out from my body.

'Well,' he said. He sounded kind.

I looked down. Ashamed. Embarrassed. I didn't want kind. 'Sorry.'

'Why?'

'I was just saying thank you. For the coat.' I tried to pull my hands away but he held them fast.

'You like it?'

'I love it.' Hadn't I already said so.

'I love you.'

I blinked in astonishment. Had he really just said that? Or, had I misheard? Our eyes locked.

'Did you hear what I said?'

'I, I think so.'

'I said I love you.'

'I love you too.'

He let go of my hands and took my face in his. Then he kissed me, rather more expertly than I had kissed him. I was in heaven.

'I'm sorry,' he said, stepping back, letting my face drop; the face he had just been cradling. 'I shouldn't have done that, or said that. I don't know what came over me. I can only apologise. My feelings…' He left the words floating in the air.

'Oh?' I was confused, bewildered.

'Maybe I should take you home.' He turned as

though looking for his keys.

'But why?'

'It's wrong. I shouldn't have done that. I'm your tutor. It's just that my feelings overtook me then. I'm sorry.'

'Don't be sorry.'

'This isn't going to work. I can't be near you and not want you.' He left the room, found his keys on the kitchen table. 'I'll take you home. Come on.'

'I don't want to go home.' I nudged the table leg with my foot. I was sulking, I knew I was. I even knew how immature it looked.

'Juliette, you're too young for me.' He sighed and looked up to the ceiling as if praying for an answer.

'I'm old enough. I'm legal. I'm sixteen.' The words trotted out with practised ease; I'd said them enough times in my head.

'Yes, but . . .'

'But what?' I didn't wait for his answer, I just wrapped my arms around his head and pulled his mouth to mine. I was sure he would succumb in the end.

When it was time to go home, the coat, along with my other clothes were draped across the chair in his bedroom. I fumbled to get my bra back on as he kissed my bare shoulders.

Alternate Thursday evenings would never be the same again.

I sneaked the coat home, hid it and later passed it off as one I had bought in the sales with my Tesco earnings. Mum said it was quite nice. It was a year later before I accidently let slip the truth and Mum and Dad expressed their extreme disapproval.

Especially Mum.

'Well done, Juliette.'

I grunt in response to Robin's praise. The sound comes from my throat. He pats my left arm. I wish he wouldn't as it's sore. I grunt again, attempting to show my displeasure.

'What you need to do now, Juliette, is move. And get those eyes open.'

I grunt again.

'Try wiggling your toes. Focus all your energy and attention on your toes.'

I try. The bed clothes are resting on my feet and I can feel the texture, or at least I think I can. I focus so hard it hurts, then miracle of miracles, I move my right toe.

I grunt to let Robin know; I just hope he is watching.

'I saw it, Juliette. I saw it. Just keep working on it.'

I grunt again. If only I could move my lips, then I might be able to speak.

'I'm going to stay with you until your parents come back, so let's work together. Move those toes.'

I'd rather move my mouth.

'Move those toes. Move those toes.' Robin sounds as though he's at a football match, but his encouragement is working, I manage another miniscule twitch. I hope he remembers to tell the nurses and Mum and Dad.

'How are we doing, Juliette?' It's nurse Jeff's voice.

'She's doing really well,' Robin says, pride in his voice. I add my grunt.

'Good stuff. I'm off soon, so I'm just going to turn you.' He's already started moving me before he's even finished the sentence. It hurts and I don't like it. I was comfortable, I was moving.

After he's finished I feel like a dead weight. Solid. Immovable.

'Good news about your MRI this morning. Congratulations.' He laughs. 'Soon have you up and about.'

MRI? I don't remember that. What's he talking about? Must have gone well if he's congratulating me.

I'll see you tomorrow.' Nurse Jeff taps my foot. I can't even twitch it in response; how annoying. 'Keep up the good work.'

I lie in the bed on my side and I am uncomfortable. I grunt but no one responds. Has Robin left without saying goodbye? I grunt again. Nothing. Where is he?

Minutes pass.

'Sorry about that, I had to nip to the men's.'

Yeah, and you could have told him I moved my foot. I sigh. It's quite audible, even through the oxygen mask.

'Then I stopped off at the nurses' station.'

I wait. He pats my left arm. Stop doing that.

'Seems your MRI went well, earlier.'

Yes. I wait. But apparently, that's it. It's annoying how I can't remember anything and I'm not able to ask questions and Robin doesn't seem to think I need more information. I think I need to concentrate on moving my mouth, not my feet. Communicating is more important than moving now.

'Let's work on moving those toes.'

I ignore him. I'm working on my mouth, but the muscles don't respond.

'Come on, Juliette. Toes. Toes.' This reminds me

of ballet class when I was little. Good toes, naughty toes. I started when I was three. I loved it. Prancing around in my pink shoes and tights, my little black leotard, the pink cross-over cardigan Mum had knitted. Mads later wore it to her first classes too, years later. We used to joke that it was indestructible. Neither of us was ever going to be a ballet dancer, but we both loved going.

'Toes. Toes.'

I ignore Robin and focus on my mouth. If I can just get some movement, maybe I can say something. Anything.

'Toes. Try harder.'

I grunt, but it's still a grunt.

'Toes. Come on, flex those toes.'

Mouth, move mouth.

'I'm not seeing any movement, Juliette.'

Oh, shut up, Robin. Mouth, move.

'Make an effort, move those toes.'

'No.' I hear a shout.

'Juliette? Was that you?' Nurse Jeff is back; I thought he'd gone home.

I struggle then manage a feeble, 'Yes.'

'Well done. Well done. Hey, I'm glad I'm running late and was here when you said your first word. Well done. I'll let them know on my way out.' His voice fades away.

I wait for Robin to congratulate me.

'No wonder your toes weren't moving.' Is he sulking? 'I suppose you were working on that rather than your toes.' He *is* sulking. He should be pleased for me.

'Yes,' I manage again.

He doesn't reply and the effort of saying those

three words has exhausted me and I'm so tired that I start to doze off. It's proper sleep too, not just the absences which I seem to have been having.

I wish I could remember the MRI scan.

Mum's voice wakes me, though she's not talking to me. Her words drift towards me, she's thanking a nurse for some good news – my speaking, I guess. I can hear the smile in her voice. Then her tone changes.

'Oh. Are you sure? Right. Okay. Well, we'll leave it at that.'

'Your parents are here, so I'll get off.' Robin's voice is little more than a whisper in my ear.

I manage a grunt in response.

'I'm tutoring tonight, so I might not make it back until the morning.'

'Yes.'

He pats my arm. 'It's good to hear you speak.' I hear the pleasure in his voice. Good. He's forgiven me for not following his instructions. 'She's all yours,' Robin says to my parents as he leaves. 'Look after her.'

'Hello Juliette.' It's Dad's voice. He wipes my hair aside and kisses me on the forehead.

I focus all my energy.

'Hi.'

Mum sniffs; she's probably crying. Even Dad's voice sounds thick with emotion when he tells me how clever I am.

It's only speaking, Dad. A feeble little laugh escapes my mouth. I've just noticed that I'm on my back again, half sitting up – I've been moved in my sleep.

'You're looking much better.'

'Yes.'

'Sorry I haven't been up for a few days; bloody Ofsted. But I can see such an improvement in you.'

'Yes.'

'It's been tough, watching you lying there.'

'More.' I need so much more and no one is telling me anything.

'You want more?'

'Yes.'

'What do you want more of?'

'More,' I say again. 'Info.'

'Start at the beginning, Brian.' That's my mum issuing instructions. Bless her.

My dad coughs to clear his throat. There's some scraping of chairs as they sit down.

'Do you know what happened? How you got here?'

'No.'

'Start at the beginning, Brian.' Mum is getting annoyed with Dad. She often gives him directions when really, she'd prefer to do it herself. I suspect she'd do a better job too.

It was Dad, under mum's instruction, who had to warn me of the dire consequences of my relationship with Robin. It was after they'd found out I'd been seeing him every other Thursday, for nearly a year. It hadn't been a happy time for anyone.

'He's far too old for you, Juliette,' Dad had said while Mum perched on the arm of his chair biting her lip.

I'd been called into the living room the morning after Robin dropped me off. We'd long ago given up the pretence of extra tutoring; I never even took my books with me any longer, not that Mum and Dad knew that. Mum's best friend, Sally, had seen us kissing goodnight outside in the car – we were getting careless, or maybe we wanted to get caught. She must have been on that phone immediately, though they probably suspected something was going on by then. We were probably too familiar, laughing and nudging each other, during our official tutoring sessions in Dad's study. We were foolhardy. We were in love.

Dad had gone through his preamble, obviously rehearsed by Mum, asking how serious this relationship was, how far it had actually gone, and the killer question; had we done anything? He kept looking at his watch, he wanted to get to work, he would be late, but he *had* to do this first.

I remember laughing out loud, which Mum and Dad interpreted as contempt but it was actually embarrassment. I couldn't believe they were asking me about sex, with Robin. No.

'I'm seventeen now,' I'd said. I'd had my birthday two months previously, at the end of August.

'Barely.' Despite delegating to Dad, Mum couldn't hold her tongue. 'You're a child. He's not.'

She was right, Robin would be thirty after Christmas. I was proud to have lost my virginity to a proper man, not like so many of my friends who had lost theirs to gangly boys at drunken parties. My boyfriend was a man.

'I'm not a child.'

'He's your teacher.' Dad struggled to keep the horror from his voice. 'It's wrong. Unethical.'

'Tutor,' I corrected. 'He's never taught me at school. Ours was a private arrangement.' Robin and I had already discussed what I would say when we were found out. We'd run over it several times, so I was quite relaxed when confronted by my parents.

'You cheeky…' my mum shook her head.

'I'm over age. Nothing illegal or wrong.' I shrugged. I was in the right. Mum and Dad couldn't tell me who I could love, or not.

'It's wrong.' Dad shook his head. 'And while you live in this house and we support you, I prefer that you don't see him again. He's far too old for you.'

'Fine.' Oh, I was so confident. 'I can move in with Robin.'

'No,' Mum yelled and started to cry.

I expected a big row, I expected some drama. At the very least I wanted to stamp up the stairs and slam my bedroom door. I was disappointed. Apart from Mum's barely audible snivelling, there was nothing. Just three people sitting in a room looking at each other.

Dad stood up. 'Think about it,' he said. 'Promise me you won't do anything hasty.' Perhaps he'd had a vision of me stomping up the stairs and packing my clothes before rushing off to Robin's.

'Okay.' I'd looked down at my shoes, my stupid school shoes.

Dad took Mum's hand and they walked out of the room in silence before disappearing into the kitchen; the door closing softly behind them.

I went up to my room and pulled off my uniform, and climbed back into bed; I couldn't even think about going to school. An hour later and I'd exchanged numerous texts with Robin. He said he would pick me up anytime I wanted, even if it was in the middle of the night.

A soft knocking on the door made me jump. No

doubt Mum would be sitting on my bed soon, begging me not to go.

'Yeah,' I called.

The door opened and I waited for Mum.

But it was Mads who tiptoed in – she was half dressed. She pulled the blankets back and climbed into bed with me. She cuddled in tight and, without thinking I wrapped by arms around her.

'Don't go. I'll miss you.' That was all she said, then she sniffed.

I thought of Mads, her warm little body snuggled up to mine, and I didn't go. At least not then.

'Well,' Dad begins as he takes a deep breath. 'You had swelling on the brain which was why you had to be sedated, drug induced coma, sedation, they called it. But you're off all that now…' his voice trails away.

'Yes?' I manage.

'You have a broken leg, it's quite bad, but they operated and,' he pauses, 'it will heal up with a bit of work. It's pinned.'

What the hell did he mean by work? I'm about to try to ask but he cuts across me and continues.

'Your arm is quite badly injured, but it's flesh, no broken bones. They've done a graft, skin.'

'And muscle,' Mum chips in.

'Yes. Of course.' He stops and I hear Mum cough as though prompting him, but he doesn't continue, so Mum takes over.

'Then you acquired an infection, because you were lying down so long you developed pneumonia. But that's better now. Oh, and you had a few broken ribs.'

What a state I am in.

'Mess,' I force out.

'Yes, you were, darling.' Mum rarely calls me darling. Mads is darling, I'm Juliette. 'But the good news is your full body scan this morning shows a lot of improvement. And your eyes look so much better. They think you'll be able to open them in a day or too.'

'Good.' It will be good to see people, to see the world again.

'And they said, not to worry about not moving much yet, the swelling on the top of your spine is still subsiding, and that will take the pressure off and, well, it should all be just fine.' Typical Mum, jolly in adversity; the flip side is that she's usually miserable when everyone else is happy.

'So, there we have it,' Dad says. He is wearing his best headmaster's reassuring persona.

'Oh, and you're not nearly so black and blue and puffy. You were unrecognisable, but not now.' Mum pats my hand.

I concentrate hard and manage to move my index finger.

'She moved. Brian. Her hand moved. She wriggled her finger. Well done. Well done. See, you're already getting better.'

'Yes.' I wish I could manage more than one word, but even that is a struggle and I am feeling overwhelmed with tiredness again. But I'm pleased I managed to move my finger.

'So, it's all good news.' Mum is convincing herself as much as me.

'Yes.'

'Sally was asking if she could come up and see you. Would that be okay?'

Sally? Ah, Sally. Mum's best friend and next-door

neighbour for most of my life. When I don't answer immediately, Mum's voice takes on a rushed, conciliatory tone.

'She doesn't have to come. If you're not ready. There's no rush. She just said she would. It's all right, she can wait.'

'No.' I imagine Sally coming up with Mum, giving Mum some support while Dad's at work. It cannot have been easy, all this, for any of them; Mum, Dad, Robin. I'm the lucky one really, I can't remember anything. 'Bring. Bring Sally.' More than one word; I'm very pleased with myself. And exhausted.

'I can bring Sally? Is tomorrow okay?'

'Yes. Bring.' I smile inside the mask. Another first. 'I will. I will.'

Chairs scrape; Mum and Dad are preparing to leave. They're making comments about the time, about how I need my rest and that Sue – they know her name – is waiting to sort me out for the night.

They're leaning over me, kissing my not-so-puffy face and Dad is holding my hand and I manage to press my finger into his palm. He tells Mum and they're both elated.

It's only as he lets go of my hand that the biggest question occurs to me and as I blurt it out the fear engulfs me and tears escape from my locked eyes.

'How? How happen?'

FIVE

I've known all along.

It wasn't a dream. Those weren't nightmares. But as Dad tells me how I hung upside down, held only by the seat belt, how I was pulled from the burning wreckage of my car, all I can wonder is how the hell I managed such a spectacular crash?

I'm crying now. Inside the mask snot dribbles into my mouth.

'There was no other vehicle involved, Juliette. So that's a good thing.'

I can't answer, even though I can't move, my whole body is wracked by sobs.

'She asked about the accident.' Dad is not talking to me, but Sue who's obviously expressed concern about me.

'Okay. Well, don't worry, we'll give her something.' She's ushering them out and they're calling their goodbyes from a distance.

I bet they're relieved to get away. I would be.

'Come on, sweetie,' Sue says. 'You're going to be just fine. And this isn't the first time you've heard about the accident, is it? We have been telling you about it right from the start.'

Have they? I don't remember. And even if that is true, so what?

'Come on, sweetie. I'm going to give you something to help you sleep.'

'I hear your parents upset you last night.' Robin sounds annoyed.

'No.'

'That's not what I hear.'

'Not their fault. Shock.'

'Well, maybe.' He pauses. 'You're doing well with the speaking.'

'Yes.'

I hear Jeff's jolly voice as he approaches.

'Here's that bloody male nurse again. It's so inappropriate.'

'Don't care.' I'm surprised at myself, but I really don't care. Everyone is looking after me, trying to get me well, so I'm grateful. I don't think I'm in a position to be fussy.

'Hi Jeff,' Robin calls with jolly insincerity.

'Hello, Juliette.' Jeff's voice is so cheerful. 'How do you feel about having a go without the mask?'

'Yes. Good.'

'You know you're doing so well. You've come on in leaps and bounds the last few days.'

'Yes.' Speaking is still such an effort.

Jeff starts fiddling with the mask, muttering to himself and suddenly it's off.

'Just breathe normally.'

'I am.'

If feels so good not have anything pressing on my face. I hadn't realised quite how tight that mask was until it was removed. Jeff starts to wipe my face and rubs my cheeks. He wipes my eyes and lifts the lids. He smiles and I can see his smile quite clearly. I smile back.

'Wonderful. You have a lovely smile.' He lets my

lids drop. 'Did your mum bring a toothbrush up for you?' I hear a drawer opening.

I've no idea whether Mum has brought me a toothbrush. I wonder why Robin couldn't have done that. He's gone quiet now that Jeff is attending to me.

Jeff starts cleaning my teeth. I can taste the toothpaste, strong and minty.

'Do you think you can spit? Here, into this tray.' He tips me forward and I try but all that comes out is a pathetic dribble. 'Good try.' I can hear the smile in his voice. 'I'll do it for you.' Again, it's like being at the dentist as Jeff sprays water into my mouth and suckers it out. I do feel a little more normal when he's finished. 'And a final flourish,' he says, slicking Vaseline around my lips. 'Lovely. I'll be back later and we can try a drink. Yeah?'

'Thank you.'

'You're welcome.' He laughs before dragging tubing across my face and positioning something under my nostrils. 'Just a little extra help, just a little bit of oxygen.'

'Thank you.'

'I'm going to put this call button here, in your hand. I know you can't use it yet, but, well, you never know. We have seen movement in your fingers. See you later.' And he's gone. I like Jeff. And Sue.

'Has he finished? Sorry, I can't be in the same space as him. He's like a black David Walliams. So in-yer-face. Anyway, I needed some air.'

'Okay.' That sounds harsh. I wish I could see Robin's face. He seems angry with me as well as Jeff.

'You do look better, though. I'll give him that. He's tidied you up.'

'Good. Thank you.'

Robin doesn't reply. I think he's sulking.

I'm tired again; the slightest little thing exhausts me. I summon all my energy to speak.

'How did I crash?'

I hear Robin's sigh. I sense his body move in exasperation.

'I don't know, Juliette. You tell me.'

'I don't remember.'

'Probably just as well. Ugh, David Walliams is coming back.' He waits until Jeff reaches us. 'Hi Jeff.' Robin's voice is high and insincere, again.

'Try a drink, Juliette. I've got a straw.' Jeff's voice is full of smiles.

I feel the straw on my lips, but I struggle to lock them around it. Jeff massages my face and together we succeed. I suck. I feel the liquid in my mouth. It's nice. But I can't swallow, even with Jeff massaging my throat.

'Don't worry, that's normal. We'll try again later.'

'Idiot.' Robin's voice is so loud in my ear that Jeff must have heard.

'Rude.'

'Don't worry, he's gone.'

Robin's voice continues but I don't hear what he's saying as I drift off again. I know this must be hard for him, he's very protective of me. But, needs must and it's not as if he can help me, he's far too squeamish.

'I don't see any point in using condoms,' I said, flinging the packet at him. We were in our bedroom; it was two weeks after the infertile revelation. 'If you can't give me a baby, why bother with these?' I hated the rubbery smell and, secretly, I hoped he was wrong and that I might fall pregnant accidently.

Without speaking he swiped the packet up, pushed it into his bedside table drawer, pulled on his dressing gown and left the room.

I lay in bed looking at the ceiling. My bedside lamp was off, his was on. I rolled over to his side to switch it off. I inhaled the scent of him, I loved it, I loved him. Was it so unreasonable to want his baby? I felt nasty and cheated. He should have told me from the beginning that he couldn't give me babies. But we'd never had that conversation.

After six years of marriage I had come to realise that there were many conversations we'd never had. He'd rarely talked about his parents, his family – and I'd never asked. His mother lived in Brazil and his father was dead, that was all he'd ever said about them. He didn't seem to have friends, only work colleagues, and even those he mostly held in contempt.

Other than pupils he was tutoring, he never brought anyone home. I had convinced myself that once we moved to the right house, the executive house that Robin so desired – I didn't care where we lived as long as I was with him – then he'd suddenly conjure up old friends, even family, maybe. But he hadn't.

Despite the size of the house, and his private study, he liked me to be out when he had pupils round. He said it looked more professional. I didn't mind. The polite animosity between Robin and my parents meant he rarely saw them. I used those two nights a week he tutored in our house to visit home, and Mads. We had our twice weekly girly giggles on those nights. I went straight from work, had tea with my family, it felt just like old times. It was easier without Robin's scowl at the table. He'd never forgiven my parents for their objections to our wedding. I don't think he ever would. And they'd never really forgiven him for taking me away.

I woke with a start; the TV was on downstairs and I'd dozed off on Robin's side of the bed. It was the middle of the night.

Robin sat in his reclining chair, his feet up, the remote in his hand. As I entered the room he looked at me, but he didn't return my smile.

'I'm sorry,' I said, holding out the olive branch. 'I was mean.'

'You were.'

'Am I forgiven?'

'Maybe.' He looked me up and down then turned back to the TV.

'It's just I don't understand why we need condoms if…' My voice trailed away as he turned his full gaze back to me, daring me to continue.

After staring at me, weighing me up, he simply said, 'hygiene.'

'Ah.' That did explain it. He was very clean. I didn't find it a problem; we just had rules about cleanliness that we'd never had in Mum and Dad's house.

We had to change the bed twice weekly; always Wednesday evenings and Saturday mornings. It wasn't an onerous task, Robin always did it. And now that we had the lovely utility room complete with tumble dryer it wasn't difficult to launder the sheets; Robin often did those himself. Other rules included dressing gowns laundered weekly, no wearing of t-shirts or tops more than once, and never, ever, ever re-wear socks or underwear. I'd once joked that it was unlikely that would happen anyway, but he reiterated that it must *never* happen.

In themselves, these were just basic things that most people did anyway, it was just that Robin was strict about these rules. He also insisted that whatever was left on the toilet roll – even if it was a nearly full – must be binned on Sunday evening. We must start the week off fresh. Towels were changed every other day. I didn't mind these rules, often it felt as though we lived in a five-star hotel and it wasn't as though the laundry was my sole responsibility, we shared it.

I had to accept his hygiene reason; we continued to use condoms even though we didn't need to. I told myself there were worse things in the world to worry about, but a tiny little part of me wondered if he really was infertile.

'What is that smell?' Robin's voice wakes me up. 'It's awful.'

'What?' I have been so deeply asleep that I struggle to wake up.

'Can't you smell it?'

I inhale as I wake, and then it hits me.

'It's shit.' Robin says, in case I'm in any doubt.

'Yes.'

'And I think it's you. Juliette, that's disgusting.'

Oh no. He's right. It is me. It's horrible. I can feel it. I am sitting in it.

'Where's that bloody Jeff when he's actually needed?' Robin's voice is far too loud. Instead of shouting, why doesn't he go and find Jeff. 'Press the buzzer.'

The buzzer? The call button. I can feel it in my

hand; I have slept clutching it. I concentrate hard, so hard it's painful. I push my thumb down but nothing happens.

'Press it harder, Juliette.'

I try. I can't. 'You do it.'

'No, you need to do it. You need to move. Press it harder. How will you manage when I'm not here if I do everything for you?'

I try and my thumb jerks against the button. I've pressed it.

'Hey hun, did you press that button?' Jeff takes the buzzer from my hand. 'I think you did. Well done. And I think I know why.' I hear the curtains being pulled around me.

'Go,' I say to Robin.

'Don't worry, I am. No desire to stay around for this, thank you very much. The sooner you're recovered, Juliette, the better. Don't think I'm going to wipe your arse when you come home.'

'Charming.'

I start to cry. How can Robin be so mean? As if this isn't demeaning and humiliating enough without him being nasty.

'Don't worry, hun. It's normal. We'll have you fresh as a daisy before your mum gets here.'

'Please don't speak,' I say through tears. I don't want any more words said, it just makes it worse.

Jeff is good, he soon has me cleaned up; he's very thorough. There's not an inch of my nether regions he hasn't wiped down. I don't know how he can do it. I don't know how I will face him once my eyes open and I'm better. This is the ultimate cringe fest.

'There you go. Just pop a clean pad on the bed and we're done.' He turns me to one side and slides something soft, yet crinkly under me. Bedcovers back on, curtains pulled back and he's gone, I'm clean but the smell still lingers.

I wonder how many times that has happened? It doesn't bear thinking about and I'm glad I can't remember. For a moment, I wonder if I will remember this time. Probably.

I lie in the bed, comfortable and clean and I start thinking. I've been unconscious for two weeks, wakeful for a few days; it's only a matter of time before I have a period. Maybe they'll use tampons. I shudder at the prospect of Jeff pulling those out. Or putting them in. I actually shudder; I feel my shoulders shake.

'Well, that's movement.' Robin's sitting beside me again. 'Well done. But it still stinks round here.'

'Shush.' The last thing I need is his judgement or his rebuke. But he's right, I did move, even if it was in response to prospective embarrassment.

'Oh, here's your mum and her friend. I'm off, I'll see you later.'

'Bye.' I'm glad he's going, but I'm worried that Mum and Sally will be treated to the stink.

'Hello darling. Mum here. I've brought Sally with me.' Mum's voice is far too cheerful, I can tell she's really trying. Then she sniffs.

'Hello Juliette.' Sally pats my hand. 'You poor thing.' I feel her stroke my face and wipe my hair to one side. I think when they're doing this – my mum, the nurses, now Sally – they're trying to cover the scars and the shaved part of my head. They probably don't even realise they're doing it.

Mum's rummaging around in the bedside locker again. 'Ah, here it is.' She's spraying air freshener around. I think she might have done this a few times before.

I laugh. It's funny.

'Good to see you laugh again,' Mum says, squeezing my shoulder.

'Yes.'

'How do you feel?' I hope Sally isn't expecting a proper answer.

'Been better.'

'Yes. I bet you have. I'm going to be honest with you, you've looked better.' Sally never minces her words, it's why she's my mum's best friend. 'You're a mass of bruises and tubes, girl. What's this one?' The question is to Mum not me as I feel a small yank at my nose.

'Feeding tube. And the one in the neck, that's for drugs and things.'

'What things?'

'I don't know. It's a main line, no central line, or something.' I can tell from Mum's tone that she'd rather not focus on it.

'Right,' Sally says in a super jolly voice, picking up on Mum's distress. 'As long as you're on the mend, that's the main thing, Juliette.'

I can't remember a time when Sally wasn't in our lives. Mum and Dad still live in the house I was born in, well, not literally born in, that was hospital, but she lived next door when they moved in and still does. She had a baby of her own, Stephen, he was nearly a year old when I was born, so she was a great support to a new mother like Mum. They had a lot in common: young babies, little money and ramshackle old houses that needed work doing on them. They became the best of friends and nearly thirty years later they still are.

Sally was a great help when I was born and an even greater help when Mads came along. And, Mum was there for Sally when her marriage broke down and her husband traded her in for a younger model.

Sally's like a second mother to me, or at least my most favourite aunt. Mum and Sally had even managed to find a job-share years ago. I went to Sally's after school when Mum was working, and Stephen came to ours when Sally was working.

Mum and Sally sit and chat, they include me, but it's nothing too taxing. Which is great. It's like old times, when I would sit at the table quietly and listen in while they dissected some situation at work.

They're talking about the dustbin collection in their street, not exactly riveting stuff, but it's normal stuff. And, no one is demanding that I move or speak.

'Once a fortnight and even then, they can't pick it all up. Drives me mad. What do we pay our council tax for?' Sally says. 'I bet it's the same where you are, Juliette.'

'Yeah, it is.' Fortunately, I don't have much to do with it, it's Robin's domain. He even has special, long, rubber gloves to deal with it. I have a sneaking suspicion he wears a mask too.

Mum and Sally chat on, I'm only half listening, but I'm enjoying it. I can almost pretend that none of this car crash, injury stuff really happened; I'm transported back to the kitchen table. And, this is certainly better than hearing Mum's monotonous reading of Pride and Prejudice. Or was it Harry Potter? No, she abandoned that after I flipped out.

After a while I zone out, but it's lovely; I'm

comfortable and cosy. Their familiar voices are so soothing.

'Wake up sleepy. You're snoring.' Mum sounds so much happier now that Sally is with her. It's been a jolly afternoon, even if I have slept through some of it.

'Sorry.'

'Were we boring you?' Sally laughs.

'No. It was nice.' I'm saying quite a lot now. I'm rather pleased with myself. Just need to move and get my eyes open.

'We're off, Dad will pop up later, on his own.'

'Okay.'

Mum leans in to kiss me goodbye, swiftly followed by Sally.

'Stephen was asking if he could come and see you. Would that be okay?'

'Stephen? Why?'

There's a tangible pause in the jollity; I imagine them exchanging glances but it could just be my imagination.

'Don't worry, I'll tell him you're not ready for male visitors.' Sally's laugh sounds hollow.

'Okay.'

They're moving away and they shout back their goodbyes. I call a bye in response, then lift my hand to wave.

I waved. I waved. I lifted my hand and waved. But, I don't think anyone saw it.

I'm elated.

But it doesn't last.

I start to imagine what I must look like. A mass of injuries and bruises, no hair, and, something I hadn't considered before, a load of tubes coming out of me.

One up my nose, which, now I think about it, explains why I don't feel hungry all the time. One in my neck – I don't even want to think about that. Then there's the catheter, that's makes me shudder. I visualise a tube draining into a big bucket of pee beneath the bed. For some reason the bucket is red – probably so people won't miss it, or kick it, or worse.

Red. The colour of my car.

What happened? How did I crash my car? Where did I crash my car? I'll ask Robin when he comes back. Maybe he's told me all about it before and I just can't remember. It's possible he's repeated the story every day since it happened.

I must have been going fast to roll the car like that, for it to end up on its roof. Did Dad say that I was dragged from a burning car? Who dragged me? Was I really wearing that black coat? It's too small and old fashioned. I never wear it. Why would I be wearing it? Or is that just my mind playing tricks? I need to ask someone if I was wearing that coat. Maybe I've already asked. Maybe they've told me a dozen times.

'Hey hun.' It's Jeff. 'Come to do your checks and turn you before I go.' He wipes my eyes. 'You been crying, Juliette?'

Have I? 'Yeah.' I shrug.

'Did you just shrug. Wow. That's excellent. Well done. I'll note than down.'

'Cool.' Well, that's progress. A hand wave and a shrug as well as the shudder. Just need to get these stupid eyes open now.

'Physio is obviously working, they'll be delighted.'

'Physio? Who? What?'

'They come every day, Juliette. They work with you. Don't you remember?'

'No.' This is awful. I have a memory like a sieve.

'Not to worry, your brain's still repairing, making new connections, finding its way past the damage.'

I don't think I like the sound of that.

'You're doing great, really you are.' He pats my hand and disappears.

I lie back and wait for Dad to come. I've no idea what time it is now, except that if Jeff is still here it must be daytime. He seems to work during the day and Sue at night; or doesn't it work like that? I don't know. There are so many questions in my head, so many puzzles.

I suppose the state of me must be why they're keeping Mads from visiting. Though, at fifteen I think she's old enough to cope with a few bruises and tubes. Mads will cheer me up. She'll tell me things about the staff, what they look like, how they walk. She's a keen observer and a bit wicked too; but in a good way, a funny way.

When Dad comes in I'm going to insist he brings Mads with him tomorrow. I'm missing her. And, I haven't seen her for weeks, even before the accident. But the last few weeks – no, it's probably months – she hasn't been in, or is leaving just as I arrive. It's a real shame; I so enjoy our silly giggles.

Last time I went I asked Mum if Mads had a boyfriend.

'I don't think so. She's too young.' I was clearing the table at the time as Mum stacked the dishwasher.

'Anyway, so where is Mads going?' I wasn't going to let it drop, though I was only teasing.

'She has exams coming up. She goes to her friend's to study.'

'You sure of that?' It was a joke, but I wished I'd never said it.

'Not everyone is like you, Juliette.' She arched her eyebrows at me. She was, of course, alluding to my deception with Robin. 'Fortunately, she doesn't need extra tuition.'

'No. Of course. I just miss seeing Mads, that's all.'

Mads still messaged me most days, but it wasn't the same as cuddling up on the sofa and laughing over something stupid. I missed her giggles, her sense of humour. I missed seeing her, in person.

After our exchange the atmosphere was tense between me and Mum; I'd dragged up the past as well as questioning Mads's integrity. I'd suggested that Mads might not be trustworthy and Mum certainly didn't like that. After I'd disappointed them with my refusal to go to university and married Robin instead, it was as though Mum gave up on me and lavished all her attention on Mads, as though she had a second chance to bring up the perfect daughter.

We sat together in an uncomfortable silence watching soaps while I waited until I could go home, waited until Robin's pupil was safely out of my house.

It was raining and cold when I left and as I drove home, I looked forward to getting indoors and warming up. I pulled up on the drive next to Robin's car and the house was in darkness apart from Robin's study.

'Hi,' I called as I hung my coat in the hall before popping my head round his door. Robin was working away on his computer. 'Your car's steaming.'

'What?' He turned and narrowed his eyes at me.

'Well, the bonnet is steaming in the rain. You been out?'

He turned back to his computer. 'Yeah. Had to drop that kid home; the rain was so heavy. He was going to walk otherwise.'

'That's good of you.'

'You putting the kettle on?'

'Can do.' I made my way into the kitchen just as my phone buzzed in my bag.

It was a message from Mads: *Just missed you. Stay later next time. Lol xxx*

I replied that I would.

I can't remember if I did.

'Hello,' Dad's voice booms. I can tell he's smiling. Maybe Mum's told him about her good visit, or maybe the nurses have told him I moved my shoulders. 'How are you?'

'Getting there.'

'You're looking even perkier than you did yesterday. It's good to see your face now.'

'Bruises, tubes and all.' I laugh. Listen to me, I'm talking properly now.

'Well, little steps.' Dad pulls up a chair. He, like Mum, sits on the opposite side to where Robin sits. That chair must dance around this bed several times a day. 'They said at the nurses' station that you moved earlier.'

'Yeah. I did.'

'Well done.'

There's an awkward silence now, because Dad doesn't really do small talk and I've got nothing to say, unless I tell him how I pooped myself – I don't think so.

'How was Ofsted?'

'Fine. Yes. Fine. Happily, over now.'

'Good.'

'Until the next time.' He sighs, then we're sitting in silence again.

'Dad, bring Mads tomorrow.'

He doesn't answer. Maybe he didn't hear me.

'Dad. Bring Mads. Please.' I want to reassure him that she's old enough to cope with a few bruises and tubes, but I haven't got the energy to go into all that. He should know she'll be fine.

I hear a long gasp, as though he's taking in air. When he starts to speak, his voice is all gurgly.

'I can't, Juliette. Madeleine is dead.'

SIX

I don't remember much after that. I don't remember Dad leaving. I just remember the howling. Heart-breaking howling. Sue came rushing over and spoke to me, or Dad, I don't know and then nothing. She probably put something in my neck tube.

But I'm awake now.

I'm not howling anymore.

I'm crying. And the sobs shake my body.

I killed Mads.

I rolled my car over and over and Mads was there with me and I killed her. I killed my baby sister.

'Mads,' I yell out between sobs. 'Mads.'

'Calm down, Juliette. You're okay.' It's Jeff again.

Have I been out that long? I wish they'd put me out forever. No wonder I stayed in a coma, I bet they've told me before. I bet that was my reaction. Unconsciousness. How can I live with myself?

'I killed Mads,' I howl.

'I said it would upset you.' Robin's soft whisper in my ear. 'I wanted to spare you this.'

'Why didn't you tell me I killed Mads?' Each word is full of dribbles and tears, barely understandable.

'It wasn't your fault.' I wasn't asking Jeff, though that's who answers. 'Just going to give you something to calm you.'

'No.' I don't deserve to be calm. I deserve to be punished. I killed my lovely little sister. Funny, cute, sweet Mads. Mads with the wicked sense of humour and fierce intelligence, much brighter than me. I killed her.

I drift. I'm calm but still conscious. The thoughts are still here. Robin is still here.

'Better?'

I have neither the energy nor the ability to answer him.

I hear myself groan.

'Don't blame yourself, Juliette. These things happen.'

No. They. Don't. How can I have survived? I wish I had died too. Or better still, died instead. What happened? How did it happen? How did I crash? I wish I could remember. But would that help? Would it change anything?

Mads is dead.

I killed Mads.

'Hello Juliette.' An unfamiliar voice. 'Physio.'

'Hi Emma.' Robin's smiley voice is back. 'You'll like Emma. She's nice.' He likes Emma.

'I know you've had an upset, so they've sedated you, so I'll just get on with it. You just relax.'

Relax. My body can do nothing else. My mind, however, is racing. Running around in circles trying to work out why Mads was in my car? Where we were going?

Emma starts to move my limbs, my torso, my head; my body is soft and compliant. There's a comforting familiarity about these movements, my body recognises them, even though it is painful. Have they been doing this every day since it happened?

How I wish this was Mads and not me.

I do not deserve to live.

I murdered Mads.

'We're done,' Emma announces. 'Your body is

healing well and you're really responding. I'll see you some time tomorrow.'

'I told you she was nice.'

'What?' My voice has returned.

'I was just saying that Emma is nice.'

'Mads is dead.'

'I know. It's very sad. Very sad. I'm sorry.'

Sad doesn't even begin to describe it. Sad. It's tragic. Mads is gone. I cannot believe I won't see her funny little face again. She'll be forever fifteen. It would have been better if I had been forever twenty-eight instead.

I feel quite, quite sick, as though I might retch. I manage to quell the feeling by breathing deeply through my nose – that extra oxygen pumping up my nostrils is probably helping.

Mads was five-and-a-half when I moved out of Mum and Dad's. She couldn't understand why I was going. In truth, neither could Mum and Dad. I'd just told them Robin had asked me to marry him.

'What's the hurry? You don't have to get married.' Dad shook his head.

'Do you?' Mum's voice climbed an octave in alarm. She didn't want to be a granny yet.

'No. No. Nobody gets married cos they have to. It's not like the old days when you were young.' I knew that would hurt, Mum didn't like being reminded of her age and she glared at me. 'I want to be with Robin.' My voice was strong, determined, emphatic.

'Well, you can be with him.' Dad gave a little head shake, he really wasn't comfortable having this conversation with me despite being a senior school deputy-head and he must have had similar conversations with pupils. 'You can still see each other. Frequently.'

'We want to be together all the time.'

'So, live with him.' Mum's voice was matter of fact. She did that, when she couldn't cope, just went into cold, rational mode. 'And still go to university.'

'I can't live with him if I go away to university.' Mum knew that.

'In the holidays…' Mum shrugged.

'Such a shame when you did so well, when you got your first choice.' Dad couldn't understand why anyone would turn down more education.

'I've told you, I've already got a job with Belton's. They'll train me and everything, and fund it. I'll be chartered without any debt.' Belton's was the best accountancy company in town and I'd been delighted when they'd offered me a position. It was entry level, but as Robin had said, I was such a lucky girl, they only took on two trainees every three years and I was one of them.

'Mmm. But you're missing out…' Mum's voice trailed away. We all knew her main motive was to get me away from Robin. We'd already had the you've-never-even-had-another-boyfriend row – more than once.

My parents gave up then, they both knew they were banging their heads against a brick wall. I was determined. I knew what I wanted from life. I wanted Robin, forever. I was eighteen. I was an adult. I could do what I liked.

Robin had proposed to me on my birthday. He'd cooked me the most amazing meal – I had no idea he was such a good cook – then got down on one knee and presented me with the ring.

'A single solitaire, for the most important girl in the world. Please be my wife.'

I was elated. I was ecstatic. We agreed we'd have the wedding as soon as we could. We didn't want anything elaborate. Robin had just moved to a new school – away from Dad's – so the best time would be the beginning of the Christmas holidays. We'd have two weeks to fit in our honeymoon then.

Of course, Mum wasn't happy about such a short engagement. There was no time to plan. How would I get a dress, the reception venue, the invitations out, in four months?

I didn't care about any of that; I just wanted to be Robin's wife.

We married in the registry office, had the reception in one of the function rooms at The Marriot – one of the smaller ones. It was lovely. There weren't many of us.

'Where's Robin's family?' The suspicion was evident in Mum's eyes.

'His mum lives in Brazil, his dad's dead, he was an only child.' I'd told her this several times before. Why she had to keep asking, I don't know.

Robin hadn't had a best man.

'I don't hold with all that,' he said.

Mads was my bridesmaid, she looked lovely in her long, pink dress, prancing around with a basket of rose petals.

'Save them for outside,' Mum had snapped, several times.

'I'm a fairy princess, spreading love and joy to all the world.' I don't know where she'd got that from, but it made me and Robin smile.

Despite Mum's concerns I'd managed to get a dress, a bargain from Monsoon's wedding department. One of the advantages of being small – I had dropped down below a size eight by then – was that there was always something in the sales for me. It was ivory, lacy and floaty. I wore a little fur shrug over it.

'You look like a fairy queen,' Mads had said. I felt like one too.

Dad bought a new suit to give me away. Mum wore a dress and coat she'd bought in America the year before, she looked elegant but her face never cracked a smile all day. Robin looked like a male model in his Italian designer suit. My heart raced when I saw him.

Mads hadn't quite realised that once I was married to Robin I wouldn't be sleeping in the room next to hers; that she wouldn't be able to climb into bed with me in the mornings before school. She cried every time I saw her for weeks. I felt mean. Robin said she could come and stay with us at weekends, he would even let her get into bed with us if it made her happy.

Mum and Dad said no.

Mum's talking in the distance; she's brought Sally with her again. I can understand why. She needs all the support she can take to cope with me after Dad's revelation last night.

Mum won't ever forgive me for killing Mads.

I won't ever forgive me for killing Mads.

I'm crying as they approach my bed. Yes, I feel sorry for myself. And guilty. Is it murder? Will the police be interviewing me when I'm well enough? Of course, they will. But what can I tell them?

I owe it to Mads to remember.

Dad said there was no other car involved. Does that mean I hit something else? The kerb? Swerved to avoid an animal? Another person? I must remember. For Mads, I must remember.

Have they had her funeral yet? Or are they waiting for me? It's weeks. If they haven't already had it, it must be soon. Can I go in a wheelchair?

Will Mum and Dad want me there?

When I was hanging upside down in my car, the seatbelt crushing my lungs, was Mads hanging upside down beside me?

A sudden horrible thought hits me.

Did Mads die instantly or did she hang there, the life ebbing out of her while I did nothing?

Or, did she survive like I did? Was she brought in here with me? Has she only just died? So many questions and no answers.

Why did she die?

Why didn't I?

'Why?' I mutter.

'Sometimes we just have to accept the way things are,' Robin whispers in my ear.

He always says that. He said that after we married when he fell out with Mum after an argument. It had been a long time coming – the confrontation. At least she saved it until we came back from honeymoon.

We were at Mum and Dad's showing them our photos – the official wedding ones, and from our honeymoon. Robin and I sat on the sofa, Mads squeezed in between us, Dad next to me. Mum hovered in the background, jumpy and pinch-faced.

We went through all the pictures; Mads pointing herself and me out on every one. 'Fairy princess. Fairy princess. Fairy Queen. Fairy princess.' Robin swiped her hand away to prevent her from marking the photos.

'Ouch,' Mads yelled, like five-year-olds do.

'Don't slap her.' Mum stood up.

'She was marking the pictures, Mum.'

'Trust you to jump to his defence.' She glared at me. 'Get away from them, Madeleine. Come on. It's time you got ready for bed.'

Mads whinged but did as she was told. Mum disappeared for twenty minutes, during which time we went through the photos twice with Dad, all of us feeling uneasy. All the while I wondered how soon we could leave without it looking like we were sulking.

Mum came back, she didn't look any happier.

She sat in the armchair opposite us. She glanced at Dad. I saw him give a little nod.

'You ruined our Christmas.' She was speaking to Robin. 'Taking our daughter away. Taking her away from her little sister. Ruined it.'

'Mum, that's not fair. We were on our honeymoon.'

'I wasn't talking to you.' Mum shot me a look of contempt before picking up where she'd left off with Robin. 'You knew what you were doing. Taking her away from us.'

I expected Robin to round on her, to give as good as he got. But he didn't. He looked at me, at Dad, at Mum, pushed the photos back into their boxes, glanced up at the clock on the wall.

'I think it's time we went.' He stood up.

'Yes, run off,' she said. God, she looked old and bitter.

I stood up. Dad stood up. Mum stood up. We all

shuffled out to the hallway and Robin and I struggled into our coats in the confined space.

'Bye.' I kissed Dad on the cheek.

Mum turned away as I approached her.

Robin opened the front door, took my arm and pulled me with him. He was outside, I was still inside when I spoke.

'Why don't you like him, Mum?'

'Can't put my finger on it. Just don't.' Her mouth was a mean, thin line.

'Come on.' Robin yanked me through the door; Mum slammed it behind us.

I cried all the way home. Robin slammed the gears all the way home – he was driving; I had only just passed my test and he declared that I was too upset to drive.

'Sometimes we just have to accept the way things are,' he said, once we were indoors.

We didn't even discuss it, even though I tried.

I rang home the next day, it was a Sunday, Dad answered. He sounded sad and embarrassed.

'Why is Mum so against Robin?' I ask him.

'I think that's something you should ask your mum.'

'Can you get her please?'

The phone went quiet, then he was back.

'She's a bit busy.'

'She won't speak to me, will she?'

'Not at the moment.'

'Can I speak to Mads, then?'

'No. Your mum says it upsets her too much. She thinks you're coming back.'

'Oh.' I wasn't even allowed to talk to Mads on the phone now.

'Your mum did say that you can pop round for tea one evening this week.'

'Cool. What day?' This, at least was progress.

'Whenever suits you.'

'I'll check with Robin.'

'No, Robin's not invited, just you.'

'Oh.' I felt a lump in my throat. 'That's mean, Dad.'

'What day do you want to come?' He wasn't going to be drawn.

'I don't know. I'm not sure I want to come without Robin.'

'Well, the offer's there.' He sighed. Mum had made this decision and put him in the horrible position of being the go-between. 'It's up to you.'

'Yeah.'

Then he pulled the killer punch. 'Mads would love it. She's really missing you.'

I had to swallow hard not to cry.

'I'll let you know if I'm coming.'

'Bye, love.' Dad put the phone down before I could even say goodbye.

When I told Robin, I expected him to criticise them, to join in with me as I ranted and raved and declared that they were being unreasonable and mean. Especially Mum.

He didn't. He just hugged me until I had cried out my frustration.

'I don't know why Mum has taken so against you, and all of sudden too.'

He shrugged. He didn't seem to be bothered at all.

'Don't worry. Go on Tuesday, I'm tutoring a new pupil at their house that night so you can pick me up on your way home. About nine.'

The pattern was set. I went to my parents for tea every Tuesday on my own. I picked Robin up at nine. Sometimes I went twice in the same week. When we moved house and Robin had his own study, the students usually came to him, so I didn't need to pick him up so often, but occasionally he still tutored in a student's home.

Mads was allowed to stay up an extra half-an-hour on the evenings I visited, and we went on like that for years. And over those years, although Mum's attitude towards Robin mellowed, she never explained why she felt the way she did and he never came with me.

After we moved to our bigger house, Mum, Dad and Mads came over for lunch one Sunday. It was a bit awkward, but I'd invited them and I think Dad had convinced Mum that they had to come. I'd cooked roast pork, apple sauce and all the trimmings and even Mum said it was excellent. Robin had offered to cook, but I wouldn't let him.

It was only as we were sat around the dining table – brand new from John Lewis, expensive, but we could afford it now I was a chartered accountant – that I realised Mum and Dad had never been to our other house; Robin's two-up-two-down. Never. I didn't make that observation out loud.

After lunch, when everyone was food drowsy in the lounge, Dad dozed off and Robin disappeared into his study; Mum, Mads and I went through the wedding photos – the first time since that fateful evening years before.

Mum selected a few photos, we'd never got round to putting them in an album. There was one of me and Dad, several of Mads and me, one of the four of us; Robin wasn't in any of them. The next time I visited they were in a lovely frame taking pride of place next to the TV. Mum saw me notice them; neither of us commented.

Mads was about twelve by then and didn't look like the fairy princess anymore, though she'd giggled at herself when we'd looked through the photos. I didn't look like the fairy queen either. I'd put weight on – according to Robin, too much. When I'd refused pudding at Mum and Dad's one week, saying I needed to lose weight, Mum had frowned and asked why.

'Robin says I'm much bigger than I was when we got married.' I'd laughed, though it did irk me; I didn't feel fat.

'Of course you are. You're a grown woman now, you were a child when you got married.'

'I was eighteen, Mum.'

'Yes, a child.' Mum raised her eyebrows and pushed the pudding towards me, it was Summer Pudding, my favourite. I picked up my spoon; I couldn't resist.

'Don't tell Robin.'

'As if,' Mum muttered to herself.

'He isn't any fatter, you know. He can still get his wedding suit on.'

'I'm sure he can. But he wasn't a child when he got married, was he? He was a man.' The way mum said those words truly showed her feelings. That was the crux of her animosity towards Robin; he was a child-stealer. And I had been the child. Mum's child.

Dad and Mads had sat silently throughout our conversation, watching us like a tennis match. I shut up then and ate my pudding.

I'm crying when Mum and Sally reach me.

'Darling, don't cry.' Mum dabs at my eyes but I can stop.

'Mads. I killed Mads.'

'What?' Mum is audibly shocked.

'In the car. I killed her. In the accident.'

Mum doesn't say anything. The chair scrapes against the floor, Mum flops down into it.

'Juliette, listen.' It's Sally's voice. 'Madeleine was already dead when you had your accident.'

That doesn't make any sense. 'Then what was she doing in the car?' I wail. None of it makes any sense.

'She wasn't in the car. She was already dead. You were on your way back from her funeral when you had your accident.'

Funeral? Funeral? I don't remember that. I don't remember anything. My brain isn't working properly, nothing works.

'Funeral?' My tiny voice says.

I hear Mum sniff. This is obviously too painful for her.

And for me.

Just as well Sally is here.

'We were at the crematorium, you know how far out of town that is. It was raining and you, for some reason, decided that you didn't want to go in the funeral car with your mum and dad.'

Did I? Why would I do that? Why would I leave my parents on their own?

'You drove. It was raining. Visibility was bad, the roads were slippery….' Her voice trails away.

I desperately try to remember, searching my brain for a clue, but I have not one recollection of that day. Hardly surprising, since I didn't even know Mads was dead. Just that thought, that Mads is gone forever, sets me off again.

'It was a lovely service,' Sally is trying so hard to soften the blow. 'Very well attended, all her friends from school came, the crem was packed out. And they all did as you suggested and wore bright clothes, because Madeleine would have liked that.'

That's true, she would.

'What was I wearing?'

'Um,' Sally stalls, pretending she has forgotten.

'Was it a black coat with great, big buttons? Too tight?'

I hear Mum gasp.

'I think it might have been.'

Why the hell was I wearing that if I'd told everyone to wear bright colours?

'Did everyone wear bright colours? Did you? Did Mum and Dad.'

Mum blows her nose.

Sally's answer is almost whispered. 'Yes.'

'Was I the only one?'

'Well, you and your husband.'

'It doesn't matter,' Mum says, patting my hand.

I have a fleeting image of the crem, there are coloured balloons, a basket weave coffin.

'Balloons?'

'Yes.' Sally's tone is a bit brighter now. 'Do you remember?'

'Music. I remember music, her favourite band.'

'That's right.' Mum is joining in, encouraging.

It seems wrong that we should be pleased I can remember something, when that something is my little sister's funeral.

'Dad did a reading. So did I.'

'Yes. You do remember.'

'We sat in the front row, Mum and Dad, me and Robin.'

'That's right.'

'Sally, you sat behind us.'

'Yes, with my son, Stephen.'

'Stephen. Yes.'

The memory of the funeral, such as it is, fades away as I remember Stephen, the boy next door.

The boy I played with in the back garden, sharing paddling pools in summer, snowmen in winter. We went to school together. Although he was almost a year older than me, his birthday in September, mine in August, we were in the same school year. He looked after me, held my hand and stuck up for me in the playground. He was the big brother I never had.

All through primary school, right up until he was eleven and I was ten, we were inseparable, unless he wanted to play football and I wanted to play Barbies.

I remember the Easter when everything changed. Stephen's dad left; on Good Friday morning. He packed his bag and said he was going, said he needed space. Sally never saw it coming or understood why, not then anyway. Later she discovered he had found someone else, someone new, someone younger. But he denied it to start off with, just said he needed some time to himself. *It's not you it's me*, he'd said.

By summer he was living on the Isle of Man, had started divorce proceedings and insisted that Stephen fly over to spend time with him. After that all Stephen's summers were spent on the Isle of Man.

Sally had to increase her hours at work, though her husband had, very generously he said, given her the house in a full-and-final settlement. Naively, she had accepted his offer.

We went to different senior schools after he came back, his dad having insisted on choosing not the local one, but one that required a long bus ride. We hardly saw each other after that, we both had new friends, new interests. Then Mads came along, more than filling the void Stephen had left.

Good of him to come to Mads's funeral, he hardly knew her.

'Stephen,' I muse out loud.

'Yes.' Sally says. 'He'd like to come and visit you.'

'Why?'

There's a pause. 'You were friends.'

As teenagers I remember animosity, especially when Robin came into my life.

'A long time ago.' I don't want strangers gawping at me now.

'That's all right.' Sally sounds disappointed. 'I'll tell him you're not ready for visitors just yet.'

'Okay.'

'Everyone all right?' Sue appears. 'Time for a few checks and a move, Juliette.'

'Is it that time already?' Mum scrapes her chair on the floor. 'Well, we'd better be getting home. Tea to cook.' She's hardly said a word and she wants to go. I don't blame her. One daughter dead, the other nearly dead. Poor Mum.

'Is Dad coming later?'

'Not tonight, he has a staff meeting.'

Kisses and hugs and they're gone. Sue messes with me and I don't even notice; I'm too busy trying to remember, trying to make sense.

Finally, I'm alone again. That's when I realise that

in the confusion, the distraction of Stephen, I don't know what happened to Mads.

Why did Mads die?

How?

SEVEN

'Has she finished now?' Robin's back.

'I think so.' I assume he's talking about Sue who's just walked away from us.

'Good. She's very loud, that one.'

'How did Mads die?'

'Do you really want to talk about this now?' He sounds upset.

'I need to know.' I force back a gulp that will turn into a sob if I let it.

'Are you sure?'

'Yes.' Why won't he just get on with it.

'She committed suicide.'

That's why. I'm stunned into silence. Then I sob.

I think I'd prefer to be dead.

'I shouldn't have told you,' Robin whispers in my ear. 'I should have sugar-coated it.'

I'm waving my arms about, I don't know why. The shock maybe.

'Well done, Juliette. You're moving.' Robin claps. He actually claps.

As if they have run out of energy my arms flop down onto my lap.

'Why?' I gulp and sniff. Instead of my arms waving aimlessly, I wish they could do something about the river of snot and tears dripping off my chin. With his stupid squeamishness about bodily fluids, including his own, Robin isn't offering to wipe my face either.

'Why what?'

'Why did she commit suicide?'

'Bullying at school. They think. Must we churn all this up again?'

'It's new to me. I don't remember any of it.'

He doesn't reply but I can imagine the pained look on his face. I wish I could see it.

'How?'

He groans. How dare he groan?

'Overdose.' His voice is quiet, almost a whisper.

Overdose? My little sister. Mads. Overdose. I cannot believe it.

'Look, I'm going to get off now. I have a pupil tonight. Will you be okay?'

'I'll have to be.' He's dropped the bombshell and now he's just leaving me alone.

He pats my arm. It's painful.

'Is that my injured arm?' I snap.

'Sorry.' His tone is just as sharp. I hear the chair scrape. 'I'll see you tomorrow, late afternoon.'

Are we having an argument while I'm lying in bed, just out of a coma, almost paralysed and my sister dead? I call a goodbye, but he doesn't reply.

How dare he be annoyed because I want to know what happened.

This has a familiar ring to it.

'I hear you've had a bad night.' Jeff moves me about to do his checks, then lifts the bedcovers. I hope I haven't shat myself again; I can't smell anything, but I've been crying so much my nose is completely blocked.

I can imagine that Mads's death has had a profound effect on all of us. Poor Mum and Dad.

What the hell could have driven her to suicide? Bullying at school, according to Robin. Is that true? If only I could remember the last time we met, or spoke on the phone. I can only recall a brief message exchange about missing each other. Surely, I've said more to her than that recently.

'I'm just going to change your catheter,' Jeff says as the curtains swish closed around me.

'Must you,' I mutter.

'Fraid so.'

He's quick and efficient, I'll give him that, but it's so demeaning and undignified.

'Done. Well done.'

'Thank you.' I feel embarrassed for being surly, embarrassed for being embarrassed. It's all so bloody horrible. 'My sister's dead,' I blurt. 'My little sister.'

'I know. I'm sorry. I'm sorry for your losses.'

'I don't know what happened. I don't remember. I feel so useless.'

Jeff pats my shoulder. Poor man, what can he say? Nothing will make it better.

He brushes my hair, wipes my face, cleans my teeth; I manage a better spit than the last time.

'Well done. Let's try you with a drink, shall we?'

'Must we?' I shouldn't be so ungrateful, but everything seems so pointless without Mads.

He doesn't answer my rhetorical question but pushes a straw into my mouth, I suck and swallow.

'That is excellent. Well done. Have some more.' He pushes the straw into my mouth again and encourages me to keep guzzling.

It's tasteless water and it's lukewarm. Not nice. I make a face indicating my displeasure.

'We'll get your mum to bring up something nicer, cordial or something, shall we?'

'Yeah.' I finish the whole glass.

'Hey hun,' Jeff says, as he's walking away. 'The best you can do for your sister…' he stalls, 'your whole family, is to get better.'

'Yeah, thanks.' I know he's right. I've got to get better for Mum, for Dad, for Robin. For Mads. And once I am better I'm going to get to the bottom of why she took an overdose, because it just doesn't add up. If she was being bullied at school, why didn't she come to me? Why didn't she confide in me? It's not like her. And if she was bullied at school I want to meet the culprits face-to-face.

I doze off and when I wake it's with a start; I've been having that dream again, the car crash dream. This time Mads is in it; she's wearing my black coat – it fits her better than it does me. She's standing on the side of the road as the car starts to roll, she's waving and smiling. Then she's looking down at my body – we're both wearing the coat. There's blood everywhere; it's the first-time blood has featured in the dream.

My heart is beating fast, I feel sick. I breathe deeply to calm myself. It's just a dream, it's just a dream. It may have happened but it's not happening now. In my mind, I sound quite reasonable.

My body is aching; the effort of thinking, the discovery of misery, it's all too much. I lift my hands to my head, rub my forehead. It's all too much.

Wait. I lifted my hands, I rubbed my head.

I move my arms around, I feel my face with my fingers, the tubes in my nose, the shaved hair, the lumps on my skull and skin. My eyes are puffballs; no wonder I cannot open them. My mouth feels almost normal though.

I wriggle my toes, flex my ankles. It is a small miracle.

'Progress,' I hiss.

But the voice in my head reminds me that it won't bring Mads back.

'It's a start.' I'm talking to myself.

'There you are,' it's Mum's voice. I wait for Sally to speak but she doesn't.

'On your own?'

'Yes. Sally's busy today.'

'Shame.' I like Sally but I don't need her to visit for my sake, but for Mum's. Sally is good for Mum. 'Next time.' I put my hand out towards where I think Mum is. I touch her face. She gasps. The skin under her eyes feels baggy and wrinkled; I imagine dark circles. Her cheeks are sunken, her skin dry.

'You're moving. That's marvellous.' She jumps up and hugs me and I am able to hug her back.

I tell Mum about moving my feet too, I tell her I'm going to work on opening my eyes. I don't tell her that Robin has told me Mads overdosed. I can't bear to upset her any further. She has suffered enough.

We find ourselves sitting in silence. I hear Mum rustling in her bag, she drops the book – Pride and Prejudice, I expect – on the bed, which hisses as the air moves from the new pressure.

'Shall I read?'

What can I say? I really don't feel like hearing about The Bennets and snooty Darcy, or silly Bingley. That all seems so trivial.

'What's Sally doing today, then?' I wonder how obvious my diversion is.

'Stephen has taken her out for a long, late lunch.'

'Stephen. Stephen.' I repeat his name, rolling it around in my mouth and in my head. 'What's he doing back here, anyway? Didn't he emigrate to America, or somewhere?'

'Canada,' Mum says, fidgeting with the book.

'Oh yeah.' I do remember. He went just after he'd finished university. He had a first-class degree in engineering, or something like that. Road building, he'd called it; he'd always been self-deprecating. Witty asides were his forte. Once, when I'd laughed at him until tears ran down my face, and told him, for about the twentieth time, how funny he was, he suddenly turned serious.

'I have to be funny, Etty.' He'd taken to calling me Etty because it was Mads's pet name for me. 'I'm not beautiful, like your husband.' He was right, he wasn't tall, dark and handsome. He was tall enough though, much taller than me, his hair was fair and already thinning, even then, but his face was pleasant enough, just nothing special. Robin looked like a movie star against the boy-next-door.

Stephen didn't dress very well either; he had that air of student-grunge about him. But he was good company and even though we'd lost touch during the years he'd spent at different schools or summering with his dad, we still had that connection from our early childhood.

He got on well with Mads too, who, like me, looked on him as a big brother. They'd become good friends during his university years, he would send her silly postcards and chat to her over the garden fence when he came home in the holidays. His dad had more children, another family by then, so wasn't demanding that Stephen spend so much time with

104

him; anyway, Stephen was an adult and could please himself.

Mads was always talking about me to Stephen – Etty this, Etty that, though invariably it was Etty and Robin this, Etty and Robin that – so Stephen usually knew what I was doing even though I only saw him occasionally, usually in the garden. He would invite me and Robin to gigs he knew about, suggest new indie bands we should hear. Robin always sneered when I relayed the invitation; I couldn't imagine Robin in some grubby pub-backroom listening to indie rock.

We were all invited to Stephen's graduation party – a grand title for a Saturday tea-buffet that carried on into the evening. Sally had invited Mum, Dad, Mads, me and Robin, as well as half the street. Robin and I had been married almost four years by then, Robin wasn't keen, but didn't want me going on my own.

Stephen brought his then girlfriend, Lucia, with him. She was a stunner, petite and dainty with thick, black hair which hung down her back like a glossy cape. Lucia was nice, everybody said so. Lucky Stephen.

'My dad's Italian,' she explained when I complimented on her beautiful clothes; *she* certainly didn't dress student-grungy. Stephen was delighted with her, putting a proprietary arm around her waist, kissing the top of her head. She seemed, to me, like a sleek, prize cat. She chatted happily to Sally, to my parents, and to Mads, who insisted on linking arms with her most of the evening until she was taken home to bed.

'Way past your bedtime,' Mum said. It was after ten and Mum had had enough herself and used Mads as an excuse to escape; Dad went with them. Mads would have been ten or so by then.

'Lucia seems lovely.' Stephen and I were in the kitchen squeezing the last drop of white wine from the box on the worktop.

'Yeah.' He had a dreamy look in his eyes, though it could have been the alcohol.

'She's very elegant and well dressed.' Unbidden, I glanced down at his clothes, a cargo-pants-rock-gods-t-shirt combo.

'Unlike me.' He nudged shoulders with me.

'I didn't mean that…'

'Yes, you did.'

'Yeah, I did.' We laughed.

Back in Sally's lounge everyone was dancing, including Robin. With Lucia. They were huddled close, whispering to each other.

I felt a twinge under my ribcage. Stephen and I stood side-by-side watching them for what was only a few seconds but felt like an eternity.

'Never mind. Dance with me.' Stephen put his arm around my waist.

'No.' I pushed him off. I marched up to Robin. I tapped him on the shoulder. He turned and glared at me, as though I were a stranger. Then smiled. But the gap between the glare and the smile was too long. 'Can we go?' My voice whined. 'I don't feel too good.'

'Until we meet again,' he held Lucia's hand in his. 'Okay. Let's go.' He turned and took my elbow.

I wanted to go and say goodbye to Mum and Dad but Robin pulled me away and towards my car. I'd driven us there, but that night Robin snatched the keys from me once I'd fumbled them out of my handbag.

'I'll have to drive. You're drunk.' I wasn't, I'd only had two glasses of wine the entire time, but maybe I was over the limit. Robin rarely drank, he said he liked to keep his wits about him. Always.

He slammed the car into gear and drove up the road.

'What was that all about?' He said as we reached the junction.

'What?' I was starting to feel foolish.

'All that. Pushing in on my dance with your friend. Acting jealous.' He spat the words as though they tasted bad.

'Not my friend,' I muttered.

'Your friend's friend, then.'

'His girlfriend. And you never dance with me. You say you don't dance.'

'And I don't, normally. But *she* asked *me*. And you were canoodling in the kitchen with your...' he deliberately paused, '*friend*.'

We were arguing over nothing. Imagined jealousies. I felt stupid. He was angry. We drove the rest of the way home in silence.

'I'm sorry,' I said as we reached our doorstep.

'You should be.' He put the key in the lock. Once inside he slammed the door behind us. 'I suppose I should be flattered that you think anyone that beautiful would want me. Your friend is certainly punching above his weight.'

I swallowed. I didn't know what to say.

The next thing I heard Stephen had gone to Canada. I assumed Lucia had gone with him.

'So, Stephen's back from Canada?'
'Yes.'

107

'On holiday?'

'No, he's back for good.'

'Why's that?'

'He said he'd had a great time over there, but wanted to live here.' The weight of Pride and Prejudice is lifted from my hissing bed. I hope Mum isn't going to read it now. 'We won't bother with this today.' She has got the message. I hear her yawn.

'Why don't you go home, Mum, and have a rest.'

'I'm fine, darling.'

'No, really. You don't need to stay. You don't have to come every day.' How stupid of me to say that.

'I do. I want to.' Of course, she does, I'm the only daughter she has left now.

For the while I've been distracted by memories of Stephen, I've almost forgotten that Mads is gone. The pain returns like a punch.

'Go and rest, Mum.'

I hear her sigh. 'If you're sure.'

'I am.' I don't want to tell her that the minute she's gone Robin will appear from wherever it is he lurks when my parents visit. Neither of them has mentioned Robin and, other than the odd polite hello, there's been no conversation between them – well not in front of me anyway. I hope they haven't had a row. It's late afternoon and that's when Robin said he'd be back.

'Your dad will be up later. He can bring the squash the nurses said you need now. So good you're drinking.' She bends over to hug and kiss me, she smells of my childhood; she smells of Mads.

'And finally, I get you to myself,' Robin says. Mum can barely have left the ward before he's back.

'How do you get here so quickly when I'm alone.

Where do you lurk?'

'Now that,' he laughs, 'would be telling.'

'Mmm.' I really can't be bothered to attempt to tease it out of him.

'What were you talking about?'

'Mum was telling me Stephen is back from Canada. He's staying here now.'

'Stephen. Your ex-boyfriend?' Trust him to think that.

'We were hardly that. Just friends.'

'He was too friendly.'

I groan inwardly, some of that groan escapes through my mouth. I wait for Robin to pounce, but he doesn't. I used to love his possessiveness. His love. Now I find it overbearing and, quite often, ridiculous. I've never given him cause to be jealous.

Robin and I sit for a while in silence before he says, 'Urgh. What's that smell?'

I sniff.

'Pure oxygen,' I say. I'm cracking a joke. He should congratulate me.

'No, it smells like body odour.'

That could be me but I'm not about to say so. Anyway, it shouldn't be me, I've been washed enough, much to my embarrassment. I wonder if I've shat myself again.

Then the smell drifts into my nostrils.

'It's food.'

'Oh God. And it's coming closer.' His tone changes. 'Hi Jeff,' he says as though they are best friends.

'Good afternoon. I thought you might like to try something solid. Well, semi-solid.' Jeff pulls something up to my bed, then his footsteps retreat.

'It's a table over the bed.' Robin says, but I've already worked that out. I run my fingers over it. 'Here he comes, lumber, lumber.' Robin can be so rude, but as Jeff reaches us he says, 'smells good, Jeff.'

'Try this. It's Cottage Pie, it's nice and soft so should slide down easily. Shall I get you started?'

I'm grateful that he hasn't suggested Robin helps me, because Robin hates doing things like that. It's just as well we've never had children because he wouldn't help with the feeding, let alone nappy changing.

'Just chew slowly and swallow when you're ready. I've got a drink for you, just water I'm afraid.' The spoon goes into my mouth and I experience the novelty of real food. It may not be my choice, or my favourite, but it tastes so good.

There's not much to chew; the texture is soft and overcooked. I swallow, afraid that I might choke but it glides down easily. I hear my stomach growl its approval.

'Juliette,' Robin hisses.

'Sorry.'

'Don't worry, hun. Your body is just saying thank you.' Jeff laughs, Robin doesn't.

After the third spoonful Jeff suggests I carry on by myself. I remind him that I can't open my eyes to see, but he just laughs, guides my hands to the bowl – yes, it's in a bowl, like baby food – gives me the spoon and watches me try.

'There you go. No problem. I'll be back when you've finished.'

I tuck in, I can't help it. I'm enjoying it.

'Looks disgusting. It's grey.'

'Shush,' I hiss at Robin.

He pushes the chair away from me. I imagine him sitting with his arms folded and scowling, but I don't care.

I'm alive. I'm moving. I'm eating and drinking.

It's a while before Jeff comes back for my bowl and he compliments me on not making much mess and congratulates me for eating it all.

'I have trifle for you now, if you want it?' Jeff lifts a straw to my mouth and I suck in water.

'Yes please.' I can't remember the last time I had trifle. Yes, I can. Christmas tea at my parents three years ago. The last time we went there for Christmas. It had been a bit of an appeasement, an effort to all get on. Robin didn't really do Christmas, he liked to spend the day at home, away from all the *commercialism and overindulgence.* I loved the overindulgence, on that occasion Mads and I had second, then third helpings of Mum's sherry trifle.

On the way home Robin commented that it was no wonder my clothes were getting tight.

I went on a bit of a diet after that. It really didn't make much difference. Mum said, when I told her, that I'd have to accept that I wasn't a sixteen-year-old-girl any longer, and so would Robin. I was twenty-five.

Robin excuses himself when Jeff comes back to clean me up – I've managed to slop some on my gown which he then changes.

When Robin comes back he starts yawning. Big theatrical yawns as if making a point.

'Why don't you get off home,' I say. There must be something in the air, Mum was tired too.

'No. I'll stay. Until your Dad gets here.'

'Thanks.'

Half an hour later Dad arrives and Robin leans in to kiss me goodbye. That's the first time he's done that since this nightmare began – as far as I can remember. I wonder if it is for Dad's benefit.

'Bye Brian, I'll leave you to it.' Robin's chair scrapes.

'I've got your squash, orange and lemon barley,' Dad says as he drags the chair into position and flumps into it. He too, sounds weary.

'Thanks Dad. I'm looking forward to that, you know how boring I find water. I'd love a cup of tea, actually.' I sound so cheerful and jolly and I'm doing it for Dad's benefit.

He takes my hand and pats it. I squeeze back before our hands part.

'Mum said you were moving now. Good work, Juliette, keep it up.' His voice sounds as though it might break.

'Yeah. Soon be up and dancing.'

'Your work rang today. Someone called Mary?'

'Marie. In HR.'

'That's it.'

I haven't thought about work at all, not once. Hardly surprising. I'm still at Belton's. Been there for ten years now. I've risen through the ranks and I love my job, and it pays very well too. That's how we could afford our lovely house. As Robin has pointed out on numerous occasions, despite his hard work, long hours, extra curricula duties and private tutoring, I'm still the main earner. He moans about teachers' salaries then reminds me that it's down to him I didn't go to university, incurring a big debt along the way, and that if I hadn't got into Belton's as a trainee, I'd probably never have got in there at all.

He's right too, because most of their staff are home grown, which is quite unusual in today's workplace. I've had offers from other companies, been headhunted more than once, but I'm happy where I am. I told Robin about the first one, he was keen for me to follow it up – the salary was a lot more than I was on at the time – but I didn't. He was angry initially, asking me if I even cared about our future. I thought that was mean. Fortunately, Belton's heard about it and offered me an increase to stay. We were all happy in the end. Especially Robin.

I didn't tell him when it happened again. I didn't pursue it either. I'm happy at Belton's.

'What did she say?'

'Just asking after you. Wishing you well, that sort of thing. Mum spoke to her. Said you were conscious now and talking. They wanted to send flowers but it's not allowed in here.'

'That's nice. Tell them thank you if they call again.'

'She asked if they could visit, but Mum said no, not yet.'

How right Mum is, I'm grateful she's put them off. Much as I like my work colleagues I don't want them seeing me like this.

'They asked if you had received the letter okay.'

'I don't know. I'm in here. I haven't seen any post.' I laugh, a little, bitter laugh. 'Not that I can see anything at the moment, unless someone props my eyes open.'

'No. I suppose not.' Dad sounds so weary.

'What was it about? Did they say?"

'It wasn't from them. It was marked *for your eyes*

only, the address, everything, was handwritten. It came in after…' he stalls. 'After Madeleine died.' Now his voice is breaking.

I reach out and squeeze his hand again. I hear him catching his breath.

'They sent it straight out to you. Before this happened. Your accident, I mean.'

'Yeah.' I don't remember any letter. Do I? 'Um. It must be at home.' I have no idea if it is, Robin hasn't said anything. I'll ask him when he comes back.

'Only Mum and I, we wondered…' his voice falters again. 'With it being handwritten, and *for your eyes only* on the envelope…' He stops.

I'm worried. I think I know what he's thinking.

'Only there wasn't anything from Madeleine. When it happened. No suicide note or anything like that. So, we wondered if the letter was from her.'

EIGHT

I try to sleep after Dad has gone, but how can I?

I go over and over in my mind, trying to remember the letter. Was it from Mads? Or are Mum and Dad just clutching at straws?

I wish Robin would hurry back. Did he say he was coming back tonight? I can't remember. Damn my brain and its inability to function properly. I want to ask him if he remembers this letter. But, surely, he would have mentioned it if he had seen it; he would have told Mum and Dad if it was from Mads.

He picks up all the post in the morning, if it comes before we go to work he sorts through it in the hall before we go, making two piles – his and mine. We rarely have time to open it until we come home, sometimes he'll open his in the car. Most days it's just bills or junk mail. Unless it's Christmas or birthdays, but now fewer people are sending cards at Christmas.

The more I think about it, the more I think that it's unlikely to be from Mads. Yes, I know she used to write *for your eyes only* on envelopes, even birthday cards, but that was when she was ten or eleven. Not now. Anyway, why write a letter when she could text or email? Why send a letter to my work? If she wanted to give me a letter, she'd do exactly that. Hand it to me. But why? It makes no sense. It's far more likely that the letter is just junk mail packaged in a way that makes you open it before you throw it in the recycling.

Mum and Dad are wrong. It's nothing.

'Sorry it's so late, we've been so busy.' It's Sue. She's wiping my face and arms.

'Late?' I had eventually dozed off and now I'm being woken by washing and moving. I have no idea of the time; I only know afternoon and evening by Mum and Dad's visits.

'Nearly midnight. Sorry.'

'That's fine.'

'I think they're going to get you out of bed tomorrow.'

'Really?'

'Sit in a chair. See how you get on.'

I don't know how I feel about that.

'You might want to have some clothes brought up, more comfortable than this gown. Leggings or tracky bottoms, a soft top.'

'Yeah. I'll get Robin to bring me something.' The good thing with Robin is he'll know exactly what to bring me.

'Don't forget underwear.' Sue chuckles. 'People often do.'

'Sue,' I say as a horrible thought occurs to me. 'How long have I been here?'

'Must be nearly three weeks.' She's moved onto my bottom half and I'm cringing. I hadn't realised I was lying in my own mess again, but I can smell it now. I'm so glad Robin isn't here.

'Have I had a period?'

'No.'

My mind is working overtime. If it's three weeks without a period then it's imminent. Oh God, how embarrassing, and messy, will that be?

'Can you give me tablets to stop it?'

'We don't usually do that. You've had enough medication. We're trying to get you off everything, not add more.' Sue half laughs. 'It'll be fine.'

I can't bear to ask how they will handle it, just the thought of Jeff fishing around with a tampon is making me shudder inside. And Robin will be horrified. Absolutely disgusted.

'Maybe it won't happen,' Sue says, sounding upbeat. 'All the trauma and shock. It's often the case.'

Is she just saying that to make me feel better?

'Who knows, you might be up to dealing with it yourself. Once you're out of bed, progress does tend to speed up.' She's definitely saying *that* to make me feel better.

Finally, she's finished, new gown on, covers rearranged and she's gone.

I doze off again and dream of Mads, her sweet little face, laughing. In the dream, she's ten or eleven and she's repeating *for your eyes only*.

'Sorry I didn't make it last night. I was so tired I fell asleep on the sofa.' Robins lips brush my face. He smells delicious; his favourite aftershave makes my nose tingle.

'That's okay.' I turn to face him, even though I still can't open my eyes to see him. I smile. And I imagine him smiling back.

'I can't stay long I need to get to work.'

'Can't you get time off.' I feel upset about how uncaring his school are being.

'I've had over a month off, what with ….'

'Mads,' I finish for him.

'Yeah, and you. Now you're on the mend and getting more visitors, well...' He pauses. 'I'll need to take more time off when you come home.'

'Yes. I suppose you will.'

His lips brush my forehead again. I must be looking better, that's twice in one visit.

The chair scrapes; he's standing up. He's going already.

'Robin, before you go.'

'What's that?'

'Did we receive a letter in the post, addressed to me, handwritten? It had *for your eyes only* on the front.'

'No. Why?'

'Oh, nothing. Just something from work.'

The chair scrapes again. 'Look, I've got to go now. I'll be late otherwise.'

'Okay.'

And he's gone. Damn, I forgot to ask him to bring me some clothes.

'I've had breakfast and lunch today.' I'm telling Mum of my progress. I'm sitting in the chair with a sheet covering my legs.

'And you are looking so much better. I've brought you some clothes.'

'Thank you. How did you know? I forgot to tell…' I'm about to say Robin but decide against it; Mum hasn't mentioned him so it's better that I don't. She's probably blaming him for all this, even if that's irrational.

'Hospital rang this morning, so I popped to yours on my way here.'

'Thank you. There's talk of me moving wards now I'm not so dependent, and having a bath. Though I'm not sure how that will work.'

'Hoist, probably. Like in old people's homes.'

'Oh God, no.'

'Does it matter?'

I think about that for a moment, and shake my head. My aim is to get well, to recover. It doesn't matter how.

'And look what I've been practising.' I reach up and force my right eye open with my fingers. 'I can see you if you're right in front of me.'

Mum smiles. It lights up her face, but behind her smile she looks as thin and haggard as my fingers discovered yesterday.

'I can't do the other eye yet, it's sort of sticky and lazy. And I can't keep this up for long because it makes my arm ache, but it's a start.'

'Well done.' She pats my knee.

'They're going to take the feeding tube out of my nose later.'

'That's wonderful. You're recovering really well now.' She's saying all the right words but her face looks so sad.

I stop holding my eye open so I won't have to see it.

'We thought we were going to lose you too.' Her voice wavers.

I hate seeing Mum like this; I need to divert her but it's difficult when I feel so miserable myself.

'Is Sally coming today?'

'Yes. She came with me, she dropped me at the door and went off to find a parking space. You know what it's like up here. Drives me nuts.'

I've diverted Mum, even if it is to moan about hospital parking.

'And it costs a fortune.' She stops, realising what she's said. 'Not that we mind, of course. Do you want me to help you get dressed?'

I think of how horrendous that would be, I don't have the energy for it. Just sitting in the chair is a major achievement. I also don't want Mum to see that I'm sitting on a big, square pad, that is akin to a nappy. She may be my mum but there are limits.

'No. I'll wait until I have a bath.'

'Good idea.' There's relief in Mum's voice. 'I've brought several outfits and your pyjamas.

'Thank you.'

Sally arrives, breathless and annoyed.

'That bloody car park. I just had a standoff with some officious arse.' She stops, evidently noticing me. 'My God, look at you.' She leans in and kisses me.

'She's having a bath later and getting dressed and moving ward.' Mum's voice glows with pride.

'Brilliant. That's just brilliant. How will they manage to bath you with that cast?' I assume Sally is talking about my leg, and I admit, I hadn't even thought about that. 'Oh, I expect they have plastic bags they'll put it in.' She laughs.

'I'm sure they'll manage.' Mum uses her best placating, upbeat voice, the one she used when we were children. It covered eating cabbage, 'it's not that bad and it's good for you,' falling over, 'no harm done, up you get,' and disappointing school reports, 'room for improvement, I suppose.' It's the voice of my childhood. And Mads's.

'Did they lift you into the chair?' It's Sally again.

'Yes.' I'll be quite happy to sit in the chair all day. I feel more human, more normal.

'Any idea when you can get out of here?' Sally

makes it sound as though I am in prison. I suppose, in some respect, I am.

'No.'

'Well, I'm off work for as long as needs be,' Mum says, positive voice again. 'So, I'll be available to look after you once you get home.'

I'm about to say that it's all taken care of and Robin will be there for me, but realise that he might need a break and it might take the two of them to start off with. Robin probably won't want Mum around at all, but if I need help going to the toilet or anything like that, Robin won't want to do it. I'm going to save that discussion and potential argument until it happens.

'Where did you go for lunch yesterday?'

'Oh, lovely place. Stephen researched it online before we went. Fab reviews. A little bistro, you've probably heard of it, Carvells.'

'Oh yes.'

'I had this lovely braised lamb, oh it in melted my mouth. Stephen had…'

'I've been there,' I cut in. 'I went with Robin on our anniversary last year.'

Someone, Sally I think, reaches over and pats my knee several times.

'What did you have?'

'Chicken.'

'Stephen had chicken, cooked in a white wine sauce. It was lovely, I tasted it. I had a wine or two, as well. Stephen didn't, he was driving.'

'Robin had steak. He sent it back.'

He said it was overcooked. He made quite a fuss. It was supposed to be our lovely anniversary dinner and he ruined it. His steak didn't look overcooked to me, he likes it medium-rare and it was still bloody inside. He was in a foul mood before we even got there, so they could do nothing right. He'd booked the restaurant weeks before and almost forgotten about it, which meant he'd had to cancel one of his private pupils at short notice.

'It's not professional, Juliette,' he hissed at me, when I dared to suggest it didn't matter.

When I'd snapped back that we could cancel the meal instead, he'd rounded on me and called me stupid.

After that the night was never going to be a rip-roaring success, which was a shame because I had already checked the dessert specials on the board and knew what I was going to have, but we left before then.

'Just as well, Juliette. You don't need to pack any more puddings in there.' He gave my stomach a cursory glare before yanking open the car door. He waited for me to get in and start the car. I'd have liked a glass of wine, or champagne even, but couldn't because I had to drive. Robin, as usual, hadn't drunk alcohol.

The evening had been a disaster and it didn't improve when we got home earlier than expected and Robin disappeared into his study and didn't come out until after I'd gone to bed. He was on his computer all evening, I could hear the frantic tapping of his keyboard. When he came to bed, I pretended to be asleep.

'We'll go there when you're better,' Sally is saying. 'A group of us.'

'Yeah, that would be nice.' I'm not sure if it will or

122

not, though.

Sally's so good for Mum, distracting her from all this misery, from missing Mads, all the while chattering on about Stephen. It's lovely to hear normal talk.

'He's not going back to Canada, he's secured himself an excellent job here, and as soon as his house is sold in Canada, he'll be looking to buy here.' Sally is excited.

'He'll be looking for a wife too,' Mum jokes.

'Plenty of time for that,' Sally says. 'He's only the same age as Juliette.'

'Nearly a year older,' I pipe up.

That year used to be so important when we were kids.

'I'll look after you because I'm older than you. I'm the oldest.' Stephen was seven then, I was six. I remember it because I'd fallen over in the grass and he had rushed to pick me up. I wasn't hurt but I had livid green stains on my knees, which Stephen spat on and rubbed away. 'I'll always look after you, Juliette. I'm the biggest and it's just us in our families.'

He was right, we were both only-children then; it would be another six years before Mads came along, but slightly less before Stephen's dad left and took him away every summer.

Mum and Sally chat on and I doze off in the chair only to be awoken by nurses wanting to move me back into bed and to remove my feeding tube.

'We'd better get out of the way,' Mum says, kissing and hugging me.

'Yes, you won't be needing an audience.' Sally, always to the point, hugs me too. 'And make sure you eat all your food.' She delivers her parting shot, 'you're very thin now.'

That makes me laugh.

Robin will be pleased.

An hour later I'm lying on my side in bed, recovering from sitting on the chair for hours and the tube removal. Jeff assured me that the tube coming out is so much easier than going in. I am grateful that I don't remember it going in, because coming out wasn't pleasant but at least it was quick.

I feel fine now. Just tired. And hungry.

'I've eaten three meals today,' I tell Robin when he whispers a hello in my ear. 'And I've opened my eye, with my hand, admittedly, but it's a start.'

'It is, it is. Well done. Watch you don't overeat, no point in getting fat again.'

I can't believe he just said that. Except that I can.

'Robin,' I say, smiling in his direction. I'm so tired I can't even summon up the energy to lift my hand to open my eye, anyway, Robin's beautiful face is indelibly imprinted in my memory and if he's grey and haggard like Mum and Dad, I don't want to see it. 'Do you know who was bullying Mads? Have the police said anything?'

He sighs, and though it's barely audible, I still hear his exasperation.

'Do you really want to churn all this up again? It just upsets you.' He pauses. 'And me.'

'I know. I'm sorry. But I do need to know everything. I can't remember anything about Mads dying. I just don't understand it. I can't believe she killed herself.'

'Well she did.' His tone is snappish.

'How?'

He doesn't answer immediately. I ask again.

'Overdose.'

'Yes, I remember you said that before. But how, what, where?' I feel as though I am playing a game with him. I'd prefer it if he would spare my feelings and just spit it all out.

'Pills. She'd been out after school. She'd been drinking. Your Mum found her next morning in her bed. Still in her school uniform. They got her to hospital but she died a few hours later.'

I gasp. I feel sick. I had assumed it was quick and clean. When Robin said overdose before, I thought painless.

'Did they try to bring her round?'

'Of course.' He snaps out the words.

'How? What did they do?'

A bitter laugh escapes his lips. 'They did everything. Defib in her bedroom. Atropine. The works. She was alive when they got her to hospital. They tried so hard. You can't blame them.'

'I'm not blaming them.' I'm blaming her. My little Mads. Why did she do it? 'Did you say she'd been drinking?' I'm sobbing now, but I'm determined to know it all.

'Yes. Shall we stop now. I told you it's upsetting.'

'No.' I almost howl. 'What was she drinking? How much?'

'Wine.'

'How much?'

'Probably three-quarters of a bottle.'

I suppose she could have been drinking; she is fifteen, the perfect age for illicit swigging from wine

125

bottles. That much would make her silly, I suppose. But suicidal? This doesn't fit with the little sister I know. But, maybe I didn't know her that well; I hadn't seen her for weeks and weeks.

'Where did she get the pills from?'

He laughs. If I had the energy I'd slap him. 'Juliette, anywhere. Internet. Street corner. School. God knows it's easy to get pills, tabs, call them what you like.'

'Is it? What was the drug? What did the police say?'

'Um. Not sure.'

'Okay,' I manage between blubbering and sniffing. I manage to get my right hand up to my face and swipe away at my nose.

'Urgh,' Robin mutters, unable to suppress his disgust.

'You can't remember what the drug was?'

'No. Sorry. But it won't bring her back, will it? All this upsetting ourselves.'

He's right. It won't. But knowing how it happened helps me. I can't explain why, but it does.

'I'll ask Mum and Dad,' I mutter.

'Why upset them? You can't bring her back. For God's sake, Juliette, give it up.'

'Sorry.' He's right, of course he is. I can't bring her back. I can't change the past. I'll never see her again. A fresh round of crying starts and it doesn't stop until I fall asleep.

When I wake Jeff is back, so it must be day. He says something about doing my eyes as he passes.

'Thanks,' I mutter back.

'You okay now?' Robin's voice is soft and tender in my ear.

126

'Have you been here all night?'

'Yeah.' He sounds drowsy.

Darling, sweet Robin. He's stayed all night. Sleeping by my bedside on a plastic, hospital chair.

'Thank you.' I wave a hand in his general direction hoping to touch his face.

'I wanted to make sure you were okay.'

'I'm okay. Well, apart from a broken leg, an injured arm and a bashed-in head.' I attempt a laugh.

'Mmm.'

'Have I gone on about Mads's death before? I mean before the car accident?'

'Yes.'

'Oh. It's just I need to know. I need to understand.'

'Yeah. I've remembered what the pills were. Co-proxamol.'

'What are they?'

'Painkillers. Strong ones.'

'That doesn't sound like the sort of drug you'd get from a dealer? Are they prescription?'

'I think so. But you could get them, if you wanted. Websites for suicides, that sort of thing.'

'I can't believe Mads would do that.' The image of her sifting through those websites on her phone just horrifies me.

'They found some in her web history on her school laptop.' He says the words quietly as if attempting to diminish them.

'Her laptop.' I imagine her sitting in her bedroom, typing in the search terms, hunting out the info. 'Poor Mads. My Mum was right.'

Mum never wanted Mads to have a laptop of her own, but Dad said that all the kids needed them for school. Mum said I hadn't. Dad reminded her there was a big gap between our schooling. I remember the withering look she'd given him.

'Can't she use your computer, in your study, like I do?'

'Yes. She can. Of course. But she must take a laptop to school. For lessons.'

The laptop was purchased and multiple safeguards were built into it. The reason for Mum's reluctance came out eventually; her friend's son had been caught watching porn on his.

'Madeleine wouldn't do that,' Dad insisted.

Mum raised her eyebrows at him, pursed her lips.

The laptop went to school most days and came back and lived in the kitchen. The agreement was that Mads did her homework on it at the kitchen table, where Mum could ensure that *it worked properly*. Those were the words said to Mads. That rule lasted a few months, then the laptop stopped coming out of Mads's bag and before long it was living up in her bedroom. She did use it for non-educational browsing, of course she did, but all I ever saw were YouTube music videos or Facebook.

'Big day today,' Jeff says, his voice as jolly as usual. 'After breakfast we're going to get that central line and catheter out, give you a bath and you can wear your proper clothes. Won't that be better?'

'Yes. Thank you.'

'And you'll be moving. And you're lucky hun, cos you've got private insurance, so you're getting a room of your own.' He laughs and pats my good leg. 'Sadly, I won't be seeing you again, but I might pop in for a chat if I get time.'

'Oh.'

'He's gone,' Robin says, 'so don't waste your breath. I need to go too.'

'Are you working today?'

'No. It's Saturday. But I need a rest and a shower.'

'Course.' I think of his power shower, then I think of my impending bath. Lifted in on a hoist, Mum had said. Not really looking forward to that.

Robin kisses me on the forehead, says goodbye and I'm alone.

During the bath I'm relieved that I can't open my eyes. I'm also grateful that it is two women who hoist me about, they also wash what's left of my hair. Once I'm dressed I do feel a lot more human. They soon have me sitting on the chair in my *new* room. It's oddly quiet. That's when I fully realise that, although I've not really been aware of other patients, I must have been in a ward with others, because there were little beeps and noises that I can no longer hear. I feel lonely.

I have my own ensuite bathroom, I've even used the toilet, albeit via a wheelchair with a toilet seat on it. Undignified, but progress and better than lying in my own mess.

I'm on my own, I've eaten lunch, I have a drinking cup beside me – a non-spill one, like a baby's.

'Here you are.' It's Emma, the physiotherapist.

'Hello.' I give her my best smile.

'Okay. Shall we get started?' It's not a question I can answer no to.

She hauls me up and plonks the frame in front of me, guiding my hands to it.

'Okay, let's see how well you can walk. There's nothing in front of you, try a few steps.'

'But I've got a broken leg. I can't put it down.'

'It's not broken, well not anymore, it's been plated, and we need to get it moving even if it's just a few small steps. Don't put too much pressure on it, but have a go.'

I try and it's agony but it's definitely better than I expected. We have several goes before she lets me sit down again. I'm puffing and panting like a steam train, but standing up felt so good even if it did make me lightheaded.

'Excellent. I can see a significant improvement.'

'Really?' I puff out.

'Hand and arm movement is not too bad, keep moving and practising. How are your eyes? Still not opening?' She pulls both my eyelids open and I can see her face quite clearly. 'Hello in there.' She smiles. 'Look left.' I can and do. 'Look right.' I can and do. 'Excellent. Keep practising. Try to get those eyes open. Try walking but only when someone else is in here with you. Wouldn't want you falling when no one's about; that's one of the disadvantages of these rooms.' She gives a half laugh as she puts the alarm call button on my lap before she goes.

And I am alone again.

I put my right hand to my right eye and force my fingers to prize open my eyelids. I can see. There is nothing wrong with my vision, it's just the lids that don't work. I let the lids drop and do the same with my left eye, but with my right arm, my left arm is still too sore to lift. I look around the room. It's bigger than I expected; all those years of Belton's paying for health insurance have finally paid off. The bed has sides, the bathroom door is ajar, there are two plastic visitor chairs. My eye, my arm and my hand start to ache. I drop my arm back down.

Mum bursts into the room.

'This is better,' she says, dragging a chair up to me. 'And you look more like your old self.' There's genuine joy in her voice. 'Well done, darling.' She kisses me on the cheek.

'I haven't really done much, just hobble across the room a couple of times. And you were right, I was hoisted into the bath.' We both laugh. 'I have managed to go to the toilet, in the bathroom.' I point in the direction of the ensuite. 'Is Dad parking the car?'

'No. He's at work.'

'On a Saturday?'

'It's Tuesday, darling. What made you think it was Saturday?'

'Oh, I don't know.' I'm not telling her that Robin told me, she'll catch him and ask him why he's telling me lies. Again.

NINE

'Your parents don't want to come to the wedding.'

'What? Why? When did they say that?'

'Your mum rang me. Let them stay away, we don't need them.' Robin smiled; a grim, straight line across his face. His eyes weren't smiling.

'But I want them to come, I want Mads as my bridesmaid.' We'd already been shopping for her dress; Mum, Mads and me.

Robin shrugged and turned away. 'Shall we have a Chinese takeaway tonight? I don't feel like cooking after this upset. Unless you do?'

I agreed to the takeaway. I hadn't moved into Robin's place at that point, I was still living at home, more to placate Mum and Dad than anything. I was in the habit of going to Robin's straight from work. I wanted to be with Robin all the time but despite Mum having said that I could live with him and not get married, both my parents vehemently disapproved of me living with him before we married. Since it wasn't long until our wedding day, I took the line of least resistance.

Later that night, after I'd pushed my Sweet and Sour around my plate, I'd checked my mobile. There was a missed call from Mum. I wouldn't be calling back, I wanted to see her face-to-face.

I sneaked in late that night, the house was in darkness, everyone was in bed. I didn't catch Mum the next morning, but I went straight home after work that evening and confronted her.

'Why won't you come to the wedding?'

She frowned at me. 'What do you mean?'

'You rang Robin and said you weren't coming.'

'When?'

'Yesterday.'

She shook her head and frowned again. Was Mum being deliberately obtuse?

'I rang Robin's home phone yesterday when you didn't answer your mobile. You weren't in from work, so I chatted to Robin.' She sighed and turned away.

'Yes. And you told him you didn't want to come to the wedding.'

'I didn't say that.' She tutted and started to lay the table, her head shaking as she laid down the placemats. 'I said, quite clearly, that I hadn't found anything suitable to wear and at this rate I wouldn't be coming. It was a joke. I laughed when I said it.'

'That's not what he understood. But if it was a misunderstanding, that's okay then.'

'He understood perfectly. He laughed and said I should wear my pyjamas as long I was there.'

'Oh.'

'He's such a liar, Juliette. You need to watch him.'

'Thanks, Mum.' I didn't attempt to hide the sarcasm in my voice. 'I'm going to Robin's now.'

'Did he give you my message?'

'Which message?' I wasn't going to say a straight no to that.

'I was ringing to see if you wanted to go late night shopping with me tonight; Debenhams are having a blue cross day and are open 'til eight. Thought I might find something for the wedding. But if you're busy, it doesn't matter. You go and have a wonderful time round there.' She smiled but I knew she wasn't wishing me a pleasant evening. I didn't go to Debenhams with her, on reflection I should have.

When I confronted Robin he too frowned his puzzlement. 'I think,' he said, 'that the pressure of being the mother of the bride is getting to her. She definitely said they didn't want to come.'

'No, she says she didn't.'

'Then, my love,' he kissed me on the nose, 'there was either confusion, or misunderstanding or both. Either way, it doesn't matter now, does it?'

I didn't want an argument over it, but at the same time I wanted more explanation, but Robin wouldn't be drawn into further discussion.

'Sally's coming in soon,' Mum is saying. 'Have you had your hair washed? It's looking quite nice.'

'For a half-baldy,' I joke.

'Well, it'll grow back. It's already starting to. Anyway, Sally is on her way, Stephen is bringing her.'

'He's not coming in with her, is he?' I feel alarmed. I like Stephen, he's such an old friend, but I don't want him seeing me like this.

'No. No. Don't worry. He wouldn't do anything to upset you.'

'Did he actually say that?' It strikes me as an odd thing to say; we're just old friends.

'Yes, he did. When we were chatting over lunch.'

'You went to lunch with him?' For some reason, I don't like this. I don't know why.

'I went to Sally's for lunch, Stephen was there.'

'Oh.'

'You're very tetchy, Juliette.' Mum sighs. 'But I

suppose that's understandable.' She pats my hand before changing the subject. 'How are your eyes?'

'Yeah, I've propped them open with my fingers, but it makes my arms ache.' I pinch my right eyelid to lift it. Mum's face comes into focus. She looks better today, not so grey and tired. 'I can't turn my head very well, it's so stiff and painful.'

'The swelling around your eyes is definitely less. Have they said how long it will take before they work properly?'

'No. Just got to keep trying.'

'Hello.' Sally bursts into the room. 'This is better. Bit quiet though.'

'No radio,' Mum and I chorus.

'Oh yes, it was playing all the time in the ward.' She drags a chair up and plonks herself down, before rustling in her bag.

'These are for you,' she says, placing something on my lap and guiding my hands to it. 'From Stephen.'

I run my hands over the punnet on my lap. 'Cherries. How did he know?' Most people would send grapes or chocolate, I hate grapes but I love cherries. I pinch my left eye open to look at the fruit, and I notice Mum and Sally exchange a silent look.

'What was that?'

'What, darling?'

'That look. Between you two.'

'What look? Don't be silly.' Mum is not a very convincing liar. They both laugh, but they're embarrassed, I can see it on their faces. 'Why don't you have one? We need to feed you up.' Mum picks a cherry out and pushes it towards my mouth.

'It's all right, Stephen washed them,' Sally says, seeing me hesitate.

I bite into the cherry, letting my eyelid go so that I can retrieve the stone and stalk from my mouth.

'Have another,' Sally urges. And I do. In fact, I have several.

'Be careful not to choke on them,' Mum says as though I were a child, but I suppose she does have a point.

Mum and Sally chat on, it's normal conversation, nothing to do with me. I don't join in but I'm enjoying hearing it. They talk about the dustbin collection, the price of parking, the state of the roads, in fact all the things our local Council are not doing properly. Then the conversation turns to Mum's work. She's a teaching assistant in a school. It's the same primary school that I went to, with Stephen. Mads went too. Mum's been there for years; she started when Mads was in year four.

Mum had trained to be a teacher, but never finished her probationary year, mainly because she really didn't like it. On the plus side, she did meet Dad during that unfinished year. She said she loved working with the children but couldn't stand the form filling and the in-school politics. When Mads was old enough, Mum went back into a school because the hours suited better than the office job-share with Sally, but chose teaching assistant instead of teacher.

'I'd have to retrain and I'd have to do the Newly Qualified Teacher year again and, really, I can't be doing with any of it.'

Teaching assistant suits her. She loves it. She's good at it. She doesn't have mountains of paperwork to do after school; there was enough of that in our house with Dad's job.

'They're being a bit difficult now about how much time I'm having off,' she tells Sally who tuts appropriately. 'I think I might give it up.' The last sentence is said so quietly that I think I'm not supposed to hear it.

'Go back to work, Mum. You don't need to come in here every day. You can pop by on the odd evening. I won't be here much longer anyway. I'm sure.' Am I?

'Yes, but you're going to need a lot of help when you get home.'

'Maybe.' I think I've stopped myself from thinking about that too much. I doubt Robin will want to wash and dress me and take me to the toilet. He'll be happy bringing me cups of tea and cooking for me, but he won't want to do the personal bit. And he'll be twitchy about taking too much time off work. I don't want to say this to Mum, she'll be angry with him. 'We'll manage,' I say, smiling and yawning.

Sally takes this as her cue to leave. She's kissing and hugging me and telling me that Stephen will get anything I want, I only have to ask.

'Tell him thanks,' I say, wondering whether Stephen really made that offer or if Sally is doing so on his behalf.

After Sally's gone, Mum and I sit in awkward silence for a minute or so. I'd be quite happy if Mum went too, I'm so tired and really wouldn't mind getting back in bed.

'Would you like me to help you?'

'What?'

'Back to bed.'

Did I say that out loud, I didn't think so? But she is my mum, maybe she's just reading the signals.

137

'Yes, please.'

Between us we stumble and fumble until I'm back under the covers. It's only a few steps but it completely exhausts me. Mum pulls her chair up to the bed. I hear the pages of a book being turned. Not Pride and Prejudice again. No.

'It just like when you were little and I used to read to you at bedtime.' Mum's voice has a faraway sound to it. 'And Madeleine,' she adds.

'Yeah.'

She pats my lap.

'I'm going to get to the bottom of it, Mum.'

'What's that?'

'What really happened to Mads. I don't believe she killed herself. I won't believe it.'

Mum gasps. I hope she's not crying. But I hear her sniff and I know she is.

'Come here.' I flap my arms in her direction and, after what seems like minutes, she leans in. I wrap her in my arms and hug her close and she hugs me back. After we've finished crying and hugging, I reiterate my promise. 'I will find out. I will.'

'You concentrate on getting better. That's what you need to do.' Mum pulls herself away from me.

'Go home, Mum. I'm tired and I don't want any more Pride and Prejudice.'

'Really?'

'Truly.'

'Thank God for that, I bloody hate that book.' My Mum rarely swears.

'Then why did you bring it?'

'I thought it was your favourite.'

'No.'

'Who brought the cherries?' Robin wakes me from a deep, dreamless sleep. It's the best sleep I can remember since this nightmare began, or at least until I became aware of it.

'Stephen,' I say without thinking.

'He's been here?' His voice is raised in annoyance.

'No. Sally brought them.'

'Then why say Stephen did?'

'I meant he sent them. With Sally.'

'Oh. Why?'

'Cos I like them.'

'How does he know that?'

'We're old friends.'

'Still, no need for him to do that.'

'There wasn't, but it's nice of him. No one's stopping you from bringing fruit or something. You haven't yet.' It suddenly dawns on me that he might have when I was unconscious. 'Have you?'

'No.'

'Well, feel free. Even Mum brought my clothes because you weren't anywhere to be seen.'

'I've been working. I told you. The bills don't pay themselves.'

'Hang on a minute. How did Mum get into the house? Were you there?' My parents have never had a key to my home, even though I've always had a key to theirs. I once suggested to Robin that it might be a good idea, but he was adamant that only we should have keys.

He doesn't answer for a moment. Then mumbles. 'I gave her a key.' Well, that's a step forward. They've hardly spoken for months, not since the last bust up over Mads revision. Dad had casually mentioned to me that, although her exams were months off, he was

139

concerned that she might need some support with her revision and that he didn't think he'd have the time. Mum didn't entirely agree with him, she thought Mads would do well anyway. We'd just finished tea, Mum was clearing up and Mads was in the living room messaging her mates on her phone.

'You,' he said, emphasising the word, 'know how it is and there are more distractions now than ever.'

'But Mads is super bright and gets good grades.' I'd almost laughed.

'Yes, but... she's at that age, easily distracted. And we think there's a boy...' Dad's voice trailed away.

'Maybe Robin could help her,' I said.

'Over my dead body,' Mum said, turning around from stacking the dishwasher.

Dad looked embarrassed. Mum was livid with anger.

'Well, I only offered.' Though I wished I hadn't.

Mum turned back to the dishwasher and continued to stack it, at the same time managing to convey anger and irritation through her movements.

I had to leave to pick Robin up not long after that, which was a relief. Foolishly I relayed the conversation to him in the car. He listened without commenting then pulled out his phone.

'Mads. Hi,' he said, 'Is your Mum there?'

'No. What are you doing?' I flapped my hand towards his phone. He leant away from me.

'Hi, Lyndsey. Just a word about my reputation.'

I couldn't hear Mum's response but it sounded angry.

'Yes. Well. Don't go slagging me off to anyone. I have a good reputation, and if you go bad mouthing me everywhere, I won't be able to keep your daughter in the luxury lifestyle she currently enjoys. Do you think nice houses pay for themselves?'

I caught the tail end of Mum's response because it was shouted. 'Stay away from Madeleine.'

He ended the call without further comment, stuffed his phone into his pocket and didn't speak. I wanted to ask him about *my* contribution to our luxury lifestyle, since I was the higher earner, but I didn't want to provoke a row. Over nothing really, just Mum's sniping. I didn't even know why she was being so nasty. It's not as if Robin would steal Mads away and marry her, like he had me. That was one of Mum's go-to arguments, whenever she was feeling mean about Robin; that he had stolen me from them. I always reminded her that I was an adult when we married and I had left willingly, more than willingly actually.

'Were you there when Mum came around?' I ask, imagining them choosing my clothes together, cooperating to help me as though I was a common cause uniting enemies.

'No.'

Okay, no cooperation then.

'Was that by arrangement?'

'No.'

He sits in silence. So do I. I am tired and all I really want to do is drift back to sleep.

'I hope Stephen isn't planning on visiting you.' Robin's voice cuts in again.

'What?' I'm not telling him that I've told Sally he can't come.

'Just saying, I don't want him here.'

'Why not?' I don't know why he's getting so

irritated.

'I don't trust him.'

'What? He's an old friend. You know that.'

'I don't like the way he looks at you.'

I sigh. And, for a second or two I'm pleased that I've been able to inhale enough air to make that sigh so loud.

'Robin, he's been in Canada for years. I can't remember the last time I saw him.'

'He was at Mads's funeral.'

'Oh yeah. I can't remember.' Although now that Robin has brought it up, something in my mind pings; a brief sensation of Stephen reaching for my hand as we stood looking at the flowers lined up at the crematorium. Or maybe that was Robin?

'And he was about before that.'

'I don't remember.'

'I do.'

'Does it really matter? Look, I'm tired. I expect that you could do with some rest too. Why don't you go home and catch up on some sleep? You've spent nights and nights here. You can take a break now I'm getting better.' I'm trying to be tactful; I want him to leave me alone. I feel an odd animosity towards Robin. I don't quite know why, maybe I'm just picking up on his ire. He seems unduly, unreasonably jealous of Stephen.

'I think I will.' He sighs too. 'Just make sure Stephen doesn't come up here.'

'Bye Robin. Have a good rest.'

'Bye.' There are no hugs, no kisses.

'I can open my eye, look.' I peer at Mum through my right eye. I've been practising all morning, after impressing the physio with my walking skills: two steps without the walker.

Mum smiles. Her eyes tear up.

'It's still an effort and I have to concentrate. When I get tired it just closes again. But they're very pleased with me.'

'Well done. We'll soon have you out of here.'

'Still a lot of work to do.' I laugh to hide my fear of leaving this place. I don't know how Robin will cope with me unless I am fully back to normal.

'I see you've eaten all the cherries.'

'I so enjoyed them. Tell Stephen thanks.'

'I will.' I can see hesitation on her face. 'He still wants to come and see you.'

'Put him off, Mum.' I'm about to add that Robin won't like it but don't.

'I will, love. But he's very concerned about you.'

'Well you and Sally can fill him in. I'm sure he's got better things to do than worry about me.'

'Yes,' Mum says quietly as she reaches into her bag.

'Not Pride and Prejudice,' I say a bit too quickly. I thought we'd dispensed with that yesterday.

She laughs. 'No. I've brought you some more fruit squash, you're running out.' She places a bottle of peach and passionfruit cordial on my table.

'Thanks,' I say a little sheepishly as I change the subject. 'No Sally today?'

'No, she's house-hunting.'

'She's moving?' This is a shock.

'No. No. For Stephen. Well, with Stephen.'

'Oh yeah. He's not going back to Canada, is he? Has he sold his house then?

'Yes. He got a call last night. So, he thought he'd

start the process here. I think he's a bit bored. He doesn't start his new job for a week or two.'

Stephen's plans seem well along and I think of what Robin said about him being around before Mads's funeral. Quite a bit before was what Robin said last night.

'Mum, how long has Stephen been back?'

'Six months.'

'And has he been staying at Sally's all that time?'

'Of course. Why?'

'Oh, just something . . .' I let my voice trail away. I don't want Mum thinking that Robin is paranoid about Stephen.

'Have I seen much of him?'

Mum doesn't answer.

'Mum?'

'Oh. Sorry. I was just thinking about something.'

'What?'

'Um, wondering if I'd put enough money on the car park. It's a one-hundred pound fine if you overstay. Isn't that scandalous. It's a hospital.'

'Yeah. Disgraceful.' I let my eye close, the effort of keeping it open is too much now.

'So, you never answered my question. Have I seen much of Stephen since he's been back?'

'Um. A bit.'

'What do you mean?' I don't like the hesitation in Mum's answers and I don't believe her concerns about her car parking ticket for one minute.

She doesn't answer.

'I think you've met up with him.'

'Have I?'

'I think so.'

'Just me and him?'

'Yes.'

'Without Robin?'

'I think so.'

'Why did I do that?'

'I don't know darling, I wasn't there.' Mum's tone is so evasive.

I think about pressing her, about forcing more information from her because I can tell from her answers that she knows more than she is saying. But I don't want to know. I am thinking the unthinkable and I don't like it.

The door bursts open and the smell of over-stewed meat wafts in.

'Here's your tea. Is it that time already? I'd better be off. Check that car park ticket and hope I don't get a fine.'

Her chair scrapes and she's hugging me and rushing to get out.

Robin's timing is impeccable. He turns up after I've been washed and changed and tucked up in bed. Just as well, I wouldn't want him to witness me going to the toilet; because I don't have the strength or flexibility yet to wipe myself. He would be disgusted. And I would be embarrassed.

His absence has given me plenty of time to think. Not that my thinking is clear; my memory is full of holes. According to the medical staff it will take a while and it's possible that I will always have gaps; there will always be parts of my life that I don't remember. I'm beginning to suspect that all has not been well between me and Robin recently. I fear I may have sought solace in Stephen's company. I hope that's all I did.

'Good day?'

'Busy,' Robin says. 'What about you? Any visitors?'

'Just Mum.'

'On her own?'

'Yeah. Just her today.'

'No more cherries?'

'No. But I can open my eye now. Look.' I blink my right eye open.

'Oh yeah. Well done.'

'Come around this side, I can't see you from here. And I can't turn my head very well, it's so stiff and painful.'

There's a delay in his response.

'I'd rather not.'

'Why not?'

'I'm looking a bit rough today.'

'What. You never look rough.' Even though I'm a little concerned by his comment I cannot believe his version of rough would match anyone else's. And, certainly not mine. I've never seen Robin look rough, even when he had flu a couple of years ago he still managed to look gorgeous, sexy even, especially when he spoke, his voice gravelly and low. I was almost disappointed when it returned to normal. 'Come on, move your chair round here and let me see you.'

'I'd really rather not.'

Now I'm alarmed. Robin is vain enough to know how good looking he is. He's always groomed and dressed immaculately. He once told me it was his USP.

He'd laughed at my ignorance when I said I didn't know what that was.

'Unique selling point,' he said.

'What?'

'You know, what makes me special. I look good.'

'Well, yes, you do. Always. But I didn't know it was a selling point. I didn't know you were for sale.'

We had giggled together, our heads touching and our breath mingling. We had only been married a month then.

'Come on, Robin. You're scaring me now.'

'Don't be silly.' His voice does not sound convincing.

Then I realise. Then it dawns on me. How could I be so stupid? I've been lying here for almost three weeks and the cause of that was a car accident. I always drive because that's how we like it, and we were coming back from Mads's funeral.

Together.

'Robin. What's the matter with you?' I hold my breath. I feel my heart beating with anxiety in my chest.

'Nothing. I'm absolutely fine.'

Of course he is. He's back at work. He's even doing his tutoring. He must be fine, he couldn't work if he wasn't. I calm down.

But there must be something or he would let me see him.

I think of my injuries, life-threatening, Mum described them as. My head and face the most damaged. Robin and I were sitting side-by-side in the car. We must have hung in our seatbelts together. With my careless – no dangerous – driving I have scarred Robin's beautiful face. There was a fire, the car caught fire. Have I burnt him?

'Are you scarred, Robin?' My voice is a tiny whisper.

'Not permanently,' he says, the hint of a smile in his voice. 'Don't worry.'

'Then show me.'

'No.'

TEN

I don't remember Robin leaving.

After his emphatic no, he refused to say anymore, he wouldn't answer my questions or show me his face. He patted my arm occasionally, my injured one, even though I have asked him not to. He must have left after I fell asleep.

'Do you think I'll ever get all my memory back?' I'm asking Emma, the physio, just as I ask every member of the medical staff.

'Maybe. Maybe not. It's hard to say. What does your doctor say?'

'Same as you. Brain damage. Blah blah blah.' I wave my arms around in exasperation.

'Good movement,' Emma says. 'Keep practising. How are your eyes?'

'Not fully cooperating.' I wink at her, not entirely on purpose.

'Keep trying.'

I'm wracked with guilt about Robin. Not only because I've scarred him, hurt him, damaged him, but because it hadn't occurred to me before to ask after his health, his injuries. What is wrong with me? Did I just assume that he walked away from that mess without a mark on him?

That's exactly what I thought. Except that I wasn't even thinking about him. Just myself.

How stupid. And selfish.

The day passes; during physio I manage more independent steps, before slumping exhausted into the chair. Emma parks the walker beside me in case I need it. My eyes still refuse to play nicely, my arms ache and my head itches. Apparently, that's a good sign: healing and hair regrowth.

'There's a rumour I might be going home later this week.' I force my right eye open and watch Mum's face.

'That's wonderful. Amazing.' She leans in and kisses me; she smells of floral perfume and talcum powder. It takes me back to my childhood, way back, even before Mads, when there was just me and Mum and Dad. I suppose that's where we've gone back to now; three where there were once four.

I can't wait to tell Robin the good news, although I have mixed feelings about it. He'll be pleased I'm recovering, but worried about how he will cope with me when I get home.

'Have they said exactly when?' Mum sounds excited.

'No. It's always vague. Or so I've been told. According to Emma…'

'Who?'

'Oh, Emma, she's my physio. She said they will just come in one day and say I can go.'

'Just like that? That doesn't seem right. Don't they have to make some sort of support available, or something?' Mum's voice now sounds more panicked than excited.

'I don't know.' I attempt a shrug, it's not very successful, my neck still doesn't work properly. 'I'll ask.'

'Yes, so will I.'

That's a shame; I was quite excited about going home, not so sure now.

'It's the night I worry about most,' Mum continues. 'Supposing you take ill in the night?'

'Yeah.' I imagine Robin running around trying to resuscitate me. He won't like that. Even taking me to the toilet in the middle of the night will not go down well with him. He won't let Mum stay overnight, I know that. He may have given her a key, but he'll draw the line at that. Despite having a four-bedroom house we only have one bedroom; the others are dressing-rooms, one each for Robin and me and a store room. 'We can always ring an ambulance,' I say hoping I don't stop breathing in the night. But I'm not sure what we'll do if I need the loo and Mum's not there.

'You're right, we'll manage,' she says, neither reassuring herself nor me. 'I'll just go and have a word…' With that she is up and out of the room.

I let my eye close, allowing it to rest while Mum's away.

'Hello.' Sally bursts into the room. 'Where's your Mum?'

'Gone to speak to someone.' I can't be bothered to go over it again.

Sally pulls up a chair and rustles in her bag.

'More cherries from Stephen.' She puts the punnet on my lap.

I open my eye, smile at her and examine the cherries. 'Washed?'

She nods.

I pop one into my mouth. I cannot resist. I tell her

to thank Stephen; she reiterates how he would like to come and visit me. My response is to stuff two cherries in my mouth, thus making it impossible for me to reply.

I would like to see him. He's a piece of normality I'd like to clutch on to. He wasn't in the car, he wasn't in the accident. I haven't done anything to hurt him, I haven't scarred his face like I have Robin's. He knew Mads but he won't be heartbroken about her death, not like Mum and Dad are, and me. It would be good to see him. But there's always the fear that I've seen too much of him already.

And Robin will not allow him to visit me at home once I'm out of here.

'Did you hear me?' Sally asks. 'I said Stephen is still keen to see you.'

'Maybe later in the week, before I go home.'

'You're going home? When? That's wonderful.'

'Not sure yet.'

'It's okay,' Mum says as she comes back. 'They'll send the district nurses round to check on you and change dressings if necessary, and give us plenty of notice. You won't just be tipped out into the street. And I've spoken to your work…'

'My work? Why?'

'They think your health insurance should cover some support too. Physio at home when you get out, that sort of thing. Good insurance that. How long have you had it?'

'Don't know. Always. It's a company perk.'

'Excellent perk.' Sally laughs before continuing. 'I'll tell Stephen soon, then, shall I?'

'Yeah.' Well, I would like to see him even if I do feel pressured into it. I sigh, not too audibly, and lift my hands to my head. I find the prickly hair and the wounds. 'Are these staples?' Horrified, I run my fingers over the hard metal edges.

'Yes.' Mum says, 'that's how they fixed it.'

'Oh. Yuk. And is this a hole?' I push my finger into the indent?'

'Yes. That's where they had one of the drains.'

'Uh no.' I don't think I want to hear any more. No wonder Robin always sits on the opposite side to my scars. Maybe that's part of why he won't move round.

'You were lucky, they said. They were able to reattach your skull because most of the swelling was at the front. Your eyes…' Mum's voice trails away.

'Don't tell me anymore.'

'There is more. When I spoke to the nurse she said they need to take the staples out soon.'

'How soon?' I am starting to feel sick at the prospect.

'Probably tomorrow morning. Do you want me to come up?'

'Yes please.'

'Oh, no. I can't. I have a dentist appointment. Damn.'

'Can't you change it?'

'I could, but I only booked it this morning. Emergency…' her voice trails away. 'I've got bad toothache.'

'Oh, poor you. You must go, Lyndsey,' Sally says.

'Yes, you must. I'll be fine.' Maybe Robin can come. Who am I kidding?

'Maybe you could come, Sally.' Mum sounds desperate.

'I've got my hospital appointment. I've waited nine months for it. It's about my bunion. But I'll come up immediately after, I'm in the same building, after all.' She laughs. 'Hopefully the timing will work.'

'Thank you.' I feel quite frightened. Quite alone. I'll mention it to Robin but he's so squeamish he'll probably refuse.

'When you get out of here, we'll get Paula round to cut your hair. If it's all short, it'll all grow back at the same pace. You'll hardly notice it then.' Paula is Mum's hairdresser, she comes to the house. Mum's had her for years and her hair always looks great. I can see the sense in what Mum's saying. And, if I'm honest I'd quite like a change. The prospect of trying to arrange my hair over the bald bits doesn't appeal. But, a nagging voice is telling me not to go short.

'I don't know, Mum. I'll see how it looks.'

'It looks godawful,' Sally says, blunt as usual. 'Juliette, have a new style. It'll really buck you up.'

I open my eye and look at Mum. She's waiting.

'I don't know. Robin wouldn't like it.'

Mum and Sally exchange glances. Mum leans over and pats my arm.

'No, he wouldn't. You see how *you* feel about it.'

'But...' Sally starts and stops. No doubt Mum has shared her dislike of Robin with her best friend, but he likes my hair long and he's my husband and after all that's happened I don't want to upset him further.

After they've gone I realise that the punnet of cherries is still on my lap. I had meant to ask Mum to put it in my bedside locker. I don't want to have the *cherry conversation* with Robin again. I haul myself up, gripping onto the back of the chair with one hand and the cherry punnet with the other and survey the distance I must travel. The walker is on the other side of the bed. Too far away for me to reach it. Mum or Sally must have moved it. Six steps. I'm sure that is all it will take. I can do it.

The first two steps are easy, now I need to let go of the chair. Four more steps. I can do it. I'll be able to grab the bed on my way. It should be easy. I let go of the chair and stand, waiting for my balance to even out. Then I step. Great. Then another step. Only two more steps and I will be there.

I feel woozy. Light-headed. The room looks spotty.

'I hear you had a fall.' Robin's voice is soft in my left ear. 'How are you?'

I open my right eye. I can't turn my head. I can't see him. I'm in bed with the sides up. I'm tucked in tight.

'I was dizzy.'

'What were you doing?'

I can hardly tell him I was hiding the cherries.

'I was trying out walking.'

'On your own? Hmm. You need to take it easy. Don't overdo it.'

'Okay.' I wonder where the cherries are now? Probably all over the floor. I hope he doesn't notice. Hopefully they've been picked up and thrown away.

'I see cherry-man has been again.'

'Sally brought them.'

'Oh yes, his mother.' The words are filled with vitriol.

'How are you now?' I ask, changing the subject.

'Me? I'm fine. I told you yesterday.' He doesn't sound fine.

'How's work?'

'Fine. Busy. You know.'

This is hard work; it should be him cajoling me, not me sweet-talking him.

We sit in uncomfortable silence. It shouldn't be like this. He's my husband. We've been married for ten years. It should be easy.

'Robin, is everything all right?'

'Hardly, Juliette. Look at you.'

'No. I know. I didn't mean me, this, I meant…' What do I mean? 'Between us. Are we okay?'

'Course we are. Look, I've been here a while watching you sleep and it's getting late. So, I think I'll get off. I've got a pupil tonight and I want to have something to eat beforehand.'

'Oh. Okay. Robin, what day is it? I lose track in here.' Mum said it was Tuesday when Robin told me it was Saturday, so I think it must be Thursday today.

'Thursday,' he says, scraping his chair as he stands up.

'Good. That's what I thought. That's good. Yeah.'

'Does it matter?'

'No. But, you know. Now I'm getting better I like to know. Only you told me it was Saturday the other day, and it wasn't.'

'I don't think I did, Juliette.'

'You did.'

'I think you misheard me. I don't remember having any conversation about what day it was. I think you're still very confused.'

Why does he sound so angry?

'Okay. You're probably right.'

'I am right. I'll see you tomorrow.'

The door opens and Jeff's jolly face comes into view. He's smiling.

'Bye Jeff,' Robin says, 'she's all yours.' As Robin leaves Jeff moves towards me and blocks my view. I've missed the opportunity to see what I've done to Robin's beautiful face.

'Hey hun, I heard you had a fall so I thought I'd pop by on my way home. I miss seeing you every day.' Jeff picks up my hand and rubs it.

'I'm okay. I was just being a bit ambitious with the walking.'

'You got to take it easy. Where's that call button?' He searches the bed until he finds it nestling between my knees. 'Here, have it where you can reach it.' He pushes it into my hands. 'Have you eaten this evening?'

Have I? I don't remember. But now he's reminded me, I do feel hungry. 'I don't think so.'

'I'll go find out. I should get off now, but I'll pop by tomorrow. You take care, hun. And no walking alone.' He laughs, so do I. Jeff's brief visit has lifted my spirits.

Damn, I forgot to ask Robin if he could come up when my staples are removed. Not that I know exactly when that is. Sometime tomorrow morning. He'll be at work. He's squeamish; it's not fair to ask him.

Five minutes later my tea arrives. I ask for what's left of the cherries too; half a punnet.

I've almost finished the cherries, when Dad arrives. He looks anxious.

'What's been happening? You fell over. They've just told us.'

'I'm fine. Don't worry. Just thought I could run before I could walk.' I laugh. I do feel fine. And a bit silly.

Mum bursts in, her face ashen.

'Juliette. They said you were walking around with the cherry punnet. Why?'

I attempt a shrug, and this time my shoulders move properly. I should be celebrating my mobility, instead I wish they'd forget about my fall. I can feel my throat clogging up. I think I might cry.

'Don't cry, darling.' Mum hugs me.

'I'm fine. Really.' I snivel into her shoulder. It feels so comforting. I wish Robin would hold me like this.

'I'll tell Sally to tell Stephen, no more cherries.'

'Don't do that?' I pull myself away. 'I love them.' I laugh as Mum pulls a pack of tissues from her handbag and hands me one, taking one herself.

We sit and chat about nothing, reminiscing about old times, times before Mads was born, times after. We don't mention her by name but she's a presence we're all aware of avoiding. Finally, I can stand it no longer.

'Why do you think she did it?' I say, watching Dad jump and Mum pale.

Mum and Dad sit silent for a moment, both deep in thought.

Dad starts his sentence with a deep breath. 'I don't think she did. Not on purpose, anyway.'

Mum shakes her head.

'Do you think she was bullied at school?' Isn't that what Robin had told me?

'Maybe.' Dad shakes his head. 'I don't know. The school haven't been particularly forthcoming. You'd think they'd know more. They say they weren't aware of any bullying. Madeleine, according to them, was a popular girl and good student.'

'She was.' Mum's voice is a squeak. 'They'd tell

you, Brian. You spoke to the Head, she'd tell you. You're colleagues. Equals.'

'I suppose so.'

'I don't know where she got the pills from.' Mum sniffs. The tissue goes up to her eyes.

'No.' Robin says such things can be sourced easily, but I'm not saying that to Mum. Why compound her misery.

'You can get anything you want these days, Lyndsey. Anything.' Dad's head is shaking again.

'On the bloody internet. We should never have let her have that phone or that bloody laptop. When it broke down a few weeks before she died we should have left it broken. I wished Stephen had never fixed it.' Mum's crying properly now. I wished I'd never said anything. But I have to know. I have to find out the truth.

'I don't think she did it. On purpose,' Dad says again.

'No,' Mum and I chorus.

'Any sign of that letter?'

'No.' I wonder how well Robin looked for it. 'But I'll have a good look when get home.' I imagine it stuffed in the letter rack, or fallen down the back of the hall table, or even dropped on Robin's desk. I doubt he's let Mum into his study; he keeps the door locked when he's not in it.

'I've looked,' Mum says. 'But I don't know your house.'

'No.' I feel sheepish. Mum and Dad should have been welcome in our home. After this is over, once I'm out of here, things are going to change.

Robin had the lock put on his study door within a week of us moving in.

159

'Pupil confidentiality, Juliette. We can't be too careful. Also, that's a brand new, expensive computer.'

'I'm hardly going to touch it.' What was he suggesting? 'I have my laptop.' Any work I did from home was fitted onto the corner of the kitchen table, Robin didn't like me to use the dining-room table; the John Lewis one.

'You're not the issue. It's if someone breaks in.' He rolled his eyes as though that was obvious and I was stupid.

'Wouldn't stop them if that's what they really wanted,' I muttered before walking away. 'Anyway, don't you have it password protected?'

'Of course,' he shouted. I was in the kitchen by then, turning on the oven, wondering what we should have for tea.

Later, as he sat typing away, I took him a cup of coffee and examined the lock. It was a substantial mortice lock, with heavy brass plates on the edge of the door and the frame. The workman had made an excellent job of it, the doors were oak, expensive and heavy, Robin had stood over him supervising the job.

'Big,' I said, idly running my finger over the two large keys, which, still on a single ring, lay on his desk. 'One for me?' I picked them up and jangled them.

'I'm a bit busy,' he said, calmly taking the keys from my fingers and tucking them into his shirt pocket. He hardly looked at me.

'Fine.' I left the room and closed the door behind me.

He stayed in his office all evening, I went to bed early and pretended to be asleep when he joined me.

We never discussed the lock on his door again, he

never gave me a key. He locked his office when he wasn't in it; he valued his pupils' confidentiality.

'Did you check Robin's desk?'

Mum and Dad exchange glances.

'Yes. I did,' Mum says and pats my hand.

'Okay.' Robin must really want to get to the bottom of it too, if he's allowing Mum into his office.

'I wish I could be here for you tomorrow. With the staples.'

'Don't worry.' I'd quite forgotten about the staples coming out. I wish Mum hadn't reminded me. 'I hope it goes okay at the dentists.'

Mum grimaces and rubs her jaw.

When it's time for them to leave, they're subdued and so am I. I miss my little sister so much.

We all miss Mads.

'We should be ready to remove your staples in about half an hour?' The very young nurse, I don't know her name, is casual and smiling. Her head popped around the door, her body still in the corridor.

'Oh. Okay.'

'I'll come and get you.'

'Thanks,' I mumble into my chest.

'You okay?'

'Yes.'

'Nervous?'

'Yes.'

'Your mum coming?'

'No. She can't.'

'Don't worry. I'll hold your hand.'

'Cool.' I don't feel cool. I feel sick.

'It doesn't hurt.'

How the hell would she know? She barely looks old enough to be out on her own.

The door closes and she's gone. I hope Sally gets here soon. I imagine her sitting in the waiting room at the bunion clinic – I don't know if such a thing exists – getting annoyed at the delay. She's not the type to sit quietly and wait patiently, she'll be asking when it's her turn. What if she's had her turn and they've sent her for tests, x-rays, scans, things like that? She could be hours.

I remember, when I was about nine, I fell off a wall and broke my arm. The wall was part of a house that was being built around the corner. It was the weekend, no builders about; all the kids played on the building site. Health and safety wasn't as strict then as it is now, there was no site fence to stop us getting in. We built castles with the sand, played snakes with coils of wire, moved bricks and blocks about, climbed the newly-built walls.

'Don't go up there, Juliette,' Stephen said. It was long before Mads had been born, so he still called me Juliette.

'I can if I want.'

'Be careful. It's too high. You're too small.'

I hated that. I knew I was small, I didn't need reminding. I didn't need him to point it out.

'Scaredy cat,' I called and the other kids joined in. 'Scaredy cat. Scaredy cat.'

I stood up on the wall to show how brave I was. None of the other kids were quite so brave, or stupid.

Then I fell, tumbling and rolling onto my arm and cracking it against a broken block. I nearly passed out with the pain.

Stephen took off his sweatshirt and tied it around me, pulling my arm into my chest. He'd been doing first-aid at cubs and pretended he knew all about broken bones, though it did ease the pain. He walked me home, his arm around my shoulders, me wailing and crying. He let us into the kitchen where we found Mum and Sally cutting out cushion covers on the table.

Mum took one look at me and frowned.

Stephen slowly undid the knot in his sweatshirt and my arm fell out, dropping in front of me. I howled. My hand was limp.

Sally blamed Stephen; he was supposed to be looking after me. She pushed him out of the kitchen and marched him home. He was grounded for a week.

I didn't blame Stephen.

Mum had to call Dad; she didn't have her own car then. He couldn't get away, so she called a taxi. At the hospital, we sat waiting in different departments; Accident and Emergency, x-ray, several others I can't remember. It went on all afternoon. Finally, I was taken to the plaster room and I left with a cast that weighed a ton. Dad had finished work by the time we were done, he collected us and Mum moaned about how much the taxi journey had cost.

It was the same arm that is injured now. Unlucky, that arm.

I imagine Sally sitting in waiting rooms, just like that.

Half an hour comes and goes and no one comes for me; no young nurse, no Sally.

Another thirty minutes pass. Maybe they've

forgotten. I'm reprieved. They can do it another day, when Mum can come.

I feel much happier now. I'm sitting in the chair, both eyes closed, my head resting against the wing.

The door bursts open; so much for my reprieve.

I wait for the nurse to say something and when she doesn't I slowly open my right eye, the left one is still not co-operating.

'Stephen?'

He looks solid and dependable. His hair is cropped short, his clothes are soft and casual.

'Etty,' he says, his voice gravelly.

A single tear rolls down his left cheek.

ELEVEN

'What are you doing here?' Do I sound ungrateful?

'My mum's held up downstairs. She sent me up instead. I'm sorry.'

'Why?'

'I'm sorry because I know you didn't want to see me.'

I look at him, his sweet face, so earnest, so genuine.

'It's not that I didn't want to see you, I didn't want you to see me.' I pause as he uses his knuckle to wipe away a tear from his cheek. 'In this state.' I add, pointing at my head, my leg, everywhere.

I want him to say that I look fine, that it's nothing, that I'll soon be back to normal, but he doesn't. He just stares at me.

'I'm not that bad, am I?' I attempt a laugh which could easily turn into a sob.

'Etty.' He steps forward, drops down to my level and grabs my hand; he pulls it up to his lips, letting them brush my skin. 'I've been so worried.'

'I'm fine.' I let my hand stay in his even though I know I shouldn't. 'There's talk of me going home soon. Although, I must accomplish some things on my own, like washing myself, and walking.' I follow my comment with another forced laugh.

Stephen nods, his face solemn.

'Anything I can do to help, anything, I'll be there

for you.'

'Thanks.' I pull my hand away now. What if Robin walked in? And I can just imagine Robin letting Stephen into our home to help. That will never happen. Just letting Mum in is a miracle.

I glance around the room, embarrassed. Stephen stands up and peers at my head.

'That's a lot of staples.'

I inhale through my nose and the sound carries around the room.

'I'm sorry. That was tactless.'

I don't get a chance to respond because the young nurse's face pops up in the door porthole. She beams at us before bringing a wheelchair in.

'We ready?' She positions the wheelchair in front of me; I would rather walk but have already proven I can't. 'Perhaps your husband could help you into the chair.'

Stephen steps forward, puts his hands under my arms and helps me up. For a moment, we're eye to eye and we exchange a knowing glance. Or is that my imagination?

Young nurse leads the way as Stephen pushes me around the corner to a little room. We go through the admin of checking that I am the correct person, then the gloves are pulled on and my head inspected. The tool to remove the staples, which looks like mini-pliers, is in the hand of the senior nurse. She introduces herself as Sharon; she will remove the staples.

'You don't need me, now you have your husband,' young nurse says, and without waiting for a reply she pushes a chair into the back of Stephen's knees and then she's gone.

'It shouldn't hurt. Let me know if it does.' Sharon pulls a bright lamp over my head. It feels warm on my shaven scalp.

Stephen takes both my hands in his. I grip and tense myself. How can it not hurt? These are lumps of metal in my head.

I feel a tug and hear a clink as the first one hits the metal bowl.

'That didn't hurt.' I'm amazed.

'No, it shouldn't. Unless there's infection. Which you don't have.'

'Thank God,' Stephen mutters.

Clink, clink, two more hit the bowl.

'Some people do this themselves at home.'

'What?'

'Obviously not when the staples are in their heads. That would be quite tricky.' She stops speaking as three more hit the bowl in quick succession. 'Or they get their relatives to do it.' She glances at Stephen who doesn't react.

For a while nobody speaks, the silence in the room is broken only by the buzzing of the lamp and the clink of staples hitting the bowl.

'There, last one.' She drops it into bowl and then starts to examine my scalp. 'Healed very well. They've been in a while. One or two were reluctant to come out.' She laughs. 'Didn't hurt though, did it?'

'No. No, it didn't. Thank you.' I let go of Stephen's hands. He stands up and moves the chair aside.

'You know the way back?' Sharon asks Stephen.

'I think so.' He laughs; it's about thirty feet away and around the corner. He grabs the wheelchair handles and manoeuvres me through the door.

Once in my room I run my hand over my scalp.

'How does it feel?'

'Lumpy. But not so tight. How does it look?'

He inspects my head, gently moving what's left of my hair to have a good look.

'Yeah. Lumpy.' He pats my shoulders with both his hands. 'Won't show when your hair grows back.

'Good.'

'You didn't correct the nurse when she thought I was your husband.'

'Neither did you.' With my good eye, I watch his face for a reaction. What am I expecting? I don't know. 'Too complicated to explain. They don't care.'

'No. I don't suppose they do.'

'And finally…' Sally bursts into the room. 'Oh, and news from your Mum, she's had the troublesome bugger extracted.'

'Poor Mum.'

'It's a back one, won't show.' Sally sits down and starts to go through her bag. 'For you. Thought now you can see a bit, you might like this.' She hands me a magazine. *Beautiful Homes*.

'Thank you.' Automatically I start to flick through it, I come across a garden picture.

'That's nice,' Stephen and I chorus before laughing.

We don't have much of a garden at home. New houses have much smaller gardens than older ones. Ours is tiny and Robin had it paved over soon after we moved in, he'd done the same in his two-up-two down house too.

'Can't be doing with gardening,' he explained to me.

I came home from work one day and it was almost

finished. He hadn't even discussed it with me beforehand.

'But I like greenery.' I sounded like a sulky child.

'Plant some pots then.' That was the end of the conversation; he went into his study to salivate over his new computer. He was still in the process of setting it up then.

I never did do those pots. My heart wasn't in it. Dad potted me up a French Lavender for my birthday later that summer, assuming that it would join others – he didn't know our garden was just block paving. The front was the same too.

'Plenty of parking space. It's always at a premium.' Robin was pleased with himself.

We'd paid the builders extra to pave the front, but I'd always assumed we'd have a back garden. Where would the children play? Of course, I didn't know then that there would be no children. Robin hadn't told me he was infertile, not then.

In our little cul-de-sac of six houses, we were the first to move in. Our next-door neighbours were next. They moved in with a three-year-old and another one on the way. Naively, I imagined we would be in that position in the near future. How silly was I?

I've often asked myself if I would have married Robin if I had known in the beginning that he couldn't have children, and, perhaps even more pertinently, that he didn't want children. I'd brought up adoption once I'd come to terms with never having my own, but Robin had been adamantly against it.

'No, Juliette. I couldn't even begin to consider it. I couldn't love a child that wasn't my own. No.'

'But..'

'No. Leave me if you don't like it.'

That was it, no further conversation, no discussion. Just no.

He knew I loved him too much to leave him, to put a hypothetical child, a fantasy child, before him. Just as I knew he would never leave me. He told me so, frequently.

So, I get on with life, I work hard, gain promotions and bonuses. Financially we are comfortable. We go on exotic holidays, have expensive cars. Robin has a silver Mercedes coupe – even though he rarely drives it. He likes me to drive him. I chose my cherry red Ford Focus which Robin derided, said it was a bit of a family car – a subconscious choice perhaps. But even he had to admit that it was a comfortable ride and useful for shopping.

I don't have that car now though. Do I?

'Penny for them,' Stephen's voice brings me back to my hospital room.

'Sorry?'

'You were miles away.'

'Yeah.' I turn another page in the magazine. Another lovely garden. I close it. 'I hear you're house-hunting.'

'We saw a lovely one last night, didn't we?' Sally says, smiling at Stephen.

'We did.' He sounds sombre. 'I suppose I should be going.' He stands up, then leans down to hug me, kiss my cheek. I hug him back and it feels so comforting. That bond of childhood friendship never fades.

I watch him leave, notice that as he shuts the door he looks sad, sadder than he has a right to.

'Is Stephen okay?' I ask Sally.

She smiles. It's that kind of odd smile that the smiler uses to mask another feeling.

'He's not ill, or something?' My voice sounds as alarmed as I feel; I hadn't expected that.

'No, no. He's fine. Don't you worry about Stephen. You just concentrate on making a full recovery.'

'Yeah. I'll do that.' But I *am* worried about Stephen. I hope he's okay. He's my oldest friend, in fact, now I think about it, aside from Robin, he's my only real friend. I have colleagues at work, people I go to lunch with, but I'm always careful what I say to them – I must maintain that air of professionalism. I suppose Stephen is the only person who knows the real me, besides Robin.

Sally spends the afternoon with me, she watches me eat my lunch, declares it unfit for human consumption – which I don't think is fair – then she slips out and brings me back a McDonald's cheeseburger. And I scoff it; I hadn't realised how hungry I was.

'Ironic, isn't it, that they have a McDonald's in the hospital?'

'Do they? I thought you were quick.'

'Yes, constantly telling us not to eat junk food…' she leaves the sentence unfinished and we laugh together. 'I'll take the rubbish away with me so you don't get caught.' We laugh again.

'You can bring me another one any time you like. But, if I'm choosing, I'd prefer a Filet-o-Fish.'

'Consider it done.'

Not that Robin will approve if he finds out. He has a real thing about junk food; he's probably right.

We flick through the magazine and chat. To be honest, she wears me out. She tells me what a big step it is for Stephen to come back, to effectively start again.

'He's built quite a reputation in his field in Canada.' Her face beams with pride.

'Then why is he coming back?' A thought suddenly occurs to me. 'Are *you* okay? Your health, I mean?'

'Oh yes. Strong as an ox.' She flexes her arm muscles to prove the point. Sally has a wiry, muscular build; she looks as though she could pop out and build a wall. Now I think about it, I think she did rebuild her front garden wall after her husband left, because he'd never got around it. 'But it will be lovely to have him back. In the same town.' She smiles to herself, the delight is evident.

'Then why did Stephen look so glum when he left? Is he worried about his new job?'

'No. Not really. They headhunted him.'

'Still it's a big step, giving up a life in another country.' I'm still puzzled as to why he's doing it.

'He'll make a success of it. I'm delighted he's staying.'

'Oh yes. Me too.' I genuinely am. Though I do wonder how often I'll be able to see my friend. 'It's a woman.' Why hadn't that occurred to me before? It's so obvious. 'He's got a girlfriend here.'

'Yes, he has.' Sally smiles.

'It must be serious if he's changing his life.'

Sally nods, there's a faraway look in her eyes.

'Well, good. I'm surprised he never married when he was in Canada. I know he's always wanted a family.' For months, I thought he had taken Lucia, the girl from the party, to Canada with him; but he hadn't. And, although I knew he'd had some very glamorous girlfriends in Canada – I'd seen them on his Facebook wall, yes, I admit I looked occasionally – none had been serious.

Stephen has never been shy about what he wants out of life. I remember the *family* conversation like it was yesterday. It was the Christmas holidays, he was sixteen, I was fifteen, it was just before Robin came into my life. Over the years we hadn't seen as much of each other as we had when we were younger, but over that Christmas break we'd spent a lot of time together, re-establishing our friendship.

It was one of those chilly days between Christmas and New Year so there was no one else about; we were hanging around the swings, taking it in turns to push each other. I went high because Stephen was big and strong, he complained that I was a pathetic pusher because I was so small. It was our constant jibe at one another – he was too big, I was too small - but it was always in good fun.

'You'll need to develop good pushing muscles if you are going to take your children to the park,' he said as I pushed him inadequately.

'I haven't got any children. Duh.' I'd yanked the seat from beneath him and he almost fell off.

'And you'll have to be more careful. Killer mother.'

'Shut up.' My fifteen-year-old self didn't want to talk about having children. I was still a child myself.

'Just saying.'

'Well don't.'

'I want a big family,' he said, evidently not shutting up. 'Four kids, maybe more.'

'What?'

'Yeah, cos then, if it doesn't work out between me and my wife, at least the kids will have each other.'

'You and your wife. Listen to you. Who's going to marry you?'

'If you can grow a bit, you can.'

I thumped him on the back and ran off. 'Like hell,' I shouted back.

He soon caught up with me, his strides twice mine. 'That hurt.'

'It was meant to. Why would I marry you?'

He shrugged, trying to appear nonchalant. 'You're my best friend,' he said.

'Round here,' I added. 'You're mine too. But not at school, obviously. I've got best friends at school.'

'Me too.'

'Well then.' I didn't really know what I meant by that. It was all a bit cringey; we both felt awkward. We walked on in silence, heading for home; it was already starting to get dark.

'You're lucky, you've got Mads.' He stood with his hand on our garden gate, pushed it open to let me in. 'If your parents ever split up, you'd have each other.'

'I'm so glad he's found *the one*.' I really am happy for him. I really am.

'Yes. Me too.' Sally starts looking around for her handbag. 'Time I was off, I think.'

When my tea arrives, I don't have much appetite; I'm too full of cheeseburger.

I try my first, almost unaided trip to the bathroom, it goes well for a first try. I've been told that I must be able to do these things before I can go home. I've also learnt that if I don't manage them in the next few days I can go to the rehab-clinic. Sally told me that is

174

where the old people who have falls go; it doesn't really appeal to me, so I'm determined to do everything I can here. I'm desperate to go home. Desperate to sleep in my own bed.

The medical staff don't seem too worried about my left eye not opening, as long as the right one works. They think it will improve in time.

I even manage to get myself into bed. All this sitting or lying around is tiring.

I'm just dozing off when Robin's voice stirs me. I don't have the energy to even open my good eye.

'I hear *Stephen* paid you a visit this morning.' He places such emphasis on Stephen's name that I can tell he's irritated.

Well, I'm irritated too. Irritated because Robin couldn't take time off work to support me. He knew I was dreading the removal of the staples; he could have taken the morning off.

'Yes,' I say, 'he came with me when they took the staples out of my head.'

There's silence for a moment.

'Couldn't your mum come?'

'No. She had an emergency dentist appointment. Sally couldn't come either, so she sent Stephen. Good of him to spare the time, wasn't it?'

I wait for Robin to respond. He won't like the way I've just spoken to him but I'm the sick one here.

'Did he bring the McDonald's too?'

Caught out. 'How do you know about that?' I thought we'd been quite discreet.

'There's a fry on the floor.' He sighs. 'You shouldn't eat that, you know. It's very fattening.'

'Apparently, I need fattening up.'

'I don't think so.'

I can't respond to that. I don't want to have the weight conversation again. Yes, I have put on weight since we married. But I don't think I'm fat. Robin prides himself on having the same thirty-two-inch waist at forty-two as he did at twenty-two – not that I knew him then.

'My mum's looking thin,' I say, diverting his attention from me. 'I suppose it's due to everything's that's happened. Mads. Me.'

'Yes. It doesn't seem to have affected your dad's belly though.'

'That's mean.' I attempt to turn away from him, but I'm tired and stiff, so he still has my left ear.

'True though.'

'Did you find the letter yet?'

'Letter?'

'The one redirected from work. The one Dad thinks might be from Mads.'

'No.'

'Have you had a really good look?'

'Yes. Of course.'

'You haven't mixed it up with the papers on your desk?'

'No.'

I don't bring up that Mum has looked on his desk; he must know, he would have to give her permission, unlock the door, but no point in annoying him about that.

'You know this bullying theory?'

'Yes.'

'Where did that come from?'

He hesitates for a minute. 'What do you mean?'

'Only the school won't confirm it and well, where did you hear it?'

'Not sure. I must have overheard it.' He pauses. 'Actually, a name was mentioned. Chloe, or something like that.'

'Chloe? But Chloe was Mads's best friend.' I've met Chloe at Mum and Dad's when she's come for tea with Mads. She's lovely. Admittedly, it's been a while since I last saw them together, but…

'You know what teenage girls are like.' He gives something that sounds like a laugh. 'Falling out with each other, usually over some boy.'

Now it's my turn not to answer. I can barely remember my teenage years; I don't think I was a typical teenager. I was only fifteen when I met Robin. He probably does know more about teenagers than I do; he teaches them every day.

When I'm well I will be having a word with Chloe. I owe it to Mads and Mum and Dad to find out the truth.

'I need to get off soon. I'll pop by tomorrow morning, early.' His chair scrapes.

'Already?'

'Yes. Another pupil.'

'Really. Can't you take a break?'

'Well, you know, bills to pay.'

'Not really. I'm sure I will still be getting paid. I'm on sick leave.'

'Okay. Well, work helps keep my mind off all this.' He gives me a quick peck on the forehead, just as the door opens.

'Hello.' It's Mum, sounding cheerier than I would expect after an extraction. Dad's cough confirms he's here too.

'I was just going,' Robin says. 'You can have your daughter all to yourselves.' I hear the door close behind him.

No one comments. Which is just as well. Chairs scrape as Mum and Dad sit down.

'How are you, Mum?'

'Not too bad.' She has a slight lisp. 'Better than it aching.'

With great effort, I pull myself up the bed and open my eye. For a second, I think my left eye opens; before closing just as rapidly. Mum's face looks puffy and her smile is lop-sided. Dad just looks tired.

'I hear you've been eating illegal food,' Dad says, forcing a grin.

'Yeah. It was Sally's fault.' I laugh. 'It was good though. Actually, there's a fry on the floor, can you find it and bin it.'

Mum gets up and looks around the room, Dad checks under the bed. They find nothing. Robin must have disposed of it.

After I've given them an update on my progress and we've talked a bit about Mum's tooth, Dad inspects my head.

'Not too bad at all,' he pronounces.

'Yes. It wasn't as bad as I thought having them out either. Stephen held my hands. That helped.'

Mum and Dad exchange the briefest of glances, but I don't miss it.

'He's a good lad, Stephen.' Dad nods.

'He is,' Mum adds.

'It was good of him; you couldn't come, Sally got held up and Robin couldn't be here either.'

Mum pats my hand. Dad looks away. Are they embarrassed on Robin's behalf?

We fall silent. We're all tired.

'Maybe you should read us a bit of Jane Austen,

Mum.' I raise my voice an octave in an attempt to sound jolly.

'After what you said last time. I don't think so. Anyway, I don't have the book with me anymore and I'm slurring.'

'Okay. I was just joking anyway.'

Dad yawns. 'Anyone mind if I go and find myself a coffee?'

'No, you go, love.' Mum pats his arm as he gets up.

'Either of you want anything?'

Coffee. That would probably perk me up. I consider it for a moment. 'No thanks,' Mum and I chorus.

'So, you had a nice time with Stephen.'

'Not really, Mum. I was having lumps of metal pulled out of my head.'

'Well, yes. I meant it was nice to see him?'

'Yeah. It was. He's such an old friend. I can't remember the last time I saw him…'

'Madeleine's funeral.'

'Oh yeah. Not that I can remember much of that. I meant before that. You know, meaningful, proper old catch-up time. Did you know he's got a girlfriend here, that's why he's moving back to the UK?'

'Yes, I did.'

'Have you met her?'

'Yes. Quite a bit.'

'What's she like? Is she nice. Of course, she's nice. He deserves someone lovely, doesn't he?'

'He does.'

'It's good that someone's having a good time in all this mess.'

'I don't think he's having a good time, Juliette.

He's very worried about you.'

'Tell him not to be. He should be enjoying himself with his girlfriend. He's buying a house here now he's sold his in Canada. And he's got his new job to look forward to.'

'Did he tell you he's delayed starting it until you're better?'

'What? No. Why?'

Mum shrugs and looks away. I'm glad Robin isn't here listening to this, he'd be annoyed about Stephen.

'Actually, Mum, while you're here on your own, I wanted to ask you something.'

Mum leans in as though she's going to hear a secret.

'Since I've been here, have I had a period?'

'Not that I know of.'

'Yeah, that's what the staff said, that I hadn't, I mean. Said it could be delayed due to the trauma. I just hope I don't have one until I get home. It won't be particularly easy then, I'm not that mobile, but at least it'll be more private.' I laugh and smile, more to reassure myself than Mum.

Mum looks away, it could be embarrassment – Mum doesn't like talking about bodily functions in too much detail – but there's something else.

'Mum, am I okay?' I'm worried now.

'You're fine, darling.' Her false cheeriness and lopsided smile are betrayed by the look in her eyes?

'No, tell me. Am I okay?'

She doesn't get the chance to answer because Dad bursts in.

'We're going to have to leave, I'm afraid. Sorry Juliette. But there's been a break in at the school and I have to go.'

'Oh no.' Mum jumps up and snatches her bag from the floor. She moves too quickly and the phrase *saved by the bell* echoes in my head.

'Oh, right. I hope everything's okay.'

'It'll be some little devil playing silly beggars.' Dad sighs; he's used to this and takes it in his stride, but the police insist he comes and inspects the damage, which is usually a broken window.

They're kissing me and they're gone.

And I'm left wondering if I have more injuries that anyone is telling me about. I pat my stomach for any tell-tale signs, any pain, any lumps or bumps, but I find nothing.

TWELVE

It would be ironic if, after all my sadness about Robin not being able to father children, I end up barren too.

Mum's face when I asked her if I was okay spoke volumes, even if her words said the opposite. Why has nobody told me? Dad told me straight about my injuries when I first came round. Maybe he couldn't bear to talk about it, or maybe he was too embarrassed. Or maybe he thought it was pointless to mention it, they already know that I will never make them grandparents. But surely the staff would have told me. Am I just being silly? Fearful for no reason?

I remember when I told Mum about Robin's sterility. Or rather, when she guessed.

She'd bumped into an old work colleague who was out with her daughter and new born grandson.

'You should have seen him, tiny. Tiny. Prem, apparently. But so cute.'

'That's nice.' I said it with a smile on my face and hoped the conversation would end there. 'Do you want me to help with tea?'

'No, that's fine. It's in the oven. Fish pie. He only weighed three pounds.' She wasn't going to be distracted. 'Can you imagine that? But he's a healthy six now. Still looks tiny. Head like this.' She formed her hands into a little ball to show how small his head was.

'Shall I lay the table?'

'Yes. Thanks. Her daughter, Zara, I think her

name is, said if we hadn't been in the middle of Asda I could have held him. Ah, I'd have loved that.' Mum's face went all gooey.

I didn't respond as I rattled around in the cutlery drawer for knives and forks.

'His name is Bryn. His dad is Welsh. He wanted a proper Welsh name for his son.'

I turned away from her and concentrated on the precise placing of the mats on the table. I wished she would shut up.

'There's not a hair on his head. Not one. He's bald. The baby, I mean. Like a cute little egg. He yawned when I was looking at him. So sweet. And his little hands were creeping out of the covers. Tiny little nails. Reminds me of you. And Madeleine.' Her voice was soft and, I suspected, she was beaming, but I couldn't look at her.

Shut up.

'Is Mads upstairs?' I'd finished laying the table and wanted to escape.

'Yes. In her room. Probably on that phone. Not sure that was such a clever idea.' Mum tutted but I was glad she was off the baby monologue.

Mads had been denied a mobile phone despite declaring that it wasn't fair, all her friends had one and she was a bit of a freak because she didn't. Dad was against it; he'd seen the effects of mobiles on teenagers, the cyber-bullying, the other horrors, but Mum had relented. She'd persuaded him it might be safer now that Mads went to school on the bus on her own. Mads became the proud owner of new mobile given to her on her twelfth birthday. I liked her having a phone too, she sent me funny little text messages throughout the day and forwarded the odd amusing picture or video – she knew better than to send me anything risqué, Mum and Dad had sworn me to tell them if she did. I'd also told Mads that if she ever encountered anything dodgy to tell me first, and I'd help her deal with it; Mum and Dad would have just taken the phone away. Fortunately, Mads had never had to come to me.

As expected when I crept upstairs I heard Mads laughing on the phone.

'Oh, Clo,' she said, 'that's so cool. You're so cool.'

I popped my head around her door.

'Oh, got to go, my big sis is here.' She ended the call and smiled at me. 'Hiya.'

'Hi.' I slumped down next to her on the bed, my old bed. She'd moved into my old room by then, but Mum had kept it empty for five years, in case I ever wanted to come back. Dad had convinced her I wouldn't. It had been redecorated for Mads. 'Having fun with your phone? What's so cool?' The instant I asked I wished I hadn't, I sounded like Mum when she was fishing for information.

'Just some stuff at school. You know.' Mads gave me an innocent smile. A smile that also let me know that's all I was getting.

I could barely remember school, never mind being twelve. What self-respecting twelve-year-old wants to tell their nearly twenty-five-year-old sister all their secrets? However innocent. It dawned on me then that I was twice Mads's age. She probably thought I'd been sent up to spy on her.

'Is tea ready? I'm starving. What is it?' She cuddled into me, maybe to let me know she didn't really think I was prying.

'Nearly. It's fish pie.'

'Cool.' Her phone pinged and she picked it up. After smiling at it, she showed me a silly video doing the rounds – a dancing chicken. I laughed with her and didn't tell her I had seen it on Facebook two weeks previously.

We were still laughing when Mum called us down for tea.

After tea, Mads disappeared up to her room, ostensibly to do her homework, more likely to play on her phone. Dad was working on some grand scheme for his school and Mum and I were alone in the kitchen again, clearing up.

'How's things?' Mum said.

'What things?'

'You, work,' she paused, 'Robin.' She said his name the way she always did, as though it hurt her to say it.

'Fine. Good.'

'Good.' She dropped a plate into the dishwasher. 'Only you seemed a bit upset earlier.'

'I'm fine.' My reply was a little too sharp, too quick.

'When I was talking about the baby.'

I shrugged and turned away, picked up a plate and went to the bin to scrape it.

'Only, you know, I'm here if you ever want to talk.'

'Thanks.' I prayed for her to change the subject. I didn't want to talk about babies, not when I would never have one of my own. I'd known for months that we would never have our own family, but I hadn't told anyone. Not anyone.

I put the plate on the worktop and turned back to the table, picking up the placemats as the tears streamed down my face. I wasted time lining them up, ensuring they were piled neatly. I didn't want Mum to see me crying. I took a deep breath to calm myself.

Who was I kidding?

Her arms were around me and she was hugging me and the whole sorry story came tumbling out.

'You didn't know before you married him?' Mum's tone suggested that it wasn't really a question, more confirmation of what she suspected. She hugged me tighter, trying to console me.

'No.'

'Most people discuss having a family before they marry, otherwise…' She never finished the sentence. 'I suppose you were too young to even think about it.'

'I suppose so.'

She pulled back and frowned.

'How does he know?'

'He's been tested.'

'Yes. But why?'

What was she getting at? I shrugged.

'I mean,' she said, 'you only get tested if you're trying for a baby and can't get pregnant. You know, to find out if it's the man or the woman.'

'Oh Mum, you always try to twist it.' I glanced up at the clock. 'I need to go, I have to pick up Robin. That wasn't strictly true, I had another half hour until I needed to leave, I just didn't want to face Mum's questions. Or my own.

She had a valid point though, didn't she?

I parked around the corner from the house Robin was tutoring in – he didn't like me to hover outside – and waited. During that extra half hour, I had plenty of opportunity to think. It had never occurred to me that testing wasn't the norm. I had just accepted what Robin said. Why wouldn't I? But now, now, Mum had sown a seed of doubt in my mind, I began to wonder.

When Robin came around the corner, he was already smiling as he walked but when he saw me his smile broadened. He jumped into the car and leaned across and kissed me on the lips.

'Good evening?' I asked.

'Very. They want me to tutor their son next term.'

'Good.'

'Extra money, every penny helps.' He pulled on his seat belt and looked pointedly at the steering wheel.

I started the car.

'We don't really need the extra money, do we. I mean we do okay. Don't we?'

'Course,' he said, his lips pursing as he turned his head away from me.

Ever since our marriage Robin had handled all the finances, even though I was supposed to be the financial whizz; I was a chartered accountant, after all. Initially, I didn't mind. In fact, I was quite happy with the arrangement initially, because, as Mum had pointed out frequently, I was a child then.

'It just keeps things tidy,' Robin had said, whenever I queried it. He also liked to handle the post, always making sure that he got to it first, no matter when it came through the door. He would sift through the letters, pick out any addressed to me and hand them over with a smile. The rest went into his study. 'Bills,' he would say. 'Nothing for you to worry about.'

So, I let him. It suited me that he looked after everything. He looked after me. Anyway, I spent all day looking at numbers, pound signs floated across my eyes in my sleep especially when we were doing an audit, so I was happy with our arrangement. Occasionally, if I asked, he would update me on our financial position. But, as he often said we had everything we wanted and needed, so I let it go.

When we got home, and before he disappeared into his study, I caught him.

'Robin, you know your infertility . . .'

I watched him flinch. 'Yeah.'

'How do you know?'

He turned an astonished look on me. He almost laughed in my face.

'How do I know what?'

'That you're infertile?'

'I was tested.'

'Why?'

He narrowed his eyes at me but didn't answer.

'Why were you tested?'

'I don't want to talk about it.' He pushed past me, went into his study and slammed the door behind him.

I sat down in the lounge and waited. I didn't put the television on, or any lights, I just sat there.

Waiting.

Twenty minutes later I heard his study door open. He came across the hall and flicked the light on.

'You're sitting in the dark.' His voice was light, his dark mood gone. He dropped down next to me on the sofa and took my hand. 'Sorry I snapped. It's just so…well you know. Upsetting. I had mumps. As an adult. It can leave a grown man infertile, so I was tested.'

'I'm your wife, you could have told me that.'

'I know, I should have. I'm sorry. Shall I make us a pot of tea?'

'Yeah.' I shrugged and watched as he left the room, his step as light as his voice.

It was a perfectly reasonable explanation.

And that's what I said to Mum the next time I saw her. She didn't comment. At all. Just lifted her head in a half nod and talked about something else. And I let her.

That all seems so trivial now, after everything that's happened. Mum will never be able to bump into an old friend in a supermarket with her own grandchild in tow. I will never make her a granny. And now, neither will Mads.

When Emma comes in to do my physiotherapy, I ask her about my injuries. She's puzzled by my questions.

'You're healing really well now. Nothing to worry about. Even that eye is starting to respond.'

'What about my stomach, my pelvis?' I can't bring myself to say reproductive organs.

She fetches a folder and flicks through it.

'No. No injuries there. Don't worry, everything's fine. Normal childbirth and all that.' She laughs as she pats my hand reassuringly before encouraging me off the bed and into full mobility training, in a gym, no less.

I thank her for the reassurance; she isn't to know that I will never experience childbirth.

After she's finished with me and returned me to my room, I'm exhausted and sit in the chair dozing off and enjoying the peace and quiet.

I jolt awake. My heart is pounding in my chest.

The dream has returned; my car spinning out of

control.

I'm remembering more detail now. I was hanging from the car ceiling, suspended by my seatbelt; the pain in my chest was excruciating. The belt was released and I was pulled out, seconds before the car caught fire.

I didn't see the face of the person pulling me out. It was a man, he was strong, it must have been Robin. I'll ask him when he comes in.

I take a deep breath and calm myself. It's over. It's finished. I'm okay. I'm almost afraid to doze again but I'm so tired. I try, without success, to keep my eyes open.

'Wear the black coat I bought you. You never wear it,' Robin's voice was insistent.

'It doesn't fit. Anyway, we've decided that black isn't appropriate.' We were getting ready for Mads's funeral.

'You've got a bright blue dress on, you should at least wear a black coat. She deserves that much respect.'

I looked at him, he wore a black suit I didn't know he had. Had he gone out and bought it especially? I couldn't be bothered to ask. Nothing mattered anymore. His white shirt looked new too, as did the narrow black tie.

'Wear it. Show some respect.' He pulled the coat out of the wardrobe and flung it at me.

'No.' I turned away and started down the stairs.

'Don't do this, Juliette. Not today of all days.' He followed me down the stairs, the coat in his hand.

I didn't reply but put my head around the lounge door to check the time. We were running late. We needed to leave.

Back in the hall I searched the coat rack for my coat, my every day, maroon coat. I couldn't find it. I turned to face Robin. He held out the black coat, spreading it so I could easily put it on.

Oh, what was the point? What did it matter? We were running late. I put my arms in the sleeves and Robin spun me around and did the buttons up.

'You need to lose a few pounds.' He kissed me on the lips, a proper kiss, as the coat strained across my chest. He looked sad, and tired, yet in his black suit, he looked like an Armani model, albeit a mature one.

I drove my car to the crematorium. Mum and Dad had wanted us to go in the funeral car with them, but Robin had said he wouldn't come. Said such cars made a sad situation worse. I didn't have the energy to argue.

I'm not really asleep, just in that halfway state. My eyes are closed. My head lolls against the chair wing. Robin's voice speaks soothingly in my ear.

'How are you today?'

'Fine,' I say, half asleep.

'Cool. I can't stay long, just popped over in my lunch break.'

'Good. Thanks. Robin,' I pause, I have to ask. 'Why were you so determined I should wear the black coat to Mads's funeral?'

I can almost hear his brain ticking over. What's that phrase? The silence is deafening.

'Black for a funeral,' he finally manages.

Is that really the best he can do? Does it even matter anymore?

'Robin, what caused our crash. How did I flip us over? Over and over?'

191

'I don't remember. Let's not churn it up again. Sometimes we just have to accept that things are the way they are.'

Not that again.

'Do we?'

'You're going to be okay, that's all that really matters.'

'Robin, was it you who pulled me out of the car?'

'Yes. Of course. I have to go.' He gives me a quick kiss on the forehead and the door closes behind him.

He's gone.

And I don't care.

I'm slumped back in the chair again when Mum and Sally arrive. They're later than usual; they're also giggly. I open my eye to see flushed faces and smiles.

'Lunchtime drink?' I say, without thinking.

'Is it that obvious?' Sally asks, as Mum hushes her.

'It was hours ago, and only the one. Actually, we've been shopping.'

'Have fun?'

'Yes. I bought you a few new things, you are so thin now, your clothes are hanging off you.'

I look down at my top and leggings. Mum's right, the last time I wore these leggings they were strained across my thighs. It was just after Christmas though, so I was at my heaviest. Robin had made a nasty comment about my immense arse.

'I've brought you chocolates,' Sally whispers. 'Thought it might make a change from healthy foods.' She giggles and lays a double-layer box of Thornton's on my lap. I feel myself start to salivate. 'Go on, open them now.'

I don't need telling twice and we're soon tucking

into the top layer. I choose first – soft centres, Mum likes toffees and Sally likes nutty ones. Which means there's no waste.

'Robin wouldn't like me eating these,' I say, forgetting it's Mum I'm talking to.

'No, he wouldn't. But he's not here, so you enjoy them.' Mum leans over and takes another for herself. 'We cleared it with the nurses.'

Sally laughs. 'I think what cleared it with the nurses was giving them a box too. Just to say thank you.'

'Thank you. Yes. I should do that when I leave.' They've been amazing, and they have the patience of saints. 'Show me these clothes then.'

Mum lifts the carrier bags from the floor and starts to pull out tops and leggings, a lovely linen cardigan, and a new pair of jeans. There's underwear too.

'Size eight,' Sally says. 'But you'll soon grow out of them.'

'But for now, they won't bag around you or fall down.' Mum holds the jeans up against me, nodding her approval.

'We'll have a few more shopping trips when you're better. Lots of new clothes and things.' Sally says, a grin spreading across her flushed face. I'm wondering if they only had the one drink.

'I've got a wardrobe full of small stuff at home.' I force a little laugh. 'The clothes are all great. Thank you.' I feel tearful. Everyone is being so kind. So helpful. I sniff to hold it in.

'What have you been doing today?' Mum's picked up on my distress and is diverting the conversation.

'Walking. A lot. And some of it without sticks. I've been to the mini-gym today too. And look.' I concentrate hard and manage to open my left eye.

Suddenly, I'm seeing in binocular vision, and using my left eye seems to be improving my vision. I put my hand over my right eye and everything is crystal clear. I let my left eye close, which it does with minimum effort on my part and peer through my right eye only; Mum's face is a little blurry. 'I think I might need glasses.' Robin will not like that. I hope I can wear contacts when I'm better.

'Worry about that later. But that's wonderful, you'll soon be back to normal. There's hardly any swelling now.'

'But glasses,' I say, making a face.

'Nothing wrong with glasses.' Sally and Mum both wear glasses.

'Yes, but you're…' I'm about to say old, but manage to change it to 'older.'

They don't care. They just laugh. This is the happiest and most relaxed I've seen Mum in years. Not that I'm advocating alcohol as a solution to our present problems.

Nothing is going to bring Mads back. Maybe if we could all understand what happened to her, we might be able to rebuild our lives.

'Mum, have you seen anything of Mads's friend, Chloe?'

Mum's face drops. I wish I hadn't let my thoughts escape through my mouth.

'Not since the funeral. Poor girl.'

'They were still friends then?'

'What do you mean? They were best friends.'

'They hadn't fallen out, or anything?' I don't want to accuse Chloe of being a bully, but, if there are any signs that Mum has noticed, it would help.

'No. They were best of friends. Just that morning,

Chloe called for Madeleine for school. They were giggling like…' her voice trails away, 'schoolgirls.' Mum's face is pale now, gone are her flushed cheeks, her own giggly smile.

Robin was convinced that Chloe was the bully; but Mum would know if that were the case, surely. The mood in the room is now sombre; I've done that, I've spoiled our fun.

'Why don't we get you into some of these clothes,' Sally says, pulling the jeans and a top out.

I allow them to dress me, it's a good diversion from my mood-killing questions about Chloe. In the end, the jeans are deemed too complicated for me to manage on my own. I might be using the bathroom unaided, but fiddly zips and buttons are still beyond me. I pull on a pair of navy leggings instead; they make my newly slim legs look amazing. Robin's going to love these.

'You look fabulous. And you'll soon fill out.' Sally runs her hands over my shoulders, smoothing the deep pink top down. She stands up. 'Anyone fancy a cup of tea? I'm going to go down to the café and get myself one. I can bring some back. They come in paper cups, but quite passable.'

'Yes, please,' Mum and I say at the same time, then smile.

After Sally has gone we sit in silence. I practise opening and closing my left eye, my right eye, then both together. It's getting easier. Mum stares off into the distance. I could kick myself for spoiling the mood. I never learn. Robin always says that I don't know when to keep my mouth shut.

'I'm sorry if I've upset you, Mum. Robin always says I'm insensitive.'

Mum flinches at the mention of Robin, but reaches over and takes my hand. 'Don't worry. Things can only get better.'

I'm about to question that but think better of it so I offer a brief smile instead.

'Still no sign of my period,' I say, changing the subject. 'So that's good. Maybe it's because I've lost so much weight. Maybe when I put weight on it'll return. Can't say I'm missing it.' I witter away then notice Mum's face.

She's staring at me, her eyes wide, her mouth forming a small O.

'What's wrong?' She's worrying me again.

'Dad said we should wait. I don't think we can.' She sighs.

'Wait for what? What's wrong?' Now I'm worried. I was right all along, there is something wrong with me. They've all been lying. Everyone, even Emma. They're all in on it.

'I know you've always wanted a family,' Mum starts but I'm already crying before she can say anymore.

Yes, I have always wanted a family. Yes, I know that Robin cannot father children. Yes, I know that he won't adopt. But, I always hoped and prayed that he might change his mind about some sort of infertility treatment, especially that one where you can find a male donor. I've fantasised that sometime in the not too distant future a baby of my own would be a possibility. Now Mum is about to tell me that will never happen.

I can hear the long cry coming from my mouth, it's drowning out a lot of her words, but Mum manages to finish what she wanted to say when I stop to draw breath.

'You're pregnant,' she says.

I stop breathing.

Then gasp.

'What did you just say?'

'You're expecting a baby. You're about six or seven weeks pregnant now.'

'But, I, we…' I don't know what to say. 'Are you sure?'

'Absolutely. Your dad said to wait until you went home, but I've wanted to tell you for days.'

'It's definite. There's no mistake?' How can this be true? It's a miracle.

Mum picks her handbag up from the floor, opens it, looks inside then pulls out an envelope. She hands it to me.

Inside the envelope are baby scans. My name is clear on the photos. It's a struggle to make any sense of the pictures, just white blobs on a grey background.

'They did them when you were still in the coma. That's the baby there. See.'

'Yeah. I think so.' I wouldn't be able to tell if Mum wasn't pointing it out.

'Congratulations.' Mum stands and hugs me. 'I'm so thrilled for you. We've got to make sure you get well and look after yourself. It's not just you now.'

'No. Yes.' I'm in shock. 'It's a miracle.'

Sally flings the door open, she's balancing three teas in paper cups on a cardboard tray.

'Here we are. I've got biscuits too.' She looks from my face to Mum's and back again. 'Everything okay?'

'I've told her.' Mum's voice is flat.

Sally puts the tea tray down, grabs hold of me and

hugs me 'til we shake. 'It's such amazing news, we're all so happy.' She lets me go and stands back, spreading across her face is the biggest grin I've ever seen.

'Yeah.' I feel overawed. 'Yeah. Robin's going to be so thrilled when I tell him.' Well, I hope he is.

THIRTEEN

Mum and Sally drank their tea and left quite quickly.

I don't know if it was my imagination but their mood seemed to drop again. Mum muttered something about the car park ticket running out, her favourite get-out now, and Sally's face looked like it had been slapped. I don't know what came over them. One minute we were happy about the baby, the next, we weren't. What do they know that I don't? What are they not telling me?

Now I am sitting here, having eaten my tea and several of the biscuits from the packet Sally brought up, waiting for Dad to come. It was Mum's passing shot as she left, that he'd be up later. On his own. It had an ominous tone.

What the hell are they not telling me?

'Lovely evening,' Jeff says as he comes in. 'Thought I'd pop by and see my favourite ex-patient.'

'Hi Jeff. Thank you. And you're my favourite nurse too.' We laugh. What liars we are.

'Get up, hun. I'm going to turn your chair around. You cannot miss this sunset.'

I stagger to my feet and wait while he turns the chair before dropping back into it. I'm facing the window now, my back to the door, so I won't see who comes in. But, it is *so* worth it. The sun is slowly sliding down the horizon. The sky is bright pink. The advantage of being on the third floor is that I can see for miles: green fields and trees below acres of sky.

'Wow.'

'Told you it was a beautiful evening. Facing west see, so…'

'Yeah. Thank you.'

'Better get off. Just wanted to make sure you didn't miss it.' He taps my shoulder.

'Jeff,' I call as he pulls the door open.

'Yes, hun.'

'Do you know I'm pregnant?'

'Hey. Congratulations.'

'But did you already know? When I was on your ward?'

There's a silence, which suggests that Jeff is thinking carefully about his reply.

'Juliette, you were in ICU, our job was to get you better.'

'Did my family tell you not to tell me?'

'Yes, hun. I must go.' The door closes quietly behind him but not before I hear Robin say hello to Jeff.

'How much of that did you hear?' Even though I'm facing the wrong way and still can't turn my head very well, I know that Jeff was answering my questions with the door open.

'All of it.'

'Spoiled my surprise.' I'm annoyed. I wanted to tell him properly. I wanted to see his face.

Robin comes and stands behind me. I feel his presence but I still lack the mobility to lift my head up and look at him.

'What surprise might that be?' He's playing along.

'We're having a baby.' I hope his grin matches mine.

He doesn't reply immediately, he must be as

overcome with emotion as I was when Mum told me.

He exhales slowly, a very long breath.

'No, Juliette. We're not.' So, they *were* hiding something. What the hell is going on?

'We are. There's a scan and everything. I know it's hard to believe, but, see, miracles do happen.' I won't be deterred. I'll keep believing it until someone tells me otherwise. 'Mum only told me this afternoon.'

'No, Juliette. No.'

'Yes. Why are you saying no? Actually, how come you don't already know?' It should have been him telling me. Not Mum. Now I'm even more confused.

'Because it's not mine. Is it?'

'Of course it is.' I feel a panic rising in my chest.

'I told you, I can't have children. I told you, I'm sterile. Remember.'

'Well. Obviously, that's not true. Not anymore.'

'Yes. It. Is. You whore.'

'What? What?' Did he just call me a whore? Surely not. 'Come round here. I need to see your face.'

But there's no reply. Nothing. He's gone. He's crept out without making a noise. He even opened and closed the door silently.

I stagger to my feet and edge around the chair. I feel shaky and upset and my emotions make walking even more difficult. It's a relief when I get to the door and cling onto it, yanking on the handle, hoping to catch Robin and bring him back.

The door is too heavy for me to open.

I'm too weak.

I press my nose against the glass in the door porthole.

'Robin. Robin,' I call but there is no sign of him.

But Dad is there, fifty feet down the corridor. He

doesn't see me. He's not alone. Stephen is with him. They are not coming towards me. They are stationary. Stephen's arms are waving. Dad is shaking his head. While I cannot see their faces clearly, I can tell that they are arguing. Stephen starts pacing, walking back and forth. His demeanour so angry.

Robin cannot have gone that way, if he had, then he would be there now. If they are arguing about me – what else can it be – then he would be part of it. He's my husband, he's my next of kin.

I bang my hand on the glass, over and over, but neither Dad nor Stephen looks my way. They just keep up their animated disagreement.

I feel all the energy drain from my body. If I am not careful I will fall to the floor.

I'm so confused. Have I imagined Mum telling me I'm pregnant? Did I imagine Robin calling me a whore?

Stephen starts to walk away, he glances back at Dad, nods and smiles. They are parting amicably. Dad turns and starts to walk towards me. His head is down, he's deep in thought.

I hobble back to my chair; I face the sunset.

'Terrific sunset,' Dad says as he comes in. 'Have you been watching it?'

'Yes,' I lie.

But Dad is as big a liar as I am when he pulls up a chair facing me and smiles his biggest, brightest smile. Not a smile he was wearing during his disagreement with Stephen.

'How are you? Mum says she's told you the wonderful news.'

'Yes. A baby. Just what I've always wanted.' How have I managed to say that and sound so flat?

'We're all so thrilled for you. Everyone.' He beams at me again.

'Not everyone,' I say, watching him. 'Not Robin.'

There's a tell-tale twitch of his left eyelid when I say Robin's name.

'Well, you're not to worry about Robin anymore.' He pats my knee.

'How can I not worry about him, Dad? Urgh.' I'm lost for words. I don't understand how Dad can be so vague, so glib, so dismissive of Robin.

'Look, Juliette, I can't stay long because Stephen wants to see you.' He pauses. 'I've sort of promised he can come along in five minutes or so, and I'll leave you to it.'

'What? What the hell are you talking about? Since when does Stephen have priority over you?'

Dad stands up. He looks flustered. It's out of character; he's the headmaster of a great big comprehensive, he deals with crap every day. Yet here, with me, he's red-faced, awkward; beads of sweat glisten on his brow.

'Are you all right, Dad. You don't look well.' Now I must worry about him too. As if I haven't got enough to fret about. It's just dawned on me that he isn't getting any younger, that he's got a stressful job, that he's just lost one daughter, and nearly lost the other one too. Poor Dad. Poor Mum.

'I'll get off.' He bends down and kisses my forehead. I can smell the angst on him; bitter, sour.

'Bye Dad,' I say, lifting a hand to wave as the door opens and closes. I don't have the energy to get up from the chair.

'He wasn't here long.' Robin's voice is calm now.

'No. He's…' I cannot tell Robin that he's gone

because Stephen is coming. I feel the panic rising again. Robin will go mad if Stephen comes waltzing in here. Not that Stephen will care, he's not in the least bit bothered by Robin. He thinks he's an absolute arse. I remember him saying that.

When did he say that?

Robin stays behind me, out of sight; he's still sulking. I can feel his ire filling the room. I wonder if he will call me a whore again?

If he says it in front of Stephen, Stephen will floor him. Of that I am sure.

How can I be so certain?

'He doesn't love you enough.' Stephen had said that. When?

I remember, yes, I remember. It was just after Christmas. This year. A mere four months ago. It was during the long, dark days of January. I'd bumped into him in the street outside Mum and Dad's. He was parking his car, so was I.

He didn't just come out and say it, not just like that. It was part of a longer conversation, a one that went on so long that we were both shivering.

We'd gone through all the jokes about bumping into each other in the street. Not that it was funny. Just breaking ice, I suppose. I'd seen Stephen over Christmas; he'd been round to Mum and Dad's with Sally when I was visiting. I thought he was just on holiday; Mum hadn't told me much about what he was doing, why he was here. Even though he'd popped round frequently when I was there, we hadn't had any conversations on our own, just Stephen and me. Until that night.

'It's so cold now.' I breathed out so he could see

my breath.

'What? This? This is nothing. You should see Canada during the winter.'

'Yeah.' I laughed. That would never happen, Robin had declared long ago that Canada was one place he never wanted to visit.

'No, really. You should. It's an amazing place for a holiday.'

'When are you going back? You've been here ages.'

'Trying to get rid of me?'

'No. No.' I laughed. 'Well, yes, a bit.' It was a joke and he got it.

'I'm thinking about staying.' He left the words hanging in the air.

'Really? What's here?'

'My mum's not getting any younger. She's on her own. I worry about her.' He shrugged.

'Don't let her hear you saying that.' I couldn't imagine Sally being old, never. She was tiny, yes, but feisty and strong. A one-woman whirlwind. 'What about your life over there?' Sally was forever telling us how great he was doing. I loved to hear it, loved hearing about his adventures as told by Sally, who claimed there was a bear around every corner. She'd been over on numerous holidays, but said she'd never want to live there.

'I can get a job here. Probably. And a house.'

'Wouldn't live with your mum then?'

'God no. We're already driving each other mad and I've only been here a few weeks. Imagine it. Could you live with your parents now? After all these years on your own?'

'No. But I don't live on my own. I'm married. Remember?' I laughed, so did he.

'How is he, your husband, Robin, is it?' He knew full well what his name was.

'Yeah, great.'

'Still teaching?'

'Of course.'

'Still tutoring?'

'Yes.'

'Is that why you're round here so often, getting out of his way?' A smirk passed over his face.

'No.' I was irritated. 'I'm visiting my parents.'

'Why doesn't he come?'

'What's it to you?' Robin never came now. It was an unspoken agreement, one I'd probably drawn up on my own; if I kept them apart then Robin and my parents couldn't argue. And it worked, Robin never asked after my parents and my Mum rarely made comments about Robin. Only rarely, though, not never.

Changing tack slightly, Stephen said, 'Hey we should all go out together, you, me, Robin. It would be fun. I've noticed some amazing new, well new to me anyway, restaurants have opened up in town since I was last here.'

'Yeah. We should.' We both knew that we wouldn't. 'Look, I'm going in. I'm freezing out here.'

'Yeah, me too. It's been great talking to you. I've missed you so much.' He realised what he'd just said and looked away, embarrassed.

'Me too.' I leant in for a hug as though it was the most natural thing in the world.

Stephen hugged me tight and whispered in my ear. 'You're lovely and I've really missed you, Etty.'

I'm not even sure he realised he was saying it out loud.

'I'll see you around, no doubt.' I pulled myself away and smiled.

'Make sure that Robin looks after you,' he called over his shoulder as he headed for his mum's front door.

'He does. He loves me.'

That's when he said it. 'Maybe. But he doesn't love you enough.'

I never got the chance to respond because Mum opened the front door, illuminating the path and beckoning me in.

'Wondered where you were. You've been out there ages.'

'I saw Stephen. We were just catching up.'

'You should have saved it for later. Sally's coming round after tea and she said she's bringing him with her.'

'Great.' Mads was already sitting at the table, knife and fork in hand. 'I love hearing him talk about Canada.' It was probably the last time she was there for tea, after that she always seemed to be off revising with her friends.

Sally and Stephen came over an hour later, we sat with them, Mads, me, Mum and Dad, in the lounge. Sally had brought a bottle of wine; she and Mum had half each. I was driving so couldn't drink, Mads wasn't allowed. She'd wailed that she was nearly sixteen. Mum didn't even reply, just rolled her eyes to the ceiling. Stephen was happy to share a pot of tea with me and Mads.

We were old friends having a laugh, it was like old times. It was as though all those years of Stephen's absence, me being married, simply rolled away. Mum and Sally were particularly giggly that night, but it was probably the wine laughing.

It was me who broke the party up, I had to leave to pick Robin up.

'I'll scrape your car.' Stephen jumped up as I was putting my coat on.

'Does it need it?'

'Oh yes,' Sally called, her sharp eyes on us both. 'The windscreen was already iced over when we came round.'

As we walked down the path to my car Stephen couldn't resist a snipe.

'Why doesn't he drive himself? Has he been banned?'

'No. He hasn't. He just likes me to drive.'

'Get in Etty and start the engine.' He took the scraper from me and I sat in the relative warmth of the car. Sally hadn't been exaggerating when she'd said my car was iced over.

It didn't take Stephen long to clear the ice, certainly not as long as it would have taken me. I pressed the button to put the window down so he could hand the scraper back.

'What did you mean earlier?' Why was I asking? What did I care what he thought?

'When?' But he knew.

'When you said that Robin doesn't love me enough. You're wrong, you know.'

'Take no notice of my ramblings, Etty. And watch out for black ice.'

'I bet it's not as bad as Canada though.'

He laughed, then his face became serious. 'No, it's not. But *we* have the tyres for it. Do be careful. I'll see you again. Soon.'

Stephen sounded so sure of himself. I liked it. I

hadn't seen much of him on that visit, unlike his last visit, which, although lasting just two weeks, seemed to have been spent entirely in Sally's garden. It was summer so I suppose that made sense. Every time I was at Mum and Dad's his head had popped over the fence. Mum and Dad liked it, they liked him, they always had, right from when he was a little boy.

'He's got a big personality and a big heart.' I remember Dad saying that on more than one occasion.

Mads loved him – the big brother she never had. Once, in an unguarded moment she had made a comment about me and Stephen.

'You should have married him instead of Robin.' The instant she said it, she'd put her hand over her mouth.

'What do you mean?' I wasn't letting her get away with that so easily.

'You know.' She shrugged, making light of it. 'You get on so well, have the same sense of humour. You know.'

'We're just friends. And I get on very well with Robin, thank you very much.'

Because of the ice I was late for Robin, he slammed into the car moaning about me being late on the coldest night of the year. I didn't respond, no point in causing an argument over nothing.

'What's happening now?' Robin says, his voice sullen.

'I don't know.' It's the best I can do. I'm weary and depressed. How can this be? I'm having a baby, I should be ecstatic. We all should. I thought we were.

'With this baby thing, I mean?'

'Don't do that.'

'Don't do what?'

'That. Be nasty.'

'Whose is it?'

'Yours as far as I know.' But that's not true. Is it? I'm beginning to remember, just little snippets. Maybe Robin's description of me earlier is correct.

There's a tentative knock on the door and when I don't answer, it opens.

'It's your hero,' Robin's bitter voice says to me, then he barks at Stephen 'You can have her. The whore is all yours.'

I wait for the outburst. I wait for the fight to start. But nothing happens. Stephen doesn't reply. The door closes quietly and Robin is gone.

'Hi Etty. You okay?'

'Great.' I let a sigh escape my lips.

'Shall I turn your chair around? You're staring out into blackness.'

'Watching the sunset…' I mutter as I haul myself up from the chair.

He rotates it then moves the chair Dad was sitting on to sit opposite me. He takes my hands in his, rubbing them gently. His hands are warm; I haven't noticed that mine are cold. I don't stop him.

'Are you excited about the baby?'

'Robin…' I shake my head as the tears start to dribble down my cheeks.

'I'm sorry. About Robin.' He offers me a tissue from the box on the bedside locker.

'It's yours?' I'm asking a question, but I already know the answer.

'Yes.' A little smile plays across his mouth. He

pulls it back. 'I realised when I saw you yesterday that you don't remember us.'

'Us.' I repeat. He's right, I don't remember the detail, but tiny pieces are beginning to float into focus.

'We've been,' he hesitates, 'seeing each other for a while.'

'And Robin?'

'You were leaving him.'

I untangle my hands from Stephen's and place them on my lap, rubbing my legs, pulling at the fabric of my new leggings, trying to connect myself back to normality. I was leaving Robin. Did he know?

'To be with you?'

'No. Ironically. No. You were leaving him anyway.'

'Why?' Would I just up and leave him? 'I mean, if not to be with you? Ah, the baby. I was leaving because of the baby.'

Stephen shakes his head. 'No. You didn't know you were pregnant. No one did.'

'Robin called me a whore.'

'Who uses a word like that? He had no right to even think it.'

'But we're married, he's my husband, yet I've been sleeping with you. That's adultery.'

I watch Stephen's face for a reaction, I can see the turmoil in his eyes. He doesn't try to deny it, doesn't correct me.

'Robin's right. I don't like the word, but the meaning…' I cannot bring myself to finish the sentence. I'm horrified at my duplicity, at my betrayal of everything I hold dear. Robin and I, we're a team. We vowed to be together forever. He promised he would never leave me, just as I promised I would

211

never leave him. And yet, apparently, I was.

'No. No.' Stephen is shaking his head. 'Robin doesn't matter now.'

'Don't you dare say that. I want you to go. Now.' I've stopped crying. I'm angry. With Stephen, with myself, with the world.

'No.'

'Yes.' I force my face to show no emotion.

He stands up.

'I'll be back soon.'

'No.'

'I won't…' His voice trails away.

He leans in to kiss me, I turn away. My best head movement yet, accomplished in anger.

The door closes softly behind him. He's gone.

I wait for Robin to burst in, imagining him lurking in the corridor. But he doesn't come back. Did he know I was leaving him? Had I told him? I wish I could remember.

I'm wailing when they give me something to help me sleep, they assure me it won't harm the baby.

I don't fall asleep immediately, but at least I am calm now. Almost numb. Is Stephen telling me the truth? Was I really leaving Robin?

Another dream. Mads is waving at me, and smiling. Robin's there too. He's grinning. He steps towards her and puts his arm around her waist, pulling her in tightly. Her smile ends. She pushes him away. He scowls.

In the dream Mads looks just like me. I hadn't realised how much alike we were. Not now. Not now that I am twenty-eight. But when I was younger.

It was Robin who had commented on it first.

Mum had sent me several photos of Mads dressed up to go to a friend's sixteenth birthday party – a proper party, in a hotel. When was that? It must have been just before she died. She looked gorgeous, her silky hair freshly straightened, her face lightly made-up. Her smile broad, her eyes so full of promise and excitement. I showed it to Robin, flicking through the pictures on my phone. He stared intently, took the phone from me and studied them. He blew Mads's face up for further scrutiny, trailing his fingers across my phone screen.

'She's wearing make-up. She's too young for that.'

'Not much. Anyway, she's not too young. She's nearly sixteen.'

'She looks just like you. Not now, obviously. But when you were young; when I first met you.' He looked wistful.

My phone pinged. Another photo of Mads from Mum, a close-up of her face. The caption said: *She looks just like you.*

Mads messaged me the next day. She sent a sad face emoticon.

Had a great time at the party but drank too many ciders. Hanging now.

Ciders? I messaged back.

Might have had gin in them. Not my idea. Won't do that again. A picture of someone retching into a toilet accompanied the message.

Glad to hear it.
Don't tell Mum.

I wake with a start just as dawn is breaking. It's early, four, or five, perhaps? There are sounds in the corridors, hospitals never really stop, just slow down for the night. I have a headache. Is that from the sleeping drug or the guilt, or the worry?

Today my left eye has caught up with my right, the lids opening in harmony, just as they were designed to. Bitter irony; I can see clearly now.

What a mess. My sister is dead. I nearly died. I'm having a baby that is not my husband's. I was leaving my husband.

Robin will want me to get rid of it. He's always said that he couldn't love a child that wasn't his own.

I cannot do that, I already love this baby. I will not get rid of it.

I must leave Robin.

FOURTEEN

If Robin makes me choose between him and the baby, there will be no choice.

I feel calm now. I've made a decision about the future. My future. My baby's future. Even though it shouldn't, the thought of leaving Robin feels right. What did Stephen say? I was leaving Robin anyway. Why? Stephen seemed ill at ease when I asked; as if he knew but didn't want to say.

Where was I going? Back to Mum and Dad's – huh, plenty of room for me there now, and the baby. Or was I going to be with Stephen?

What has Robin done that had made me want to leave him? Something pings in the back of my mind, a memory, a thought. But it's elusive, like a helium balloon that repeatedly floats out of my reach. And I don't have the energy to stretch up and grab it.

I'm having a baby. Stephen's baby. When did that happen? Just how pregnant am I? Six, seven weeks? I'm sure that's what Mum said.

I'm still not clear whether Robin already knew about the baby. He didn't seem shocked when I told him or, more correctly, when he overheard me discussing it with Jeff. It would explain Robin's off hand manner with me. Now that I think about it, he hasn't been particularly pleasant or helpful since I regained consciousness. He hasn't brought me any clothes from home – Mum did that. In fact, he's quite often been nasty. Is he always like that? Am I only noticing it now? Have I already moved out of our home? Is that why he didn't bring my clothes, because they are no longer there? No, Mum went to our house to fetch my things.

There are so many questions swirling around in my head and I can answer so few of them myself.

I don't know why I was leaving Robin and yet, I know it is the right thing to do. I should feel devastated. Yet I don't.

Am I cold-hearted?

There will be practical things to sort out. The house. We will have to sell it and split the proceeds. What will be a fair split? Despite Robin's extra tuition jobs, I am the major earner. But the equity from his first house – the two-up-two-down – funded the deposit. I foresee expensive legal bills on the horizon. But I must be fair. And so must he.

While neither of us will want to lose the house, I suspect that Robin's attachment will be greater than mine. In truth, it's always felt more like his home than mine.

I cannot believe I am allowing myself to think like this. We've been together for so long. I have, no, had, never been with anyone else. Robin loved that about me, that he was my first, my only. He used to say that it made him love me more.

He called me his virgin bride even though I wasn't a virgin when we married. But, I had only been with him.

'There's no greater honour for a man, Juliette, than being a girl's first lover.' He'd said it after that first time, the night he gave me the coat as an early Christmas present. The coat I wore to Mads's funeral. Even he said I was too fat for it. Well, it's gone now.

216

And I am thin.

A sudden, sharp prick of memory hits me; we were arguing in the car on the way back from the funeral. Is that how we crashed? His hands were on the wheel. Was he trying to pull us back to safety when I veered off course? What made me do that? I hope we weren't arguing about the coat. If only I could remember. My head spins with confusion.

I shift uncomfortably in the bed. I am tired. It's too early to be awake. If I close my eyes will I go back to sleep?

'I knew you'd go off with him eventually.' Robin's voice is pin-sharp in my ear.

I try to open my eyes. I try to turn to him. But nothing works. I feel the panic pressing down on my chest, the pressure so strong that I cannot take even one breath.

Is he suffocating me? Is that why I cannot move? Is he killing me?

I wake. A nightmare. Robin would not do that.

I pant, inhaling deeply. I open my eyes, turn my head a little. There is no Robin.

Maybe now that the truth is out, now that he knows about the baby, now that I know about the baby, he will not visit me anymore.

How has it come to this? Robin was the love of my life.

Where will I go when I leave hospital? Will Robin allow me to go home?

Breakfast comes early in hospital. I've chosen cereal and yogurt. It's preceded by warm, sweet tea and a dry biscuit. I'm hungry. I must be getting better; I still feel hungry after I've devoured the breakfast.

'There's someone to see you,' the auxiliary who collects my breakfast dishes says. She looks flustered and tired. 'Is he allowed in?'

I suppose she's asking because it's so early, though Robin has been here early, and late, before. It can't be Robin. It must be Stephen.

'Yes. Thank you.' I sound so pompous.

Stephen looks tired and anxious but when he leans in and kisses my cheek his hair smells of shampoo and his face is freshly shaven.

'Sorry it's so early. I couldn't sleep. I'm sorry about yesterday. About being so blunt, just blurting everything out like that.'

I shake my head, not because I'm disapproving but because I don't know what to say.

He pulls up a chair and takes my hand.

'I'm so sorry for everything that's happened. For Mads. For Robin. For everything.'

'Not your fault,' I manage. Then, alarmed. 'Is it?'

'No. No. To some extent you and I are innocent bystanders.'

'Not so innocent.'

'No.' He looks down, embarrassed.

'There are so many holes in my memory, so many gaps, I don't really know what's happened recently. You said I was leaving Robin but not to be with you. Why was I leaving him?'

Stephen shifts in his chair. He glances away.

'For God's sake just tell me.'

'You caught him.'

'Caught him?' The meaning of those words hangs in the air. 'Doing what?' I add, but it's obvious. 'Tell me.'

'You went to pick him up from his tutoring job.

But you were early, you couldn't get a parking space in your usual place, so you drove around the block, you went past the house.' Stephen stops speaking.

'And I caught him. And I told you?'

'Yes. Later.'

'Tell me what I told you. I cannot remember. What was he doing?'

Stephen's Adam's apple bobs in his throat as he swallows. 'Kissing her goodbye.'

'Who?' I'm dreading the answer but deep down I know.

'His pupil.'

'How did I know it was his pupil?' It might have been someone else. That *is* possible. Would it make it any better?

'She was wearing school uniform.'

'How old?'

'We found out later. Fourteen.'

I gasp.

'What kind of kiss?' It could have been a quick goodbye cheek peck.

'You said,' Stephen stalls, and I squeeze his hands to force him on. 'You said it was a full on, mouths locked together, arms around each other kiss.'

'I obviously got a good look.'

'I'm so sorry.' Stephen, reading the anguish on my face, squeezes my hands back.

'Definitely not your fault.'

'Not yours either,' he says, sharply. 'Don't go blaming yourself.'

'But why?' I'm overwhelmed and yet numb at the same time. 'Where were her parents?'

'Not there, apparently. They trusted Robin.'

'What happened next? Do you know?'

Stephen nods. He looks solemn and pale. He's obviously been through this before with me, no doubt we turned it over and examined it from every angle.

'We weren't together at that point, you and I. For what it's worth. Just so you know.'

Does it have any worth? I don't know. I shrug – a movement I couldn't make a week ago. I raise my eyebrows – a first – a gesture to urge him on.

'You parked around the corner and waited for him as usual. You drove home without mentioning it. You waited until you were indoors then you confronted him.' Stephen stops.

'Then?'

'He laughed in your face. Called you hysterical and delusional. You said, he almost convinced you that you had imagined it.'

I can imagine Robin laughing at me. I can feel his derision, his mocking.

'You were my confidante?'

'Yeah.' He looks down at our intertwined hands.

'How long after that did I sleep with you?' I want to know if it was an instant act of revenge.

'A while. Weeks. I won't pretend it wasn't a factor. For you. Not me.'

'Did I leave him then?'

'No. No. You were still with him when the accident happened, but you were planning on leaving shortly after the funeral. Perhaps that's what you were discussing when it happened.'

Good God. Did I cause our accident because I told Robin I was leaving? It is all my fault. Everything.

'What else did I say?' I feel so weary.

'You threatened him. You said you would expose him. You asked if there had been others. He laughed. He denied it over and over. But, you told me that you thought you had scared him.'

Maybe I had, maybe I hadn't. I try to imagine Robin's reaction to such an accusation, and the threat of exposure.

Deep down inside I believe Stephen, but, God, it hurts.

'Mum must be pleased,' I mutter, thinking aloud.

'I don't think she knows.'

'What?'

'I certainly never told anyone, you didn't as far as I'm aware and I doubt Robin did.'

'But your mum and my mum know the baby is yours?' They haven't said as much but now I know why their faces looked so pinched when I mentioned Robin in relation to being pregnant.

'Yes. They know about us.'

'So, I'm the adulterer. I'm the one in the wrong.'

'They're not judging you, they're pleased.'

That figures, Mum has always hated Robin, and loved Stephen. I bet she's ecstatic.

Emma bursts in lugging her giant bag of tricks, and all conversation between Stephen and me stops.

'Sorry I'm earlier than usual, but we've got a lot to do today.' She smiles at me then turns to Stephen and gives him a lovely, pleasant look that says, *get out now*.

He takes the hint and leaves, telling me he'll be back later.

'Your husband seems lovely,' Emma says as she starts pulling me about, she's stretching my neck and arms today.

'Yeah,' I say. Only now I know that Robin isn't so

lovely. And neither am I.

'Sorry I had to break you apart like that, but lots to do.'

That's when I realise that she thinks Stephen is my husband. I'm about to correct her, but think better of it. She'll just be embarrassed, and to be honest, so will I.

We go through all my exercises, I walk unaided for a record number of steps, chugging along the corridor, smiling like an idiot, and Emma tells me how proud she is of my progress.

'Everyone is very impressed with your recovery. When I think about what you were like when I first saw you.' She raises her eyes to the ceiling. 'I'm not sure if you realise I have been working with you from day one, well maybe day two, give or take my days off.'

'No?' I hadn't even thought about it.

'Yes, I was doing your daily chest physio. I apologise if I hurt you.'

'I don't think you did.' I smile. I have no recollection.

'Well, you groaned plenty every time I thumped your chest, but we had to clear those lungs. You picked up an infection when I had a few days off.' She rolls her eyes. 'But hey, look at you now. Just brilliant.'

'It's thanks to everyone in here,' I say, knowing full well how true this is.

'A good mental attitude helps too, and a willingness to try.' She helps me back onto the bed. 'There, I think we're done. Now I think that you should manage with a walking stick around your home to start off with.' She pulls a folder out of her giant bag and flicks it open. 'I've prepared a suggested action plan for you which you need to pass onto your own physio.'

'My what?'

'I understand that your insurance is paying for a physio to come to your home from tomorrow. That's brilliant because,' her voice drops, 'between you and me, I think you'd have to wait a while on the NHS.' She pushes the plan – a couple of pages of A4 with copious notes and body diagrams on it – at me. 'Just hand this to your physio and they'll take it from there. Have you got any questions?' She starts stuffing her bag shut and zipping it up.

'When am I going home?'

'Tomorrow.' She gives me a lovely smile.

'Oh. I didn't know.' Did I? Has someone told me? It had been mentioned but nothing specific was said. No definite date.

'It's been lovely working with you, Juliette. You take care and keep up the good work.' Her hand is on the door.

'Thank you, Emma. For helping me. For everything.'

'My pleasure.' And she's gone.

I lie back on the bed and close my eyes. As usual, after Emma's visit, I am exhausted. I just need to rest and recover.

'I see he's been here.' Robin's voice is in my ear.

I can't bear to open my eyes and look at him. I feel both guilty and angry.

'Who?' I say this just to rile him.

'Your lover boy. Him. Your old friend. Your neighbour. He's always tried to come between us. Conniving bastard.'

'Shut up.' I can't believe I've just said that to Robin.

'Oh, he's made you so brave,' Robin spits in my ear.

'No, he's made me remember. I remember seeing you kissing one of your pupils on her doorstep while her parents were out. A child. Was she the only one?'

There's silence for a minute, Robin is, no doubt, working on his reply.

'Bullshit,' he says. 'Laughable lies.'

'I don't find it funny.'

'Huh. It's a sick joke.'

'Sick. Yes. By the way, I'm coming home tomorrow.'

I wait for him to think about that.

'I won't be wiping your arse.'

So much vitriol. I'm beginning to wonder if he ever loved me. Maybe. But maybe not enough. What happened to *in sickness and in health*?

'I'm not asking you to. My Mum will be with us. She might stay overnight.' I've managed to wipe my own backside but I'm not telling Robin that.

'Over my dead body. She's interfered enough. Go and stay at your parents until you're better.'

'No. I'm coming home. To my home.' Even if it often doesn't feel like my home.

The door slams and he is gone.

In his place the aroma of lunch, served at 11.30am today. I open my eyes, put the bed up and smile. The lunch, mashed potato and mashed chicken, accompanied by very dark, chopped green beans, is placed on the overbed table in front of me. I promise myself that from tomorrow I will have my favourite foods, especially if Mum is cooking.

After lunch, I hobble over to the bathroom then, on my return, settle myself in the chair.

When I get home, I will be able to use my phone, catch up with people, let them know I'm okay. It was in my handbag, wasn't it? Where's my handbag? I must have had it with me when I crashed the car. Damn. It must have gone up in flames. When I get home, I'll organise a replacement phone, and credit and debit cards. What else was in my handbag? And what about my car? A wreck now. Since he isn't willing to help me physically he can make himself useful, he can sort out the insurance. He may have already done that. He likes to look after all the household bills, insurance for the cars, our joint bank account. I don't mind. He's good at it, keeps a spreadsheet on his computer. He's showed it to me, to my accountant's mind it seems simple, but it does the job.

Maybe, there's already a brand-new car sitting on the drive, waiting for me. I smile at the prospect. I shudder at the prospect. Will I ever want to drive again? Should I?

I still don't know how it happened. Am I dangerous? Will I lose my licence? The police must be involved - will they visit me when I get home?

I feel the panic and fear in my body.

Robin will have to deal with them. Just as he will have to tolerate Mum's presence in our home.

And what about Mads? I promised Mum and Dad that I would find out what happened? Why she killed herself? I need to find her friend, Chloe, and ask her. Was Mads really being bullied by Chloe? Robin seemed convinced she was. I don't know how Robin would know, but he sounded so sure.

'We've just heard the news.' Mum and Sally burst into my room. 'Tomorrow. Isn't that wonderful.'

'Yeah. I think so.' Part of me can't wait to get home, part of me is petrified.

'You can always come and stay with us,' Mum says, pulling her jacket off and dragging a chair over. 'We've got plenty of room…' She realises what she's said and slumps into the chair.

'And me and Stephen will be on hand to help.' Sally tries to lift the mood again.

'I ought to go home. I think I should go to my own home.' Robin may not like it, but it's my house too. I may be about to leave him – am I? But that doesn't mean I can't enjoy the comfort of my own home while I'm recovering.

'Well.' Mum forces a smile. 'I can stay if you like. We'll just have to sort me out a bed.' She beams the best smile she can muster, but sorrow shows in her eyes.

'You can borrow that put-you-up bed I've got. It's very comfortable.'

'Oh yes. Good idea.'

'Stephen can bring it over. He'll want to be there anyway, make sure you're okay,' Sally says to me.

Robin won't like that. He won't like that at all. He probably won't allow Stephen over the threshold. But *I* didn't like seeing Robin kissing his child-pupil.

'I bet you're looking forward to getting out of here.' Sally glances around the hospital room that has become my sanctuary, only I hadn't quite realised how safe I feel here.

I give Sally a nervous smile by way of response.

Mum looks anxious too.

They start talking about the baby, it's obvious that Stephen has told them that I now know the baby is his. Sally is as thrilled at the prospect of being a granny as Mum is. It makes me pleased too, to see them so happy. And Dad deserves something lovely to look forward to.

When they start talking about the sex of the baby and possible names, I have to rein them in.

'It's early days. Let's not get too carried away.' I worry that I will lose this baby, that the injuries I have sustained will affect it.

Sally's and Mum's faces drop. I've killed the mood, which wasn't my intention; I was just exercising a bit of caution.

After they've gone I haul myself back onto the bed. I lie back and half expect Robin to come bursting in.

I don't relish the prospect of another row with him, another slanging match. How we will manage when I go home tomorrow, I do not know. I could take the soft option, I could go to my parents. I'm giving it serious consideration, but why should I leave my home? It's as much mine as his. Yes, I admit, I have committed adultery. But so has he. Probably.

I lower the bed and close my eyes. I'm not asleep but it's peaceful and quiet. I breathe deeply and attempt to meditate, something Emma has suggested when I find the situation overwhelming. A little sleep might be nice, but instead I find myself reliving the accident. I've been through it so many times in my dreams that it has lost its power to appall me now. I'm watching myself being hauled out of the car, laid on the ground. Robin is laid alongside me. There is not a mark on his beautiful face. It was only my head which took the beating.

Who pulled us out?

The black coat, spattered with blood, is straining across my chest. Robin looks immaculate. I realise all this is happening in my imagination, because I could never have had this view.

Someone is calling my name, shaking my shoulders gently as I lie on the ground. It's grass, damp grass. I can almost smell it.

The voice is Stephen's.

Did Stephen pull me out of the car? And Robin?

I rouse myself and I'm agitated. I need to get to a phone. I need to speak to Stephen.

I wander out of my room, try to locate the nurses' station. The corridors all look the same. I don't really know where I am.

'Hey, hun. What you doing?' It's Jeff. Thank God, it's Jeff. 'I hear you're going home tomorrow. I'm on my way home myself, so was coming to say good bye and good luck to my favourite patient.'

'I'm lost. I'm looking for a phone.'

'Let me help you.' He takes me by the arm and steers me back to my room, settles me in the chair.

'But I need a phone.'

'Hey, you can use mine.' He pulls a mobile from his pocket and offers it to me. 'I'll get us some tea.'

I don't know Stephen's mobile number. I don't know Sally's home number. I ring Mum and Dad's landline instead. But no one's home. I leave a garbled message asking Stephen to come and see me as soon as he can. Mum will fret, so I add, 'nothing to worry about.'

Jeff comes back with sweet tea, and biscuits, sits down and drinks with me. We talk about nothing, but it makes me feel better, calmer.

'I got to get out of here. I've got a blind date tonight.' He pockets his phone. 'And he'd better be hot.'

'Thanks, Jeff. For everything.'

'Just doing my job, hun.' Then he whispers, 'But you are my favourite ex-patient.'

An hour later and I've eaten my last hospital supper, and still no Stephen. I'm calmer now, the urgency is gone, but the need to know is still strong.

Finally, he comes rushing in.

'Did you get my message?'

'Yes, eventually. I'm sorry. I tried to call you back, I forgot you haven't got your mobile. Stupid of me.' He swings a little gift bag in front of me. 'For you, until you get your own sorted.' A pay-as-you-go mobile peaks out of the top of the bag. 'I've done all the stuff, set it up, put the important numbers in it. It's not top of the range, just useful.'

'It is. Thank you.' I put my arms out and he falls into them, hugging me hard.

'I wish I'd thought of it sooner. It'll need charging. I'll plug it in.'

I watch him find a plug and set the phone to charge. I wait until he is finished and sitting in front of me. His earnest face waits for me to speak.

'I think I've remembered something about the accident. It was you, wasn't it, who pulled us out of the car.'

'Yes. It was.' How solemn his face looks. 'You were first out of the car park. Your parents, my Mum,

229

others were still looking at the flowers, walking up and down that covered pathway. Your mum said she wanted to take some home. Your dad wasn't sure. Then I saw you and Robin, roaring away.'

'So, you followed?'

'Yes. Not immediately, probably six or seven minutes later. We were meeting in the pub, you know The Bellwether Inn, your parents had booked a room there.'

'Yes, it's the nearest to the crem.' I do remember we had booked it. I went with Mum and Dad to arrange it, I helped them choose the food from a special funeral menu.

'You'd already crashed by the time I caught up with you. You were opposite the pub, wrong side of the road, upside down.' He stops.

'Go on. Tell me.'

'You were hanging upside down. Both of you. Just your seatbelts keeping you in. I got you out first. You were badly injured, but you kept asking about Robin. I went back and got him. Then the car burst into flames.' He stops again.

'You saved my life.' I take his hands, I squeeze them. 'Please tell me everything.'

'You looked bad, far worse than him. You were gasping, your eyes fluttering, then they rolled into the back of your head. I was shaking you and calling your name and rubbing you and begging you not to die.' He stops again, his eyes glistening. He takes a deep breath. 'I'll never forget that. Never.'

'No.'

'I did all those first aid things, tilted your head back so you could breathe better. I couldn't let you die.'

'You didn't. Thank you.' I'm crying now. 'I remember bits of it.' Flashes, disjointed pieces.

His face is ashen. His eyes search mine.

'I'm sorry. I couldn't help Robin more.'

'You got him out.' I half laugh. I don't know why. 'He's all right now.'

'Well, I suppose.'

'He knows about you. He's really mad about the baby. He's not happy I'm coming home tomorrow. We've had a row.'

'When?' Stephen's brow furrows.

'This morning, after you left. He came, he didn't stay long, just long enough to be nasty.' I try to make light of it. 'Told me to go to my mum's, I'm not. Why should I?'

'This happened today?'

'Yeah, this morning. I said.'

'No, Juliette. It can't have. You're getting confused. I was here this morning, early, remember?'

'Yes. Then Emma chased you off and as soon as she'd gone, Robin came in. I expect he was lurking in the corridor, hiding out until she'd gone. He's here every time I'm alone, he never leaves me alone.'

'No.' He shakes his head several times. 'That's not right.'

'Yes, it is. You weren't here.'

'Juliette, neither was Robin.'

'He was.'

'He wasn't. He can't have been. He died in the crash.'

FIFTEEN

I am not going home tomorrow. Maybe not the next day either.

I had to be sedated.

I didn't believe Stephen, he was lying. I couldn't understand why he was being so cruel. He rang my parents. He fetched a nurse. He explained it to her, she looked shocked. She paged a doctor who looked flustered as he assured me it was true.

Between wailing and shaking I asked why no one had told me.

'They did tell you. Several times. You even discussed his funeral.' Stephen had tried to hug me, tried to make it better. I pushed him off.

'No. No. One. Told. Me.' I was hysterical by then.

'That explains why you took it so well. You weren't hearing it. Oh, Etty.' Stephen tried to comfort me again, hugging me, stroking my head. I pushed him off. Again.

They put in an emergency call to the psychiatric unit. Four hours later Dr Bev something or other turned up – I couldn't pronounce her surname. Four hours was a super-fast response, apparently. There was a dirty mark on her pale pink top. I focused on that as she told me again that Robin was dead, that I had been told several times previously. She said I'd blocked it out.

Now we are sitting here, just the two of us. Dr Bev and me. Stephen has gone. He looked sad, he looked sorry. And so he should.

I've decided that the mark on Dr Bev's top is either chocolate or gravy. I survey her face, her whole body as she says things I don't want to hear. She is thin, very tall, her hair a dirty-blond and it might have started the day, or the day before, or even the evening before, curly. Now it's lank, with kinks. She continually wipes it to one side. She's tired, she suppresses a yawn more than once. I feel sorry for her; I know how she feels.

Once, I had to deal with a bankrupt case. I'd been lumbered with the account by one of the partners – he didn't want to deal with *grim accounts* any more. The bankruptee, a woman in her late forties, immaculately groomed and obviously used to the finer things in life, couldn't believe that she had run out of funds. She swore blind that no one had told her, that as her accountants it was our fault, our responsibility. I showed her the proof – the seven letters we'd sent her drawing her attention to her situation, our copy of the letter sent to her from HMRC telling her she owed tens of thousands in unpaid tax. She sat blinking at me, her mouth opening to speak then closing before the words escaped. She looked like a fish.

It took several meetings and many tissues before she finally accepted the truth. I felt stressed every time I saw her name on my appointment list. I dreaded our interchanges; sometimes they developed into arguments. Eventually she saw the light.

So, I know how Dr Bev feels. But this time, I am

right and she is wrong, so it's not the same as my bankruptcy case.

We've been talking for over an hour now and she still can't get me to believe her. That's because she is wrong. She makes occasional notes that I cannot read.

'If he's dead,' I say, leaning in towards her sallow face. 'How come he's been visiting me every day. Even today.'

She scrutinises my face, weighing me up. I see her take a sly glance at her watch, her eyes darting away when she sees that I have noticed.

'Have you seen him?'

I stop in my tracks.

Have. I. Seen. Him?

'No.' My voice is a little whisper.

She doesn't say anything, just waits for my own answer to sink into my brain.

'No, he usually sits on the side of the bed that I can't turn to. Before that I couldn't open my eyes. That's why I haven't seen him.' Dismiss that if you can.

'That's very convenient. Don't you think?'

'What?'

'He sits where you cannot see him.'

'I've only been able to open my eyes a few days. It's not that…' My voice trails away, not that what? I don't even know how to finish that sentence.

She doesn't respond, just stares at me. I don't know whether this is a psychiatrist's tactic or because she is tired.

'But I hear his voice quite clearly and he has plenty to say.'

'Yes.' She nods. I don't like the way she nods, I fight the urge to slap her stupid face. 'Has anyone else seen him?'

'Yes, some of the nursing staff must have seen him. Sue, Jeff, Emma. He often chats to them if they come in when he's here.' I fold my arms. Get out of that one, Dr Bev.

'No one else has seen him. He died as a result of his injuries at the scene of the accident.'

That's not right.

'Maybe it wasn't him. Maybe there's been some big mistake and it was someone else.'

'Who?'

'I don't know.'

'O-k-a-y.'

I hate the way she drags that word out. She flicks through her notes, her scruffy, illegible handwriting annoys me.

'Let's just suppose that he is dead.'

'He's not.'

'For the sake of what I'm saying, let's just suppose that there was no mistake and your husband…' She flicks through her notes for his name.

'Robin,' I snap.

'Yes. Robin. Yes. Let's suppose that he is dead and that the voice you've been hearing is your own subconscious talking to you.'

'That's just stupid.'

'Mmm. Let's just suppose that's what's happening.'

'What? As though I'm haunting myself?' I would laugh if only I could. How stupid. How ridiculous.

'Yes. Let's suppose that's how it is.'

'It isn't.'

She glances at her watch again then scribbles something down.

'Does he tell you anything you don't already

235

know.'

'Of course he does.'

'Give me an example.'

I can't think straight. I shake my head. 'I can't think of one at the moment.'

'Okay. What I want you to do is think back over everything he's said and try to find something that he's told you that you didn't already know.'

'Yes. I know. He told me my sister was being bullied by her best friend, Chloe. And, he told me who was approaching my bed before I could see – when I couldn't open my eyes, I mean. I didn't know who they were, but he told me.'

'O-k-a-y. Do you think that you might have already known about the bullying? Or that you might have been told who these people were but, due to your brain injury, you might have forgotten?'

'No. I don't. How could I know about Chloe? And, I couldn't see these people even if I did know them. Which I didn't.'

'Do you think it's possible that you picked up on their voices as they approached, that you identified them without realising then,' she stalls, blinks then remembers his name. 'Robin's voice gives you that information?'

'No.'

She doesn't sigh, but I can tell she wants to. She looks even more tired than I feel. I'm sick of this.

'Okay, we're going to leave it there. I'm going to make an appointment for you in clinic tomorrow and we'll see how you're doing then.' She stands up, gives me a weak smile and turns to leave. As she opens the door Jeff appears. Has he been waiting outside?

'Jeff, Jeff. Tell her you've met Robin.'

Jeff looks at me, then at Dr Bev. They exchange that pitying look – and it's for me.

'Tell her, Jeff.'

'I've never met your husband, hun.' He steps aside to let Dr Bev out, then comes in and sits down in the seat she's just vacated.

'But you've had conversations with him.'

'No, hun. I haven't.

'But he's spoken to you and you answered.'

'No, hun.'

'But I heard you.'

Jeff shakes his head.

'You think I'm mad too, don't you?'

'No, hun. You've had a big accident, a lot of damage.' He taps his head. 'The mind plays tricks.' He takes my hands in his; he has large hands, they're warm and soft, and podgy. 'When I was a kid I had a dog, he was a good dog, RexTex we called him, I don't know why. He slept under my bed, not on it, my ma wouldn't allow that. Every night he snuffled and scuffled and scratched the carpet beneath my bed until it was threadbare. He'd bark at any noise, even my sister going to the toilet in the night. Then he died. He was old. But I kept on hearing him scratching under my bed when I was asleep, even barking at noises. I'm not comparing RexTex to you husband, but the mind plays tricks, especially when we're grieving.'

'Yeah, well, that could be anything, that scratching sound. Robin speaks to me. And you.' It's a bloody conspiracy, I just don't know why they're doing it.

Jeff changes the subject, talks about the weather, helps me shuffle around my room then up and down the corridor because he says I've been confined to one space for too long. I get up quite a pace and I'm only using a walking stick, albeit one which has three-pronged feet. He takes me down to the Costa Coffee and buys me a tea. He doesn't mention Robin again. Or RexTex. Neither do I.

Mum and Dad are sitting in my room when Jeff escorts me back, he leaves me at the door. Mum and Dad watch me shuffle in; I'm exhausted now and I feel about a hundred and eighty. Their faces are creased with anxiety but they force false smiles for my benefit.

'No doubt you've heard they all think I'm insane?' I flop into the chair.

'No one thinks that, love.' Dad pats my knee.

'Well, I'm not going home tomorrow. I'm seeing the nutcase doctor instead.'

Mum and Dad don't know what to say to that. I realise how stupid and immature it sounds.

'Why didn't you tell me Robin was dead?'

'We did, darling. Over and over.' Mum's eyes don't quite meet mine.

'I don't remember that.' I shake by head and raise my eyebrows as though I am presenting proof.

'The doctor says that you've blocked it out.'

There's a silence now as we all look anywhere but at each other. After five very uncomfortable minutes I speak.

'Is he really dead, Mum? Did you see him?'

Mum shakes her head as Dad slowly nods his.

'What?' I'm looking at Dad for more and he's looking solemn.

'I identified his body.'

'Why you?' As I say it I realise that there would be no one else until his mother came over from Brazil.

'Where's his mother?'

'There wasn't anyone else. You could hardly do it. And we don't know where his mother is.' Mum looks livid now as though talking about this has churned up so many feelings for her that she cannot contain herself. 'You should be grateful your Dad did it.'

'I am. I am. It's just I can't believe it. He's been here, in this room and the ICU, with me, every day. How can he be dead?'

'It's your subconscious speaking.' Mum and Dad have obviously been given the same version as me.

'I can't believe he's dead. I won't believe it.'

'You can see his body,' Mum says in such a flat way that I almost don't understand the words.

'What? What?'

'You can see his body, anytime you like. He's at the chapel of rest.' Tears fill Mum's eyes, then mine.

I remember. We visited Mads in the chapel of rest. Her little body laid out in the basket-weave coffin. She was wearing her favourite smart jeans and a bright pink top. Mum had only bought the top for her the week before she'd died, she'd worn it non-stop. It was in the laundry basket and Mum had had to wash it before they could put it on her corpse.

Robin and I met Mum and Dad there; Mum and Dad went in first and we went in when they came out. Robin had kissed Mads on the lips; I couldn't do that. When I touched her, she was hard and cold; not Mads at all. Mads had gone. She looked odd too, her face posed, her lips closed, she never shut up so that wasn't like her. She looked thin, thinner than she had been the last time I'd seen her, but that had been many weeks before.

They'd wrapped a blue silk scarf around her neck,

tucked it under her chin. It wasn't hers. I poked it with my nail.

'To cover the scar, I suppose.' Although the t-shirt didn't have a low neck, it wouldn't have covered the post-mortem stitch-line.

'Don't.' Robin pulled my hand away, scowling at me.

'She's too thin.' I surprised myself when I said that; it sounded like a judgement.

'She's beautiful.' Robin kissed her again, on the forehead this time. 'Forever young.'

It was my turn to pull him away; I couldn't wait to get out of that chilly room with its odour of air freshener and new carpet.

'You should have said a proper goodbye, you'll regret that you didn't later.' He'd waited until we were outside in the car park before delivering his wisdom.

'Too late now.'

'How does he look?' I search Mum and Dad's faces for a clue.

'He looks fine. Like he always did.' Mum delivers her verdict without emotion. 'Not a mark on him, that you can see.' She hasn't seen him so Dad must have told her.

'How?' What I want to ask is how he can be dead but have no marks on him while I am alive and looking such a mess. 'What killed him?'

'Massive trauma to the chest. Steering wheel. His air bag saved his face, yours saved your body.' Dad doesn't look at me when he speaks, he's looking away, remembering.

'Stephen pulled him out.' I'm musing aloud rather than asking a question. I'm crying again, forcing words out between sobs and dribbles.

'Yes. He did. He pulled you out too. Saved your life.'

'He pulled me out first. Maybe if he had pulled Robin out first he'd still be alive.' Am I already accepting that Robin is dead?

'Don't blame Stephen.'

'I'm not blaming him, Mum.' Is that true?

'Stephen's outside,' Dad says.

'What does he want?' I don't know how I feel about Stephen. I don't know if I want to see him.

'He wants to make sure you're okay.'

'I'm blatantly not okay, am I? My dead husband is haunting me and I'm pregnant by another man. And let's not even mention the crash, the mess I'm in physically and my poor, dead, little sister.'

Mum and Dad don't react, not even when I mention Mads. They are either very good at playing poker face or they are wrung out of all emotion. They are just staring, not at each other, not at me; just staring.

'Well, he's there if you want to see him.' Mum stands up and waits for Dad to do the same.

'Are you going? Now?'

'Yes. You're tired.' Mum already has her hand on the door handle.

'No.' I am tired but my head is spinning. 'I won't sleep.'

'We're tired,' Mum says, without looking at me. 'Stephen is here for you.'

'But what if Robin comes back?' There, I've said it. My greatest fear is spoken.

'That's why Stephen is here, to make sure Robin can't come back. I'll send him in.' Mum opens the

241

door.

'Robin won't come back. He's gone, love. You need to accept that, and believe it, because they won't let you out until you do.' Dad kisses me on the cheek and follows Mum through the door. They don't wait for me to protest. They're gone, closing the door behind them.

Minutes pass and there is no Stephen. He's probably conspiring with Mum and Dad. I'm starting to think that none of this is real.

None of it.

'How you doing?' Stephen asks from the doorway before he comes in.

'How do you think?'

He sits in the chair that Dad sat in, reaches over for my hands but I pull them away.

'Am I imagining all of this? Are you real? Are Mum and Dad real? Is any of it real?' I feel sick. Is that real?

'Oh Etty. I'm so sorry about Robin.' He tries to grab my hands again. I clutch them to my chest and out of his reach.

'Are you? Are you?' Snot dribbles out of my nose.

'Yes. No one wanted this. Any of it.'

'If you'd got him out first he might have survived.' There, I've said it to his face. My accusation.

'Maybe.'

'You're not even denying it.'

'If you want me to say that I chose you over him, then I will. I did. I always would. I don't want to speak ill of the dead but Robin was a controlling bastard.'

'You don't know him.'

Stephen stands up, goes over to the window and

242

presses his forehead against the glass. I don't know what he's looking at; it's dark outside.

'I may not have known him like you did, but what I did know, I didn't like. He didn't treat you well.'

'You don't know about us. You don't know anything.'

'He groomed you.'

'What? What shit is this?'

'He groomed you. You were a child; he was an adult.'

'You sound like my bloody mum, is that where this is coming from?' I'm angry, so angry that I can't even cry anymore.

'He did such a good job that you can't even see it.'

'Get out. Get out.' Now I'm screaming.

'I am sorry he's dead, because now you're going to turn him into some latter-day saint. He wasn't a saint, Etty.'

'Just get out.' My voice is hoarse now.

'I'll be down the corridor if you want me, there's a little family waiting room.'

'You're not family.'

'I'll be here all night.'

He's gone before I can scream at him again.

A nurse comes in to check on me, no doubt Stephen sent her. No doubt he told her I was hysterical. She says they can give me something to help me sleep. She offers to sit with me for a few minutes. She offers to help me into bed. I decline all her offers. I prefer to sit in the chair.

I don't know what's real anymore.

Now I'm alone. Now it's quiet. It's late. I'm alone in my room. If I close my eyes will Robin speak to me? I won't close my eyes.

I think he might be dead.

What did Dr Bev ask? Oh yes: Did he tell me anything I didn't know? She couldn't even remember his name. I don't know anything anymore. I don't know what I don't know.

I'm so tired but I daren't close my eyes; just in case. But I'm so tired and my eyes are stinging.

Gasp. I was asleep.

The nightmare that isn't a dream. The car spinning: wheels, roof, over and over. The black coat that doesn't fit me, the large buttons straining. Robin by my side on the grass verge. Stephen's face close to mine. Robin makes a sound, a gurgle, a choke. He was alive.

And now he isn't.

If I tell the psychiatrist that, will she let me go home? Home, our home. Do I want to go home? I don't know what to do.

I thought I was a mess before, but I'm an even bigger, fucked-up mess that I thought I was.

If I'm hearing voices does that make me a psycho?

I wish I could remember what happened in the car.

Maybe I'll never remember, maybe I'll have to accept that. Maybe I'm blotting it out, after all, I've successfully blocked out Robin's death, even though, apparently, I've been told several times about it.

Is that true? Is it real? Is anything real?

I get up from the chair and shuffle to the bathroom, greet myself in the mirror. I look like a ghost. I look like a monster. Made of bits.

'I am a ghost,' I say to my reflection. 'I don't need you haunting me, Robin.' I shake as I wait for his response. It doesn't come.

I shuffle along the corridor, my three-pronged walking stick squeaks along the floor. I'm looking for the family room. I'm looking for Stephen. I must tell him something.

He jumps up when I enter the room. He looks as grey and tired as I do. He smiles, but not too much – I suppose he's worried I'll take offence – no one can ever be jolly again because my husband is dead.

I stand. I don't move. I just stare. Stephen steps forward and wraps me in his arms; it's nice. I can feel the softness of his shirt against my cheek. I could sleep like this, safe in his arms. Safe and alive.

We sway. I close my eyes and we sway. We could be dancing; the slow dance at the end of the evening, the last couple on the dance floor. I can almost hear the music. It's lovely.

I break the spell.

'If Robin really is dead…'

'He is.'

'Shush.' I take a deep breath, I must say this. 'If Robin really is dead, then I killed him. I'm a murderer. That's why he's haunting me.'

SIXTEEN

'No. No.'

'Listen. Have the police said anything? Do you think they think I did it on purpose?'

'No. No. You've got this all wrong.'

I pull back from Stephen, reach up and place my hand across his mouth. I don't want him to confuse me, I don't want him to speak until it's clear in my head.

'Do you think I did do it on purpose? That's what it must look like. I'm having your baby, not that they would have known that, not then anyway; and I'm leaving him. Not that they know that, do they? Has anyone told them? What did you say when they questioned you?'

Stephen pulls my hand away from his mouth. He's smiling.

He's smiling.

'What the hell is there to smile about?' Another thought occurs to me. 'Shit, do you think I did do it on purpose?'

He almost laughs.

'You've got this all wrong. You haven't killed anyone. Not by accident and not deliberately.'

He wouldn't lie to me, not Stephen.

'Etty, you didn't do anything. You weren't driving. Robin was.'

I feel my knees buckle, but Stephen catches me.

'Are you sure? He never drives when I'm there.'

246

'Quite sure. I pulled you both out, remember.'

We sit down, side by side on plastic padded chairs that squeak as we move. Stephen puts his arm around me and I slide down and snuggle into his shoulder. I let my eyelids droop and allow myself to doze, safe in his arms.

'It saved my life.' I'm awake and sitting up, sitting forward.

'What do you mean?'

'Because I wasn't driving. I've just remembered what Mum and Dad said, Robin was killed by the force of the steering wheel hitting his chest.'

I nestle back down in Stephen's embrace before lunging out again.

'If I'd been driving we might not have had the accident. We'd probably both be fine. None of this would have happened.'

'You don't know that.'

'No, but…'

Stephen cuts across me. 'If I had bought a lottery ticket I could be a millionaire now.'

'What? That's not the same. Not the same at all.'

'My point is that you can't second guess what might or might not have been. There's no point in torturing yourself any further.'

I slump back into his arms.

'You're right. But why was he driving? He never drives.'

'You'll probably never know. You were very upset when you left. Maybe too upset to drive.'

'Yeah. That's probably it.'

'Why do you always drive?'

'Robin likes it.'

'Always struck me as odd. He could drive. You

both had cars. Yet he wanted you to ferry him about.'

'It was fine. I didn't mind. I have a bigger car.' I stop, correct myself. 'Had. I had a bigger car.'

'We'll sort that.'

'Doesn't matter now. Nothing matters now.'

'You matter. Our baby matters.'

He probably says more but I doze off and when I stir because I'm uncomfortable, Stephen coaxes me back to my hospital room and into bed.

My appointment with the psychiatrist is at 3.15pm. The psychiatry department is at the far end of the hospital, too far to walk. I'm sitting in a wheelchair in the waiting room. The porter who brought me has parked me next to the extra wide chairs. No one sits in them, even the fat man who is perspiring despite the chilly aircon. I look at the other patients wondering if they are as mad as me, then mentally rebuke myself for judging others. Everyone looks miserable; two men, quite young, flick through their phones.

3.15 comes and goes. The waiting room seems to get fuller but no one leaves for their appointment. On the wall, a sign says something about various clinics running at the same time and people may not appear to be seen in turn. A nice get out.

At 4.20 my name is called. I start to wheel myself behind the nurse who called me, but it's a struggle, she glances back, sees me and comes back to push me. I feel like a giant baby.

It's Dr Bev again. She's washed her hair. As per hospital protocol, we check who we are and why we're here. Dr Bev offers me a smile and asks how I am. I say I'm fine. She's wearing a name badge today, she might have been wearing it yesterday, but I never noticed. I scan her name, breaking it down into syllables, San-ustra-ma-lam. I practise it in my head while she speaks. Only as she finishes do I realise I haven't heard a word she's saying.

'Um.'

'O-k-a-y.' There it is again, that long okay giving her time to think. She tries again. 'How do you feel about your husband's death?'

This I can answer. 'Sad. Sorry. Guilty.' I hadn't meant to say guilty, it just fell out, but she picks up on it.

'Guilty?'

'Yeah. He was driving. It should have been me.'

We have a lengthy discussion then about guilt, blame, what might have been, what could have happened. She doesn't ask me if I still think he's alive, she doesn't ask me if I believe he is haunting me and I don't mention it either. She tells me grief and bereavement play tricks on the mind, she goes on to give examples. There's a box of tissues on the table and I use several.

After thirty-seven minutes, we finish. I can be exact about the time because there is a large clock on the wall which we both glance at periodically. Its loud tick fills the room during gaps in our conversation, its echo eerie.

I don't know if I feel any better afterwards, I can't really tell. I have to wait for someone to take me back to my room. After thirty minutes, I realise this could be a long wait; fortunately, I have the phone Stephen gave me in my pocket. I ring him first. He's already in the hospital, waiting for me in my room; he comes straight down to collect me.

'How did it go?' he asks as he wheels me along the endless hospital corridors.

'Okay. I think. She never asked me if I believed in ghosts.' I hear my nervous laugh rebound off the walls.

Stephen echoes my laugh – hollow.

'I have another appointment tomorrow.'

'Does that mean you can't go home yet?'

'Yes. But she did say that if I'm still making progress, whatever that means, then I can go home and only see her as an outpatient. If it's necessary.'

'That's good.' Stephen tries to sound encouraging; we're all trying.

When we reach my room, and despite it being covered, my evening meal is congealing on the overbed table. We both take a long look at it.

'There's a café downstairs.'

'And a McDonald's,' I add, grinning.

'I'm sure you shouldn't have that, but what the hell.' He wheels me straight towards the lift.

I feel small and insignificant as I sit among people dressed in normal clothes instead of hospital uniforms. I suppose some are patients, but most are visitors. Stephen parks me at a table while he queues up for our food.

'I know I shouldn't say this,' I say, taking my second bite of Filet-o-fish, 'but this is so good, even these salty fries are yummy.' I think of Robin and how he would disapprove.

'Everything in moderation,' Stephen says, tucking into a double cheeseburger.

'That doesn't look moderate.'

'Won't be making a habit of it.'

'No.'

'I supersized our meals.' He grins at me and there's the cheeky, clever kid I used to know, all grown up. I wonder if he still sees the kid in me.

'What?' I pretend horror at the same time as helping myself to another handful of fries.

Back up in my room and feeling full to the point of bursting, I'm grateful to see that the congealed meal has gone.

Stephen helps me out of the wheelchair and into my chair; sitting for so long has made my legs wobbly.

'I'll need a walk before bed,' I say, making no attempt to get up.

Stephen sits down opposite me, he picks up the magazine Sally brought and we flick through it together. We're easy company, no need for heavy conversation, silence is simple and comfortable.

'I still can't believe he's gone.' I kill the mood.

'No. It's a shock.'

'I need to see him.'

Stephen blinks at me, I can see thoughts flicking through his mind.

'I'll take you,' he says, eventually.

'Thank you. I need to go soon. As soon as possible. The psychiatrist says it will help me.'

Stephen nods, he gives me a thin smile, but his eyes are solemn.

'Okay. As soon as you're out of here we'll arrange it. And the funeral.'

Oh God, I hadn't thought about the funeral. How will I be able to cope with that. Who will come?

'Mum won't come,' I voice my thought out loud.

'She will. She'll come for you if not for him.'

'Mmm. Maybe. I need to track down his mum, she's in Brazil.'

'I'll help with that.'

'Thank you.'

When Mum and Dad arrive Stephen leaves. He kisses me on the cheek, reminds me I can ring him at any time and goes.

Mum looks pale, Dad looks tired.

'How did it go?' Mum asks. She doesn't need to even explain what she means.

'Okay. No, probably better than okay, but I have to go back tomorrow.'

'Oh. So you're not going home yet?'

'No. Should be soon though.'

We sit in silence but it's not the comfortable silence I enjoyed with Stephen. Mum, evidently thinking hard, starts to speak.

'When you do get out of here, do you still want to go to your house?'

I hadn't thought about it; I'd been pleasantly distracted by Stephen.

'I don't know, Mum. What do you think I should do?' From the look on her face I know she's given it a lot of thought.

'Come and stay with us. We'd like that, wouldn't we Brian?'

'Yes.' Dad doesn't sound as enthusiastic as Mum but he'll be at work most of the time.

'I will need to go to mine to collect things, but we'll see how it goes.'

'You'll want to see Robin too, I suppose.' Mum sounds resigned.

'Yes. The psychiatrist thinks it will help.'

'Right.' Dad looks miserable, he assumes the burden will fall on him.

'It's okay, Stephen will take me.'

'Probably for the best.' Dad brightens after hearing that.

After another ten minutes, during which we all yawn, Mum and Dad leave. I think I'm as relieved as they are. This is horrible for me but it's just as awful for them. Worse, with Mads gone.

Once I'm in bed I find, despite feeling exhausted, I don't fall asleep immediately. My mind is whirling, there's so much to do; Robin's funeral will be a trial, as will sorting out all his belongings. One thing I'm feeling both relieved and guilty about is how accepting I am of Robin's death, now I'm over the shock. I wouldn't admit it to anyone but a tiny part of me is almost thankful; no messy divorce, no explanations, no recriminations. What a bad person I must be.

Even though my memory is hazy and my recall of incidents and reasons cloudy, I know, deep down inside, that something happened between us in that car. We were arguing. I just don't remember why.

I've been thinking about Stephen's assertion that Robin groomed me. I dismissed it as nonsense when he said it, but the seed has been sown and it's making me look at our relationship. I feel disloyal for even thinking like this, but now I start to look there are so many times in the past when Robin needed to be in control. Of me.

The black coat at my little sister's funeral was one such occasion. And, just why did he always want me to drive? Stephen has churned up questions in my mind that, maybe were always there.

Even at the start of our relationship he called the

tune; it was Robin who coaxed – that is the word – me to apply for a job at Belton's instead of applying to university. Even though I'd always wanted to go to university, he persuaded me it was a waste of time – and I never questioned it. He'd told me, several times, that it's down to him that I got such a good, early start there, and had done so well. My hard work, talent and ability always seemed irrelevant to him.

The more I think about it, the more I realise that Robin has always been in charge. He opened the post, managed our bank accounts – despite me being the chartered accountant. He decided when we should move and where we should live, just as he decided where we went on holiday. And I just accepted it.

Have I been a fool all these years?

I'm dismissed by Dr Bev at our appointment the next day; she says I can go home, though I need to come back as an outpatient next week. When I get back to the waiting room, this time a porter is on hand to wheel me back. The ward sister is waiting for me in my room.

'You can go home,' she says, her bright smile spreading across her face.

'Yes, but how did you know?' It's barely ten minutes since I was told.

'The NHS is efficient sometimes.' Her laugh is genuine. 'You can go now, if you like. I'm sure you'd like to get home and sleep in your own bed tonight.'

I don't like to tell her that sleeping in my own bed, on my own, is the last thing I want to do.

'Who shall I ring to help you?' It seems, whether I like it or not, I am going home today.

'It's okay. I have a phone.'

'Great. I'll let you get on with it, while I do your discharge paperwork.'

After she's gone I ring Mum but she doesn't answer and I leave a message. Then I remember Stephen telling me to ring at any time.

It doesn't take him long to pack my few belongings and stuff them into the leather holdall he's brought with him. Then he goes off to find the ward sister but comes back without her.

'She's doing your stuff but it might be a while.' He rolls his eyes.

'Typical.' I slump back down into my chair. 'She was virtually pushing me out of the door and now she's not ready.'

When Mum rings me back I tell her what's going on. She sounds relieved that she doesn't have to come for me. I don't like to think of the pressure I'm putting Mum and Dad under. The sooner I can get back to my own home the better – even though I am dreading it.

We wait for another hour during which Stephen checks at the nurses' station several times, until one of the nurses reminds him that sick patients take priority over discharged ones.

'That was me told,' he says, recalling the words. 'It felt like a bit of slap in the face.' He contorts his face in pain. I laugh. He always makes me laugh.

Eventually I'm discharged with my copy of a letter for my GP, another outpatient appointment – this time to see the doctor I've been under since my accident – and strict instructions to take painkillers if I need them but only paracetamol as I'm pregnant.

'Oh.' We're outside and a chilly wind catches me

by surprise. Stephen helps me out of the hospital wheelchair we've borrowed and ushers me to his nearby car; he's parked in the mother and baby spaces.

'That's naughty,' I admonish.

'Mother.' He points at my face. 'Baby.' He points at my middle.

Mother and baby; that's something else I must get used to. It still seems unreal. Surreal.

Mum's waiting for me when we pull up outside her house. She's standing on the doorstep, her arms wrapped around her body, keeping herself warm. She must have been watching out of the window and seen us come down the road.

Stephen grabs the bag he's lent me and helps me to Mum and Dad's front door.

'I'll leave you to get settled.' He kisses me lightly on the forehead. Stephen has a smell about him, it's not aftershave or anything like that, it's him and I realise that I love it. He's so very different from Robin.

Mum takes my bag and leaves it on the bottom of the stairs as we go through to the kitchen. She's made a pot of tea and there's a cake on the table.

'That looks lovely.' It's chocolate sponge with buttercream filling and frosting. 'My favourite.'

'I know. That's why I baked it. We've not had many nice occasions for cake recently.' Mum smiles but her face looks weary. She steps forward and gives me a hug. 'It's good to have you home.' She hangs onto me for a long time and I inhale the familiar scent that is my mum.

'Is Dad home from work yet?'

'Yes. Been and gone out again. He'll be home

again soon.'

'Have you already had tea?' Much as I relish the prospect of the cake, I really want something savoury.

'Yes. Haven't you?'

When Mum realises I've missed my evening meal in the confusion of being discharged she produces the leftover lasagne that she and Dad had. Even reheated it's delicious.

'I made it with you in mind,' Mum tells me when I say how much I love her lasagne. When you didn't come home sooner I assumed you'd eaten.'

'Never mind, I'm enjoying it now.' I even have a second helping, then follow it up with a large slice of cake. I lean back in my chair and pat my stomach. It's sticking out. 'Food baby.' I laugh, more to myself than Mum.

'I suppose we should take your stuff upstairs.' Mum's voice sounds weary again.

'Yeah.' I stand, clutching onto my stick and the dining chair for support. I don't think I want to go upstairs. I don't think I can face Mads's room. After I left and Mads moved into my old room, Mum turned Mads's old room into her sewing room. She has her sewing machine, cutting table and mannequin in there; there's no room for a bed.

Upstairs, my bag in her hand, Mum leads the way. I follow, clomping along with my walking stick.

Mum has tidied a lot of Mads's stuff away, but there's still a lot of her personality in the room. The bedding she chose, the blinds instead of curtains, her music system, her books, they're all still here.

I lean on my stick and stand in the doorway; I can hear my heart beating. Mum stands in front of me, she's still carrying my bag but her shoulders are

257

hunched high, almost to her ears. Neither of us speaks as we stare into Mads's room, her life.

I can't sleep in this room. It's not mine. It's wrong. It's too soon. This is the bed where Mads overdosed. This is where Mum and Dad found her.

I can't sleep here.

'I've changed the bed,' Mum's voice croaks. She gulps and sniffs. She's crying silently.

So am I.

As we continue our soundless sobs I know I should say something; I have to let her off.

'I can't…' I start.

'No,' she finishes as I turn around and start back towards the stairs. I can see Mum once I'm on the stairs, she hasn't moved, she's still holding my bag, but her shoulders are shaking and she's starting to howl.

I drag myself back, exhaustion is getting the better of me now, and I wrap my arms around my mum. Together we slide onto Mads's bed and wait for our grief to subside; not that it will ever go away. We're both lost in our own thoughts and memories of Mads, we're together, yet alone.

The rapping on the front door brings us back to the present. I jump up, or rather, I attempt to jump up. Mum beats me to it. She pulls a tissue from her pocket and offers it to me. I take it, knowing that she'll have another tucked somewhere else. She does, there's one up her sleeve, she whips it out like a conjuror performing a trick.

We blow our noses and sniff in unison as the knocking on the door starts again.

Mum gets to the door first. She's greeted by Stephen and Sally's expectant, yet hesitant faces. Once inside, they read the situation easily; red eyes are hard to hide.

Sally takes Mum into the kitchen; the kettle is filled and soon boiling. Stephen puts an arm around my shoulders and I lean into him.

'Tough time?'

'Yeah.' I sigh.

'Can't stay here?'

'Not in Mads's room. Can't go to my house either.'

'No.'

'No.' I echo.

'Mum's changed the bed in my room. Hoovered and dusted it too.'

'Mmm.' I don't know what to say.

'You sleep at ours at night, then come round here during the day. Takes the pressure off you all. You, your mum and dad.'

'What about you?'

'I'll sleep in our spare room. Don't worry about me.'

'Okay.' Despite us having an affair, despite my carrying his baby; it seems wrong for us to sleep together. Yet. Now. Here. It makes me wonder where our baby was conceived; I hope it wasn't in the back of a car.

We go into the lounge and we sit on the sofa and I put the TV on because it's easier than talking or thinking. We watch a quiz I've never seen before because Robin hated quiz shows. Stephen explains the game to me and we talk about it as though it really matters, as though there's nothing more important for us to discuss. Oh, the sanctuary of the banal.

Sally comes in carrying a tray of coffees, Mum trundles along behind her with the biscuit tin.

259

'We thought perhaps you should sleep at ours?' Sally makes a statement that sounds like a question.

'Yeah. Okay.'

Mum offers up a meek little smile, at the same time nodding.

'That's settled then.' Sally takes the biscuit tin from Mum's hands and opens it. We all eat biscuits we don't want and smile without any joy.

By nine pm I'm asleep against Stephen's shoulder; it's not a comfortable sleep. By ten pm I'm in Stephen's old bedroom. It's a match for Mads's room and separated only by the thickness of a wall, yet it seems a thousand miles away. Thank God.

Someone, Stephen? Mum? Sally? has brought more of my clothes from my house. I pull on my favourite pyjamas, thick and soft – Robin hated them and would only tolerate them on the coldest of nights and even then, he would protest – before stumbling along to the bathroom. Unlike Mum and Dad's, it's been modernised; a sleek design and super bright lighting highlights the wreck that stares out at me from the mirror.

I look like I've been stitched together from bits of other people. My eyes, despite being *normal* are still puffy and bruised, my face is gaunt, my hair, well I don't think it's a style that will catch on. I'll be wearing hats for the foreseeable future.

A soft knock on the door as I'm easing myself down brings an unexpected smile to my face.

Stephen comes in and sits on the bed.

'How are you doing?'

'Okay. Thank you.'

'It'll get easier.'

'I bloody hope so.' I hadn't expected that to come

out so loud.

He half smiles.

'Oh Etty.' He pats my leg over the duvet. 'How's my bed?'

'Not bad.' I wriggle around. 'Actually, quite comfortable. Certainly, better than the hospital ones.'

'New mattress.'

'For me?' How sweet.

'No. For me. Last time I was here I had backache, so bought that just before I went back.'

'Cool,' I mutter for want of something better to say.

'We'll get through this. Together. I'll always be here for you.' He pats my leg again.

I feel panicked. It's too soon to be playing happy families with Stephen. Far too soon. Alarm must show on my face.

'No pressure. No hurry. At your pace.'

'Okay. Thanks.' I sound ungrateful.

'Your mum says for you to be round there by ten at the latest. Paula's coming. Something about hair.' Stephen shakes his head affecting not to understand, suggesting my hair is fine when we all know it isn't.

'Thanks. I have physio at eleven.' I grimace. 'I also need to arrange to see Robin.'

'Already done. Tomorrow afternoon. I'll take you.'

'Thank you.'

He kisses me lightly on the forehead, opens his mouth to speak then changes his mind. He was probably going to say something stupid like *sweet dreams*.

I won't be having those.

I imagine Robin's dead body in the chapel of rest. He's probably been wondering where the hell I am.

SEVENTEEN

Robin visits me in my dreams. Even in Stephen's bed. He's not saying or doing anything much, just visiting.

It was inevitable that he would. When I saw the psychiatrist yesterday she asked me if I'd had any more visits from Robin. I told her I hadn't. Not when I'm conscious anyway. But he visits me in my dreams. Dr Bev had said it was to be expected, that my mind was still processing his death. She encouraged me to talk about my dreams. I won't be doing that. Mum won't want to hear it and neither will Stephen.

I shake off the night's memories and hobble along the landing. Sally's beautiful bathroom doesn't have a bath but it does have a double shower. This is so much better for me, I don't have to bend too much, I can wash my hair with ease. But, it also reminds me of home; mine and Robin's home and Robin's power shower.

I turn up at Mum's just as Paula arrives. We've met before, a long time ago; I instantly recognise her face, but I doubt she remembers mine. Paula is visibly shocked by my head with its scalping and scars, but she does her best to hide her horror. My hair is still wet from my shower which means Paula won't have to wash it. She lifts strands and lays them back down with care, as though they might fall out.

'I think the best thing to do would be to cut what's left quite short.'

'How short?' I think of Robin, then dismiss his

preference.

'Well, not as short as…' she stumbles for the words. 'The rest. But short enough that it doesn't look so odd.'

'Do what you can.' I sound so glib. 'Anything will be an improvement and I can always wear a hat.'

I see a little smile on Paula's face as she takes the tools of her trade from her bag. A cape swirls around my shoulders, a rubber mat is laid snug to my neck where barely a week ago tubes had protruded; so, this is progress. Paula combs my hair with care and a little nervousness.

'It'll soon grow. You've already got over quarter of an inch regrowth. Was it shaved off completely?'

'Yes.' It's Mum who answers for me.

Paula snips away and I enjoy the sensation and attention; I'm finding it quite relaxing. I let my eyes close and almost drift off.

'That's much better,' Mum pronounces when it's finished. 'It rather suits you, Juliette.' Mum holds up a mirror for me to see.

'Elfin or gamine, maybe.' Paula stands back to examine her own handiwork. 'I've left this front section a little longer and swept it to the side. And, this style will only look better as the rest grows.'

'It's great. Thank you.' I don't recognise myself in the mirror. My face, no, my whole head, looks tiny. I look like a teenager. Robin always said he liked my hair long, that it kept me looking young, but he was wrong; this is the style which has wiped away the years.

'You look like a young Audrey Hepburn,' Mum says as Paula removes the cape. 'Go up and see what make-up Madeleine has; do yourself up a bit.' I think

Mum might have, just for a moment, forgotten Mads is dead. But I go upstairs anyway and I find Mads's make-up and I cover my sallow complexion and sunken eyes, and I use a soft gloss on my lips which makes me look as though I might break out into a broad smile at any moment.

I admire myself in the mirror; in a dim light I could pass for almost normal. I pop the lip gloss into my pocket; it's good to have a little something of hers with me.

Before I go downstairs I flick through Mads's things; her notebooks stacked neatly on her desk, her hairbrushes on the dressing-table. I don't know what I'm expecting to find – Mum and Dad will have been through everything, as well as the police probably. I open a drawer, her phone, inside a plastic bag, lies inert and dead. I remove it from the bag and push it deep inside my pocket next to my own phone, my temporary phone. In the corner her school bag gapes open, her laptop, in a police plastic bag pokes out. Mum or Dad must have put it back there.

'How much do I owe you?' I say to a waiting Paula when I go back downstairs.

'Nothing. Bless you.' She heads for the door.

'No, but…' I say to her retreating form.

'Really, nothing.' She laughs. 'I'll charge you double when your hair grows back.'

'Okay.'

'No. I was joking. You look fab by the way.' And she's gone; Mum closing the front door behind her.

'You do look much better. Even your clothes.'

I'm wearing a pair of jeans that I haven't been able to get on for a couple of years, now they fit perfectly.

Robin was right, I had become fat.

'Did you bring these?' I pull at the jeans.

'Yes. I looked around for small stuff that would fit you now. Might as well wear it while you can.'

'What, before I get fat again?'

'No. You've never been fat. You're pregnant, darling and you will get bigger.'

Pregnant. I'd almost forgotten.

By the time Stephen arrives at Mum's I've met my new physiotherapist, had lunch and reapplied the lip gloss.

'Wow. Is that you, Etty? You look amazing.'

'Doesn't she just.' Mum beams.

'You ready?'

'Yes,' I say as I shake my head. I'm apprehensive and I'm also conscious of my absence of hair, nothing brushes my shoulders or falls over my eyes. Odd feelings.

'It'll be okay.' He helps me on with my coat. I've decided not to wear a hat.

'Do you want me to come with you?' Mum's words say one thing but her voice gives her reluctance away.

'No. No.' I give her a kiss and a hug.

'Mum hates Robin, you know.' We're in his car and Stephen is pulling away as I say it.

'Mmm.' A nice non-committal response.

'I think Dad does too.'

'Yeah.' Stephen pretends to concentrate on turning left.

'And you.'

He glances at me but doesn't speak; he doesn't

265

need to.

We pull up outside the chapel of rest; it's a newish building tacked onto the back of a Victorian end-terrace. Opposite, a primary school playground is full of children playing netball, there's pushing and shoving as they attempt to get the ball in the net. A school and a funeral home; an incongruous pairing.

The car park is small and Stephen has to park someone in, but the alternative is parking in the street and that looked busy. I sit in the car and take deep breaths. Stephen comes around to my side and opens the door. I don't get out.

'We don't have to do this today.' His voice is soft, caring.

'Yes. I do.' I take the hand he offers and haul myself out of the car; my accident injuries suddenly rendering me immobile. Then I remind myself that I'm still alive. Robin is dead.

The black portico door looks solid and impassable. Stephen rings the bell and we wait for what seems an age before it is opened.

'You have an appointment?' There's a neat professional smile behind the soft voice of the man in black waistcoat and pin-striped trousers.

'Yes, we do.' Stephen explains who we are and why we are here. Thank God for Stephen.

We're ushered into a little room filled with low-slung waiting-room chairs. They're dark green, as is the thick pile carpet and the curtains; the walls are painted pale green. I feel as though I'm deep in a forest. In the corner, a coffee machine and paper cups sit awaiting duty.

'Can I offer you a coffee?' The soft voice asks.

A farcical part of me wants to ask him if he can? For how would we know?

'Not for me,' Stephen speaks first, his voice quiet.

'No, thank you.'

Soft voice excuses himself and goes off to find our funeral arranger.

Beverley comes in and introduces herself as Bev. Another Bev. This could be confusing, but probably only for me.

We go through a few formalities, all of us speaking in hushed tones, before she asks if I would like to see the deceased's body. At this point Robin doesn't seem to have a name. When I confirm I do want to see him we are ushered out of the dark green room and into a more open waiting area.

'I'll just pop through and make sure they're ready for you.' The way she says *they* makes me think there are several deceased people waiting to be seen. She disappears through another door, then seconds later, she *pops* back.

'You can go through when you're ready. Take as long as you like. There's no rush. When you're finished, just ring the bell.' She points to the tiny brass bell on the table, the type usually seen in hotel receptions. Then Bev disappears through a different door.

I inhale deeply. Stephen stands and waits.

'Do you want to go in alone?'

Do I? I don't know.

'How long has he been here?'

'Since it happened. Four weeks or so.'

I stand still. I don't know what to do. I want to see Robin. I don't want to see Robin.

I must see Robin.

It might not be him.

'Come with me.'

Stephen takes my hand and squeezes it. He pushes the door open and we go in together.

It's chilly in the room and there's an overwhelming scent of air freshener, just like when Mads was here. There's the same green carpet and curtains in this room as in the meeting room. There are no chairs. A lidless coffin sits in the middle of the room on a pair of trestle legs.

I take a tiny step forward, then stop. I glance at Stephen, he's still holding my hand but he's looking down at his shoes. I inch forward and Stephen has to come with me.

I gasp when I see Robin's face. He looks perfect, pale, but perfect. His hair is neat and brushed, his lips are slightly parted. He could be asleep. From his neck to his feet he is covered in a cream cloth – a shroud, I suppose.

I lean over the coffin, I peer at his face. He looks like Robin but I can see, quite clearly, that Robin isn't there.

'He's gone.'

I'm crying but not making a noise; silent tears run down my face, yet I don't feel distressed. It's strange.

'It's him.' I say as though I'm being expected to confirm his identity. Stephen squeezes my hand in response.

With my free hand, I stroke Robin's beautiful face. It's rock solid and cold. I pull my hand away as though I've been stung.

But I feel compelled to say goodbye. I touch his lips lightly with my finger. They're hard, it's odd. His lips were always so soft, his mouth so sweet.

'Rest in peace, Robin,' I hear myself say. Then I squeeze Stephen's hand and we back out of the room, closing the door behind us. Once back in the waiting room, I feel I can breathe properly again.

'You okay?'

'Yeah. I'm okay.' And I am, amazingly I am. Poor Robin. It isn't fair that he died and I lived. It isn't fair at all, but deep down inside I know that fair or not, it's right. I feel numb. I should be wailing and crying, but I just feel numb.

'Shall I?' Stephen's hand hovers over the brass bell and I nod my agreement.

Bev arrives like a spectre who has been hovering in the ether. Pop, and she's here.

'Would you like to discuss the arrangements now?' She pauses and smiles. 'Or another time?'

'Let's do it now.' I sound so rude. 'Please,' I add to soften it.

We're ushered back into the green-green meeting room. Coffee is offered and this time we accept. Bev produces a long checklist and gives us a little speech about funerals. I hope Stephen is paying attention because most of it is washing over me.

A catalogue of coffins is produced, it seems the one he is currently in isn't his. I don't want to dwell on that too much. I choose one which is dark and smart, something he would choose himself. I wonder if it really matters. He isn't here to care. A hearse is ordered, a service is arranged – just the one at the crematorium. Would we like a notice in the newspaper? A part of me shudders when I say yes.

'We need to contact his mum and see if he has any other family.'

'Okay.' Stephen squeezes my knee before starting the car. I shift uncomfortably in my seat; I have a new cast which, despite its lightness, nips at my ankle. 'I think we need to go to my house to do that.'

'Today?'

I shake my head. Enough is enough. I'm tired.

Later, when I'm tucked up alone in Stephen's bed I think of Robin's face, so elegant, so smooth. It floats across my eyes as I drift into sleep.

I sleep well, I sleep deep. And Robin doesn't visit me.

When I wake I feel happy, but only for a moment, only until reality kicks in and I remember what is happening in my life. Then I think of the little person growing inside me, and that happy feeling returns, momentarily.

Mum is nervous about me going to the house. She's glad I'm not going alone, pleased that Stephen is accompanying me, relieved that she doesn't have to come herself.

'You could leave it, go another day. There's no real rush.' She's trying her best to dissuade me.

'The funeral is next week. I need to try to track his mum down. The last I heard she was in Brazil.'

'Have you ever met her?' Mum has that sceptical tone in her voice, not unusual when she talks about Robin.

'No.'

Mum purses her lips, allows herself a little nod.

'You might as well say it, Mum. Get it out.' I know she's wondering why I'm bothering.

'No. No. You do what you need to do.' Whether she's aware of it or not, I'm not sure, but her eyes roll

270

up to the ceiling.

'Well how would you feel if it was me dead and no one bothered to tell you?' The words are out without me thinking and now I wish I could take them back, but it's too late. How insensitive can I be? 'I'm sorry.' I rush to her, wrap my arms around her. She remains impassive and unmoving.

'Ready Etty?' Stephen lumbers into Mum's kitchen via the back door.

'Yes, go on. Get off.' Suddenly Mum is smiley and pleasant. 'Don't forget we're all eating at Sally's tonight. Make sure you're back by six.' Now Mum's almost pushing us out of the door.

'Everything okay? With you and your mum, I mean?' Stephen holds the car door open for me.

'Just put my foot in it. Cast and all. You know.' I don't want to say any more and Stephen doesn't press me.

I feel myself start to shake as we pull into my street and I see the house, our house, mine and Robin's. It looks so normal. Just like it does every day when we come home from work; Robin's car on the drive.

I gasp suddenly realising that I don't have any keys. Is that a deliberate mistake on my part?

'Okay?'

'No keys,' I say.

'I have your keys. Your mum gave them to me.'

'How did… where did she get them from?'

'Your handbag.'

'My handbag.' I knew Mum must have had keys, she'd collected clothes for me. I just didn't realise she had my handbag, the one I had on that day. I shiver – someone has just walked over my grave.

271

Inside there's post on the doormat, Stephen picks it up and adds it to the growing pile on the hall table. Robin wouldn't like that, he never let the post hang around; it was always dealt with efficiently. Now it will be my responsibility.

I pick up the letters and flick through them, I'm not really seeing the detail. I'm looking for the one forwarded from work, I'm looking for the one with Mads's handwriting on it. *For your eyes only*. It's not here; I drop the post back on the table.

Stephen takes my hand and steps towards the sitting room. I freeze. I don't want to go any further. I don't want to stay. I want to leave, go back to Mum's, go back to Sally's, back to Stephen's bedroom. I want to go home.

This is my home.

'We can do this another day.' Stephen steps back towards the front door.

I think of the funeral in eight days' time, I think of Robin's mum in Brazil. No one has told her that her son is dead.

'No. We must find Robin's mum's phone number.'

The lounge looks just as it did the day of Mads's funeral.

'I was going to wear that one.' I point at my maroon coat, folded neatly on a chair where Robin must have hidden it before he made me wear the black one.

Stephen gives a little shrug, he doesn't say anything. What is there to say? Would we still have crashed if I'd worn a different coat?

'Do you have an address book? Where would it be?'

I glance around the lounge, it's minimalist and

everything in here is Robin. The black leather sofas devoid of scatter cushions because Robin didn't like them, the lamps and matching tables, the music system, the ultra-thin TV hung on the wall above the sound-bar, a selection of remotes neatly stacked on the unit that houses the Sky box. Everything chosen by Robin. Nothing of me.

'Address book?' Stephen prompts.

'I didn't have one. I have everything on my phone.'

'Yeah. Me too.'

'Where's Robin's phone?' Did it survive the accident? Was it returned to us? Who would have it.

We wander through the dining room; I run my finger along the soft dust accumulating on the expensive John Lewis table. In the kitchen, everything is where it should be, tidy, minimalist. Robin. So little of me. How have I never noticed before?

We're back in the hall and I notice for the first time that Robin's study door is open. I stop and stare.

I step forward and stab the door with my hand and wait while it drifts open. I half expect him to be sitting at his computer.

Stephen, patient, respectful Stephen, waits.

'You go in,' I say eventually.

'If you're sure.'

'Yeah.'

I step aside and let Stephen pass me. It's wrong. No one should go in there. It's Robin's room, his private study.

'His phone's here.'

I'm still standing in the hall but I lean into the room. I can't see anything. I must step over the threshold, violate Robin's sanctuary. The first step is the hardest, then the spell is broken.

On his desk a neat pile of post, larger than the one in the hall. Mum, or maybe Dad, has been through this pile, looking for the letter they believe Mads sent to me.

Stephen holds up a plastic bag, inside Robin's phone and keys, his wallet, his wedding ring.

I hear myself gasp. Stephen snatches Robin's office chair and wheels it under me just as my knees give way, even my three-pronged stick won't save me. He fetches me water from the kitchen, looks on with genuine concern in his eyes.

'I'm okay.' I've gulped half a glass of water. 'It's just the shock. You know. Seeing his things like that.'

'Yeah. Sorry. I…'

I wave his apology away.

'The phone's flat.'

'Let's go now. Bring it with us. Charge it at yours.'

'Do you want to bring anything else? More clothes.'

The prospect of going upstairs frightens me. I shake my head and get up. I want to leave. That's all I want to do.

Stephen brings the plastic bag full of Robin's personal effects and I sit in the car while he locks the front door.

Back at Stephen's we plug the phone in and wait while it charges enough for us to switch it on. It takes about ten minutes, but it has been flat for weeks now. We watch it fire up together and wait for the home screen to show; a black screen waiting for a password.

'Is that right?' Stephen's face screws up in puzzlement.

'I don't know. I've never really looked at Robin's phone. We tend,' I correct myself, 'tended to keep our phones to ourselves.'

'Okay.' Stephen doesn't try very hard to keep the judgement from his voice.

'What's that supposed to mean?'

'What?'

'Your face. The way you said okay.' I'm annoyed.

'I just think it's odd. That's all. Don't you?'

'Never thought about it.' That's true, I haven't. Robin was a private person in many ways and I respected that.

'Did you never share photos or funny videos or stuff like that?'

I think for a moment. 'No. Not with Robin. Only with Mads.' And even then, not in a long time. We used to take photos and send them to each other while we sat side-by-side on Mum and Dad's sofa. 'Actually, that reminds me, I've got Mads's phone too. It needs charging. It's upstairs.'

'Don't suppose you know the password?' Stephen has Robin's phone in his hands and is stabbing away at the number keypad.

'No.'

'Okay, let's try some obvious ones, date of birth, his and yours, that sort of thing.'

We try a few combinations but nothing works and I'm starting to despair.

'We should have looked through the desk drawers. He might have stuff in there.' I lean back on Sally's sofa and sigh.

'I'll just do a few random numbers.' Stephen starts stabbing away.

'Four numbers, how many combinations? Must be

thousands. You'll never get it.' I get up and lumber upstairs to retrieve Mads's phone.

Stephen is still stabbing numbers into the phone when I return.

'Any luck?'

'Not yet.'

'I hope you're writing them down so you know what you've tried.' I can see that he isn't.

'I'm going through the numbers methodically.'

'Right.' I plug Mads's phone in. 'This is hopeless. Is there anywhere we can take it to bypass the password?'

'Don't know.' Stephen puts the phone down and sighs. 'I'll Google it in a minute.'

We're pinning all our hopes of finding Robin's mum's contact details, on getting access to his contact list. I hope we're not wasting our time.

'Maybe we should have switched his computer on and had a look on there.' I wished I'd thought of that when we were at my house.

'Do you know the password for that?'

'No. Maybe it doesn't have one.'

Stephen looks at me over the rim of his cup and raises his eyebrows.

'Here,' he says, passing his phone to me, 'you Google it while I try a few more combinations.'

'Password?'

'Guess.'

'I don't know.'

'You do. It's always been the same, Etty.'

'I don't know. Just tell me.'

'You know it.' He's laughing now.

I type in 3889 and it opens immediately, the numbers equating to the letters.

276

'E-T-T-Y.' I laugh. 'You're so predictable.'

'Yeah. And so should Robin be.' Stephen's brow furrows as he has another go at Robin's phone. 'Urgh,' he groans. 'I thought that might be it.'

'What?'

'I put Etty in his too.'

'He never called me Etty. He hated that you did.'

'Did he have a pet name for you?'

'No.' I think about that, Robin never called me anything other than Juliette.

'Got it,' Stephen says, holding the phone up.

'What? What was it?'

'6237.' He looks sheepish. I don't know why.

'That's random.'

'Yeah.' Stephen offers me a smile. I can see he's trying to keep the pity out of it but he's so transparent his emotions always show on his face.

Stephen's phone is still in my hand and has returned to the locked screen. I look at the numbers for a long time, trying to work out the significance of 6237. Finally, it dawns on me.

'M-A-D-S. It's Mads.' I gasp and put my hand up to my mouth. I can't believe it.

'It could be anything. Probably coincidence.'

'You tried Mads though, didn't you?'

Stephen looks down and mutters into his lap.

'What made you try that? Why?'

He looks up and shrugs. 'Just a guess.'

'Why? Why Mads? What does it mean?'

'Shall we look through the contacts?'

'What made you try Mads?'

'Just a feeling. Nothing really.'

'I don't believe that. Why Mads? What made you even think of her name?' I'm starting to feel hot and uncomfortable now. 'Say something. Tell me.'

'No evidence. Really. Just a feeling.'

I lean over and push him, urging him to speak.

'I'm sorry, but I never liked the way he looked at her. He watched her too closely.'

As he says it, a horrible sinking feeling envelops me.

EIGHTEEN

'We've had this conversation before, haven't we?' It has such a familiar ring to it.

'Similar,' Stephen says, quietly.

'What do you mean?'

'You had your suspicions.' He leaves the words hanging in the air.

'I don't remember, so tell me.' I'm annoyed with him, I'm frustrated by my own poor memory, I'm horrified by what I think might have happened between Mads and Robin.

'After Mads died you started having suspicions about Robin and Mads. You said it fitted with her never being at home when you visited.'

'Did I have any evidence?'

'No.'

'It doesn't fit. I always dropped Robin off and picked him up. I even saw him kissing that girl on the doorstep that time, didn't I?' I dropped him off before six, I picked him up before ten, was there enough time for him to see Mads? What about the nights when he tutored from home? Was Mads visiting him then? His need for frequent bedclothes changing makes me wince.

'You said it was just a feeling.' Stephen sighs. I wish he wouldn't do that.

'And what do you think?'

'That's not fair. You know there's never been any love lost between me and Robin.'

'Yes. Well. That aside. What do you think? What's your gut feeling?'

'Same. I think,' he mutters before flicking through Robin's phone.

'Have we fed each other's suspicions to justify our own actions?' I'm thinking aloud but it's a valid question for Stephen. If Robin's been unfaithful, it's perfectly acceptable for me to commit adultery as well. Isn't it?

'Maybe.' He looks sheepish and that's how I feel too. But underneath that I feel agitated. What the hell made me think Robin was doing anything - I shudder at the thought – with my little sister? 'Then there's the password to his phone.' Stephen adds.

'Just a bunch of numbers.' I'm defending Robin; he can't defend himself.

'And letters.'

'Let me see that phone.' I hold my hand out and Stephen passes it over. While we've been talking it's locked itself again. I type in the numbers, the numbers that translate to the letters that spell MADS. I feel sick. I start to flick through the contacts, I find Mads's mobile, but that's not unreasonable; my little sister is Robin's sister-in-law. 'There's no history of messages or calls between them.' I feel relieved.

'WhatsApp?'

'Not listed as a WhatsApp contact.' I feel almost smug. 'Perhaps I was just being paranoid, or…'

'Yes?'

'Justifying our affair by thinking vile things about my husband.' That is plausible, so horribly plausible that I feel nauseous and ashamed.

'Yeah. Probably.'

'You don't think so?' I'm annoyed with Stephen,

it's as though he wants us to find something vile out about Robin.

'I don't know what to think. You were the one who said it to me, I never said it to you, not first anyway.'

'But you've always suspected it?' How dare he?

Stephen doesn't say anything, but gets up and heads for the kitchen, leaving the door open behind him. I hear him filling the kettle, switching it on, the clank of cups and spoons. When he comes back he's carrying a tray, he lays it down on the coffee table without a word.

'You said Robin groomed me.' My accusatory tone fills the room.

Stephen gives me a quizzical glance over his coffee cup.

'When I was in hospital, you said he groomed me.'

'Yeah. I shouldn't have said that.'

'Is it what you think?'

'It doesn't matter what I think.'

'It is what you think. Isn't it?'

'You were young, you were easily swayed. He was attractive, even I could see that, especially then, when he was younger. What would he have been then? Our age, now?'

'Yeah.' Robin was twenty-eight, just as I am now. I think about my feelings for Robin, I was consumed with love for him. He was all I thought about, morning, noon and night. He was all I ever wanted. I was sixteen. 'I don't think he groomed me,' I snap. 'I was over the age of consent.'

'Yeah. I shouldn't have said it.'

'Then, why did you?'

'No excuse. I was just worried about you. In that

hospital. Nearly dead.' His voice is soft and sad and I'm forgetting the effect the accident must have had on him; he pulled us from the wreckage, watched it go up in flames as we lay on the grass verge. He saved my life. And he was sorry he couldn't save Robin's.

I offer Stephen a weak smile as we sit and sip our coffee in silence. It's all so bloody miserable. I put my cup down and pick up Robin's phone again, I type in the treacherous password and begin to flick through his contacts.

'Here it is: Mother.' I flash the phone at Stephen before pressing dial. 'It's ringing.' Now I'm dreading it being answered, I'm going to have to tell Robin's mother that her son is dead. I shouldn't be doing this over the phone but I can hardly travel to Brazil.

'Hello, Robin.' The voice sounds weary.

'Oh, hello. It's not Robin. I'm sorry. I don't think we've ever met.' I know we haven't, she couldn't come to our wedding. 'I'm Juliette, Robin's wife.' I wait for her to say something.

'Oh.' There's a pause. 'Oh,' she says again. 'His wife?'

'Yes. I'm really sorry, I've got some sad news for you.'

There's silence at the other end.

'Are you still there?'

'Yes. Is he all right? Is he ill? I haven't seen him for weeks, he missed his usual visit.'

'His visit?' I shouldn't be diverted from the purpose of this call, but I don't understand how Robin can have visited Brazil without me knowing.

'Yes, regular as clockwork. First Saturday of the month. He didn't come this month. Is he all right?'

'No. I'm sorry. He's not. Robin died in a car

accident four weeks ago. I'm so sorry.'

'And you didn't think to tell me earlier?' Her tone is bitter and snappy.

'No. I'm sorry. I couldn't.' I'm crying now. It's not unreasonable of her to be angry, but I'm doing my best to break it gently. Stephen takes the phone from me and leaves the room. I hear his voice as he talks to Robin's mother but I cannot hear what is being said. When he comes back he drops the phone on the coffee table and sits down next to me, his arm goes around my shoulder.

'You okay?'

'Thank you. For that.'

'I should have made that call. It was never going to be easy.'

'Did you tell her about the funeral? Will she be able to make it?' Part of me still believes that she is in Brazil, but the rational part of me knows that cannot be true.

'She wants to see his body. I'm taking her tomorrow. She wants to meet you there too. I haven't made any promises, just said I'd ask you.'

I don't want to meet her and yet, at the same time, I do. I'd like to know when she came back from Brazil. I'd like to know why I've never met her.

'What time?'

At eleven the next morning we're sitting in a little cul-de-sac of tiny bungalows, barely ten miles from where Robin and I live. The gardens are open plan and neat, the grass is the same length across them all, the bushes beneath the front windows are the same. It dawns on me that these are communal gardens and probably maintained by gardeners.

283

'Do you think this is sheltered housing?' I try to guess how old Robin's mum is. He was forty-two so it's feasible that she could be anything between sixty and eighty.

'Looks like it.' Stephen glances at the clock on the dashboard. 'It's time. Should I go and knock for her? Maybe she's a bit infirm.'

'Yeah. If you don't mind.' I can't face the thought of knocking on her front door myself.

Just as Stephen puts his hand on the handle to open his car door the front door of Robin's mother's house bursts open and a woman steps out. She is neither elderly, nor infirm.

'My God, that *is* Robin's mother.' Stephen takes the words right out of my mouth. I think we had both imagined old and frail, but this woman is tall, slim, perhaps mid-sixties, but youthful. Her hair is styled into a dark bob, her face is elegantly made up. She wears a dark trouser suit, a soft pink blouse, and carries a large handbag. She only needs a pair of sunglasses to look like a model for a middle-aged ladies' fashion advert. *She* is where Robin got his looks from.

Stephen jumps out of the car and moves towards her. Courtesy propels me from my seat too, though it takes rather longer for me to struggle out and by the time I do she is standing on the pavement waiting for me.

I shuffle forward awkwardly and offer my hand, she glances at it before extending hers.

'I'm Juliette,' I say. 'I'm pleased to me you, despite the circumstances.'

'Caroline. Likewise.' She glances up and down the street. 'Shall we get on?' At first, I think she is asking

284

me if we'll get on, as in be friends, then I realise she means that we should get going.

I offer her the front seat in the car. She glances at the back doors, then looks me up and down, her eyes resting on my cast, and refuses.

'It's very nice round here.' I don't know what else to say as we drive down the street.

'Yes. It's pleasant enough. Lot of old people though.'

'You don't seem…' I'm about to say old, then realise how rude that sounds.

'I'm the warden. It's sheltered housing and, among other duties, it's my job to see that no one dies on their own in the night.' She gives a stiff little laugh; she's as uncomfortable as I am.

I turn around as best I can and give her a smile which I try to endow with empathy.

'I'm so sorry we're having to meet in these circumstances. And I'm so sorry I couldn't let you know sooner about Robin…' My voice trails away, I feel a catch in my throat.

'Yes. Well.' She grips the handbag on her lap and turns to look out of the window. The atmosphere inside the car is fraught; we all wish we were somewhere else. The silence seems to go on forever. I'm grateful when Stephen finally breaks it.

'How long have you been back from Brazil?'

'I beg your pardon?' Caroline leans forward to hear Stephen better as he raises his voice.

'I said, how long have you been back from Brazil?'

'I haven't been to Brazil.'

Stephen and I exchange confused glances before Stephen turns his attention back to the road.

'Oh. There's obviously a misunderstanding. Robin

said you were in Brazil; that's why you couldn't come to our wedding.'

'I've never been to Brazil, it's not somewhere I would holiday.' I can feel her annoyance.

'No,' Stephen counters. 'We thought you lived there.'

'No. Never.'

We're getting off to a good start.

None of us speaks anymore during the twenty-minute drive to the chapel of rest until we pull up in the car park.

'Do you want us to come in with you?' Stephen waits for Caroline to answer. Her response is to look us up and down several times before nodding.

Stephen leads the way, he rings the bell and we wait. When it's answered it's by someone we haven't met before, but they wear the same uniform, the same expression on their face as the undertakers we met yesterday. I can hardly tell them apart.

We're ushered into the same green waiting room, then told to visit the deceased for as long as we like. Then, we're left on our own; the door to the room where Robin lies is ajar. Robin's mother stares as if expecting him to walk through it. I know how she feels.

'Do you want some privacy?' Stephen keeps his voice low as he speaks to Caroline.

She shakes her head several times but says nothing.

'Would you like me to come in with you?' Stephen offers.

Caroline shakes her head again, then points at me. I feel my heart sink then thud against my ribcage.

'You want me to come with you?' My voice is a squeak. I'm horrified. I've seen Robin, I thought I would not have to see him again.

Caroline nods, then links her arm through mine. I hope she does not falter because my balance is not good enough to hold us both up even with my three-pronged walking stick. Stephen steps aside to let us pass; to see my husband's corpse.

She gasps when she sees him. I do not look at his face, just fix my gaze on the skirting board behind the coffin. I breathe slowly and deeply and tell myself this will soon be over.

Out of the corner of my eye I see Caroline run a finger along his nose, then rest it on his lips. I hear her take a deep breath.

'Car accident, did you say?'

'Yes.' I glance into her eyes; they are dead, as I suspect mine look too.

'Not a mark on him. He looks beautiful. Don't you think?'

'Yes. I do.' I'm still not looking at him.

'What killed him?'

'Trauma to the chest' I'm repeating what I've been told, it's sounds so impersonal. 'The steering wheel…'

'Was he driving?' she cuts in.

I nod.

'Silly boy,' she says, lifting her finger from his lips. 'Inevitable.' I want to ask why, but dare not. She turns to leave, and, still linked to her, so do I.

In the waiting room Stephen mouths 'okay?' at me behind Caroline's back. I widen my eyes in response. Now is not the time for conversation. Caroline lets go of me and slumps into a chair.

'I could murder a cup of tea,' she says.

'Me too.' I agree too hastily.

'There's a pub across the road; I'm sure they do tea

and coffee,' Stephen offers.

'Is there anything I need to sign before we go?' Caroline looks to Stephen for an answer.

'No. Everything's taken care of.' He's using a soft, reassuring voice on her.

Stephen shuffles us out and towards the pub.

We're soon seated. Stephen has a cappuccino and Caroline and I have individual pots of tea; two cups each. I'm pleased about that but my bladder won't be; I seem to be going a lot lately. Mum has told me it's often the case in early pregnancy, even though most people think it only happens later.

'Did you say you've never been to Brazil?' Stephen asks Caroline. He's picking a scab and, while I want to know what's going on, a part of me wishes he would just let it be.

'No. No. What is this with Brazil?'

'You've never lived there?'

'No. Why do you keep asking?' Caroline sounds tired, irritable.

Stephen flicks his eyes in my direction; having started this, he now expects me to carry on. Caroline stares at me and waits.

'Robin told me you lived in Brazil, that's why you couldn't come to our wedding.'

I hear her sigh.

'Maybe he was confusing the places. Or you misheard. My sister lives in Basildon, I often visit her. When was this?'

I definitely did not mishear. Robin had told me several times, over the years, that his mother lived in Brazil.

'Ten years ago. Christmas time.' As I say the words I watch her face.

Her mouth doesn't exactly drop open, her eyes don't widen, but I watch the shock register on her face. She starts to speak twice but the words don't come out. She swallows.

'You've been married ten years?'

'Yeah.' I look down at my hands, twiddle my wedding ring. I feel so embarrassed. I think she had no idea I even existed until yesterday.

'Ten years, ten years,' her voice echoes as she shakes her head. She turns to Stephen. 'Who did you say you were again?'

'Stephen. I'm Etty's, err, Juliette's friend. We grew up together.'

'R-i-g-h-t. Good of you to help with my son's funeral.'

'Err, yes.' I can tell from the look on his face that he wants to say there's no one else to do it, but he manages to restrain himself.

'Would you like to do anything, say anything? Have you any preferences for the service?' I'm offering an olive branch that I hope she'll take.

'No. No. You go ahead. It's all a bit...odd. Many coming?' She looks at me expectantly as she takes a sip of tea.

'I don't know. We only arranged it yesterday. There's a notice going into the paper, probably today, and we'll ring his school with the details. I'm sure some of his colleagues will want to come.'

'You didn't know Robin was married, did you?' Stephen can't resist stabbing.

'No.' She half smiles at Stephen. 'But nothing my son does surprises me.' She turns to me. 'Any children.'

'No.' I feel my face flush.

'Just as well, he's not too good with children.' She stares into the distance.

'But he's a teacher.' Stephen can't resist another stab.

'Yes. Well. Yes.' She pours her second cup of tea. 'Where's the wake, afterwards?'

'Umm, err…' We haven't arranged a wake because we assumed there would be just us and Mum and Dad and Sally.

'Not arranged yet?'

'No. Not yet,' Stephen answers, smooth and calm.

'Okay. Well, I'll organise that. We can use the community room we have in the sheltered housing. You'll have to pay for the catering, but I'll get them to bill you direct. Message me your address?' She knocks back her second cup of tea, puts the cup down and looks around for her handbag. 'That was a bit cold, that one.' She stands up. It's time to go.

The atmosphere in the car on the journey back is not as tense as before, but there's no small talk, no pleasantries.

We pull up outside her bungalow, Caroline gets out and stands on the pavement. I wind down the window and Stephen leans over me to speak to her.

'Do you need a lift to the crem?' he asks.

'No. No. I'll see you there.' She walks down the path and puts the key in the door, as she opens it she turns. 'I'll tell the others.' Then she's gone, the door closing behind her.

'The others?'

'There must be more relatives.'

'Robin never mentioned anyone.'

'He said she lived in Brazil.'

'Yeah.' And he never told her about me.

We go straight through to Mum's kitchen when we get back. She's sitting drinking tea at the table.

'Just made a pot. Want one?'

We decline in unison. I tell Mum about Robin's mum. I tell her about Brazil, or rather, not Brazil, and about Robin's mum not knowing about me.

Mum doesn't say anything, just gives me the look and offers a weak smile. And her words from years ago echo in my mind: *he's such a liar.*

Later, when Stephen and I are alone in Sally's lounge, I remember Mads phone.

'You left it in here. It's fully charged now.'

'Have you looked through it?'

'No,' Stephen says and he sounds indignant.

'Shall we look through it now?' I've been through Robin's phone again and again. I don't know what I'm expecting to find, I don't know what I want to find, but so far, I've found nothing of interest, except, of course, his mother. Now I face the same quest with Mads's phone.

Mads's phone doesn't have a password, she's chosen a pattern instead.

'Any idea what it might be?' Stephen asks, looking over my shoulder.

'M, I suspect.' I give a small laugh. 'I'll try that first.' It works.

I scroll through Mads's messages and contacts; there's nothing that jumps out at me. When I find Chloe's number I drop her a message. Stephen watches me intently, then frowns.

'Chloe. She was Mads's best friend, but Robin said she had bullied Mads.' Was that true? Did Robin really say that, or was it me putting words into imaginary Robin's mouth?

'What did you say?'

'Nothing really, just asked how she was, wondered if she wanted to meet up?'

'And if she doesn't reply?'

'I don't know. Just clutching at straws really. I cannot believe that Mads would kill herself. And, if she did, I need to know why.'

'Of course.' Stephen looks solemn.

'Oh, do you know what we did with Robin's wallet? We brought it back with us, didn't we?' I remember it being in the plastic bag with his phone.

Stephen gets up and opens the sideboard drawer; he pulls the plastic bag out and brings it over to me.

Robin's wallet has fifteen pounds and some change in it, as well as his credit and debit cards.

'I suppose I'll have to cancel these.' I sigh.

'We could go to yours and go through stuff tomorrow if you like, there may be bills and things that need paying.'

'Yeah. I'll have to catch up with our bank accounts. Robin handled all that.' I stop myself from sighing again.

'I can help you.' He pauses. 'If you want me to, I mean.'

'Thanks.' I start to stuff the cards back into Robin's wallet, jamming them in, but they don't all fit. I groan my irritation.

'What's wrong?'

'They won't go back in.' I pull them out. 'Something's in the way.'

'Your winning lottery ticket,' Stephen laughs as I pull out the offending jammer.

It's a photograph, printed on paper. Of me. I smile. I never knew he carried a photo of me in his wallet. I remember that photo, remember when it was taken; we were at the zoo, Robin, me and Mads. We're all in it but it's been folded so that only I show. Mads used to have a copy stuck to her bedroom mirror. It was taken on her phone; Robin must have asked for a copy too.

I turn it over. The rest of the photo: Mads and Robin – he has his arm around her shoulder.

'At least he didn't cut you off,' Stephen says to reassure me.

'He's just folded it to fit in his wallet.' It hadn't occurred to me until Stephen cast doubt. I stuff it all back into the wallet, then the wallet, still bulging, into the plastic bag. I pop Robin's and Mads's phones in too. I can't face going through Mads's phone anymore tonight.

'I think I'll get off to bed now. Good night.' I take the bag with me.

'Etty,' Stephen calls after me. 'You okay?'

'Yeah, just tired.' Which is true, but I also feel irritated by Stephen, by Robin and, even by Mads.

The second visit to my house isn't any easier than the first. I have a go at Robin's computer, but, inevitably it's password protected. We go through the same rigmarole trying to guess the password but with no luck this time; thankfully, it isn't MADS.

'It'll be something more complicated.' Stephen states the obvious. 'Any ideas?'

'No. Never touched it.' I regard the computer with disdain; this whole room is alien to me. I'm beginning to think I never knew Robin at all. 'We might as well go.'

'I don't mind having a few random goes.' Stephen offers me a smile.

'Really?'

'It worked last time. Failing that, I have a friend who could probably crack it. I could ring him.'

'Okay.' I drift back into the lounge and flop down on the sofa. I stare out of the window and watch the road; it's a cul-de-sac, there's not much traffic. It's strangely soothing though, just staring and not thinking. Just sitting.

I've no idea how long I've been sitting here, I'm vaguely aware of the sound of Stephen clicking the keyboard in the study across the hall. Then he speaks on the phone; the doors are open but his voice is soft so I don't hear exactly what he says.

Suddenly he's in the lounge, brandishing a small notebook and smiling. 'Cracked it, with a bit of help from my friend.'

'What was it?' I ask this but I'm not sure I want to know.

'I don't know, we bypassed it and now I've removed it. There was no other way. I hope that's okay.'

'We didn't have much choice really, did we?' I stand up. 'Thank you,' I add.

He offers me the notebook, I flick through it. It's a list of user names and passwords.

'Where was it?' I've never seen it before, though it is logical that such a book exists, I have one at work for the few systems and websites I use.

'It was clipped under the desk, quite clever really.'

'But you found it.'

'Almost by accident, I knocked against it when I

was on the phone.'

'Well, that's lucky.' I sit down and start working my way through the book. There are the inevitable shopping sites, eBay and Amazon included, then I find what I really want, our bank accounts.

'Shall I make us a coffee while you're doing that?'

'There's no milk,' I say, half surprised he hasn't realised that; there's been no one here for weeks.

Stephen pats my shoulder and smiles. 'There is. I brought some with us. It's in your fridge.'

While Stephen's in the kitchen I go through our accounts, they're as I expected. We have several savings accounts, and a joint account which both our salaries are paid into and all our direct debits are paid from. The amounts in them are as I expect also, because, although I never took an active role in their maintenance, Robin always kept me informed of our current financial status. He was very proud of his ability to make the most of our money.

As I flick through the direct debits, I'm grateful that they all seem to be ticking along and I don't need to worry about the gas or electric being cut off. I've just moved off the list of direct debits when I notice it; a standing order, a regular monthly sum of over a thousand pounds. I can't imagine what utility that must be paying for – half the street? Perhaps it's to a savings account. But, when I investigate further I find the recipient is referenced as Carly.

'You okay?' Stephen asks as he brings our coffees in from the kitchen. 'Only you look very pale. You feeling all right? Do you need something to eat? I brought biscuits too.'

I shake my head and stare at the online-banking screen. Stephen follows my gaze and leans over my shoulder.

'Wow. That's a lot. Who the hell is Carly?'

'I have no idea.'

NINETEEN

'Did he ever mention a Carly?'

'No. Never.' I search my brain. Did he? No? I'd remember if he'd told me we were paying someone over a thousand a month. 'No,' I repeat.

'That's a lot of money.'

'Yes.' I turn back to the screen and start hunting through the transactions. The payments go back months and months. I find the button that allows me to look at previous years' statements. I go back to last year, the year before, five years before, seven years before. 'I can't go back any further,' I murmur.

'What's that?'

'I've gone back years and the payments are there every month, they've gone up over the years, but they never fail. Look, seven years ago it was eight-hundred-and-forty, a year later it was eight-hundred-and-ninety. What does it mean?'

'Loan repayment?' Stephen says.

'No,' we chorus. We both know it's not.

'He's paying for something? What's his mother's name again?'

'Caroline, as you full well know.'

'Carly – Caroline. It could be her. That's quite feasible. Perhaps he pays her rent for her, or something.'

'Mmm. Maybe.' I'm not convinced, surely if she's a sheltered housing warden her rent would be included in her salary, or at least, very low. 'I'll have to ask her, but I'll have to choose my time. I don't think it's now. Do you?'

'No. I don't remember seeing a Carly on his phone. Do you?'

'No. I'll have a look later.' Robin's phone is still in my bedroom at Sally's, along with Mads's, both stuffed in the same plastic bag. 'That reminds me, I need to go upstairs and get another handbag, Mum's put the one I had the day of the funeral somewhere, so I've been using my pockets to carry stuff around. Not ideal.'

He laughs and shrugs. 'Do it all the time, Etty.'

'Yeah, well…' I manage a smile before turning my attention back to the computer. 'I've had enough of this. There's enough in the joint account for me not to worry about the mortgage and bills. My salary is still being paid while I'm off sick. Thank God.' I close the online-banking down and stand up. I've stiffened up and I need to use the desk to haul myself straight. 'I need to let Robin's school know about the funeral, in case they miss the notice in the paper.'

'I can do that. If it helps. I'll shut this down too while you go upstairs.'

'Thank you.' I turn to leave, then look back as Stephen sits down in Robin's chair, at Robin's desk, using Robin's computer. So wrong.

Stephen looks up and sees me staring. Our eyes meet briefly before he looks away. Can he read my mind?

'Etty, about your mortgage…'

'Yeah?'

'Don't you have insurance to pay it off?'

'My God, yes. We do. I'll have to sort that out.'

Upstairs looks just as it should. Our bedroom is neat and tidy, the bed made before we left for Mads's funeral. The décor is minimalist: beige walls, dark wood bed with integrated bedside tables and lamps, beige and brown bedding. A wall of dark wardrobes, flat and with no handles – they just touch open – is the only other furniture. Everything is hidden inside, my make-up, my shoes, my clothes, my handbags, even our full-length mirror. Robin's clothes and shoes. Robin's life. I ping the doors open and survey myself in the mirror. I'm thin. Too thin. I'm pale, even with make-up on. I'm almost bald in places although my short hair suits my face shape. I force myself to smile.

At least I'm alive.

I run my finger along the windowsill, a thin layer of dust has settled in our absence. Robin would not like that.

The room is bland. It has no personality. It is beige. Even the carpet. The stain is tiny; a dot smaller than a thumbnail. Hot chocolate. Faint from scrubbing. We had a rule about drinks in bed, and food. Or rather Robin made a rule and I broke it. Only on that one occasion. When was it? The memory comes back, vivid, sharp, painful, but my poor brain struggles to place it exactly. I think it is recently.

I was cold and tired; I went to bed first. I took hot chocolate and lay in bed enjoying it. I felt warm and cosy.

I didn't even notice the drip until Robin came in and caught me with the cup to my lips.

'What are you doing? You know we don't have food or drink in the bedroom.'

'I know, but I was cold. Anyway, I've finished it now.' I turned to put the cup on my bedside table.

His eyes followed my action, his hands followed the cup. He snatched it up.

'I'll take it downstairs,' he snapped. 'What's that? You've dripped it on the carpet. For God's sake, Juliette. This is why we have rules about this sort of thing. You've ruined the damn carpet. I can't afford to be replacing carpets because of your sloppiness.'

'Hardly shows,' I said, glancing down at it. I was stung; he still behaved as though he owned everything, paid for everything – even after all these years together.

'Clean it up while I get rid of this.' He held the cup as though it were something rancid. He was still muttering about rules and slovenliness as he stomped down the stairs.

I didn't want to get out of bed. I was warm. I was comfortable. I dragged myself out, found a pack of wet wipes among my make-up, rubbed at the offending stain. I was still at it when he came back.

'That's not good enough,' he barked. 'Here.' He thrust a bowl of water and a brush at me. 'Then you can mop it up with this.' He threw a kitchen roll at me; it bounced off my back.

On my knees I cleaned and dabbed, then took the bowl and brush downstairs.

He was sitting up in bed when I came back; his mouth set in a grim line of annoyance. I was cold and miserable. Inside I seethed. I didn't sleep well.

He started the row up again the next morning when he saw that I had dumped the bowl and brush in the kitchen sink.

'Shut the fuck up,' I shouted, shocked at my own

defiance. 'You get yourself to work. I'm going now.' I stormed off, spent the day incensed and aggrieved. I didn't go home after work; I went to Mum and Dad's. Sally was there, with Stephen.

I stayed at Mum's that night, sleeping on the sofa. When I went home the next day, a Saturday, with a hangover, neither Robin nor I mentioned our row or my absence. We silently colluded in our pretence that nothing had happened.

I slump onto our bed. There are so many things to do. I need to make a proper list. Stephen's right about the insurance, but, now I'm forced to think about it, that's just the tip of the iceberg. When we moved into this house we made wills, I need to find them, then there's probate, credit cards, Robin's phone, God knows what else. I hear myself sigh. It's all too much.

And, there's the funeral to get through yet.

'Etty.' Stephen appears in the doorway, his voice is soft and sympathetic, as though he has heard everything going on in my head. 'Are you okay?'

'Yeah.' I get up; it's an effort. 'So much to do.'

'I'll help. Whatever I can do, just ask.'

'I know. Thank you.' I stop and look at him, his kind, pleasant face looks wrong in this room. 'In case I haven't said it before, I don't know how I'd get through this without you.'

'Come on, Etty. Find this handbag you were talking about and let's go.'

I eat with Mum and Dad that evening, just the three of us. I tell them about the Carly payments and watch as Mum tries her best not to let the judgement show on her face.

'Say it, Mum.' I almost laugh.

'Nothing,' she says, getting up and starting to clear our plates from the table.

'Say what's on your mind. Go on. I don't mind.'

Mum shakes her head and keeps her lips firmly shut; I can see it's an effort.

'I'll say it,' Dad says. 'It's maintenance for an ex-wife.'

There it is, the elephant in the room, the words that neither Stephen nor I dared to say.

'Or a child.' Mum finally breaks her silence.

'I told you Robin couldn't have children. He was sterile.'

'Oh yes.' Mum brings pudding to the table. 'Only yogurts, I'm afraid.'

'I still think ex-wife,' Dad is adamant.

'Well, whatever it is, no, was, it will be stopping soon.'

'Can you do that?'

'Yes. I can. I will. After the funeral.' If it's urgent or important, someone will contact me, then I'll get to the bottom of it. I will stop further payments. I make a mental note to add it to the list I've begun in a notebook Sally has given me.

'When's your next appointment with the psychiatrist?' Mum tactfully changes the subject.

'Tomorrow. Afternoon.'

'Do you need a lift?'

'No. Stephen is going to take me.'

'He's a good lad,' Dad says, inspecting the yogurts Mum has brought to the table then pushing them away. They're all rhubarb, Mum and I pounce on them. 'I haven't had one of these for years.' I lick the inside of the lid in anticipation of the pot contents; I

302

don't want to waste a drop. 'Robin hated yogurts.'

Neither of my parents comment. They're right, I see it now. Just because Robin didn't like them doesn't mean that I shouldn't have had yogurts. I feel my throat tightening. I will not cry. It's a stupid thing to get upset about. Anyway, I can do what I like now.

'Mum,' I say, resolving that the future is the only place I should focus on, 'what did you say you did with my handbag?'

Mum gives me a quizzical look. 'Oh, that one,' she says, realisation dawning. 'It's upstairs, I'll get it shortly.'

The bag is a small, black shoulder bag. I remember now how I'd snatched it from my wardrobe after Robin and I had had the *black coat* argument. I had intended to use my usual, dark brown bag. I remember hastily stuffing the essentials into the black one as we left.

Mum lays in on the table in front of me; inside my purse, my phone – the battery flat – a pack of tissues and my keys. The light-grey lining is streaked with blood; probably the reason why she has kept it hidden for so long.

'Oh,' I say, pulling the keys out. I now realise that I've been using Robin's keys to get into our house. Obvious really, his bunch contains the key to his study. Though that was already unlocked by Mum or Dad – my excuse for not noticing.

'Amazing this survived the accident and the fire.' I close the bag. I am going to throw it away when I've emptied it.

'You were wearing it when Stephen pulled you out.'

'Oh.' I must have jumped into the car in a hurry if

I was still wearing my bag; I usually take it off, it's uncomfortable beneath the seat belt. 'What about Robin's keys? Weren't they in the ignition?'

'Police gave them to us.' Dad shrugs.

'But the car went up in flames, didn't it?'

'Y-e-s,' Dad says, his voice sounding cautious. 'Don't know. Obviously, they retrieved them in one piece.'

I take the bag and its contents back to Sally's.

'I'm off to bed,' I say as I pop my head through the lounge door. Stephen and Sally are going through Sally's iPad together; they look so cosy, mother and son, their heads together.

'Sleep tight,' Sally says, smiling.

Stephen waves and smiles too.

They both turn back to the iPad and start giggling.

'What's so funny?'

'Just YouTube. Nothing really. Just silly.'

'It's a puppy in a dress and it's dancing. Really silly and really funny. Come and have a look.' Sally rewinds the video for me and waits for me to come in close enough before she presses play.

It is silly and it is funny but I hardly manage a laugh.

'I said it was silly,' Sally says, evidently feeling the need to justify herself. 'But Stephen's just fixed my iPad so I'm catching up on silliness.' She looks up to the ceiling, excusing herself. 'He's good with computers. He's even fixed my old laptop, though only so he can use it himself. Do you want to see another video? I can probably find a better one.'

'No thanks, I'm really tired. Night.' I can't bear the prospect of more dancing dogs.

Once in my room – Stephen's room – I put my

phone on to charge and decant the remainder of the contents into my other handbag. I look around for a bin to stuff the black handbag in, but there isn't one so I wedge it into the drawer Stephen has cleared for me. I'll do it tomorrow.

Then I pick Robin's phone up out of the drawer. A quick glance through his contacts confirms that there is no Carly present. I stall over Caroline, his mother's number, and stop myself from ringing her. Now is not the time.

I pick up Mads's phone. It's still charged, and has been waiting in the drawer. I check again that there's nothing from Robin, not hidden with a fake name or code; I'm pleased and relieved to find there isn't, or at least nothing that I can see. There's a string of messages between Mads and Chloe, her friend, or bully – if Robin is to be believed. Except it wasn't Robin saying those things, it was me, my subconscious.

I flick through the messages feeling like a voyeur; the last one from Chloe particularly poignant.

Chloe: *Mads, reply to me. I'm going to do that thing if you don't. xx*

I saw this message before but it didn't resonate with me then like it does now. I check the time and date; Mads would never reply, she was already dead by then.

My own message to Chloe asking her to contact me has not been answered.

I flick further back, it's the usual school girl thing, talking about some boy they like, don't like. A pair of shoes they both want. There's no sign of bullying, no sign of animosity. The messages are frequent and friendly.

305

One catches my eye.

Mads: *Hope you're keeping my thing safe. xx*

Chloe replies, assuring that she is. Could the thing referred to in both messages be *the letter*?

But I am beginning to wonder if this mythical letter really exists? Was it from Mads? The only mention of it was from my work. It's too late to ring them now. I drop a quick email to my assistant asking if she knows anything about it. It may be pointless but it's worth a try. All I know about the letter is that it was handwritten and had *For your eyes only* on the envelope. That's why Mum and Dad are convinced it is from Mads.

I remember the first time she heard that phrase, she was about eight. I'd popped round one rainy Sunday afternoon, on my own as usual, to spend some time with Mum, Dad and Mads while Robin was marking books. We were watching a Sunday afternoon film on TV, the old Bond movie, *For Your Eyes Only*. Mads had loved the theme song, sang it for weeks afterwards and she loved the sentiment, used it repeatedly. Every Christmas and birthday card had it printed on the envelope, she'd done that for years, she'd been twelve before she grew out of it.

Was the letter from her? Or was it just a clever piece of junk mail? Why send it to me at work? Why send a letter at all, when she could message or email me? Something light and flimsy, like a gossamer-winged moth, flutters across my subconscious, an elusive memory perhaps. But it's gone before I can catch it, before I can make sense of it. Damn my useless memory.

I look through Mads's Facebook feed. I catch my breath when I see the dozens of RIP messages from her friends. I can't bear to do it now but I know I must shut down all her social media accounts; fortunately, they are all logged in on her phone. I grab my notebook and add it to my to do list.

I put the phones away and get ready for bed.

I sleep in the next morning. It's eleven by the time I've showered and dressed. Breakfast awaits me in Sally's kitchen and I help myself to cereal and toast. There's a note from Stephen; he's running errands with Sally this morning but he'll be back in time to take me for my appointment this afternoon.

I use the time I'm alone to start on the list: I cancel Robin's credit cards, his phone contract. I can't do the complicated items like mortgage and insurance until I go back to the house to find the paperwork. And I need his death certificate, there must be a death certificate, who registered it? I add this to my ever-growing list.

An email pings into my inbox; it's from my assistant at work. Yes, she remembers the letter, she forwarded it to me immediately. She's so sorry it's gone astray. Yes, it had *For your eyes only*, on the envelope. It was handwritten. She gives me a date which is four days after Mads died.

I know little more than I did before, except that it was sent after Mads died. It's all I can think about during my home physiotherapy session. I've improved so much that I don't need another visit for a week.

Chloe. She must have sent that letter.

I find her number on Mads's phone and ring her. I'll leave a voicemail if she doesn't answer; it's the middle of the day and she's probably at school

307

anyway. But the call is neither answered nor goes to voicemail; the number is unobtainable.

Stephen sits with me in the waiting room as I wait for my appointment to see Dr Bev. I survey the other patients, again wondering if they are all as bonkers, or more so, than I am? I check myself, I shouldn't be so judgemental. But the man who is quietly talking to himself suddenly lets out a loud howl, and I think, despite my apparent haunting, that I'm getting better.

I'm only twenty minutes past my appointment time when I sit down in front of Dr Bev. She looks tired. I feel sorry for her and before I know what I'm saying I'm asking after her health before she asks after mine. We both laugh and I see a sweet side to her, she suddenly looks much younger than I thought she was.

We chat, or that what it feels like, chatting with a new friend. We talk about Robin, we talk about the accident and Mads and Stephen. She empathises in all the right places.

'I hope you're giving yourself some space and some rest,' she says.

'Well, you know.' I half shrug and smile. 'Funerals and stuff.'

'It can all wait. All that sorting things out, it won't bring him back. Allow yourself time to grieve for your husband, and your sister.'

Grieve. I think about that in the car on the way out of the hospital. The overriding feeling I have is one of numbness. I haven't allowed myself to grieve, not for Robin anyway. And, probably not for Mads; I had two weeks between her death and my accident. Although I have vague memories of cryfests during that time, even I know that's not enough. Poor Mum and Dad, they can't have had much time either. As for grieving for Robin, I now realise I haven't allowed myself to do that; I was leaving him anyway so I have no right to grieve. He was probably an adulterer. Was he messing about with Mads? There are so many reasons not to grieve, so many unanswered questions.

But he was my husband for ten years. He was the love of my life.

'How did it go?' Stephen is pulling the car onto the main road; he's had the sensitivity not to ask me until now.

'Okay. Yeah. Okay. I don't have to go back unless I feel I need to. Then I can just ring for an appointment.'

'Wow. That's good. Isn't it.'

'Yeah.' Is it? I don't know. 'Can we pop by my house on the way home?' I've surprised myself with my request, but I need some answers and I feel they are in my own house. If Robin was having an affair there must be evidence, or at least clues somewhere. And who the hell is Carly? An ex-wife? A mistress?

'Yeah. Sure.' He sounds puzzled.

'Maybe there's something in his email about Carly, on his computer or somewhere.'

'Worth a look,' Stephen says, indicating and turning the car in the direction of my house. Mine and Robin's.

We sit on the drive for a moment or two as I fumble my keys out of my handbag. I'm shaking as I get out of the car and the keys jangle in my hand.

'Here.' Stephen takes the keys. 'Let me.'

I follow him up the path, wait while he unlocks the door then follow him into the house. I stop in the hall.

'Someone's been here.'

'What?' Stephen turns and frowns.

I look down at the hall table, stare at the post laid on it. 'That's today's post. Look at the postmark. How can it be there? It should be on the door mat.'

Stephen steps back and puts his arm around me, he squeezes my shoulder and pulls me into him.

'Oh, Etty. I just picked that up when we came in.'

'Did you? I didn't see you do that.'

'No? You've had a difficult afternoon. Perhaps we should just go home.'

I stand and wait for a moment, trying to recall him picking up the post. He's right, I am tired.

'No. Let's stay. Let's see if we can find anything.' I push the handle on Robin's study. 'That bloody letter would be a start.'

'What letter?

'The one supposedly from Mads.'

'Oh yeah.' Stephen grimaces as though dispelling a myth.

'It's real. I've checked. Doesn't mean it is from Mads, but it does exist.'

'Okay. Oh, by the way, I rang Robin's school. They knew about the funeral already, saw the notice in the paper.'

'Good. Is anyone coming?'

'Yeah. The head and some others, depends if they can get cover.' He raises his eyes to the ceiling. 'Difficult for them, you know.' He says it as though he's quoting.

'Oh well. Whatever.' There will be Mum and Dad, Sally and Stephen and me, and Robin's mother plus the others, whoever and how many that may be. I'm almost past caring.

I sit down at Robin's computer and switch it on. I go to his email and I'm glad that it logs on immediately, no need for a password. His inbox is full of mail, accumulating over the weeks since he died. I hear myself sigh. Most of it is junk mail. I start to scroll through – this will take ages.

'You could search it.' Stephen is leaning over my shoulder.

'Yeah?' I know I can. Why didn't I do that? I feel my energy sapping away.

'Would you like me to?'

'Yeah.'

He leans over and takes the keyboard, speedily tapping away.

'Nothing,' he says as we watch the search go through Robin's emails. 'No Carly.'

'Good.' Is it?

'Do you want to search anywhere else?'

'Like where?'

'Documents? Internet history. Other email accounts?' He shrugs.

'Are there other email accounts?'

'I don't know. We'd have to look.'

'I wouldn't know how to.' I use a computer every day at work, who doesn't? But hunting around looking for stuff you don't even know exists, well, I wouldn't know where to start. We have an IT department at work for that.

'No. Well, I'm no expert but we could have a look. Fumble around.'

'Fumble.' I smile. So does he. We're flirting. Odd really, given our circumstances. Odd, yet right.

I get up and offer him the chair. 'Go on. You

fumble while I have a good look for this letter. It must be here somewhere.' I try a flirtatious laugh but this time it doesn't quite work.

I go through the pile of post again, finding nothing but bills. I will need to tackle these, but not now. I hunt through the kitchen drawers – I'm really clutching at straws here, we never put paperwork in the kitchen, but…

I check our bedroom, the spare rooms, the sitting room, dining room, every damn room. Finally, I drift back into Robin's study to find Stephen frowning at the screen.

'Find anything?' I ask.

'Not really.'

'No Carly?'

'No.'

'Anything else?' I'm asking because he's still staring at the screen.

'Nothing you'd want to see.'

I lean over him, staring at the screen. He flicks the internet browser off.

'What? If you've found something, let me see.'

'Just some dodgy websites on the internet history.'

'Dodgy?'

'Bit porny and stuff.'

'Really?' I don't want to believe it. 'Show me.'

'No.'

'Show me. I want to see.'

Sighing, Stephen opens the browser and flicks up the history, it shows a list but he doesn't click on any of the links. There are several *sexy schoolgirl* links. I shudder.

'Have you clicked on any?'

'God, no.'

Then, further down the list I notice *lethal suicide drugs*, *suicide drug recipe, painless suicide*.

'Oh my God, what's that?'

Stephen turns and his eyes meet mine. 'You don't want to look at those.' He closes the browser.

'Have you?'

He nods slowly.

'Do you think he bought stuff? Do you think he…' I can't bring myself to say it.

'I don't know. It's hardly going to be like Amazon where you get a receipt and notification of delivery.'

'What would it be like then?'

'I don't know.' He shuts the computer down. 'Did you find the letter?'

'No. I think it must have got thrown away. Or not got here, more likely. Lost in the post. It'll turn up next year, you know, like you read about in the media.' I affect a laugh, I'm trying to be jolly but I can't stop thinking about those websites. It'll just be some clever marketing ploy and nothing to do with Mads. 'Do you think…?'

'Let's go.' Stephen, cuts in, as he stands up and rubs his back, stretches his arms above his head. 'All this has made me feel…' he shakes his head and groans.

'Yes, but…' But what?

'Come on.' He takes my arm and leads me out.

We're in the car before I finish my train of thought. 'Do you think we should tell someone? The police?'

Stephen turns and looks at me as he starts the car.

'Tell them what?'

'Those websites. You know.'

He turns the engine off, takes my hands in his.

313

'Etty. If, and it's a big if, those sites mean anything, what's the point? It won't bring Mads back, will it? Robin won't stand trial for it, will he? All it will cause it heartache. Is that what you want, having all your private business in the media, all over the internet? What about your mum and dad?'

'The police won't release it to the media.'

'Course they won't. Bet it'll get there though, somehow.'

'Maybe. But we should tell Mum and Dad.'

'Really? You don't think they've suffered enough. Would it help them to know that their son-in-law might have murdered their daughter? Will it bring her back?'

'No, but…'

'Don't do anything, not yet. Wait. Think about the consequences. Think about the pain. More pain, heaped upon pain. I'm sorry you had to see that list. No need to inflict it on them. Is there?'

'I don't know.'

'Don't do anything. Don't.'

'Mmm.'

'We should all be focusing on the future, our baby, our life together. Give your parents something lovely to look forward to. There's scans to look forward to, we could get one of those 3-D ones done. Shall we find out the sex?'

'I don't know.' I think about the baby, this tiny little being that has already survived so much, growing inside me.

'Your husband was a controlling bastard but he's gone now. Let's put away our suspicions and focus on the future.'

'Yeah.' He's right, of course he is.

'Let's get through this bloody funeral and move on.'

'Yeah,' I say, agreeing with him. Of course, he's right.

'And let's give it a week or two before we sort your stuff out here. Let's give ourselves a bit of breathing space.'

'Yeah. Okay. Yes.' He's definitely right on that one. It's exactly what Dr Bev said.

We haven't bothered with a funeral car. Dad drives the five of us in his car; Mum, Sally and I cosy up in the back, Stephen rides shotgun next to dad.

Shotgun, that had been Stephen's joke, as though we were driving into hostile territory.

Robin arrives in the hearse direct from the chapel of rest, it waits outside for us to enter first.

It's cold in the crem; heavy rain overnight has made the air damp and chilly.

'Soon warm up,' Stephen says, hugging me then grimacing as he realises how distasteful his remark is. Black humour, I suppose.

There's no sign of Robin's mum or *the others*, as we take our seats across the front row on the right-hand side. Maybe they've changed their minds. I worry that I might have given them the wrong date.

'Where is she?' I whisper to Stephen. 'We did tell her the right time, didn't we?'

'We did.'

There's just us. Five people. Five people: one is indifferent towards Robin and three hate him. But he was the love of my life.

We've been sitting here for two minutes when the door opens. I turn, expecting to see Robin's lonely coffin approach, but I'm wrong. A gaggle of girls burst through the door. School girls. They pile into the back row on our side.

The website addresses flash before my eyes.

More people come in, I recognise Robin's headteacher; he's accompanied by two others, teachers I assume.

Robin's mother wears sunglasses and a black hat; self-consciously I touch my own head, wrapped in a dark scarf to hide my scars. Caroline's shoes tip-tap down the centre aisle and she sits in the front row on the left-hand side. I'm so mesmerised by her that I hardly notice *the others* until they sit down. Four rows. There are four rows. Fifteen, perhaps twenty people?

Next to Caroline a tall man with abundant grey hair blocks my view of anyone beyond him; maybe there is no one beyond him. The people in the rows behind her look like black crows, their faces indiscernible, their heads bowed.

The music we have chosen plays as Robin's flower-bedecked coffin is wheeled down the aisle.

Words are said, music is played, it seems to go on forever yet at the same time it is over in no time and soon we're standing outside waiting for the coffin flowers to be brought out into the garden – more draughty outside corridor – of remembrance.

There are more flowers than *we* ordered.

There are more people that I expected.

'I'm so sorry about Robin.' It's his headteacher, he's taking my hand in both of his. 'He was very popular. He is sadly missed at school.'

I bet he is; I glance over at the gaggle of school girls.

He introduces me to his colleagues, they shake my

hands and spout their platitudes. They're so, so, sorry.

I smile and nod and thank and bite my lips. They wouldn't be sorry if they knew the half of it. Not sorry at all.

Robin's mother approaches, presses a hand on my shoulder when she reaches me.

'Juliette,' she says.

'This is Robin's headteacher,' I say, wishing they would all go away. Where is Stephen when I need him?

'I'm Caroline, Robin's mother.' More hand shaking, more sorrow. 'And this is Robin's father.' The grey-haired man steps forward, ignores the headmaster and gripping my shoulders, pulls me in tight. He stifles a sob in my ear. 'And this is Robin's daughter, Carly.'

TWENTY

Carly. Unmistakably Robin's daughter. She even has his lop-sided grin. Her eyes are red-rimmed and doleful. She looks at me from under her eyelashes.

Mum, Dad, Sally, Stephen and I are silent, dumbfounded. Time seems to stand still.

Then the heavens open and despite being undercover we soon realise that the rain is hitting the ground with such force that it rebounds, trying its best to soak us.

Everyone makes a dash for their cars.

We sit in Dad's car, the windows misting over, our coats damp and clinging to us. When no one else speaks I realise they are waiting for me to say something.

'I didn't see that coming.'

Mum puckers her lips as if the words *I told you so* are fighting to escape.

'I thought his father was dead.'

'We all did, Sally,' Dad says. 'Because that's what Robin told us.'

Mum puckers again. *Liar* is battling its way out of her mouth. I can't help but admire her restraint.

'He looked like he'd had a stroke,' Dad continues. 'Did you notice that?'

It's only Stephen who says yes.

Dad starts the car, flicking on the windscreen demister and the wipers. We sit and watch as our view clears.

'We'd better get along to this thing then, or they'll think we're not coming.'

'Must we?' Mum spits then clamps her mouth shut again.

No one answers but Sally pats Mum's hand.

'Let's just get it over with,' I say and I pray there are no more revelations.

The community room is large and airy. It's obvious it's for old people; the high wing back chairs have been pushed to the edges to make way for the tables that are laden with food.

'Where the hell did these all come from?' Sally voices all our thoughts. There must be fifty people in the room. I don't think they were all at the funeral.

Caroline spots us, raises a hand in welcome, finishes her conversation with an elderly woman, then comes over. We're hovering around the food table by the time she reaches us. She's carrying a glass of white wine.

'You didn't know about Carly,' she says, by way of a greeting. It's hard to tell if she is pleased or disappointed.

'No.' I can't be bothered to dress it up or prevaricate.

'His daughter by his first marriage.' Caroline puts her wine glass on the table and helps herself to a plate, napkin and fork, she picks up a sausage roll, a scotch egg, a tiny triangle of sandwich and dumps them on her plate.

'First marriage?' Mum says. She is fighting the sound of triumph from her voice.

'Yes. He was very young. So was Carly's mother. Too young.' Caroline rolls her eyes.

'How old is Carly?' Stephen picks up a plate and helps himself to food.

'Twenty-one. Just finishing university.'

'Did Robin see her much?' Stephen again.

'Monthly. At least. Sometimes he'd pop round in the evenings. Less the last few years what with her being away. At university, I mean.' She arches her eyebrows.

'Robin said he couldn't have children.' I wish Stephen wouldn't dig but at the same time I want to know. I think.

'Well, no, not now.' Caroline laughs and picks up her glass of wine, takes a long, slow sip. 'Not after Carly. He went off and had the snip.' She makes a scissor movement with her fingers and laughs. 'Not that he told anyone. Not his wife. Not then anyway. But that's our Robin.' She turns to me. 'Always secretive, as you no doubt know.'

I manage a noncommittal smile.

'After all, he didn't tell us about you. Although, I had guessed there was someone. When did you marry again?'

'Ten years ago.'

Caroline shrugs her shoulders and sighs. Either she doesn't care or she's an amazing actor. I can't tell, but I don't think I'm bothered either way.

'Is she here?' Mum says.

'Carly. Yes. Over there. She has some friends with her, for support. It's hardest for her, I think. Losing her dad.'

'I meant his first wife,' Mum persists.

'God, no. They hated each other. She'll probably dance on his grave.' She grimaces. 'Well, you know what I mean, grind his ashes, or something.'

'How young was she?' I ask, my voice tiny.

'Sixteen, when she had Carly. Barely legal.' She

rolls her eyes again. 'How old were you when you *got together*? Legal?' We all know what she means when she says *got together*.

'Robin said his father was dead.' Dad cuts in, saving me from answering as Mum turns her face away.

'Mmm. Well, to Robin, I suppose he was. They haven't seen each other for years. We divorced when Robin was eleven. He was a drinker,' she adds as she knocks back the rest of her wine. 'But I've seen more of the old sod since he had his strokes. He nearly died then. Maybe that's what Robin meant.' She smiles, a brief, hollow smile.

'He also said you lived in Brazil.' Dad won't let this go.

'So I hear. Odd that. I wonder why he chose Brazil, I've never been there.'

'He said that was why you couldn't come to our wedding.'

'Robin. Eh? What can I say?' I don't think Caroline cares what he's said, or not said, about anyone. 'Anyway, eat and drink your fill before these old buggers swoop on it. You're paying the bill, after all.'

'Who are all these people?' Dad says.

'Some are distant family, you know the sort that crawl out from their caves for a funeral. Some are the olds from the sheltered housing. I thought it might be jollier with more people. His teacher friends are over there if you want to talk to them.' She pushes her plate into an empty space on the table, grips her wine glass and wanders off in search of a refill.

'Is she drunk? Already?' Mum's voice is censorious.

No one answers.

'She's coming over.' I watch as Carly detaches herself from her friends and heads straight for me. She's beautiful, like Robin. She has his slim build, his hair. She is so obviously his daughter.

'Hello,' she says to me. 'We didn't get a chance to talk.'

'No.' I want to turn and leave, right now. Then I remember that none of this is her fault. 'We didn't. I'm Juliette, Robin's wife.'

'I know. Caroline told me.'

'I thought she was your grandmother,' Mum snaps, her tone judgemental.

'She is. She doesn't like being called granny. You know…'

'Not really, dear.' Mum picks up a plate and starts to fill it. She nudges Sally to do the same.

'Caroline says you're at university?' I feel the need to know more, however painful.

'Yeah. Finishing soon. Yay.' There's a false little smile, she's trying so hard to be jolly. Aren't we all? Well, not jolly, civil.

'Well, I hope you do well.'

'Me too. I sort of owe it to dad. I didn't really want to go. He persuaded me. And I've really enjoyed it.'

'That was good of him.' Mum is back and butting in. She won't have forgotten how he dissuaded me from going to university.

'Yeah, I'm really lucky. He's been helping me with the costs, no student debt for me, thanks to Dad.' She sniffs and waves her hands across her face to fight away the tears, then she smiles, putting on a brave face.

I feel the knife in my heart. I want to tell her that

I've been helping with the costs too, that *I've* probably paid the lion's share. Instead, I force a smile. The polite part of me knows I should ask what she's studying, what she plans to do when she finishes, but I just cannot bring myself to ask.

'I should get back to my friends. It's been nice meeting you.' Sensing my discomfort, my misery, she leans in for a brief air hug; she has more empathy than her father.

'You too, Carly,' Mum says for me as I smile inanely at Carly's retreating form. She even has Robin's walk.

Mum pushes plates at me and Dad.

'I'm not hungry.' I push the plate back at her.

'You may not be, but that little one in there probably is.' She pats my middle. 'Anyway, you're paying for it.'

I catch Mum and Sally talking about the funeral in Mum's kitchen the next day. I've let myself in and I creep along the hallway, listening as they dissect the horrors of the previous day.

'Nothing surprised me. Nothing.' Mum's voice is pure vitriol.

'No.' Sally agrees.

'I always thought he was a shit. Always.'

'Yes.'

'A liar. A liar from the very beginning.'

'You were right,' I say and Mum and Sally jump as they turn to cast their guilty stares at me; caught in the act. 'Carry on. You're not saying anything I don't feel.'

'Have you had breakfast?' Mum changes the subject.

'Yeah. At Sally's. Really, you don't need to stop. You can't say anything that can make it any worse. He was a liar. You always said that, Mum. He had this whole other life going on before me and during me.'

'The lying little shit,' Mum mutters as she comes to me and wraps her arms around me. 'Never mind, it's all over now. No more lies.'

'Yeah.' I hug her back and let the tears flow. They flow for me, for the life I thought I had, for the life I might have had. They even flow for Robin. My mind is in turmoil. Caroline. Robin's father. First wife. Carly. What next? No more. Please no more.

Mum has no tears for him. She had always had the measure of Robin and she had been right all along.

There's a knock on the door and Stephen appears.

'You ready?' he asks Sally.

'Is that the time? I hadn't realised. Hospital appointment.' Sally jumps up. 'Pre-assessment before the actual op. I've been offered a late cancellation and I've jumped at it. Could be any day now.' She grabs her jacket from the chair.

'You okay?' Stephen takes over from Mum and hugs me. 'I've got to take Mum but maybe we could do something later?'

'Something?'

'I don't know. Walk in the sunshine, get some fresh air. It's not raining today.'

'Yeah. Good idea.' I sound vague because that's how I feel. Vague. And bewildered.

'You haven't got any other plans?'

'No. No. I might go back to bed, I didn't sleep well. I've got a headache.'

'Well, wait for me to come back. We'll do something together.'

'You don't have to stay with me, I could be up there hours.' Sally pulls on her jacket and starts down the hallway.

'Just as easy to stay,' Stephen calls to Sally, kissing me lightly on the cheek before following her to the front door.

After they've gone I have a cup of tea with Mum. We don't talk, just sit in silence, both staring, both lost in our own thoughts.

'Can you take anything for your headache? Paracetamol?'

'I already have. It's going off now.' I think about going to bed but the prospect of lying there, not sleeping and just churning everything over doesn't entice me.

'Oh, I bumped into Chloe's mum when I went to Asda last night. Chloe's doing a lot better.'

'Is she? What was wrong with her?'

'She had a bit of a breakdown after …' Mum's voice falters. 'Madeleine… you know.'

'Poor girl.' That explains why she wasn't answering her phone.

'Yes, not helped by all that nasty business.'

I screw my face up in question. 'What's that?'

'Phone calls late at night from a withheld number and threatening messages. She had to get a new phone number.'

'I tried ringing her old number. That explains it. I want to talk to her.'

'Better not.' Mum gets up to clear the cups away. 'Leave the poor girl alone.'

'But she might know something. About Mads,' I add.

'Leave it. The police spoke to her. Took her to the

station and everything. Quite traumatic. Just leave it.'

'Okay,' I promise, and I will for now.

'Mum, do you know where Robin's death certificate is? I need it for the bank and stuff.'

Mum stops and stares at me. Is she thinking, trying to remember where's she put it? 'No, Stephen sorted it out, thank God. Me and Dad…' Her voice fades away as she shudders.

'Maybe it's at the house, I'll ask him later.' I change the subject. 'I think I might go back to bed.'

'You should. Take it easy. It's been nonstop shocks since you came out of hospital. And you're pregnant too. Have you made an appointment with the doctor about it?'

'No. Too soon.' I get up, give Mum a quick kiss and escape before she can start nagging about prenatal care and vitamins. Me having a baby seems unreal, almost a fantasy. Just like the life I thought I had.

Back at Sally's I go up to Stephen's room and flop on the bed. As expected, I don't fall asleep. My mind churns. I flip through my growing to-do list. I should tackle more of it.

I will go to my house. I call a taxi, grab my jacket, and, just as an afterthought I fish the black, blood-splattered handbag out of the drawer and stuff it inside my big handbag. I might as well take it back and add it to my others. It's Chanel and it seems a shame to throw it away. I doubt I'll ever use it again, but maybe the blood will clean off, maybe I can sell it on eBay.

There's a lot of my life I would like to get rid of, sell off.

I find Robin's death certificate quite easily, in an envelope in Robin's in-tray – that almost makes me laugh. Stephen, bless him, has had the foresight to get several copies too. I must reimburse him for the cost.

I start going through Robin's desk, I'm pretty sure the bottom drawer, the one with suspension files hanging in it contains bills and household paperwork.

I'm right, and thirty minutes later I have all the documents I need; Robin's need to be in control means that everything is neatly filed and annotated. I find our wills, straight forward; everything is left to me. No mention of his other family.

I start with my car insurance and make the phone call – I soon wish I hadn't bothered, it goes on and on. But, at least they are already aware of the accident, it's on the national database. When I finally finish the call, fully aware that the claim is only just started, I feel drained of all energy. I cannot bear to call anyone else yet. In the meantime, I can drive Robin's car, they said, except I can't, not with a cast on my leg.

In the kitchen, I wonder if the milk Stephen brought is still in the fridge and still drinkable. A quick sniff tells me it is.

I take my tea upstairs with me, together with my handbags. I have some wet wipes upstairs that might get the blood stain out. They don't but I try cold water in the bathroom then dab it with toilet roll; it's definitely working. More water and it's clean. In my bedroom, I get the hairdryer on it and when I've finished it's as good as new.

I remember when I got this bag, I didn't want it especially, but Robin insisted. It was very expensive. He paid. I've hardly used it, last time, before that day, was at Belton's staff Christmas Ball.

I check the bag to ensure it's empty. I don't want to sell it full of snotty tissues and cloakroom tickets. A quick couple of pictures on my phone and it's on eBay. There, done.

I feel a weight move from my shoulders.

'First of many,' I say aloud, grabbing another bag and a pair of boots. They're going too; I never chose them, I never wear them.

I go into the spare room we use for storage and find a box. The bags and boots get consigned to the box and are joined by more. *The selling box*, I mentally label it. I don't find much in my handbags, the odd pen, an old lipstick – they go in the bin.

Just as I throw another bag onto the pile I glimpse the Chanel bag that started this cathartic spree.

'Side pocket,' I say, grabbing the bag and unzipping the forgotten compartment. I pull out a scribbly envelope.

For your eyes only stares at me and I feel panic rising in my chest.

I shake.

This is it.

The letter.

My hands hover over it.

I wish I wasn't alone.

Downstairs the front door opens and closes.

I am not alone.

I am being burgled?

My heart is thumping in my throat.

I stand up and scrabble around for my phone, finding it under the laden *selling box*. I still have the letter in my hand, I stuff it into my jeans pocket. I've taken so many photos and been on eBay so many times that my phone is flashing low battery. It'll let me make an emergency call though, won't it?

It will. I lean on the windowsill as I dial 999, imagining that my voice will not be heard downstairs if I'm facing outside. I'm asked to choose the service I need when I see it.

Stephen's car.

On the driveway.

I end the call.

The carpet on the stairs is thick, it masks my steps as I descend.

'Hello,' I say when I find him in Robin's study, his back to me as he is going through the items I've laid out on the desk.

He freezes, just for a moment, then turns and smiles.

'I thought you might be here when you weren't at home.'

'Yeah. You know.' I shrug. 'Spur of the moment thing. Is Sally done at the hospital?'

'No. She's going to be ages. She'll message me when she's ready.'

'How did you get in?'

He blinks several times as though I've asked something stupid or the answer is so obvious that he can't believe I'm asking.

'It wasn't locked.'

'Oh God. Wasn't it? I thought it was.' I really need to concentrate on what I'm doing. 'I didn't hear you knock.'

'I rang the doorbell, maybe the battery's flat. Then I tried the door. And here I am.' He lifts his arms up as though he's a magician. 'I see you've been sorting your documents out.'

'Yeah.' I slide around him and plonk myself on the

desk chair. 'Sorted out my car claim. That's one off my list, dozens to go.'

'Baby steps.'

'Yeah. I know.'

'Any sign of the mysterious letter?'

I'm about to tell him but then I don't. I want to read it on my own. I want to know if it is from Mads and I want to decide alone whether I'm going to share it with Mum and Dad if it is.

'No. Then I decided to sort out my handbags and shoes.' I don't tell him that I rang 999.

'Really?' He laughs. 'I suppose that's a good diversion.'

'Something like that.' I laugh now. I can see why Stephen, or anyone really, would think it's a waste of time when I have so many other things to do.

'I can take you home if you're ready?' He reaches for the keys he obviously dropped onto Robin's desk when he came in.

But I grab them first. I hold them behind my back. A look of irritation flashes across his face, then it's gone.

'You want to play silly buggers? Okay.' He tickles me under the arms. Fortunately, I'm not very ticklish. When that doesn't work he grips my arms behind my back and tries to extricate his keys. I grip them tighter, laughing. He stops, smiles, then comes in for the killer move, a kiss. One hell of a kiss; even though I'm sitting down my knees go weak. This is why I was leaving Robin. 'There,' he says. 'I've been wanting to do that for so long.'

'Yeah.' I'm almost breathless.

'Keys.' He holds out his hand.

I drop them into his grasp, sweeping my eyes over

them as I do, it's a casual, unconscious act. I notice the gold one, longer than the rest, I remember its sharp-edged feel in my hand.

He gets a message from Sally just as we arrive at her house, he drops me off and turns around to go and pick her up. I stand on the kerb and wave him off before letting myself into her house. I creep up to my bedroom – Stephen's bedroom – and, even though I know I'm alone, I close the door behind me.

The letter is even more crumpled since it's been screwed up in my pocket. I smooth it out. My hands are shaking again. Should I go next door to Mum, open it with her? No. It could be rubbish. Or it could be upsetting. Why was it in my handbag? I must have had it that day, in the car, in the accident.

I have the vaguest memory of it. Reaching into the glove compartment for tissues. That's where I kept them. Stephen had said I was upset when I left, I remember, I was; we'd just cremated my little sister. It was my car but I wasn't driving. I also remember that. I do.

And that's where the letter was. Stuffed in the glove compartment. We were rowing about it before I had even opened it. But it had already been opened. Robin had opened it.

And now I must open it.

For your eyes only.

Dear Etty

If you're reading this letter then it means something horrible has happened to me.

If you're reading this letter it means Chloe has had to send it to you. It's addressed to your work so Robin won't get it first, cos I know he's like that. I've put for your eyes only on it so your assistant won't open it.

A wave of nausea engulfs me, I breathe deeply until it passes.

And I can't text you or email you, cos he will read them too, cos he goes through your phone.

Does he? Did he? What had Robin told her? I didn't know he read my messages or my emails.

I'm in love with Stephen. We're a couple. He loves me.

I read this line several times. Has she put the wrong name in? Does she mean Robin? Is that any better?

We've been together since the summer when Stephen was over from Canada. As I'm writing this Stephen is making arrangements to move back here for good

I flick back to the top of the letter, she has dated it; it's just after Stephen came back from Canada permanently. She definitely means Stephen. I am so confused.

Now that he's back we're going to be together, in our own house and everything. I've wanted to tell you cos I know you'll understand cos it's only the same age difference as between you and Robin, but Stephen says it's better to wait until it's all settled, until I'm sixteen otherwise he'll get done for sleeping with a minor, but I wanted to, it was my idea. He says we've got to win Mum, Dad and Sally over too. Lol.

Is this true? Or is she fantasising?

But now Robin has found out and he's mad. Stephen says that Robin hates him and doesn't want him to be happy and that's why he's being nasty. Stephen also thinks that Robin wants me for himself. Robin has emailed me. He says that if I tell you or try to be with Stephen that he will kill us both.

My heart thumps in my chest. I do not know what to believe. This is definitely from Mads, her handwriting is so familiar to me and so is her signature. But it cannot be true, any of it. She must have been delusional.

So, if you get this letter and something has happened to me and Stephen, go to the police and tell them it is Robin.
Love and kisses xxxxxx and I hope this never gets sent.
Mads.

I read the letter over and over.

I am shaking with shock and fear and I don't know what to do.

But now I remember.

Robin denied it. He snatched the letter from me and stuffed it into his inside jacket pocket. We were on the way to the funeral, not leaving. I sat through Mads's funeral knowing about that letter, its contents burning in Robin's suit pocket. That was why we left in such a hurry, Robin ushering me away before I could cause a scene. That was why he was driving.

And that's what we were arguing about in the car. I remember. He screamed at me that he didn't even know about Mads and Stephen until he read the letter himself. He claimed that he opened it in haste as he often opens the post in the car on the drive to work if it comes soon enough. That part, at least, is true. He said he didn't notice it was addressed to me. Liar.

Why hadn't he shown it to me? He said he thought Mads must have been mentally ill. He wanted to speak to Stephen first. Stephen had laughed in his face.

I remember Robin's contorted, angry face, his white knuckles on the steering wheel as I grabbed the letter from him and read it aloud before stuffing it into its envelope and zipping it into the side pocket of my handbag. We were screaming and shouting at each other. I didn't believe him, I yelled through my tears as Robin made a grab for my handbag.

We hit the kerb on one side, spinning across the road; we were going too fast.

The front door bangs closed; Stephen and Sally are back from the hospital. Stephen calls my name. I push the letter and envelope back into my jeans pocket, lie down on the bed, facing away from the door and wait.

A tentative knock.

'Yeah,' I call, my voice weak.

'Etty, you okay?'

'Yeah. Just got a bit of a headache.'

'Okay. Only I thought we might go out for that walk soon.'

'Yeah. Maybe later. I just need a rest now.'

'Well, I'm just going to pop out and pick up Mum's shopping. Is there anything I can get you?'

'No. Thank you. I'll be fine after a sleep.'

'O-k-a-y.'

Stephen closes the door quietly behind him and I wait until he's outside starting up his car before I ring for a taxi, my second of the day.

TWENTY-ONE

I let myself into my house. This time I'm conscious of locking the door behind me; I try the handle to ensure I have locked it. I've brought Robin's and Mads's phones with me.

I use Robin's printer/scanner/copier to make several copies of the letter. They're colour and impressively like the original. I haven't planned what I'm going to do with the copies but I want them for back up, just in case. In case of what, I don't know. I look for somewhere to keep them safe, finally stuffing them into the bottom drawer of Robin's desk, in among the gas and electric bills.

I fire up Robin's computer and start hunting through his emails. He only appears to have one account; I go through the sent mail but can find nothing to Mads. He's either deleted it or had another account somewhere.

On his phone? I flick through it. He must have deleted the email account, because there are none set up. His only account is on his computer.

I check Mads's phone, she has only one email account on hers. I scroll back through her emails, it takes ages for them to load as it pulls up the old ones. I am at the point of giving up when it catches my eye. A gmail account with Robin's full name.

That wasn't very clever Robin.

The language is nasty, the message just as Mads described in her letter to me; a death threat if she continues to see Stephen.

335

My entire body aches with the horror of it all. Why did Robin even care? How did he find out? I had no idea.

My phone pings. It's Stephen asking where I am? He's worried about me, bless him. I'll reply later.

I still don't know if I believe Mads's story about the two of them. Why would she lie? She was a teenager, she could have had an unrequited crush on Stephen. She could have imagined feelings in his actions. Did she kill herself when she realised he didn't feel the same?

My phone rings. It's Stephen. I let it ring out then listen to his message: he's worried about me. Am I all right? Can I ring back as soon as I pick this up?

No, I can't. I need to absorb everything in Mads's letter, I need to get to the truth. I need to understand.

Were Stephen and Mads really having an affair? Could it be called that? Mads was only fifteen, yes, nearly sixteen, but still not legal. That would fit with what she says in her letter. Or, is it all a silly schoolgirl crush? A fantasy?

And what about Robin's part in this? Threatening to kill them both – had I not read his email I would think this was Mads's fantasy. But why would he bother? Why wouldn't he just tell me? If any of it were true then just telling me, knowing that I would tell Mum and Dad, would end it. It would be a bigger punishment, especially for Stephen, than killing them.

Yet, Mads is dead. Apparent suicide. But I do not, and I will never, believe she killed herself.

I think about the horrible list of websites Robin had visited, among them the suicide drugs. Why would he do that?

A car pulls up on the drive.

Stephen.

I fumble with my phone. I'm nervous. I shouldn't be, I remind myself; this is sweet, genuine, dependable Stephen.

He rings the bell. It works this time. I do not answer. I wait. I know the door is locked.

Then the door opens.

'Etty,' he calls out.

I don't answer. I wait.

'Etty,' he calls again. From the sound of his voice he's shouting up the stairs.

'In here,' I shout back.

The study door opens.

'What you doing here? I thought we were going out. I've been ringing you and messaging you.' He smiles at me. 'You okay?'

'Still got my headache.' I offer a weak smile back.

'Let's go home. Get something to eat. Get some fresh air.' He wraps an arm around my shoulders, pulls me in tight.

'How did you get in?'

'What?'

'You rang the doorbell, I didn't answer, yet you let yourself in.'

Stephen's comforting arm drops from my shoulder.

'You didn't lock the door again.' He laughs.

'I did.'

He stiffens and I can tell that he doesn't know what to say, how to reply.

'Do you have a key?' If he lies to me now all is lost.

'Yes.' He looks down, like a naughty, little boy.

'Why didn't you say?'

'It seemed a bit sneaky. But I thought I could help. You know. Maybe find that letter you're all so desperate to see. Put all your minds, especially your parents', at rest.'

I look him up and down; he's the same old Stephen I've always known, and liked, and respected, and maybe been a little in love with. Always.

'Yeah. I can see that.' I smile at him. He looks reassured. 'Where did you get it from?'

'What?' He's frowning now.

'The key? Your key to my house. Where did it come from?' I remember the feel of his keys in my hand, the sharp edges of the new one.

I watch a blush travel up his face. 'You don't want to know.' He shakes his head, shrugging off a bad memory.

'I do.'

'No.' He shakes his head again.

'Tell me. Tell me, now.'

He sighs and begins to pace; Robin's study isn't large enough for more than three steps in any direction.

'Okay.' He interlaces his hands in front of him. 'When you had the accident, after I pulled you out and I went back for Robin, I turned the engine off. Obviously, I thought it might be safer. I just stuffed the keys in my pocket and pulled Robin out.' He grimaces.

'But I have Robin's keys, the police gave them to Mum and Dad.'

'Yeah, I gave them to the police.'

'But not before you made a copy.'

'Yeah.' He looks down at his feet. His naughty little boy act again. 'I thought if I could find the letter, you know…'

I wait and I watch and I think.

'But no one knew about the letter then. It was weeks before Mum and Dad became aware of it.'

'Mads mentioned it.' He looks sheepish now.

'Really? Did she tell you what was in it?'

'Something about Robin threatening to kill her. I told her he was probably bluffing. She said it would be posted by her friend if anything happened to her. At the time, I told her she was being silly. I wish I'd taken her seriously now, I might have saved her life. But I didn't believe that Robin was stupid enough to put something like that in writing.'

'Robin? What in writing?'

I watch Stephen's eyes flicker back and forth. 'He sent her some nasty emails, so she said. I wish I'd listened, I could have saved her.' He rubs his face in his hands, pushing back his hair, so much thinner than Robin's.

'She says that in the letter.'

'You found it?'

'Yeah.'

He spins round looking for it. It's on the desk. He snatches it up and starts to read. His head shakes rapidly as he scans the lines.

'Oh my God. Oh my God. I …' He stops and rereads the letter. 'None of this is true, Etty.'

'I remember Robin saying that too. In the car. That day.'

'Well, there…'

'It fits though, doesn't it, with why you and she were so chummy last summer. Every time we were in the garden you popped out too.'

'Yeah, to see you. It's always been you. I've always

wanted you, Etty. Not Mads.'

'But you couldn't have me, could you? So you had the next best thing, didn't you? My baby sister. And you promised her the earth.'

'No Etty, it's just her fantasy. I don't know why she's said these things.'

'I found an email from Robin, so that part is true. *If* it came from Robin, only I can't find that account on his computer or his phone.'

'Probably deleted it. Or used webmail.'

'Yeah, that's what I thought. I expect the police will be able to find it even if it has been deleted.'

'You're not going to the police with this, are you? What's the point? Mads is dead and so is Robin. He's had his punishment.' Stephen offers a grim smile.

'If Robin did drug her to death, I want to know.'

'Maybe it was accidental. Maybe he didn't mean to do it.'

'Why are you defending him?'

'I'm not. Just, you know . . .' he shrugs. 'Thinking out loud. You don't want to go to the police. It'll be all over the internet, raked over in public, everyone will know your business. Have you told anyone else? Have you told your parents?'

'No. I wanted to understand what it all meant before I told anyone.'

'Think about your parents. What will this do to them? Think about our unborn baby.'

'Oh, I have been. And I remember that one, drunken night. One night. It was just days before Mads died. You took me to the pub. I'd had a blazing row with Robin over something stupid and you were there, a shoulder to cry on. We drank far too much. Or maybe it was just me who drank too much.'

Stephen shakes his head. His eyes moisten. 'Don't, Etty,' he says. 'Don't.'

But I carry on, undeterred. 'I remember the inept fumbling on the way home, the quick fuck in the back of the car when you'd driven round the back of Sainsbury's car park, by the recycling bins, because it was darkest there. I remember it all now. Sleazy and tacky.'

'It wasn't like that. Not at all. You're making our love sound cheap and nasty. Stop this insanity now.' His face is turning puce.

'I wasn't leaving Robin, was I? I hadn't seen him kissing anyone, had I? You planted that thought in my brain-damaged head. Didn't you?'

It's odd, because tears are rolling down my face and yet I am not sobbing or wailing. I should be, but I'm not.

'Etty. What's wrong with you? Where is this coming from?' I see a little tremor in his hands.

'When you thought you had me you didn't need Mads anymore, did you? So you got rid of her. You. Not Robin.'

'Rubbish. What about the email from him? What about those websites?' He folds his arms in triumph; evidence presented. 'This is all a messy misunderstanding, a mistake.'

'Was it you who made those searches on Robin's computer? You who visited those websites? You pretended you were inexperienced on computers, but you fixed Sally's, you even fixed Mads's laptop – were you laying trails even then? I bet you changed the password on Robin's phone too. Didn't you?'

'Etty, this is insane. Can you hear yourself? You've been very ill. Head trauma. You're paranoid.'

'The letter. Parts of it are true. The part about you and Mads is true.'

Stephen is shaking his head. He looks at me with his soulful, doleful eyes.

'Etty, please…'

'No.' I hold up my hand. 'That letter. It sort of fits. It shouldn't, but it does. I don't want to believe it and yet . . .'

He glances around the room, he's still holding the letter in his hand. 'Then don't. It's all lies.' He flaps it at me. 'If this is the problem, let's get rid of the problem.' He pushes the letter into Robin's paper shredder. We both watch it disappear. 'Cross-cut,' he says, satisfied. 'So now there's no going back. We can only go forward, you, me and our baby.'

'That would be nice,' I hear myself say, I sound so reasonable.

'It will be.'

'I made copies.'

'Why?'

I shrug.

'Where are they?' His eyes sweep the desk before he drops down and starts opening the drawers and scrabbling around inside them. He finds the copies and feeds them into the shredder. 'Any more?'

I shake my head. 'No more copies.'

'There, that's done with. We can move on. Forget this nonsense.' He gives me a shy smile. There he is, Stephen, my best friend.

'Yeah. Maybe.'

'I'm afraid Mads was living up to her name.'

'Why did you have to say that? Even if it was true, why did you have to say it?'

'I don't know. Relief it's all over, I suppose.

You've found the letter, it's nonsense and no more harm is done.'

'It's not though, is it?'

'What do you mean?'

'It's not over. I've called the police.'

He blinks at me, several times.

'Are you insane? They'll think so.'

'Did you threaten Chloe?'

'What? Who?'

'Mads's best friend. You have threatened her, haven't you?'

'No, of course not.'

'When did you find out about the letter? When did Mads tell you about it? Or was it Chloe who told you?'

'Urgh. That stupid bitch.' He flings his arms out in a dismissive gesture. 'I doubt the police will be able to piece that stupid, lying letter back together anyway. They'll see you and know you're not right in the head.' He jabs a finger at his own head. It's a gesture so reminiscent of childhood.

'They won't need to piece it together.' I wonder if my voice sounds as hard and cold as I now feel.

'You said there weren't any more copies.' He looks alarmed.

'There aren't. Not paper ones anyway. I emailed it to myself and to you.'

'We can delete it.' He folds his arms. 'No harm done.' He smiles and I see sweet, genuine Stephen shining through.

There's no sound when the police cars pull up, just a flash of blue light filling Robin's study.

'I don't believe you've done this,' Stephen says, staring at me. 'It's not too late, you can say it's all a big mistake.'

I shake my head. I'm sobbing now.

'She was in our way. Don't you see that? I did it for you. For us. What about our baby? Don't you care?' His voice comes out in one long babble now before he steps forward and hugs me tight. His mouth comes close to my ear and he whispers. 'Robin was still alive, lived for ages. I watched him choke on his own blood. I watched a bubble of blood form and pop as he gasped his last. I didn't turn him onto his side. I let him die. I didn't ring the ambulance until he'd gone.' He pulls back and smiles at me, shaking his head as four police officers burst in. 'Etty, you're insane.' He turns to the police. 'She's been in a really bad accident, she's brain damaged. Look at her.'

They do look. And they listen. And, after an hour we both go to the station to *help them with their enquiries*.

Later that day they search Sally's house and they take away her laptop, the one Stephen has fixed.

EPILOGUE

I managed to give evidence at Stephen's trial. I was nearly nine months pregnant with his child. He didn't meet my gaze but, sometimes, I caught him staring at me; his look reproachful, resentful and confused. Even now, he still cannot understand why I put my sister and my husband before him.

Stephen was right about the media. They all covered it. To the national dailies it was just another tawdry case, quite minor really; consigned to a side column on inside pages. Only our local evening newspaper gave it any prominence; dragging our names and his across the front page, featuring it in their online newsfeed.

He was charged with perverting the course of justice. The police had hoped for assisting suicide but there wasn't enough evidence. We wanted him tried for murder, or, at least, manslaughter – realistically there was never any chance of either. The CPS threw out the charge against him for sleeping with a minor; Mads's letter wasn't proof enough that it happened and even if it had, her age, her apparent willingness would be in Stephen's favour.

Stephen denied everything; absolutely everything.

He thought he was clever. He thought he had covered his tracks. But the police digital forensics specialists provided the damning evidence: the planting of website addresses on Robin's computer after his death; on Mads's laptop during the time

Stephen was fixing it, and, the creation of an email account in Robin's name. Sally had gasped her horror when she realised it was on her laptop that the vile email had been sent to Mads; the laptop Stephen had fixed for her but used himself.

Perverting the course of justice was the best we could hope for, it covered fabricating evidence, it carried a possible life sentence.

I wasn't in court to hear the guilty verdict, neither was Mum, but Dad sat through it until the bitter end.

I was in labour as the jury deliberated, giving birth as they announced their verdict, gazing into my new-born daughter's scrunched-up face as Stephen was taken back to the cells below the court. Mum was by my side, her face filled with love and hope, erasing a little of the misery Mads's absence will always cause.

It was another two weeks before Stephen was sentenced and Dad was present for that too, watching his face intently, hoping for some sign of remorse. But there was none.

He was still denying everything to everyone, even after the verdict. Sally so desperately wanted to believe him; don't we all want to believe our child is good, not evil?

I am convinced, as are the police, that he supplied Mads with the drugs. We'll never know how he persuaded her to take them. I've lain awake so many nights and wondered if she even knew she had. He had tricked her? But how?

He didn't get life. He was sentenced to three years. Three derisory years for murdering my little sister. With time off for good behaviour he will be out in eighteen months.

For Robin's death, he goes unpunished. He denied

what he had said to me and there was no evidence, no proof. It didn't even come up at court.

But, for us, he will always be a murderer. A double murderer.

I didn't go to the sentencing, neither did Mum. We were too busy looking after our darling Grace and packing up ready for our move. Mum and Dad's house, the house where so many memories lurk in the shadows, sold quickly. As did my house; Robin chose well, it made a handsome profit. With the mortgage paid off by the insurance policy and a nice income from another insurance policy, I am a wealthy woman. Wealthy enough to put one-hundred-thousand pounds into a trust for Robin's daughter, Carly. It's the least she deserves. She'll get the money when she's twenty-five, I've told her it's a legacy from her father, there's no need for her to know that he left her nothing in his will.

Robin's mother wanted to keep in touch, wanted to meet the baby. But I cannot do it, there is no connection between Grace and Robin's family. No genetics. Nothing. And there never will be.

It's harder with Sally. She chose not to meet her granddaughter, which was difficult as we were still living next door to her when Grace was born. We crept around and kept indoors, grateful that it was winter and the weather disinclined us to venture out. Sally said that she could not bear to meet her then never see her again. Sally said she must bear some of the blame for Stephen's actions, we think she is being too hard on herself. He is an adult. She clings to the belief that he is misunderstood.

She kept to herself after it all came out, no longer

the gregarious, outspoken Sally. She said that despite his failings, Stephen was still her son and she would wait for him, provide a home for him when he comes out of prison.

Stephen has vowed that when his is free he will find us, find his daughter. For this reason, we didn't tell Sally where we were going or what we were called – we have changed our surname by deed poll.

We moved when Grace was four weeks old.

'Grace looks more like you every day.' Mum's smile says it all, she's grateful that our darling girl looks less and less like Stephen. She was his image when she was born, so shockingly like him that it made both Mum and I gasp when we saw her scrunched-up, pink face for the first time. 'She reminds me so much of you at that age.' Mum says, her face taking on a wistful look. 'And Madeleine,' she adds.

We have photographs of Mads everywhere, photographs of the four of us, Mum, Dad, me, Mads. In the photos we're laughing, but for a long time the laughter went out of our world. Grace has brought it back.

We live in a rambling old house along a quiet lane in an anonymous village in Devon. It's not on the tourist map, though there is beach a mere thirty-minute stroll away, but it's down a narrow lane that is only accessible on foot. We put Grace in her pushchair, load up the basket beneath it and take a picnic with us; we go summer and winter. There's no car park, no café, no beach huts in the tiny bay, just an ancient public toilet where sand drifts under the door and council cleaning takes place once a month –

we're all grateful for Victorian plumbing.

We've thrown ourselves into village life. Mum has joined the Women's Institute, all those years of dressmaking with Sally on the kitchen table have come in useful. Mum bakes amazing cakes too, the WI sells them by the slice for charity. She spends as much time as possible with Grace and she's happy. She deserves to be happy. We all do.

Dad, retired now, looks better; he's lost weight, he's tanned and the stress-laden bags under his eyes are gone. He's joined the Parish Council; he loves it. We have a dog now – Robin would never allow that – it's Dad's job to take him for his daily walks.

I work two half-days a week in the local shop; the plan is that I will train to take over the post office when the present postmaster retires. That's many years in the future and assumes that the post office will escape closure. I try not to plan too far ahead, I just want to enjoy the present.

Grace is twenty-one months now. She toddles and talks and points and climbs. She is the best thing to come out of our misery. When she's older Grace will attend the village school. She will never know her father – I'll tell her he died before she was born.

I have sworn off men. I am such a poor picker: one control freak and one murderer, both with paedophilic tendencies. I don't need another man in my life. I blame myself for some of what happened; I was naïve, I was stubborn. I was young and foolish. I hope that now I am a mother I have grown up. Mum and Dad blame themselves too; for not stopping me seeing Robin, for being fooled by Stephen, for not knowing about Mads and Stephen.

Oh, the guilt we all carry.

I attend counselling sessions, it helps. I don't talk about the specifics, how can I? The constant fear of Stephen finding us is always there.

But most days we're happy, Mum, Dad, me and Grace. It's us against the world and we've made a good life.

From the outside I look fine; my hair has grown and covers my scars. But, the past still haunts me; when I wake in the night, when I think of Mads. And Robin. And Stephen. Everything that happened will always be there hiding behind my smiling eyes. It never leaves me.

And, Stephen is free now.

THE END

Grab a Freebie

Wondered what Stephen was thinking?

You can grab this short, companion piece to

Never Leaves Me, for FREE.

Type this link into your browser:

http://bit.ly/2lAFBlZ

ONE LAST THING…

Thank you so much for reading this book. I really do appreciate it. I am an Indie Author, not backed by a big publishing company, so every time a reader buys one of my books, I am genuinely thrilled. I've worked hard to eliminate any typos and errors, but if you spot any, please let me know: cjmorrowauthor@gmail.com

If you have enjoyed this book please leave a review on Amazon and/or Goodreads, and if you think your friends would enjoy reading it, please share it with them.

Many thanks

CJ

ABOUT THE AUTHOR

I am a writer, word weaver, lover of things curious, unseen and unexplainable, as well as a general wordy person. I'm always watching, listening and laughing – mostly at myself.

I love to write about everyday life as though viewed side on – I like to catch the object that moves in the corner of your eye then vanishes when you turn. I'm fascinated by the ordinary man, or woman, who isn't quite what they seem. I see magic or mystery in every situation and relationship. I adore synchronicity – I see it everywhere. Life intrigues me and in my experience fact is often stranger than fiction.

I write across several genres; this is my first psychological thriller. I hope you have enjoyed it.

When I don't like what's going on in the world, I write another one. Join me.